SARAH MASON

Caught in the Crossfire

First edition

ISBN: 979-8-9992950-2-6

This book was professionally typeset on Reedsy.
Find out more at reedsy.com

Would I survive at Basgiath?
No.

Would I win the Hunger Games?
Absolutely not.

Would I get out of the Maze?
Let's be honest—no.

Do I thirst after morally gray, outlaw men
with bad tempers and wicked tongues?
Every. Damn. Time.

To all my BookTok girlies who can relate—
this one's for you.

If you ever wished Elliot got with Olivia,
or that Susan fell for Prince Caspian,
you're in good company.

Caution to the reader

This story doesn't play nice. It's raw, reckless, and unapologetically dirty. Yes. There is sex in the first chapter. I am not sorry; you've been warned.

Expect violence, explicit sexual content, and power dynamics that toe the line between control and surrender.
There's bondage, dominance and submission, breath play, strong language, and blood on the badge.
You'll find crooked cops, drug deals gone sideways, and a system just as flawed as the people trying to survive it.

Every act of intimacy is consensual—but that doesn't mean it's gentle.
Every choice has consequences—but that doesn't mean it's clean.

You can't report the author for emotional damage, but you *can* take a break if it hits too close to home.

As always... your mental health matters more than any story. Read with caution. Or better yet, read like you mean it.

1

Caught in the Crossfire Playlist

Cause that's totally a thing now, and I am obsessed.

Control • Halsey
Blood // Water • grandson
WITCH • Devon Cole
The Way I Do • Bishop Briggs
Last First Kiss • Rowan Pierce
Cop Car • Keith Urban
Skinny Little Missy • Nickelback
Steal My Thunder • Conner Smith
Lose Control • Teddy Swims
5150 • Dierks Bentley
Dani California • Red Hot Chili Peppers
White Horse • Chris Stapleton
Shotgun Rider • Tim McGraw
Let It Go • James Bay
The Devil's Backbone • The Civil Wars
Good Girl (Praise) • Nation Haven
BONUS - Hurricane • Band of Heathens

CHAPTER 1 ⊙ OWEN

N ew Orleans after midnight hummed like a low-grade
fever. The air stuck to your skin, the streetlights bled,
and everyone who was still awake had a reason.
Mine was bourbon.

The bar I found myself at more often than I cared to admit
was one of those places you stumbled across by accident. No
sign, no name—just a cracked door and the sound of an old
record player losing its will to live.

The bartender didn't bother looking up when I walked in.
I didn't know his name, and he probably didn't know mine.
My boots stuck to the floor as I weaved across the dance floor,
fending off too-drunk tourists and regulars who had come
looking for an escape, just like me.

I took my usual stool in the corner, back against the peeling
wall, and a view of the door.

The barkeep may not have known my name, but he knew
what I drank, and that was just fine with me. I accepted the
bourbon he slid me with a nod. My team had just pieced
together one hell of a case. They were probably over at the 10/7,
a cop bar not too far from headquarters. It was everything I
didn't want or need. Loud and boisterous, full of cops looking
to let off steam—posturing, bragging, bad jokes recycled from

the last dozen cases. Too much noise, too much testosterone, and the unmistakable sense that everyone was one drink away from either a confession or a fistfight.

Harper, my lead detective, had tried dragging me along, as per usual, but I'd gotten good at fending him off lately. I had just taken a sip of the cheap liquor, ready to let the bourbon do its thing, when the door swung open.

And she walked in.

Five-one, maybe. Boots, boot cut jeans, and a sheepskin collar on her worn jacket. Midnight hair piled on the top of her head like it had been wrangled into submission. She didn't scan the room the way most people did; she *felt* it, like she could read the temperature by instinct. Her smile was friendly but firm as she, too, made her way through the dance floor to the bar, and the jukebox switched to an old soul track, bass low and slow. She ordered something clear, tossed cash, and never looked my way.

She threw back the shot, grabbed a beer, and let the beat lure her back out to the floor. Then she started to move. Not a performance. Just her body remembering music.

Half the room stared. She didn't care. She wasn't dancing for them. She was dancing like she and the rhythm were old friends, eyes closed, head tipped back as she swayed. My grip tightened on the glass before I realized it, mouth dry despite the liquor.

When the song ended, and her drink was empty, she made her way to the bar again. I signaled the bartender against my better judgment. "Whatever she's having."

He nodded, poured, and slid it down to her.

She looked at the drink like it had insulted her, then at me.

And sent it back with a shake of her head.

4

Fair. I'd have done the same.

But the air changed. Static now. Every second after that felt like waiting for a match to strike.

The next song kicked on, and the floor came alive at the tune of a popular dance song. She turned, eyes finding me through the dim light, and sipped her drink. The one she had ordered, not the one I sent her. No smile. Just a dare. She looked me up and down and bit her lower lip like she was thinking. Then she strutted straight over and stopped close enough that I could make out the ink that crawled over her shoulder and ended by her collarbone. She tossed her coat over the chair, then leaned on the back of it, arms braced on the frame.

"You dance, Officer?"

I didn't ask how she knew.

"Not really."

"Better late than never." Her small hand wrapped around my wrist.

I pulled back. "I'm good."

She paused, tilting her head. The tip of her tongue traced the edge of her top teeth, eyes steady on mine—not playful. Evaluating.

"If you were good, you wouldn't have bought me that drink. Besides, I wasn't asking." She winked at me, finished her drink, and this time, when she pulled me forward, I let her.

The floor was small. The crowd didn't matter. At first, I kept my distance. I didn't dance. Not my thing. But those brown eyes were bright with mischief, and her cheeks were flushed pink. She leaned up on her tiptoes, and I bent towards her to catch what she was saying. "If I didn't know any better, I'd say you were scared. Don't worry, honey. I'll be gentle."

She spun away from me before I could respond, and the song

5

changed again. All thoughts of protest left my mind the second she backed up, her back to my chest. Her ass was at just the right height, and I had a feeling she knew exactly what she was doing when she swayed against me.

Fuck.

She tilted her head back, looking up at me, and smirked. My hand found its way under her shirt, and when she didn't immediately bolt away, I spread my palm over the warm expanse of her belly, right above the waistband of her jeans. She was still moving her damned hips, and I told myself I was just trying to still her before we both did something we might regret. But instead of holding her in place, I pulled her to me until she was close enough that she could feel what she was doing to me. Her ass was any man's dream, and it was rubbing me just right. She broke eye contact then, turning her head slightly, like she was steadying herself.

So, I put my other hand around her throat and tilted her face back to me. Her pupils dilated as I squeezed just a little before easing off the pressure, keeping my hand around her pretty throat. She relaxed in my hold, and we let the beat carry us with not an inch of space between us.

For three minutes, the world shrank to sweat, sound, and breath—everything else drowned out by hunger. The song died, but neither of us stepped away. When my thumb dipped beneath her waistband and stroked her skin, her breath caught, and she stood on her tiptoes again. "Want to get out of here?"

I hadn't been with anyone since my divorce. And now here she was... walking in like she owned the room, clocking me almost as quickly as I clocked her. I knew better, but still the words came from my lips. "Lead the way."

We found ourselves at the motel across the street, and the

night clerk barely glanced at us as I all but threw some cash at him. After grabbing the key he slid to us, she led me by my hand down the hall. Even under those ugly-as-sin flickering yellow lights, she shone. Rich black hair and a body that belonged on the cover of some catalogue. But it was her eyes that did it for me. Warm and intelligent, bright with desire, and sparking every time they met mine… yeah, I followed her down that hallway all too willingly.

She was on me the second I got the door open, and I kicked it shut as she pressed her lips to mine.

Fuck. *Yes.*

I picked her up, and she wrapped her legs around my waist as she pressed her tongue against my lips. It was raw and messy— a clashing of teeth and lust as we devoured each other. The way my hands cupped her ass was a perfect fit, and I was so fucking hard, I was surprised my damn zipper didn't give out. She moaned into my mouth when I pressed her against the wall, using it for leverage as I tore off her shirt and she tore off mine. Her hands roamed my abdomen eagerly, and I kissed my way down her neck before biting the top of her breast right by her bra. She bucked when I sank my teeth into her, just a nip, and moaned again. She was light enough that when I picked her up again, I was able to carry her with one arm, so the other worked at getting that damned bra off.

I wasn't gentle when I tossed her down on the bed and braced myself over her. I kissed her neck again and then moved my mouth back to her chest. When I licked her pale pink nipple, she whimpered, and I nipped at it too. She wrapped her hands in my hair and pulled me to her. I groaned low in my throat as she traced my jaw with featherlight kisses until she got to my ear. When she nipped me back, I lowered my hips until they

7

were rubbing against her. There were entirely too many clothes still on both of us.

She reached for the buckle of my jeans, but I stopped her. "It's Owen."

She blinked at me, those gorgeous eyes hazy with need. "Huh?"

I reached between us and cupped her sex. She tossed her head back into the pillows, then cut her eyes back to me when I didn't move. "When you scream my name, it's Owen."

She smiled. "What if I'm not a screamer?"

It was my turn to smile, and the grin I gave her was predatorial. "You will be." I pressed the heel of my hand into her pussy. "When I get these off, I bet I'll find you already soaked for me."

She raised an eyebrow. "Why don't you hurry up and find out?"

I tried, and failed, not to rush as I ripped her jeans off her and revealed tanned and toned legs. I kept my own jeans on as I spread her knees for me and looked back up at her when I caught sight of the wet spot on her panties. She watched me through hooded eyes as I leaned down and blew on it. I chuckled when she shivered, and she said, "Owen?"

"Yeah, *mon péché*?"

"It's Casey. For when you moan mine."

"Is that so?" I pulled her panties off and tossed them to where I had thrown her jeans. She was fucking glistening for me, and I couldn't resist running a singular finger through her slit. She hissed and pressed her hips forward. "So wet for me, Casey. You want to know something, baby?" I leaned down and kissed her inner thigh. "I haven't had dinner yet, and I'm fucking starving."

In one smooth motion, I grabbed her hips and flipped us until she was kneeling over me. "Take what you need from me." She bit her lip, and I saw a flash of uncertainty in her eyes, so I guided her hips until her pussy was right over my chin. "Sit, *mon péché*."

She shivered but didn't move, so I tightened my grip on her hips and began to rock her body back and forth. My tongue darted out, and I licked her cunt from top to bottom as I moved her, and this time the moan that came from her lips was wanton and unabashedly loud. I encouraged her further by sucking her clit into my mouth and then nipping it like I had done her breast. She bucked in my hold before finally sinking down and straddling my face, rubbing her pussy across my lips like I had wanted her to do. I licked her again, and again, until she was using my mouth without hesitation, one hand propped against the headboard as she chased her high on my tongue. "Owen... fuck, Owen."

She couldn't see it, but I couldn't stop the grin that came as I dragged my teeth across her sensitive slit. Her hands found mine, where they still braced her hips, and moved them up until they were cupping her tits. *That's it, baby. Take what you want from me.*

I knew she was close; she was practically soaking my chin. I squeezed her breasts and then pinched her nipples between my thumb and forefinger as I pushed my tongue inside her cunt. She jerked when she came, her body stiffening as she ground out a bruising rhythm on my chin, warm and slick beneath my mouth. I groaned deep in my throat, letting her ride it out as she shivered in my hold. When she was done, she slowed to a stop. Moving my hands back to her hips, I twisted us until we were back to our original position. I backed off the bed, and she watched me as I stood and took my jeans off. When my cock sprang free, she licked her lips and stretched languidly on the bed.

"I'm clean. Are you on birth control?"

She hesitated, then nodded.

"Good, 'cause I want to feel your pussy squeeze my cock when you shatter around me."

I sank onto my knees between her thighs and lifted her ass in the air as I drove into her in one go. She yelled, her back bowing off the bed as I settled myself deep inside her. "Fuck, baby. That's it. You're so fucking tight."

She moaned in response as I began to slowly thrust in and out of her, letting her adjust, but her hips rose to meet mine every time until she looked at me. "You can't break me. Show me what you've got."

I growled. "Careful what you wish for." I pulled out until just the tip was inside her, her cunt squeezing my cock like it was trying to keep me inside. For a second, I held us both in place. A thin sheen of sweat covered her skin from having ridden my face until she came all over it. I licked my lips, still tasting her, then slammed myself to the hilt inside her warmth. Her eyes widened, but I wasn't done. Not nearly. I pulled out and drove back in, over and over, until she was thrashing in the sheets. "Take it, baby. I want my cock coated in your sweetness when you come. Fucking take it."

She reached for me, but I grabbed her wrists with one hand and pinned them above her head, and used the other to wrap around her throat. Squeezing just enough, like I had done back at the bar. Her cunt became impossibly tight, and I fucked her even harder. Faster. She started to yell.

"Owen! Fuck! Owen, oh my God, yes. Please, yes. More, please. Owen..." Her words grew mangled, dissolving into shouts as I grew feral with the need to fill her.

Her eyes rolled into the back of her head as her pussy squeezed me so tight I saw fucking stars. Someone in another room banged on the wall, but I ignored them, moving both my hands back to her hips before going still and spilling myself inside her. She was panting, her pussy dripping when I pulled out. A mixture of her cum and mine. I swiped my finger through it, coating my thumb in the thick, wet mess. I brought it to her lips, and her dark brown eyes never left mine as she wrapped those lips around my finger and sucked. "Knew you would scream for me."

I withdrew my finger with a pop, my cock twitching at the sight, and she grinned at me. "Don't think the neighbors appreciated it."

I shrugged. "Fuck 'em."

I moved to get out of bed, but she pulled me back. "Stay."

I glanced down at her. "I'm not much of a cuddler."

"Not much of a dancer either, but look where that got you. Stay." I glanced at the door, and she leaned towards me. "Just once won't kill you, Owen."

Knowing better, and knowing I would curse myself for it later, I gave in and lay back down beside her. She propped herself up on an elbow and watched me arrange the pillows until they almost didn't feel like typical motel rocks. Grabbing the blanket from where it had fallen to the floor, she covered us both and then lay on her side. I couldn't keep my eyes off her.

"I'm no expert in cuddling by any means, but I don't think that's how you do it."

She opened one bleary eye, raising an eyebrow at me. When I grabbed her and pulled her to me, she squealed before sighing and curling into my side, resting her head on my chest. Two seconds later, she was asleep. I traced the tattoo on her shoulder.

A whirl of color, blues and greens. A horse-like creature with the tail of a fish, leaping over a wave. Bet there was a story behind that. She shivered under my touch as I followed the line of ink down her spine. It pulled at me, quiet and hypnotic, until I gave in and closed my eyes. Much to my surprise, I fell asleep shortly after.

two weeks later

I was halfway through a report I didn't believe when Thibodeaux's voice barked from his office.

"Bishop!" His was the kind of voice that made you question every life choice leading up to that moment.

I sighed, frowning at Harper, who tutted at me and shook his head as I moved towards the oak door marked "Deputy Chief." The coffee on my desk had already gone cold enough to qualify as evidence, so I didn't regret leaving it behind.

I pushed the door open and then shut it behind me before stopping in front of his desk. He didn't look up from the file in front of him. "Sit."

Always "sit." Never "good morning," never "how's your blood pressure, Owen?" Just *sit*.

I sat.

"You're getting a partner."

I scoffed. "No, I'm not."

"Yes, you are." He finally looked up. "Joint tasking with Vice."

Fantastic. Nothing like being babysat by the loudest and most fucking worthless department in the building. "Vice?" I repeated. "Sir, I work homicides. The orangutans down there wouldn't know a fucking knife wound from a bullet hole."

"Don't get poetic with me. You've got dead girls showing up with needle marks. Vice has the living ones who still might talk.

You and Detective Chambers are going to play nice."

"Chambers?" I knew that name, had heard it whispered throughout the whole fucking precinct. Word was she got bumped up fast, skipped over a few bitter old-timers.

He nodded, oblivious. "Casey Chambers. Runs point in Vice. Smart. Fast. Bit of a wild card, but the best they've got."

Of course she is.

Before I could come up with an excuse, the door opened.

She walked in looking like caffeine personified—black hair pinned back, blazer wrinkled, dark circles under eyes that were still too damn bright.

And then she saw me.

It was one of those slow-motion moments where logic died before sound caught up. Her expression twitched—confusion first, then realization, then something else.

Casey tried to hold it in. She really did. Her shoulders started to shake. That adorable little button nose started to twitch, reminding me of a rabbit. Then she snorted. Loud.

"Something funny, Sergeant Chambers?" Thibodeaux asked without looking up.

She coughed, then broke entirely, laughter spilling out like she'd been holding it in for days. "It's not"—she wheezed between laughs, hand pressed to her chest—"it's not funny, really—it's not—oh my God—"

She bent double, one hand braced on her knee, the other in the air like she was trying to summon oxygen. "I swear, Chief, I'm—trying—to stop—"

Thibodeaux looked up at her then, brow furrowed and jaw ajar like he was trying to figure out if he needed to call psych. "Should I come back when we're done with the comedy routine? The one I'm apparently missing out on."

13

She straightened, still hiccupping through her grin, eyes watering. "No, sir. Sorry, sir. I just—of all the people"—another snort—"I mean, it's a *big* city."

"Evidently not big enough," I muttered. That didn't help. She clapped a hand over her mouth, muffling another burst of laughter.

Thibodeaux sighed the way men did when they remembered retirement was still too far away.

"Bishop, Chambers. You're attached at the hip until this is closed. The Vice angle, the bodies—they're connected. Work it, write it up, and don't burn my precinct down."

"Yes, sir," I said.

"Yes, sir," Casey echoed, voice still wobbling, brown eyes dancing with mirth.

He dismissed us with a wave, and she bolted into the hallway. For a minute, neither of us said a word. Every time she glanced at me, she started giggling again. I sighed, shaking my head and walking back towards my desk.

"You done?" I asked over my shoulder.

"Almost," she said, then snorted again. "Nope. Nope, not yet."

"Glad to see this is a serious partnership."

"I'm serious," she said, still laughing. "It's just—what are the odds? I mean—two weeks ago, we were—" She stopped herself, realizing the chief's walls had ears. "Never mind. Long odds. Very long odds."

"Long enough I'd call it bad luck."

"Oh, don't be dramatic. It's not *that* bad."

"Remind me to revoke your optimism card."

She grinned, finally breathing again. "Sorry. I promise, I'm done." Then, under her breath: "It's just really, really funny."

I sighed. "You should get more sleep."

14

"I tried. The universe said no."

We stopped by the elevator. The fluorescent light above us buzzed like it had opinions.

She glanced sideways at me, humor dimming to something almost soft. "For what it's worth, Owen... I am good at my job."

"Good," I said. "Because you just became my problem."

She smiled, crooked and dangerous. "Hmm, that implies that you think you're somehow in charge. Adorable."

I stared at her. "Say again?"

The elevator dinged, and she stepped in without replying. She turned as the doors closed and shot me a wink before disappearing from view.

And that's when I knew it. To be honest, I should have fucking known how screwed I was the second I let myself fall asleep beside her. Not just beside her. Holding her.

I wasn't going to survive this partnership.

Fuck.

CHAPTER 2 ✦ CASEY

I tried to regain my composure as I left Homicide. But come the fuck on... I could still hear myself moaning his name. And the things the man could do with his tongue.

Why, *why*, did he look twice as good in the daylight? I could think of about a dozen different uses for those handcuffs on his hip. *No. Bad Casey. Focus. You are above this. He was a one-night stand.*

A gloriously hot, seared-into-my-memory one-night stand. I had gone to that bar looking for a way to forget and got a lot more than I'd bargained for.

Who knew I liked older men?

Fuck. I needed a coffee. I drove my squad car to my favorite drive-thru near Vice and prayed that Owen fucking Bishop would be as easy to work with as he was to look at. Judging by the way he'd watched me choke on air when I couldn't keep the laughter from bubbling up, my money was on probably not.

The drive-thru beignet stand on Magazine was a local miracle—open twenty-four hours, serving enough powdered sugar to smother a horse and coffee so strong it could power a generator. The kind of place that didn't ask questions if you looked like you hadn't slept which was convenient, because I hadn't. "Large café au lait," I said into the speaker, "and... six beignets. No, make it a dozen. It's for a meeting."

The speaker crackled. "Sure it is, cher."

The caffeine burned my tongue, which was probably karma for everything else I'd done in the last twelve hours. I told myself the coffee was for the hiccups. Or the headache. Or the mountain of paperwork waiting back at Vice. Definitely not because I needed something—anything—to drown out the memory of a certain homicide detective's voice rasping my name like it was a sin. I peeled out of the lot and tore a corner off a beignet before the light even turned green. The city hummed around me—horns, jazz, humidity, the scent of rain and regret.

I devoured the still-warm treat and groaned. If sugar was a religion, I had been born again. When I pulled into the Vice building's cracked parking lot, my pulse had finally slowed to something resembling normal. The air outside smelled like oil and wet pavement. The box of beignets was supposed to be a peace offering.

Or a bribe.

Or maybe a distraction from the fact that I'd spent the morning replaying the way his hands felt on my skin.

Whatever worked.

I nudged the door open with my hip, juggling the pastry box and a gallon of coffee that was dangerously close to spilling. Someone's radio crackled about a bust on Bourbon and a few people outside my team yelled a greeting, probably hoping for a beignet.

Jordan Delaney looked up from his desk the second I stepped in, eyes narrowing like a bloodhound catching the scent of guilt.

"Ooo, a bribe!" he said, pushing back from his chair. "Who'd you piss off this time?"

"Everyone, as always," I said, dropping the box on the nearest flat surface. Powdered sugar puffed up like smoke. "But the good news is, you're easily bought."

"True," he said, lifting the lid and inhaling. "But you only bring pastries when you've done something stupid or dangerous. Sometimes both."

I took a long sip of coffee and stared at the floor. "Define stupid."

Jordan snorted. "Oh, this is going to be good."

The door banged open behind us, and the rest of my squad trickled in—Ramos grumbling about parking, Nguyen juggling a tablet and a breakfast burrito, and Sanders already scowling at the noise.

I straightened. "All right, kids, gather round. We've got a case, and apparently, we're sharing it."

"We've got a joint assignment. Homicide's drowning in dead girls. Chief says we're throwing them a life raft."

Collective groan. Always the same one—part outrage, part resignation.

Ramos rubbed a hand over his face. "Every time we 'collaborate,' someone ends up in Internal Affairs."

"Then maybe don't shoot anyone this round," I said sweetly.

Nguyen perked up from behind his tablet. "Do we at least get hazard pay?"

Jordan laughed. "Hazard pay? For working with Homicide? We should get therapy vouchers."

"Cute." I rolled my eyes. "Anyway, the victims are all late-twenties, suspected overdoses with matching needle marks. Homicide's looking for a killer. We're looking for a supplier. We work together until somebody gets a name."

Sanders leaned back in her chair. "Translation: we do the legwork while they take the credit."

I didn't deny it. "Pretty much. Nguyen, can you put the girls up on the board?" I never called them victims. Never.

With a few swipes on his beloved tablet, Nguyen managed to wrangle the finicky and outdated technology into submission. A few seconds later, three pictures were staring back at us, each girl as pretty as the last. Same haunted eyes, same sad smiles. I shook my head. *Who did this to you?* From the brief I had scanned over before heading to Homicide, I knew they'd been clean for months before this. They wouldn't have just overdosed.

"Case?"

I turned to look at Jordan. "I want to know everything. Take apart every inch of their lives, and put them back together. Find out what pieces of the puzzle are missing, and what pieces fit a little too well."

My team nodded as I handed out assignments. Ramos to canvass the halfway houses, Nguyen to pull arrest records, Jordan to chase down the corner dealers. Sanders grumbled but took notes like a pro. We were meeting with Homicide first thing tomorrow, and I wanted to show up with more than just a little something.

Moments like this reminded me why I fought so hard to run Vice—why I'd put up with the politics, the patronizing, the whispers about sleeping my way to a desk with my name on it. I didn't take the job to just sit around and look pretty. I took it because someone had to care enough to dig through the rot.

Jordan must have seen the shift in my face because his usual grin softened. "We'll get him, Case."

I nodded once, sharp. "Damn right we will."

The bullpen had emptied, the echo of voices fading down the hall until all that was left was the hum of the old AC and the soft tick of the clock on the wall. My office door stayed cracked—habit, authority without distance—but the quiet still felt heavy. I dropped into my chair, the case file open but unread, and let my mind drift to two weeks ago. Jordan's kitchen had smelled like basil and garlic and the kind of comfort I never managed to recreate in my own apartment. His husband, Marco, stirred sauce on the stove while Jordan stood at the counter holding an eggplant in one hand and a banana in the other.

"So," he said, deadpan. "Just for science—are we talking banana big or *eggplant* big?"

"Jordan!"

He waggled the produce. "Don't make me guess. I'm a visual learner."

I snatched a dog toy off the floor—a squeaky chicken, of all things—and winged it at his head. It bounced off harmlessly as the rumble of Marco's laughter and the sound of the chicken filled the space.

Jordan waited expectantly, produce still held aloft.

"Fine… eggplant."

Jordan gasped theatrically, pressing the eggplant to his chest before turning to Marco, who watched the theatrics with a raised eyebrow. "Don't worry, baby. You'll always be my favorite eggplant!"

Marco shook his head and turned back to the stove. "Better be. Or we may need to rethink this whole marriage thing."

Jordan had teased me endlessly the rest of the night. I wasn't typically a one-night stand kind of girl… but when temptation struck, she struck. Hard.

A soft knock at the door pulled me back to the present.

"Hey, boss lady." Jordan leaned against the frame, coffee in hand, grin dialed somewhere between innocent and *I know something.* "So tell me what had you bringing in bribes this morning. Because I know it's not just a joint case."

I sighed, pushing the file aside. "You are never going to believe who runs Homicide."

"Can I get a hint?"

"About six foot tall. Met him two weeks ago at that sleazy bar over off North…"

Jordan's eyes widened. "No!"

"Oh yes."

"You're kidding."

"Do I look like I'm kidding?"

He covered his mouth, half-laughing, half-groaning. "Case… you don't do anything halfway, do you?"

"Shut up."

"I'm not judging, I'm just—damn. You really know how to pick the complicated ones."

I pointed at the door. "Out."

He didn't move. "Was it at least worth it?"

"Jordan!"

He threw up his hands in surrender, still grinning. "Fine, fine. I'm going to head to Scottie's, see if he's heard anything."

Scottie was one of Jordan's informants, a homeless man over on 7th. "Good idea."

"You know what else might be a good idea? Round two!"

"Out! Get out before I transfer you to cold cases or some shit."

Jordan beat a hasty retreat out the door but tossed over his shoulder, "You would never. You love me."

I groaned, sliding a hand across my face and sinking down in my chair. I spent the rest of the day putting the case together as my team moved in and out of the bullpen. Occasionally, I would get a text as one of them moved from one lead to the next. Using what I knew and what they sent me, I managed to make a mosaic of sticky notes on the far wall. What led where, what led nowhere. What made no sense, and what felt right. I let everyone go home, staring at a wall would do no one any good tonight. They were all to meet me in the morning at Homicide, 8 a.m. sharp. Glancing at the room one last time, I sighed and shut off the light before locking the door behind me.

Tuesday was wet. Hurricane season tended to do that here. I glared at the dark sky outside my house before glancing at my phone as it buzzed on the passenger seat: a text from Jordan.

Jordan: You alive?

Me: Define alive.

Jordan: Did you at least bring food? We're meeting them in fifteen. Don't make me go in hungry—you know how I get.

I snorted.

Me: Already on it, drama queen.

The rest of the drive was muscle memory—traffic lights, jazz bleeding from open shop doors, humidity clinging like a desperate ex. When I pulled up to Homicide HQ, the mirrored glass doors flashed defiantly in the light pushing its way through the clouds. I'd walked into ambushes that felt less dangerous.

Jordan was waiting in the lobby with the team, sleeves rolled, tie already loosened. He grinned the second he spotted the bag. "My hero."

"Don't push it," I said, passing out the coffees I had snagged on the way here.

We pushed through the double doors together. The instant I saw him, the world shrank. Owen Bishop, standing near the chief's office, sleeves rolled, forearms crossed, looking every inch like bad news in daylight. His head turned at the sound of our footsteps, and for half a heartbeat, neither of us moved. His blue-green eyes looked me up and down, and when they met mine, I couldn't help but smirk. He frowned.

Jordan froze mid-sip, the recognition dawning on his face like a sunrise of pure chaos. Then he choked. Hard.

"Jordan?" I hissed, thumping his back.

He wheezed, trying to breathe, then gasped out one cursed word between coughs. "Eggplant!"

The sound echoed through the bullpen.

Every detective in Homicide turned to stare.

Sanders glared at a nearby detective. Nguyen hid behind his tablet. Jordan looked like he was seeing God. Owen closed his eyes and muttered something that sounded like a prayer. Ramos glanced between Jordan, Owen, and me like he was trying to put two and two together.

Then a voice from the desks muttered, "Real professional, Vice. Glad to see you brought the circus."

I froze, then turned toward the speaker—a smug middle-aged detective with a crooked tie and a face that begged for consequences. I didn't raise my voice. Didn't need to.

"Say that again."

The man's smirk faltered.

"Please. I'd love to know what counts as professional in a department that can't close its own cases without help."

Jordan stage whispered, "Oh no. She's doing the face."

Ramos drove an elbow into his side. I turned my back on the detective as he spluttered and frowned at Jordan, who immediately shut up. Really not how I wanted this to start. Fucking eggplants, man.

The bullpen had gone dead quiet. The Homicide detective I'd verbally filleted looked like he was reconsidering his life choices.

I smoothed my jacket, rolled my shoulders, and cracked my neck. "All right," I said brightly, voice slicing through the silence. "Since Homicide is apparently allergic to basic manners, how about we try this again? My team's Vice. Yours is Homicide. We both hate paperwork, we're all underpaid, and we've got a body count stacking like bad debt. So let's call a truce, yeah?"

No one answered.

I raised an eyebrow then marched to the front of the room, planting myself beside Owen like I owned the place. He didn't look at me, just crossed his arms and stared down like I was a problem he couldn't quite solve.

"Breakfast is on me," I said. "Get your orders in. You can hate me after you've had carbs. But don't say shit about my team. That is all."

There was a beat of stunned silence... and then, slowly, the tension cracked. One of the homicide rookies snorted. Someone else muttered, "I'll take extra bacon." Even the detective I'd dressed down earlier found something fascinating on his desk instead of meeting my eyes.

Owen's captain stepped out of his office, surveyed the scene, and muttered something about diplomacy before retreating.

And just like that, the room started moving again. Maps were pinned, case files opened, and for the first time since Vice and Homicide had been thrown into this unholy alliance, it didn't feel like open war. Jordan and a Homicide detective—Harper, according to his badge—were already arguing over the best way to organize the evidence board. Jordan favored color-coded chaos. Harper wanted military order. Jordan was my second, Harper was evidently Owen's. They were halfway to murder themselves as I leaned back against a desk, arms folded, hiding a grin.

"Entertained?"

Owen's voice cut through the noise, low and smooth enough to raise goose bumps.

I looked up. He was watching me, one brow raised, that infuriating calm of a man who'd seen too much and cared too little.

"So, you're in charge now?" he asked. The tone wasn't mocking—not exactly. It was that gravelly mix of challenge and curiosity that made me want to hit him and kiss him in equal measure.

I tilted my head, a smirk tugging at my mouth before muttering. "You sure didn't seem to mind it the other night."

Owen's jaw flexed, but his eyes didn't waver. He stepped in close enough that the air between them went hot and narrow. "We'll see about that, *ma louve.*"

My pulse stuttered. I turned sharply to face him. "What did you just call me?"

His mouth curved, slow and deliberate. "You heard me."

I let out a soft, humorless laugh. "Guess I shouldn't be surprised. You've always had a way with French."

His brow lifted—just a fraction—and there it was: that flicker of recognition. The memory slid between us like smoke, unwanted and undeniable, making it hard to breathe.

He moved past me then, close enough that his shoulder brushed mine. Then he leaned down, breath ghosting my ear. "*Alors tu n'oublieras pas,*" he murmured. "*Je me souviens de ton goût.*"

That tone of his hit like a live wire—soft, dangerous, and devastatingly personal. The building could've fucking imploded, and I was pretty sure I wouldn't have been able to move. My brain said, "Bad news." My heart and that thing between my legs said, "Take me; I'm yours." My throat went dry, stomach flipping like it was an acrobat during the final performance at the circus. I scrambled to piece his words together, my high school French class working double time. What I did manage to figure out had me weak in the knees.

"Watch it, Bishop," I managed, voice thin but sharp.

He straightened, not looking back. "I was."

I glanced around the room and found Jordan grinning at me. I glared at him and he went back to arguing with Harper. For once, I was at a loss. What the hell was I going to do now? Asshole speaking French like a damn poet. Dammit. Damn him. And damn my wet panties.

I needed air. Or an exorcism.

Instead, I grabbed the case file off the desk nearest me and pretended to study it like it held the meaning of life. The room was alive now—murmurs, chairs scraping, papers shuffling— but I could still feel his presence like static against my skin. Every time I looked up, his team looked back at me like I was an experiment they weren't sure would explode or save the day.

Fine. Let them watch. I'd worked too damn hard to care what a bunch of Homicide boys thought of me.

"Ramos," I said, sliding the file toward him. "Pull the pharmacy logs for any oxy prescriptions filled under these names. If you can't get the warrant fast enough, call Michelle at Narcotics. She owes me a favor."

One of Owen's detectives raised an eyebrow. "You've got favors with Narcotics?"

"Baby, I've got favors everywhere."

That earned a snort from Crawford, another Homicide detective I had never met. "Guess Vice has its uses after all."

I looked over at him, slow and deliberate. "We do. Mostly cleaning up after Homicide."

The grin dropped off his face, replaced with a sheepish cough.

"Relax," I said. "You're not the worst I've worked with. Yet." I shot him an easy grin.

He blinked, then grinned back despite himself. "You're somethin' else, Chambers."

"Damn right." I pushed my notes to the side and made my way across the room.

The bulletin board was a mess of photos and maps—victims' faces, abandoned buildings, red string chaos. Harper and Jordan were still mid-debate over how to organize it, their argument escalating fast.

"It's a visual hierarchy issue," Jordan said, waving a marker like a weapon. "We color-code by timeline, not by location."

"That makes no damn sense," Harper shot back. "We group by geography—hot zones first, then radiate out."

"Hot zones?" Jordan barked a laugh. "What is this, a military op? You gonna start calling me 'Private Cupcake' next?"

I stepped between them, grabbing the marker from Jordan's hand. "You're both wrong." Two sets of eyes glared at me. I ignored them, rearranging photos with fast precision. "Timeline across the top, geography down the side. That way, we track who met where *and* when. Overlap the names, see who connects." I pinned the last photo and stepped back. The board, once a disaster, suddenly made sense. Jordan blinked. Harper gave a low whistle.

I smirked. "You're welcome."

Even Owen's head tilted just slightly, assessing. Approval clearly wasn't his style, but I caught the faintest curve of his mouth before he looked away.

The next few hours blurred into motion. Coffee cups multiplied. Files grew teeth. My team blended with his in a way no one had expected—bickering, yes, but productive. Nguyen traded data with Crawford. Ramos and a homicide detective compared witness statements. Even Sanders, my resident grump, found common ground with a Homicide detective over shitty jazz and whiskey.

By 4 p.m., we had managed to not kill each other and made a modicum of progress.

"Chambers!" Harper called from across the room. "Your people are terrifyingly efficient."

"It's a survival skill," I said, flipping a page. "Learn it or get buried under red tape."

He grinned. "No wonder Bishop looks half impressed, half annoyed."

I glanced up then, finding Owen frowning at us. "That's just his face."

That earned a bark of laughter. Maybe they were starting to get it.

Because for all their old-school swagger and backroom bullshit, they respected results. And I delivered. Every damn time.

It wasn't about proving myself anymore. It hadn't been for a long time. It was about reminding them *why* I'd already earned my place.

Eventually, the captain barked for everyone to clock out. By that point, I was running on fumes and pure spite. The room thinned, detectives trailing out with muttered good nights and empty cups. Owen was still at his desk, scribbling something into a report. Our eyes met briefly. He didn't say a word. Just that slight, knowing smirk before he went back to writing.

Cocky bastard.

Jordan appeared beside me like a well-timed devil on my shoulder, sipping the dregs of his coffee. "Sooo…" he drawled, drawing the word out like he was winding up. "What did tall, dark, and homicide whisper to you earlier? Because I caught the French, and my gay ass is only fluent in *innuendo*."

I groaned. "You're not gonna let that go, are you?"

"Not unless it involves blackmail material or emotional trauma. Spill."

I sighed, leaning back against the desk. "He said, *'Alors tu n'oublieras pas. Je me souviens de ton goût.'*"

Jordan blinked slowly. "Okay, I understood maybe half of that. One word sounded like food. Should I be aroused or concerned?"

I rubbed my forehead. "Translation: 'I remember your taste.' And some stuff about not forgetting. I think." I tried, and failed, to sound casual like it hadn't been a shot straight to my core.

He nearly dropped his cup. "He said that? Out loud? In *French?*"

"Quietly. But yes."

Jordan fanned himself. "Okay, well, I take back everything I said about straight men having no game. That's art. That's a masters in foreplay."

"Jordan."

"I'm just saying. You could teach a class on bad decisions, but that one? That one I'd audit."

I threw a crumpled sticky note at his face. "Go home before I arrest you for being insufferable."

He grinned, heading for the door. "You would be lost without me."

"Questionable."

When the last of them had left, the silence hit different. Heavy, but not unwelcome. I sank into a chair, stared at the half-clean board, and let the day settle. Owen still sat in his office; I had refused a spare one, preferring to be in the thick of it. The desk I had been given gave me direct line of sight to him. He had his back to me and was yelling at someone on the phone. I gathered my things and made my way to my car, navigating the slick streets and boozy tourists with ease.

Finally home, I crawled into bed, my muscles aching in that good way—earned exhaustion. I turned off the light and stared at the ceiling fan spinning lazy circles above me. The sound of the city outside was a heartbeat I couldn't turn off. I told myself I was thinking about the case. The connections. The timeline. The missing link. But when I closed my eyes, I didn't see evidence. I saw blue-green eyes and the shadow of a smirk.

And I heard his voice again—low, dark, and French. *Alors tu n'oublieras pas.*

I groaned, and rolled over, burying my face in my pillow.

Get it together, Case. Fucking poets.

CHAPTER 3 ◆ CASEY

O n Wednesday, another body turned up. I got the news as I was brushing my teeth, and when I glanced down at my phone as it buzzed next to the sink, I grimaced. The address wasn't too far from me, so I sent Jordan and Ramos a text to meet me there. I hurried to put my boots on, casting a forlorn glance at my coffee pot, which had yet to magically refill despite my many prayers. A few of my neighbors greeted me as I made my way onto the relatively quiet street, and I took a second to coo over the new baby that had become familiar background noise at 2 a.m. when I was poring over cases instead of sleeping. Her poor parents. I gave Mom a smile and felt a pang of empathy at the bags under her eyes. *Me too, sis. Me too.*

When I pulled up to the scene, I frowned when I saw another Explorer already there. Owen got out and I told myself that the twinge in my stomach was jealousy over his SUV being in a lot better shape than mine... and definitely not my traitorous body reacting to the way he got out and stepped onto the street. A simple movement, fluid and almost predatorial. I shook my head. *Predatorial? Really, Case?*

Christ, I needed to get a hobby. But, alas, with his back to me I couldn't resist the temptation to ogle the way he filled those Levi's.

"See something you like?"

"Fuck! Jordan! You creeper."

"You know, it's funny, but usually I can't surprise you, with your Supergirl hearing and all, but it would appear I've found your kryptonite."

His smile was downright gleeful, and I scoffed. "I have no idea what you're talking about."

Jordan fell into step beside me as I headed towards the mess of yellow tape. "Girl, please. Listen, I don't blame you. If I wasn't a married man..."

"And if he wasn't straight as an oak."

Jordan winked. "You would know. Betcha can't wait to climb that tree. Again."

I smacked him on the back of the head, and he fell quiet as we got close enough for everyone else to hear us. I felt a twinge of guilt; this was neither the time nor the place. I saw Ramos approaching from across the lot and nodded at him. I ducked under the yellow caution tape and knelt by Owen, who was beside the covered body. He glanced at me before returning his attention to the poor girl in front of us. She was covered with a sheet of plastic and I pulled on a pair of gloves before reaching for it.

"ME says time of death is around 0300."

I made a general sound of acknowledgment as I tilted her wrist towards me. Sure enough, the track marks were blatantly obvious against her pale skin. She couldn't have been more than what? Nineteen? Twenty? I closed my eyes as I pressed a gentle hand on her shoulder and whispered, "May you find peace."

I stood and glanced around us. "This doesn't make sense, Owen. We're in the middle of a downtown private parking lot.

One, there should be at least a few cars here. But there are none. And two... this is not a place anyone would come to get high. This whole thing is wrong."

He stood, and I was reminded of just how big the man was as he joined me in surveying our surroundings. "She was obviously dumped here."

"No shit. But why here? Why like this? If they wanted to make it look like an overdose, I know of at least five spots off the top of my head, within ten minutes of here, people go to dose up. She's fully clothed, makeup barely smeared. She's young."

"She doesn't look like your typical addict."

I shook my head, glancing back at her. *What secrets would you tell me if you could, kid?* Her hair still had curl. Not street frizz. Styled. Nail beds clean, not picked raw. Tiny rhinestone stud in her nose—not irritated, not crusted. Well kept. She hadn't been out here long. I brushed my thumb along her jaw. Cool to the touch, muscles starting to stiffen—early rigor. Death maybe four or five hours out. "Rigor's creeping in," I murmured.

Owen crouched beside me, scanning her hands. "Tracks are fresh. She didn't die where she was dropped."

"Yeah. Look at her shoes."

He glanced. Beige wedges. "So?"

"So nobody from this parish steps out in open-toe anything at night unless she's trying to impress somebody with a guest list and air conditioning. She's dressed to go inside. She did not walk two blocks on this trash asphalt in those. She didn't make it here on her own."

He considered that. I watched his jaw work like he was chewing what I told him, separating fact from fiction.

I swallowed hard, pulled my gaze off her body and away from

him, and started scanning the lot itself. Not much to it. Private parking behind a shuttered law firm. Chain-link fence on two sides. Brick wall on the third. Access from the alley. One busted camera on the southwest corner that might as well have been a decorative birdhouse.

Wait. There. Tiny smear on the asphalt about six feet from her heel. Drag arc. I glanced at the shoes and immediately clocked a matching scuff. "Owen?" I said quietly.

"Yeah."

"This was careful."

"Yeah," he said again, lower.

"Overdoses aren't careful."

"No," he said. "They're not."

Whoever brought her here knew the cameras were dead. Meaning whoever brought her here had done this enough to be comfortable doing it in a ghost lot two minutes from Bourbon without blinking. I swallowed. For one moment, it wasn't Vice vs. Homicide. We were just two people trying to figure out who the fuck had the audacity to pull shit like this in *our* city and why. Just two sergeants looking down at a kid someone threw away like she wasn't somebody's whole world.

"He's not just moving dope," I murmured. "He's using these girls like a means to an end. They're not the reason, not the end game. Just a step in this shitty scheme he's plotting."

Owen went still.

There it was. The jump. The click in his head. Not just dead junkies. "Say that again," he said, voice low.

"He didn't shoot her up and run. He gave her something measured, watched her go under, and then put her down easy. He carried her. See that drag arc by her heel?" I pointed with one gloved finger. "That's not stumble scrape. That's dead weight skid from a controlled lift. He didn't panic. He placed her."

"Why here?" he asked.

I turned in a slow circle, scanning the lot, the fence line, the alley mouth. My brain wouldn't let it go. "You're Homicide," I said, eyes still moving. "You tell me."

He didn't bristle. He just hunched down, elbows on his knees, and looked at her the way real detectives looked at bodies—like they're still talking. "Last girl," he said quietly, "was left under the I-10 overpass."

"Mm."

"And the one before that was propped in the doorway of that needle exchange on St. Claude."

"Yes," I said softly. "Somewhere she'd be found fast."

"And now this one?" Owen lifted his eyes to mine. "Corporate address. Private lot. Security cameras, even if they're fried. Somebody's lawyer's gonna see this one."

I watched the gears turn in his head as he realized what I had. This was deliberate placement in zones that escalated who paid attention: outreach workers, then the public, now the suits. Like a ladder. Like pressure.

I felt my stomach turn. "He's forcing eyes on them."

"Yeah," Owen said. His jaw flexed. "This isn't cleanup. This is escalation."

My throat went tight. "Big."

"Bigger than a corner dealer," he agreed.

"Jordan," I called, without looking away from Owen. "I want you checking strip cams up and down Poydras, Canal, Carondelet, anything pointing east the last four hours. Don't send a request through the system. Just go knock. Bartenders pay more attention than half the uniforms anyway. See if anybody clocked a vehicle rolling slow."

Jordan nodded, already moving. "Got it."

"Ramos," I said. "Canvass the building. Talk to whoever manages this lot, find out who pays for towing. If this is reserved exec parking, I want that list before we leave. Top floor, partners, whoever they're wining and dining. The dump spots are climbing tax brackets. And why in the fuck is this lot empty?"

That earned me a look from Owen. "You think that's deliberate? Seems like a stretch."

"I don't know yet," I snapped, too sharp because I was mad at the dead girl and the stupid shoes and the whole goddamn machine, not at him. I took a breath. Softer: "Give me an hour."

Halfway back, my phone buzzed. Jordan: *We got something.*

I let it sit. If I read it now, I'd be pulling U-turns like a lunatic. My pulse hadn't slowed since the scene. I was running too hot, and walking into Homicide made everything feel tighter, louder, wrong. I blew through the bullpen like a heat-seeking missile, barely registering the way Harper lifted his hands like, "Oop, incoming storm front."

Owen caught up with me easily, his stride twice as long as mine. He glanced at me, and I said, "Jordan just texted me. We've got something. An address." I didn't bother waiting for him to respond.

I threw Thibodeaux's door open without knocking.

He looked up the second I blew in, saw my face, and didn't waste time pretending this was social. Good. He might have been a grumpy bastard, but he wasn't stupid. "What've we got?" he asked.

"Another girl," I said. "Staged in a private lot two blocks off Canal. Same arm, same injection site. No struggle, no blood, no sign she ever even braced for it. She was carried and placed. Cleaned up after."

"Christ," he muttered.

Owen stepped in behind me. He didn't take the chair. He stayed standing. Territory move. "And it's bigger than dope," he said. "He's escalating where he drops them. Overpass, nonprofit doorway… now corporate property. Somebody's trying to get noticed."

Thibodeaux's gaze cut sharp. "By whom?"

"By somebody at that level," I said. "He doesn't dump in alley trash. He drops her where she lands in paperwork. That's deliberate. That's pressure. This is leverage."

Thibodeaux frowned. "Leverage for what?"

"Don't know yet," I said. "But—"

Owen crossed his arms. "Vice has an address."

Thibodeaux looked between us. "And?"

I rolled my eyes. "You gonna tell *your golden boy* to let me finish a sentence—"

"Not a golden boy," Owen snapped.

I smiled without humor. "Calm down, Bishop."

"Both of you shut the hell up," Thibodeaux said mildly. He turned to me. "Address?"

"There's a spot in the Lower Nine I've been circling for weeks," I said. "Guys call it a 'clinic.' It's not a clinic. It's a locked room. Girls get 'helped' shooting clean and then disappear for a day or two. Half come back strung out and jumpy. The other half don't come back at all."

"You think that's where they're getting dosed?" Thibodeaux asked.

"I think that's where they're getting handled," I said. "And I think whoever's running it is the one staging these girls like warning flyers."

Thibodeaux grunted. "We got enough for a warrant?"

"For a warrant?" I scoffed. "No. For a knock and pull? Yes."

"No," Owen said immediately.

I turned on him. "Excuse me?"

He took a step in. Not aggressive—just assertive. He lowered his voice and leveled me with a look that probably made lesser women crumble. I narrowed my eyes. "You're not going in there without Homicide."

"Watch me," I said.

"No," he repeated, calm in that way that made men dangerous. "This is my dead girl. My scene. My case. You don't just cut me out and run an off-book raid because it makes you feel useful."

That hit like a slap.

My fists clenched. "Fuck you, Bishop. You think this is about me feeling useful? You think I'm looking for a gold star? There might be a girl in there still breathing right now. I am not sitting on my hands to make you feel important on a write-up."

Owen dragged a hand over his jaw and leaned in, toe to toe with me now. His eyes were pale and furious and doing alarming things to my pulse. "God, you're arrogant."

"You think Vice promotes girls who just look good on paper?"

His jaw ticked. "Don't push me."

"Then get out of my way," I hissed. "I don't need your permission to pull a girl out of a room."

"You need my presence," he growled.

I blinked. "I'm sorry, what?"

He leaned in, voice a razor. "You find a live girl in there? That's not possession. That's not solicitation. That's kidnapping. That's homicide-in-progress. They're evidence. They're witnesses. The second you lay hands on that room, it's not just

Vice anymore—it's murder. You want to make a case, you bring
me. You want to put this asshole in a cage for life instead of
eighteen months and a plea deal? You bring me."

Dammit.

That was infuriatingly fair.

I hated that it was fair. But I knew Homicide's reputation.
Owen's reputation. And, though I would never admit it aloud, I
knew I was a bit too stubborn for my own good sometimes. So
I was preparing a biting retort when Thibodeaux interrupted.

"Here's how this is going to go so neither of your unions
eats me alive: minimal entry team, no uniforms, no sirens. I'm
not putting SWAT on a rumor. We do this quiet, we do this
clean, otherwise Internal will have me crucified in front of City
Hall and the Times-Picayune will spell my name wrong. So,
congratulations. Joint op. Homicide rides with Vice." He jabbed
a finger at Owen. "You take Harper, Crawford, and Bishop—"

"I am Bishop," Owen said tightly.

"Then take your damn self and three others. Chambers, you
take your usual squad. You run point because this is your
playground. Bishop, you're backup and evidence lockdown
the second the scene is stable. You two will work together or I
will staple you together. Do we understand each other?"

I opened my mouth. Owen opened his.

Thibodeaux slammed his palm on the desk. "Do we. Understand. Each other."

I snapped my jaw shut. "Yes, Chief."

Owen ground out, "Yes, Chief."

"Good," Thibodeaux said. "Get out of my office."

Owen held my gaze another beat. He looked like he wanted
to argue more. I probably looked like I wanted to bite him.
Which, honestly, not inaccurate.

I shoved into the shitty women's locker room down the hall that still smelled like mold and lemon cleaner and old perfume from whoever had this space in 2003. Jordan hovered in the doorway like the world's nosiest guard dog.

"You good?" he asked.

"No," I said honestly, tearing my work shirt off and yanking a sports bra from my go bag. "Hold the door."

He held it with his back and continued talking through the crack like I wasn't standing there in my bra and tattoos.

"You know what bothers me about Bishop?" Jordan said casually. "He's got that broody homicide swagger that says '*I don't talk about my feelings, but I definitely brood about them under a streetlight with a cigarette.*'"

I snorted. "You done?"

"No. Because somehow that man makes morally questionable look *hot*. Like, *we-bury-bodies-by-the-river* hot. And I find that deeply upsetting."

"Jordan."

"What? I'm venting."

"I know," I muttered, wriggling into my heavy, black cargo pants with reinforced knees and so many pockets I could probably pack a weekend bag in them.

I changed my boots out, swapping my favorite, cute brown ankle ones for a heavier black pair. These had soles thick enough to stomp glass. Weight I could use if I needed to put someone through drywall. I strapped on my vest last, hanging my badge from my neck and tucking it out of the way. Holster refit low against my ribs so I could draw without flashing metal at first glance. We weren't going in screaming "police," not unless we had to. First priority was to get the girls calm, not make them think they were being raided. Scared girls bolt.

Bolting girls get hurt.

"Hey," Jordan said gently. "You're good."

I blew out a breath. "Yeah. I will be. Let's do this shit."

We stepped into the hall at the same time Homicide came around the corner from their locker room. And I'll say this: I had not prepared myself for what Owen looked like geared. This was not dress-shirt-with-rolled-sleeves Owen. Nor bourbon-and-grit Owen.

This was Sergeant Owen Bishop. Homicide's rogue golden boy. Fitted black tee under tactical plate carrier. Glock seated at his hip like an extension of his hand. Veins popping in his forearms where he'd cinched his gloves on too tight. His jaw was locked, his eyes cutting through the room like a blade. He saw me at the same time I saw him. His eyes went dark. Not shock, not awe, not "oh wow, you clean up nice."

Please. He's not a rookie.

It was possession.

He didn't touch me. Didn't say it. But it was in his face clear as day: *Mine.*

Heat curled low in my stomach like it lived there.

Jordan muttered under his breath, "Ooooh someone looks like he just found religion."

"Shut up," I whispered.

Owen's gaze dipped to my boots, climbed slow—cargo pants, vest, throat, mouth, eyes. He stopped at my mouth just half a second too long. "You good to move?" he asked, voice low.

"Always," I said.

His mouth twitched, just the corner. "Let's go to work," he said.

The "clinic" wasn't marked. It sat behind an old muffler place off Claiborne, cinderblock walls, back door with a rusted hasp

41

and a padlock that had been cut so many times it hung on spite instead of metal. No patrol cars. No sirens. No light bar. We rolled up dark, two unmarked sedans, and pent-up energy with a side of anger issues.

"Check comms," I whispered.

"Copy," Jordan murmured behind me.

"Copy," Harper echoed from cover on the right.

Ramos: "Copy."

Sanders: "Copy."

"All right," I whispered. "Same thing as we talked about. I knock first, I talk first. We're 'help.' We're 'safe.' We are not cops unless we have to be cops. Goal is to get the girls calm and out before anybody gets stupid. Jordan, you're extraction and immediate med. Ramos, you float between us and Sanders. Harper, you're hall cover. Crawford, back door—nobody runs. Bishop—"

"On you," he said.

God. The way he said that.

Keep it together, Case.

I eased up to the door and listened. Muffled male voices. One higher, whining. One low. A woman crying underneath it, too soft and too even to be normal crying. That drugged sob. I hated that sound.

Hated it.

I knocked twice. Sharp. Familiar. The talking inside cut. I pitched my voice low, warm, tired. The voice I used on girls when I found them under bridges or shaking behind gas stations. "Hey, baby," I called through the door. "It's Casey. You in there?"

Silence.

Then: "Who the fuck is that?" Male. Annoyed.

"Casey," I repeated, sugar-sweet. "Open up. Pretty please,

love."

I heard shuffling. Whispering. The chain scraped. The door cracked. The second I saw we weren't staring down a barrel, I shoved.

We were in.

Everything happened at once.

Guy #1—skinny, tatted to hell, glove still on one hand—stumbled back with a curse. Owen was on him instantly. And I mean instantly. He didn't hesitate, didn't announce, didn't ask. He grabbed the guy by the throat, slammed him into the wall so hard drywall dust coughed into the air, and growled right in his face, "Move and I take your windpipe. Don't test me."

Temper, temper. My whole lower body lit up like a fuse. I told myself it was the adrenaline.

Guy #2 at the table went for something in a drawer. Sanders lunged past me, wrenched his arm behind his back, and bounced his forehead off the shitty card table.

My eyes went to the figure on the busted vinyl couch. She was slumped sideways, tank top hanging off one shoulder, lips pale. Her pupils were pinpricks. Breathing shallow. Sweat plastered the hair to her forehead.

"Hey, sweetheart," I breathed, dropping to my knees in front of her. "Hey. Hey. You with me? Can you hear me?"

Her eyes fluttered. Her mouth worked. A tiny, wrecked sound came out that sounded like "please."

"I got you," I whispered. "You're okay. You're okay. I'm gonna get you up, all right? We're leaving. Nobody here's gonna touch you again." Her fingers twitched weakly at the hem of my vest like she was trying to hold on. "Ramos!" I snapped without looking. "Blankets, med bag. Now. Sanders, get over here now, I need eyes."

Ramos blew through the doorway with the go bag and a thin gray thermal. I wrapped it around her shoulders like she wasn't basically cooking from the inside out. "You're okay," I said again, softer. "Breathe for me."

And then I heard it.

From the back.

A small sound. Not loud. Not a scream. Just a muffled sob. My body went cold as my head snapped in that direction.

"Bishop." My voice dropped to gravel. "With me."

He dropped his guy like he was trash.

We moved down a short, narrow hall. Owen slid ahead of me at the last second to take the corner first—because of course he did, control freak—and pushed the half-latched door with his boot.

There were no windows to bring light to the dark, damp room. As my eyes adjusted, part of me wished they hadn't. The space heater in the corner was doing nothing to fight back the chill. A chill I felt in my heart when I noticed the two girls on the bare mattress shoved into a corner. One was curled on her side, shaking so hard the whole mattress rattled. Couldn't be more than twenty-three, tops. Fresh track marks. Tear tracks on her face. Knees to her chest like she was trying to make herself smaller than air. The other one? Too still. On her back. Mouth parted. Lips edging blue.

"No," I whispered, already moving. I hit my knees and pressed two fingers to her throat. Nothing. My stomach tried to fall straight through the floor. "Shit. Shit. Shit." I tilted her chin, checked her airway. Clear. "Ramos!" I yelled, voice cracking. "Narcan! Now!"

I started compressions. Hard. Fast. Center mass. I'd done this more times than I wanted to admit and it never, ever got easier.

Owen was already kneeling on her other side, one hand cradling her head so it didn't slam against the bare floor every time my palms drove into her sternum. Ramos slid in, dropped to the floor next to us, and jammed the first dose of Narcan into her thigh. "C'mon, c'mon, c'mon," he muttered.

Thirty compressions. Breath. Thirty compressions. Breath.

"Breathe, baby," I begged, staring down at her face. "Please breathe for me. I got you. You're okay. Don't do this. Don't you quit on me tonight."

Then she jerked. Sucked in an ugly, rattling gasp so violent her whole body arched off the mattress, smacking into Owen's forearm. She started coughing, gagging, panicking.

"There you go," I gasped, stupidly close to crying. I smoothed a hand over her hair. Gentle. "There you go. That's it. That's it, sweetheart. You're all right. Keep breathing. We got you."

Her eyes snapped open, wide and wild. She tried to sit up, hands clawing, breath tearing out of her in fast, panicked sobs. "Don't let him touch me again," she choked. "Please, please, please, please—"

"He's done," I said, and I don't think I've ever meant anything more in my life. My voice dropped to a promise. "You hear me? He is done. He's never laying hands on you again. I swear it."

Her sob broke. Her body just crumpled. I caught her and pulled her against me. Behind me, I heard Owen exhale. Slow. Like he'd been holding his breath the entire time and finally let it go.

I glanced up at him. He wasn't looking at the suspect in the other room. He wasn't looking at Ramos or Jordan or anybody else. He was looking at me. Like I'd just torn his ribcage open with my bare hands and rearranged what was inside. My throat went dry. He swallowed. His voice came out low, rough. "Tell me which one's mine."

I blinked. "What?"

"Which one did it," he said quietly. Not loud. Lethal. "Which one put hands on them. Which one thinks he gets to walk out of here. Point and I'll handle it."

Something deep in me purred.

"Gloves," I breathed. Don't ask me how I knew. I just did.

His mouth curved into something feral. "Copy that." He made his way down the hallway and from the grunts and shouts of pain, it sounded like Owen had thrown protocol out the window.

Ramos and I helped both girls outside, gently ushering them to safety. I carried the one I had had to bring back to life. She was small enough that I could get her up in my arms with her head against my shoulder like a kid. She kept grabbing weakly at the strap of my vest, fingers flexing, then going slack. Jordan took the shaking girl. Ramos and Sanders hovered like mother hens, already on the phone with EMS, rattling off vitals, calling in possible trafficking victims without using the words "trafficking victims" over open radio.

Harper had Glove Guy in cuffs against the hood of the car when I cleared the back door. I smirked when I saw the busted lip and the eye that would be black come morning. Crawford had the other asshole bent over the trunk next to him, face mashed so hard into metal it was gonna leave a mark. Owen's team wasn't gentle, which was shocking to no one.

The block was still quiet. No sirens yet. No cruisers. Just us and a handful of porch watchers down the street pretending not to stare. We settled the girls in the back of our van with blankets and oxygen. Ramos climbed in with them and shut the doors behind him, giving them as much privacy as possible in a parking lot under a streetlight. For about ten seconds, nobody talked.

That happens sometimes after a pull. The air feels thick. Your ears ring. Everything gets a little too loud and a little too far away at the same time. You come off the high and your body tries to decide between passing out or throwing up. The world had gone quiet—sirens faded, radios muffled, the hum in my ears finally drowning itself out. I looked around for a quiet corner, and found it against the side of an empty SUV. I leaned against it, bracing my hands on my knees.

They'd all call her a victim. The news, the reports, my fucking captain. Even Deputy Chief Thibodeaux. But I couldn't.

Victim meant powerless.

Victim meant waiting to be saved.

And I'd been that girl once—too many times, too many houses that didn't want me. The kind of girl who learned to disappear before someone could hurt her again. If you called them victims, you started to believe they were already lost.

I didn't do lost. I found the bastards who made them bleed. My chest tightened—sharp, sudden. Panic clawed at the edges of my lungs, like it had been waiting its turn. I forced myself to breathe. One. Two. Three. In through the nose, out through the mouth.

I was fine. I had to be. A shadow slid into my space. I didn't have to look up to know who it was. I could feel him. Owen didn't touch me. He just stood there, close enough that his vest brushed my arm and his body blocked me from the street like a wall.

"Breathe," he muttered.

"I am," I whispered.

47

"Then do it again."

Bossy bastard. I did it again. The black sparks at the edge of my vision backed off. I let my head thunk very lightly against the side of the Explorer. Just for a second. Just for me.

"Casey," he said quietly.

"Mmh."

His voice dropped even lower. "Look at me."

I opened my eyes and turned my head. He was right there. Close enough I could see the little crease at the corner of his mouth. Close enough to smell sweat and gun oil and whatever spicy aftershave he used. He held my gaze, something fierce and unfinished burning there, before his expression shuttered like a door slammed closed. His shoulders squared, decision made. Then he turned and started to walk away.

Which, frankly, really pissed me off. Fuck this. Fuck that.

"You don't get to do that," I said quietly.

He stopped, looked over his shoulder. I didn't think he was going to reply, but then his jaw flexed and he said, "Do what?"

"Pretend that night didn't mean anything."

"It didn't," he said—too fast, too sharp.

I smiled, slow and humorless. "You sure about that, Bishop? Because every time you look at me, I can *feel* you trying to convince yourself."

He turned back to me, closing the space in two long strides. "You're out of line."

"You mean the line we crossed weeks ago? I couldn't refuse this assignment, nor would I want to. But you? You've been in the game longer. You've got favors you could've cashed in. But you didn't. Why do you think that is?"

For a beat, he just stood there, chest rising and falling, like he couldn't decide whether to walk out or burn the whole damn room down.

"We need to shut this down. Walk away," he said finally, voice low. "It's the right thing to do. The easiest."

"For whom?"

"Me. You. Both of us."

"Well, I don't know about you, but I've never been a fan of paved roads. I prefer gravel."

He stared at me—that cop stare meant to make people break. I didn't. I just stared back. *Yeah, I can do it too buddy.*

"Goddamn it," he muttered.

And then he did it. He broke. But he didn't ask. Owen Bishop was not a man who asked. He reached up, bracketed my jaw with one big, rough palm, and leaned in. The first brush of his mouth wasn't polite. It wasn't exploratory. It was surrender.

Heat slammed through me so fast I actually made a sound— low in my throat, automatic, traitorous. His thumb slid under my chin, angling my face up, and he kissed me like we weren't at a crime scene, like he'd been holding this in his teeth since the motel and it had finally snapped.

I grabbed his vest. I had to. My knees weren't doing shit. He groaned into my mouth when I yanked him closer. That sound? I'd be chasing it for the rest of my life.

He pulled away just long enough to breathe against my lips. His voice was wrecked gravel. "This is mine," he muttered. "You understand me?"

Cocky, possessive, absolutely insufferable man.

"Big talk," I whispered, heartbeat slamming, mouth still brushing his. "You planning on backing it up, Sergeant?"

His answering smile was pure sin. "Oh, you have no idea, *ma louve.*"

I swallowed a laugh. It came out shaky. "We are gonna be a

problem."

He smirked, and I couldn't resist kissing him again, not caring who might have been watching—or what it would cost later.

CHAPTER 4 ◉ OWEN

Evidence bags were stacked in uneven towers around the bullpen, and my detectives milled around in the familiar rhythm of a precinct after a bust. CSU had gone home hours ago, leaving more questions than answers. The squad looked half-dead—Harper typing with one hand while rubbing his neck with the other, Ramos arguing with the vending machine because it ate his dollar again. I kicked Jordan's chair as I walked past, and he jerked awake with a grunt.

Casey was the only one still sharp. Or at least trying to be. She was perched on the corner of my desk, hair tied high, boot tapping a rhythm. She had the ME's preliminary spread out in front of her like a poker hand.

Three bodies in eight days, all in places you couldn't *not* find them—under an overpass, in the doorway of a needle exchange, in a parking lot beside a law firm. It wasn't rage killing. It wasn't sexual. It wasn't sloppy. It was loud.

Whoever was doing this didn't want to hide. That was the part that pissed me off.

I leaned against the doorframe, watching Casey gnaw on a pen, apparently oblivious to me as she frowned at the report in her hands. I took the opportunity to watch her; something about the way her black hair gleamed in the light calmed me. Which was ridiculous. This wasn't the kind of job—and she wasn't the kind of partner—that should have come with calming side effects.

"This mix is wrong," she said, mostly to herself.

"What mix?"

She pointed with the pen she had been chewing on. "Tox screen. Benzos, fentanyl analog, xylazine—horse tranquilizer. Nobody's cut dope like this since early last year."

"Maybe nostalgia's back in style."

She gave me a look. "Cute. No, look at the ratios. It's too specific to be random. I've seen this exact combo before."

I should've been annoyed by her tone. I wasn't. I'd seen her barking at dealers, lieutenants, rookies, and a federal prosecutor in the last forty-eight hours. The snapping wasn't disrespect. It was bleed-off so she didn't rupture. I leaned closer, scanning the report but not seeing anything familiar. "Where?"

"That's the problem." She tapped the page again, faster. "It's right there in my head. I just can't grab it."

She'd been like this since we got back—pacing, muttering, chewing on a case file like a dog with a bone. The rest of us were winding down. She was winding up.

"Casey," I said, voice low enough to keep it between us. "Go home. You've been running since dawn."

She snorted. "Sleep is for slackers."

"You're about to fall on your face."

"Wouldn't be the first time." She gave a dry grin that didn't touch her eyes.

I caught myself watching the curve of her mouth a second too long and turned away. The kiss from earlier—the one behind the SUV when everyone was shouting—was still burning a hole in my skull. One bad second, too much adrenaline, and we'd crossed a line we shouldn't have. She hadn't mentioned it. Neither had I.

Harper came by with a fresh cup of sludge masquerading as coffee. "You two gonna glare that report into confession, or can I turn off the lights?"

"Shut up, Harper," we said in unison.

He grinned. "Cute. Couples therapy's Thursdays, by the way."

Casey flipped him off without looking up. Harper laughed his way out of the room.

When the door swung closed, she sighed, shoulders dropping. "It's not random, Owen. This formula—it's like déjà vu."

"Write it down," I told her. "Your brain'll hand it to you at 3 a.m. when you least want it."

She sighed before murmuring, "So bossy." She hopped off my desk, and her shoulder brushed mine as she walked past. The clock on the wall read 23:48. The city outside was still buzzing—sirens in the distance, thunder rolling over the river.

"You sure you don't want me to drive you home?" I asked.

She shook her head. "I'll be fine. But thanks."

For a long minute, I just stood there, staring at the empty space she'd left behind, listening to the rain start against the windows. I watched her go and told myself it was just because she still had my copy of the ME findings in her hand. Liar.

Thursday hit like a hangover that wouldn't quit. The air in the bullpen was swamp-thick, the AC working overtime just to push heat around. Every desk looked the same—cold coffee, half-eaten takeout, eyes gone glassy from too many hours staring at the same damn case files.

Casey was everywhere at once. She'd been glaring at that tox report for almost two days now, pacing around the bull pen like she could shake an answer loose by sheer will. You could see it eating at her—every muscle coiled, every pen cap mangled. She hadn't said it out loud, but she was taking the case personally. Maybe too personally.

We ran interviews all morning. Nothing but noise.

One of the street runners we'd hauled in wouldn't stop fidgeting, so I took the chair across from him and let my silence do the talking. The trick was to give them the quiet—they'd fill it eventually. Casey leaned against the wall, arms folded, watching me work. She was learning that sometimes shouting didn't move the needle. The kid kept insisting he didn't know anything about "the dead girls" or "the new mix," but every time I mentioned the word "product," his knee bounced faster.

"Look at me," I said, voice flat. "You're selling garbage that's killing people. That make you proud, or just stupid?"

He stared at the floor, but still didn't talk. I slammed my hand on the table, making him jump before leaning forward and letting my voice drop low. "Here's what's gonna happen. You keep running your mouth in circles, and I'm gonna make sure every dealer in this parish knows you gave us names. You start talking, maybe I forget to mention your name at all."

Casey gave me a look—maybe a warning, maybe something more. She let the silence drag, then spoke, calm and sharp. "Bay Street. That ring a bell?"

The runner blinked, hesitated, then nodded once. "Maybe. Used to be a drop spot. Not anymore."

"Why not?" I asked.

He shifted in his chair. "Bad batch. People started dropping. Word spread. Nobody wants to touch it."

Casey's eyes narrowed. "Bad batch, huh?" She scribbled something in her notebook, muttering under her breath. I could almost see her mind working—fast, focused, already chasing threads none of us could see yet. I didn't press. Sometimes it was better to stay quiet and let her think. Casey smiled, but there wasn't a drop of warmth in it. "Appreciate the honesty, sweetheart."

The kid tried to grin back, but she was already turning for the door, and I recognized the fire in her eyes—she was already ten steps ahead. Outside, Ramos was leaning against the wall, arms folded, tie long gone. "You two sure know how to make a guy look lazy."

I raised an eyebrow. "You could've come in and helped."

He shrugged, easy. "Nah, you've got the scary act handled. I'm better with charm."

Casey rolled her eyes, but she was smiling now, the kind that softened her whole face. "Sure, Ramos. Next time you can bat your lashes at a criminal and see how far that gets you."

He laughed, hands up in surrender. "Just sayin', Homicide could use a gentler touch sometimes."

"Tell that to the morgue," I said.

His smile faltered, just a flicker. Then it was back. "Fair point."

When he walked off, Casey sighed, rubbing the bridge of her nose. "You think he's right?"

"About charm?"

"About the morgue." Her eyes found mine. "You think this is gonna end before we run out of bodies?"

I wanted to lie. I didn't. "No."

She nodded once, sharp, then pushed off the wall. "Then we better work faster."

By Friday night, we hadn't slept, hadn't eaten anything that didn't come in a Styrofoam box, and hadn't found a damn thing worth celebrating. So, when Harper texted about drinks with

Vice at the 10/7, I surprised myself when instead of heading home, I took the turn for the bar. Not because I wanted to drink. Because I wanted to see her somewhere that didn't smell like death and coffee. That should've been my cue to turn the car around. I didn't.

The 10/7 was one of those New Orleans bars that smelled like a hangover before you even walked in. The place was already bleeding light onto the sidewalk, a swampy glow that looked like bad decisions and cheap beer. You could taste the fryer grease in the air, hear a half-broken jukebox cycling through every "dad rock" hit from before I made detective. The neon lights buzzed like mosquitoes. I didn't go to bars much anymore. Last time I'd been here, I still wore a wedding ring and thought I was working late for the good of the city. Turns out, I was just avoiding home. Tonight, I didn't have an excuse.

Harper clocked me first. "Jesus Christ, look who decided to mingle with the living."

Ramos whistled. "Didn't think you knew where this place was, Bishop."

Crawford didn't even look up from his beer. "Oh, he does. I vaguely remember him coming here when he was hiding from his wife."

I shook my head. "Cute. You girls done?" I motioned to the barkeep and a few seconds later a waitress stopped by our table long enough to slide me a bottle, condensation already rolling down it. I turned just enough to catch Harper elbowing Ramos like a school kid.

I hadn't planned on staying. I figured I'd make a lap, pretend to care, then ghost out. But then I saw her. Casey was already there—front and center, leaning against the bar in a tank top, that same sheep skin jacket, and worn jeans, hair down and wild.

She was laughing at something Jordan said, head thrown back, eyes bright. Completely at ease, like the weight she carried during the week had finally slipped off her shoulders.

"Well, if there's no wife to hide from... what could possibly drag you out here?" Harper followed my line of sight. "Ah. There it is. Mystery solved."

"Shut up," I said, but it didn't matter. He'd already caught me.

She saw me before I could look away. One eyebrow lifted. Then she smiled—that same sharp, knowing grin that I was willing to bet had gotten her both in and out of trouble—and started walking over.

Jordan whispered something in her ear and she laughed. When she reached the table, Harper sat back and said, "Well, hell. Didn't expect to see Homicide and Vice in the same watering hole without a brawl."

Casey smirked. "Give it five minutes."

Jordan frowned. "Bitch, you invited us."

Sanders shook her head before stealing Ramos's drink, and Nguyen claimed a spot in the corner with an expression that said he had been dragged here against his will.

Me too, bud. Kind of.

"Sit," I said, jerking my chin toward the empty stool beside me.

She did, like it was the most natural thing in the world. "Thought you were a whiskey guy," she said.

"Sometimes."

"Just not here."

"Not usually."

She waved the waitress over. "Round for the table, please." Everyone except me cheered, I just kept watching her.

Different bar.

Same woman.

Same line we shouldn't cross.

I declined the bright blue shot of whatever the hell it was and watched as Harper choked on it. It shut him up for all of five seconds before he said, "So, Sergeant, you coming out of retirement tonight? Maybe we'll get lucky and see you dance." I glared. "Not unless someone's dying."

And for a while, it was almost normal. If normal was Vice and Homicide together without being at each other's throats. Casey had my whole damn team wrapped around her finger, and I just sat back as we drank the week away. The noise of the bar swallowed the world outside—the bad cases, the bodies, the damn tox screen that had been haunting her. She laughed with Jordan over something stupid, her head tipping back, throat exposed, hair brushing her shoulders. I caught myself watching again.

"Careful," Harper muttered, low enough only I could hear. "You're starting to look human."

"Shut up," I said, but there was no heat in it.

Then, with only a couple hours before last call, the karaoke machine kicked on.

It started with a drunk rookie butchering "Sweet Child O' Mine," and by the second chorus, everyone was yelling instead of singing. Casey and Jordan were cheering him on, and I figured that'd be the end of it—until Jordan turned to her with a devilish look. Which she returned before standing and pulling him with her. Jordan wobbled on his feet but she steadied him and with encouragement from the whole table, they headed to the stage.

The first beats of "Love Me Like You Do" came through the old speakers—way too loud, and not the kind of music you would usually hear in a room full of cops. A song I only knew 'cause my ex wife had been obsessed with it. Jordan was pretending to be Casey's backup singer. When she started singing—off-key, off-tempo, full voice anyway—the entire bar howled.

It was chaos. Beautiful, stupid chaos.

She was waving her arms, hair flying, trying to hit notes no human should attempt. The mic squealed. She laughed so hard she had to grab Jordan's shoulder to stay upright. And I couldn't look away. Maybe it was the relief of seeing her unguarded for once. Maybe it was the way she didn't care that she sounded awful. Maybe I was just a fool. For the first time all week, something in my chest shifted—loosened just enough to be a problem.

Halfway through the song, she spotted me watching. Held my gaze. And sang the next line straight at me: *"My head's spinnin' around, I can't see clear no more. What are you waiting for?"*

Fuck. I was cooked.

She laughed, big and bright, right into the mic. When the song ended, everyone was clapping, half ironically, half in love with her. She gave a dramatic bow and handed off the microphone. When she came back to the table, she dropped onto the stool beside me, flushed and smiling, breathless. "What?"

"Nothing."

"You're judging me."

"I'm... observing."

"You sure you don't wanna sing one?"

"I'm sure I want to keep my dignity."

"You lost that years ago," she said, smirking into her drink.

Jordan leaned across the table, eyes gleaming. "So, is this what foreplay looks like for detectives, or am I missing something?"

"Keep talking, Delaney," I said. "See what happens."

59

He grinned. "I like my chances."

I ignored him, turned back to her. She was tracing circles on her beer label, humming under her breath. Same damn song.

"You done terrorizing the sound system?" I asked.

"Depends," she said. "You done pretending you don't like me?"

I looked away, grabbed my drink. Ignored the way her smile faltered when I refused to respond. The whole table was watching us both now. I glanced back at her, noted the spark of anger in her eyes before she shoved it down.

"Yeah," she said, pushing off the stool. "Figured as much."

She started to leave, then stopped. "Next time, Bishop, try showing up *before* last call. I might even save you a dance."

Then she was gone—just a flash of denim and wild hair in the neon light—leaving me sitting there with a half-empty beer and a head full of bad ideas. Ideas I should've shut down weeks ago. And hadn't.

Harper waited until the door shut behind her, then looked at me. "You're so screwed."

"Go to hell," I muttered.

He clinked his bottle against mine. "Cheers to bad decisions."

I drank to that, though it didn't taste like victory. The noise of the bar rolled on without me—laughter, music, the faint echo of her voice singing something off-key. I stayed just long enough for the bottle to run dry, then left the same way I'd come in: through the smoke, past the jukebox, out into the night. I made it home, and the quiet felt even heavier than usual.

I showered, letting the water run hot until the mirror fogged, took two ibuprofen and told myself I wasn't sore because I was getting old. I threw myself in bed sometime after 1 a.m. and let the ceiling fan rattle me toward unconsciousness.

I was mostly asleep when someone tried to break my door down.

CHAPTER 5 ⊙ OWEN

T hree hard, fast pounds. Not timid. Not neighbor polite. I was awake, armed, and moving before the thinking part of my brain caught up.

"Owen! Open the door!"

Casey.

I exhaled, not relief exactly, just recalibration. Gun still in my hand, I checked the peephole out of habit. Sure enough: her. Ponytail now half falling out, tank top, fuzzy pajama pants with stupid little cartoon cats all over them, flip flops instead of boots... I glanced at the stove clock as I slid the deadbolt back. 2:17 a.m.

I cracked the door and stared at her. "You better be shot," I said.

She blew past me like she lived there. Like she was blissfully unaware of how bad a decision this was.

"I figured it out!"

"I'm serious, Chambers. How the fuck do you even know where I live?"

"I've got skills." She tossed the words over her shoulder without even looking at me, kicking her shoes off next to where my boots were. Old habits.

I shut the door before heading back to my room and putting

my gun away. Running a hand through my hair and resigning myself to whatever this was, I followed the noise until I found her in the kitchen. My place used to look like a home. You could see the bones of that if you squinted. You could also see exactly where she'd stopped touching it. There were patches on the wall from where pictures used to hang. Throw pillows I didn't buy and never bothered to get rid of. And dining chairs that matched and a table that didn't because the original table left with the ring.

Now there was also Casey, barefoot on my tile, dropping a manila folder on that table like it was a live grenade.

"Okay," she said.

"Okay what?"

"I figured it out."

"You said that already."

She ignored me. Crumpled papers were yanked from a tired-looking folder and scattered across the scratched wood: toxicology screens, evidence logs, crappy photocopies of forms with black smudges where signatures used to be before someone ran them through a copier twelve times. Her hands were moving fast. She had that look again—pupils wide, jaw tight, some kind of electric hum under her skin. That relentless, restless *go* in her. It was 2 a.m. and she looked awake from the bones out. She smelled like some coconut shampoo and something woodsy, and I told myself I was just getting a better look at the papers in front of her when I leaned in.

"Listen, look," she said, and she pointed without looking up, like she was conducting me. "I knew that toxic mix was familiar. It was killing me. I went home, I showered, I tried to lie down, and my brain was just doing that screechy modem dial-up noise in my head. Could not shut off. So I got up. I pulled seizure logs for the last six months. Every batch we hit that didn't match normal street cut."

"You have seizure logs at home?"

She shot me an offended look. "Obviously."

"Obviously," I echoed.

She slapped one stapled packet down in front of me and tapped it hard enough to rattle the table. "Bay Street warehouse. Three months ago. We hit them on a tip they were stretching fentanyl with benzos and horse tranq, trying to get girls hooked faster and keep them under longer. We pulled eight bricks. All stamped the same. Our lab flagged the cut ratio because it's nasty, even for this city."

I skimmed the lines of typed lab notes. There it was in black and white: fentanyl analog variant, diazepam derivative, xylazine. Same ugly mix. Same levels. Same weird outlier contaminant our ME circled because he didn't recognize it.

"Keep reading," she said.

"I can read without supervision."

"Can you? Because every time I've seen you fill out a use-of-force report, you've looked like you're trying to do calculus with your off-hand—"

"Casey."

She shut up. For two seconds.

Her voice dropped. "It's the same cut. It's not just close. It's exact."

I looked up at her. "So, the same batch that was in that warehouse three months ago is back on the street now."

"Yes," she said, like she'd been waiting for me to say it out loud so it became real. Her eyes were bright and mean and scared. "Except it shouldn't be. That's why I'm here."

"Explain," I said.

She flipped to another page, this one an evidence destruction order—grainy photocopy, black boxes, chain-of-custody table down the left. She stabbed at it with her finger. "See that? Logged at Vice. Weighed, cataloged, signed into lockup. That's my sergeant's signature on intake. That's mine on verification. Then that"—she tapped lower—"is the destruction authorization. It got signed out two days later for 'incineration.'"

Her voice curled around that last word like it tasted bad.

"So it's supposed to be gone," I said slowly.

"It's supposed to be ash."

"Maybe somebody skimmed before it hit the furnace. That happens."

Her eyes cut to me. "Not eight bricks."

Fair. You don't just "skim" eight bricks. You can't misplace that. That's weight. That's money. And if that much weight walked out of an evidence cage, it didn't walk alone.

I felt my jaw tighten. "Who had access?"

"Vice," she said flatly. "Which means me. Which means my people."

She held my gaze when she said it, chin lifted like she was daring me to say what both of us already knew. "It means somebody in Vice," I said instead.

Her mouth twitched. It wasn't a smile. "Split that hair however helps you sleep, Bishop."

"You didn't sign the release," I said, tapping the bottom of the form. Different signature. Different handwriting.

"Doesn't matter," she said. "I'm still top of that page. My name is on 'verification.' That's enough to get me crucified if this goes public."

Her shoulders were shaking—tiny, constant vibrations like she was holding herself so tight she might crack. All that loud, reckless energy from the bar was gone. What was left was something rawer. Guilt. Fury. Fear wrapped in armor. Casey never came in soft. She came in swinging. Watching her shake instead of swing was worse than any body bag.

I stepped in closer. "Tell me what your head's doing right now."

She blinked. "What?"

"You're spiraling. Talk."

Her laugh was sharp and ugly. "Oh, I'm spiraling? Wow, I hadn't noticed. Thank you, Dr. Phil. That's so helpful."

"Casey."

That shut her up again. I took a second to marvel at how one word from me was enough to move her. To make her listen. Which was saying a lot for a woman who had a hard time taking orders from anyone.

She dragged both hands over her face, pressing her fingers into her eyes hard enough they left red crescents on her cheeks when she dropped them. For a few seconds she just breathed, fast and shaky. Then, quiet: "He's not just dumping bodies, Owen. He's... talking to us."

"Go on."

"He's putting these girls in places we have to see. Under an overpass. The stash house. That damn parking lot. That's not hiding. That's putting them where the city has to file paperwork. Where the press can get pretty pictures."

"Yeah."

"He's saying, 'look what you let happen.'" She tapped the tox screen again with the back of her knuckle. "He's using *our* batch. He's literally poisoning them with evidence we're on record as 'destroying' and then displaying them like, 'Hey Vice, hey Homicide, hey City Hall—still feel good about that press

66

conference you gave about cleaning up the streets?'" Her voice frayed on the last word.

I let that sit a beat. Let her breathe. Then: "Okay. Let's assume you're right—"

"I *am* right."

"Let's assume you're right," I repeated, because if I gave her that win right now, she'd blow apart. "What does that make him?"

Her mouth opened. Closed.

I took a breath, let it out slow. "He's not random. He's not chaotic. He's not a thrill killer. He's a message with legs. He thinks he's a crusader."

Her throat flexed. "He is a crusader."

"Careful," I said quietly.

"I'm serious," she snapped, eyes flashing. "You think this city gives a shit about dead girls nobody can name? You think anybody upstairs does more than sigh and do the math on how much the OD report is gonna cost them in PR if some councilman's wife sees it on the news? We log 'suspected overdose,' we move on, the world keeps spinning. He knows that. He knows if he doesn't make noise, nobody listens. So now he's making noise. With us. With what we 'lost track of.' He's not wrong about that part."

I studied her. "You sympathizing with my killer, Chambers?"

"I'm sympathizing with somebody who begged us to listen and got ignored until he picked up a needle and started screaming," she shot back. Then, softer, almost to herself: "I can't lose another one."

There it was.

Before I could think better of it, I reached up and touched her. The second my hand made contact, I knew I'd crossed it.

Not the professional line. The one I wasn't sure I'd ever find my way back across. My hand fit perfectly on the back of her neck, just below her hair. Warm skin under my palm, still a little damp from sweat and New Orleans air. Her pulse jumped hard against my fingers. Her eyes snapped to mine like I'd grabbed her by the spine. "Hey," I said, and my voice came out lower than I meant. "Look at me."

"I *am* looking at you."

"Then hear me: this is not on you."

Her laugh cracked. "Right."

"It's not. If you'd known that shit didn't get destroyed, you would've lit your own evidence cage on fire and thrown whoever touched it through the front window of the precinct. I've seen you go for throats over less."

Her mouth fought a smile and lost for half a second. "You don't know me like that."

I huffed. "Chambers, I've known you for two weeks, and I already know you're the kind of person who'd fistfight God in a Walmart parking lot if He looked at one of your CIs wrong."

That got me a sound. A tiny one, barely there, but it was real. Her shoulders dropped a fraction. She swayed forward like gravity pulled her. I should've stepped back. I didn't. We were too close now. My hand was still on her neck; her fingers were curled in the hem of my T-shirt like she hadn't even realized she was doing it. Her eyes flicked down to my mouth. Slowly. Thought about it. Flicked back up.

"This is a bad idea," she whispered.

"Yeah," I said.

Her breath hitched. "Tell me to leave."

Yeah, I probably should. Instead, I said, "C'mere."

She made a sound low in her throat and melted into me like

she had been waiting for someone else to take the weight from her shoulders.

When she kissed me, it wasn't like the first time.

The bar hookup all those weeks ago had been heat and hunger and the kind of impulsive stupidity you swear you'll never repeat. This wasn't that. This was desperate. This was relief. This was her shaking in my hands and trying to climb out of her skin and into mine because she'd been holding this together with her bare fingers for days, and they were finally slipping.

I didn't pretend I was stronger than that. I didn't pretend I was noble. I dragged her in by the back of the neck, swallowed her little gasp, and felt the bottom drop out of both of us. Fuck. I don't know how I'd convinced myself I didn't need this. Or why she'd been the one to prove me wrong.

The taste of her. The little sound she made when I threaded my fingers in her hair and tilted her head back to give myself better access. The way her body melded into mine until I could feel the heat of her body through our clothes. I moved my hand from her neck to her hip, and pulled her into me as I brought my other hand to her throat. My hands were big enough around her slender neck that my thumb could trace her jawline from the tip of her ear to her chin. She moaned and I walked her back until she was pressed up against my counter.

I picked her up and sat her on the worn surface, running my hands from her ass to her calves. I grabbed them and wrapped her legs around me. She pulled away from me, looking up at me with a question in her eyes. Was I sure? I answered her the only way I knew how.

By pressing a kiss to her exposed collarbone and whispering, *"Laisse-moi être ta distraction."*

She shivered then slipped her hands under my shirt, running

69

them along my abdomen. I growled, suddenly irritated by the fabric between us and she froze, misunderstanding the reason for the sound. I all but tore my shirt off before leaning in and nipping at the delicate skin of her shoulder. Her shirt was quick to follow. I covered her skin in near frantic kisses, in a desperate attempt to memorize her taste. She was panting now and had a hand wrapped in my hair, which she pulled on until I rose and kissed her pretty, pink lips. I pulled away from her, basking in the sight of her flushed cheeks and bright eyes.

"Fuck, Owen, why'd you stop?"

I chuckled, "Because, *ma louve*, I want to see you in my bed. Now." I stepped back, and she hopped off the counter with a soft smile.

"You ever going to tell me what all those fancy words mean?"

I pulled her with me as I headed for the hallway and gave her a wolfish grin, "Look it up."

She laughed. I couldn't remember the last time I'd had a woman in my room. And suddenly I realized she was everything—what I'd been chasing before, and what I hadn't known I wanted until now. I saw the moment she hesitated and gently pushed her further in. Stepping up behind her, I wrapped my arms around her waist and whispered in her ear. "Strip for me, baby. Let me see you."

She shivered as I stepped back, watching her every move. She turned to me, taking a backwards step to the bed. I watched as her confidence grew with every second I stayed still. Until she tossed her panties at me and I caught them easily. She sat on the bed, and tilted her head. Those expressive eyes of hers challenged me, and the smile she gave me was all sin. But I stayed where I was. "Spread your legs."

Her mouth formed a small "O," and I swear my cock got even

harder at the thought of her swallowing me until I touched the back of her throat. But not yet. She bit her lip but slowly did as I asked, exposing herself to me. I raised an eyebrow, wanting to see what she would do next. I could see how wet she was, knew she was probably dying for some friction. I took my time taking off my gray sweats I had gone to bed in. She never looked away, but I grinned when I heard her whimper as I pulled out my aching cock. I fisted myself, so hard it hurt, and she licked her lips. Then she dropped a hand between her legs, and ran a finger through her glistening slit. Just like I wanted.

"That's my girl."

Her eyes were hooded, and they widened at my praise. This time when she touched herself it was firmer, and she tossed her head back on a moan. She pushed a finger inside herself, then another. Her hips started rocking against her hand, and she was panting again. I could hear the sound her fingers made as she pumped them in and out of herself. She was close. Her eyes closed, and I took a step closer. When she pressed another finger against her clit, I moved and grabbed her wrist. Her eyes flew up, brown eyes so molten they glowed like a dark amber. She pulled against my grip and practically growled at me. "Owen!"

"You thought I was going to let you come without me? Not a chance, baby." I put my mouth to her wet fingers and sucked on them until they were clean. Dropping her hand, I lifted her and tossed her further back onto the sheets. When I climbed into the bed with her, she whimpered, and I leaned down to kiss her, letting her taste herself on my tongue. *"Ma louve. Mon péché.* Do you know how crazy you drive me? How many times I've thought about you?"

I coated myself in her arousal.

71

"Bent over my desk."

I slid in the tip and then pulled out.

"Handcuffed to my bed."

I pushed into her, groaning at the way her warm cunt squeezed me. Her eyes fluttered closed, and she pushed her head back into the pillows.

"Riding my cock, and moaning my name."

I wrapped my hand around her slender throat, pulled out, waited until she opened her eyes and looked at me, then slammed back in.

"Owen!" She reached behind her, bracing one hand against the head board and using the other to dig into my back. I knew she was going to leave marks. She wasn't being gentle but then again, neither was I. Hand still around her throat, I used the other to pull one of her legs up and over my shoulder. I loved how flexible she was and bent my head to the side, kissing the soft hollow just behind her knee.

"Owen, please."

Fuck, the way she panted my name. I couldn't hold myself back anymore. Using her throat and leg for leverage, I pounded into her relentlessly. Every time I bottomed out in her pussy, it shuddered around me and squeezed like a vise. She started cursing, muttering what sounded like a prayer. I growled, tightening my grip on her throat and watching the way her eyes rolled.

When her cunt grew impossibly tight, I knew she was right there. I moved my hands to her hips, stabilizing her as she drew in a sharp breath and shattered around me. I was right there with her, riding it out until she grew still under me, a fine sheen of sweat on her tan skin. Then I pulled out before I finished, and she whimpered. I kissed her again, then traced her jawline like I had all those weeks ago. I made my way to her breasts, pulling the taut peak into my mouth, and her back bowed off the bed. I licked, sucked, and bit my way down to her pussy until I could press my tongue against her clit. She pulled at my hair until I looked up at her.

"Owen, baby, I can't."

"Can't what?"

"I can't come again."

Not breaking eye contact, I said, "Wanna bet?"

Then I licked her from top to bottom. She shouted, hand finding its way into my hair again. She yanked on my head, raising her hips and pressing her pussy against my face. I chuckled before pushing my tongue against her inner walls. When I replaced my tongue with my fingers, she groaned. Pumping in and out, spreading her, loving the little sounds she made. I got three fingers in before she started rocking against my hand, riding it like she wished it were my cock.

"Who do you belong to?"

She was trembling, and for a second I wasn't sure she would respond. Then she said, "No one."

I stilled and leaned over her until we were almost nose to nose. She gave me a sexy grin, then I nipped her earlobe and pinched her clit at the same time. Hard. She yelped. "Who do you belong to, Casey?"

"Owen, please."

"Who?" I pressed my finger against her clit again.

I saw the moment she gave in and relished it. "You. I belong to you."

"That's right, *ma louve*." I settled myself between her thighs again and then slid slowly inside of her. Torturing her. She shuddered. "My pussy. My girl. Every little whimper and moan.

73

Mine." In and out, then I pinched her clit again.

She shattered, screaming my name and dragging her nails down my back. I came with a snarl, shoving my cock as deep inside her cunt as I could. For a minute, I swear I couldn't see past the stunning woman under me. Then I wrapped my arms around her, twisting us both until I was under her and she lay on top of me. My cock grew soft inside her but neither of us moved. I ran my hands up and down her back until eventually, her breathing slowed and she was asleep. Her legs were entwined with mine and before I knew it, I was asleep too.

When I woke up, it was quiet, same as before, but not empty. The hum under it had changed. It was gray outside—that pre-dawn hour where the streetlights were still on but the sky behind them was starting to go pale. My blinds cut the light into stripes across the floor. The air tasted familiar, but under it was something sweeter that I wouldn't think too hard about, because if I did, I was going to drag her back to bed, and we did not have time for that. I pulled on the sweats I had discarded last night and headed downstairs.

My kitchen table looked like a murder board had exploded. And Casey was in my kitchen wearing one of my shirts. I had never seen anything look so damn right. It wasn't sexy, not the way you'd sell it in a movie. It was one of my old button-ups, sleeves rolled sloppily to her elbows, hem hitting mid-thigh. The collar sat wrong on her because it wasn't cut for her shoulders. Her hair was a wreck—bun half fallen out, curls and wisps sticking out in every direction like she'd been electrocuted. I smirked, knowing I was the reason for her scattered appearance. I leaned against the doorway and just watched her for a second.

She was muttering to herself, voice rough with sleep and

74

overuse. "Okay, so if we pull chain-of-custody from Bay Street and line that up against payroll and overtime, maybe we get who suddenly got cute with the money… come on, pour, you bastard—"

I hated that coffee pot, but had never gotten a new one. You had to press a button on the handle for it to pour. Some dumb-as-hell safety feature. I watched her fight it for a moment… then she jammed her finger against the button just right and coffee overflowed the mug.

"Son of a bitch—!" She jerked back, coffee splashing down the front of the shirt.

That was my cue, apparently.

"Burn yourself in my kitchen and I gotta file paperwork," I said, voice still gravelly with sleep.

She jumped like I'd fired a round. "Jesus, make noise when you walk!"

"I did. You're just too busy cussing out appliances to notice." I pushed off the doorway and crossed to her, grabbing a dish towel from the oven handle and offering it. "Here."

She took it, blotting at the coffee stain. My shirt now had a brown splash down the placket and across the hem. On her, it looked indecent in a way that made my brain fog for a second.

She looked down, then up at me, deadpan. "Sorry. I'll dry-clean it."

I snorted. "That shirt's older than half my rookies. If it survives this, it deserves a medal."

Her mouth twitched. "Looks better on me anyway."

"I didn't say it didn't."

I stepped in closer to take the ruined towel from her, close enough to catch the scent of coffee and skin. The collar of the shirt slipped off her shoulder when she moved, exposing a curl

75

of color—blue and green, wet-paint bright against bare skin. Without thinking, I hooked a finger under the fabric, pulled it a little farther aside, and pressed a kiss to the spot just above the ink.

"What's the story with that?" I asked, tracing the edge with my thumb before I turned away to clean the spill.

"Hippocampus," she said finally. "Greek sea horse. Poseidon's steed, and ferrier of souls."

I looked back at her—the shirt slipping off one shoulder, that ink catching the light.

"Figures," I said. "You'd pick something born from the ocean. Wild. Free. Untamed."

Her mouth curved, just barely. "Better than being leashed."

"Wouldn't suit you anyway," I said.

She huffed a laugh, shaking her head. "You don't even know me, Bishop."

"Sure I do," I said, rinsing the mug. "You drink your coffee too sweet, you talk to evidence, and you don't back down from anyone. I know enough."

When I looked back, she was watching me—soft, wary, like she couldn't decide whether to kiss me or hit me. Then she was setting the mug down, climbing up to sit on the edge of my counter like she'd done it a thousand times. Like she'd done last night. Bare legs swinging, my shirt riding up just a touch with every little movement. Her toes brushed the cabinet door. I tried very hard not to look like I was staring and probably failed.

Her voice went business again. "Okay. We need to talk strategy."

"Good morning to you, too." I started a new pot of coffee and rested my crossed arms on the counter next to her, my elbow brushing her bare thigh.

"Good morning," she said automatically, then added, "Strategy."

I sighed, dragging a hand over my face. "Fine. Talk."

She pointed at the mess on the table with her mug. "We've got proof that batch never got destroyed. We've got bodies with that exact signature in their system. We've got a killer who's doing public drops to force attention."

"Yeah."

"And we've got a leak," she said, eyes hard. "In Vice."

"In your unit," I corrected quietly—enough to tell her what I meant: *I believe you.* Her jaw flexed, but she nodded.

"So, we do this quiet," she said. "No captains. No Internal Affairs. Not yet."

My eyebrows went up. "You really wanna sit on 'somebody in my division diverted eight bricks of poison and is now indirectly responsible for a bunch of bodies' and not tell Thibodeaux?"

Her look said *don't be stupid.* "I tell Thibodeaux, he kicks it to my captain. Captain loops in Legal. Legal panics, everything gets labeled 'pending review,' and the trail dies before we even start. Leak vanishes. Product vanishes. And our guy?" She flicked two fingers like she was tapping ash. "He escalates. Because the only way he can make us listen is body count."

She wasn't wrong. I hated how not-wrong she was. I scrubbed the back of my neck and looked over the paperwork. "So you want to hunt this from both directions."

"Exactly," she said, brightening, like I'd just gotten the right answer in class. "You quietly pull chain-of-custody on the Bay Street seizure. Who signed, who logged, who transported, who had keys. You run your Homicide background voodoo on them—gambling debt, sudden cash, divorce payments magically current. Anything that smells like side money."

"And you?"

She took a drink of coffee, winced when it burned, powered through anyway. "I work my people. Street side. See if anyone's heard about product with the crown stamp still moving. See if any of my confidentials suddenly got generous donations. See if anybody's running scared of a guy they shouldn't be scared of." She swallowed and added, quieter, "And I start looking at my own house without looking like I'm looking at my own house."

That last part came out tight.

"Casey."

Her eyes flicked to mine.

"Be careful."

She gave me a look like *obviously*. But under it was something else. Something softer. Something that said thank you without her mouth having to form the words.

"I'll handle my end," I told her. "You handle yours. We don't go upstairs until we've got a name and something solid to nail them on so they can't just resign and disappear quietly to Florida."

"Florida's too miserable," she muttered.

I almost smiled.

For a second, we just sat in it. Morning creeping into the edges of the blinds. My coffeepot hissing. The AC clicking on and then off again because this house leaked air like a busted lung. Her on my counter in my shirt, swinging her legs, pretending she wasn't watching me watch her.

I could feel the shift. The line we'd already crossed wasn't just physical. We'd locked into something else. Something I shouldn't name. Something that'd get us both burned alive if we weren't careful. So, naturally, I decided to be responsible.

"Casey," I said.

"Mhm?"

"This doesn't leave this room."

Her mouth curved, slow and lethal. "Which part? The conspiracy to expose a dirty cop in my unit, or the part where you said 'c'mere' and then—"

I kissed her, partly just to shut her up. Mostly just 'cause I wanted to.

She was grinning now, full teeth. "Relax. I'm not telling Harper anything. He'd choke on his own tongue, and then I'd have to resuscitate him, and HR would get involved. Too much paperwork."

I groaned. "You're a menace."

"I know." She slid off the counter. My shirt shifted on her hips, and I actually had to look away for a second like I was a teenager and not a grown man with kids on the job calling me sir.

"Also," she added lightly, "Don't take it personal."

I turned to her. "Take what personal?"

She leaned up, pressed a quick kiss to the corner of my mouth like it was nothing, like it wasn't going to sit in my skin for the rest of the day burning like a brand. "All the shit Jordan is going to give you," she said against my jaw.

Then she grabbed her stack of paperwork, my spare hoodie from the back of a chair, and her stupid cat pajama pants from where they'd landed, and started for the door barefoot with her mug in her hand like she was just heading out to grab the mail.

"I thought you said you wouldn't tell anyone," I called after her.

She looked back, one eyebrow up. "I said I wouldn't tell

Harper. Best friends are off the table, handsome."

For fuck's sake. My brain short-circuited at the way she said it. She might as well have said, "Mine."

"Next time," I said, "you call before you show up at two in the damn morning."

Her grin went smug. "Where's the fun in that?"

Then she was gone. Door clicking shut behind her. House going quiet again.

I stood there in my kitchen, bare feet on tile that needed mopping, coffee cooling in the pot, paperwork bleeding across my table, the air still thick with her, and let the reality catch up: Someone in Vice was dirty. Three girls were dead. And I was in this now—not because I was Homicide, not because I was good at my job, not because this would look great on paper with the captain. I was in because of her. I'd spent years convincing myself I didn't need anyone. Turns out, I'd just been sober.

And Casey Chambers was one hell of a relapse.

CHAPTER 6 ◆ CASEY

Monday morning was any other day. Except for the part where everybody shut up when I walked in. Not subtle, either. Full sitcom. Ramos was mid-story at Harper's desk—something about his neighbor, a busted air conditioner, and a shirtless repair guy—and he just... stopped talking. Froze with his hands still up like a mime. Harper saw me, saw the look on my face, then immediately dropped his eyes to his computer and pretended to type. I knew he was pretending because Harper didn't even type that fast on forms IA might read.

And Jordan? Jordan looked like he'd been waiting for this since sunrise.

He was leaned back in my chair—my chair—feet up on my desk, sipping my coffee, scrolling through my notes on my tablet like he paid my car insurance. He brightened like a raccoon that just found an unlocked trash can.

"There she is," he announced. "My favorite girl. My queen. My reason for believing in romance again."

"Get your feet off my desk," I said.

"That's the tone," he said, pointing at me with a to-go cup from the coffee shop down the street—my usual, made exactly the way I liked it. I still hadn't figured out who kept leaving them for me, but I had a good guess. "That's it right there. That post-sin glow. I knew it."

"Jordan."

"You're humming," he went on, ignoring me the same way toddlers ignore speed limits. "You only hum when you slept. Or when you got railed. And you, Miss I-Haven't-Slept-Since-January, do not look rested."

"Jordan."

He leaned in, eyes wide and delighted. "So. On a scale of one to 'I am going to have to pretend I didn't hear this on the stand one day,' how illegal do I need to consider it?"

I plucked the coffee out of his hand, went to take a sip, and made a face. "Did you drink this?"

"Of course I drank it. I thought it was mine. I thought you brought me coffee because you loved me. But apparently, you're out here betraying me."

"Move," I said.

He did not move. He just scooted over an inch, patted the edge of my own chair like he was offering me space on a park bench. "So, you gonna tell me who it is, or am I supposed to guess like it's Clue? I feel like it's Clue. I feel like this is 'Sergeant Bishop in the evidence cage with the attitude.'"

Ramos made a coughing noise that sounded suspiciously like "oh my God," and then pretended to reorganize a stack of case files that did not need reorganizing. I didn't look at Owen. That would've been too much. I could feel him, though. You know how you know when there's a cop car behind you even before you see the lights? It was like that. Presence. Weight. A hum at the edge of my skin.

I was not thinking about his mouth. I was absolutely not thinking about his hands. I was busy.

Working. Professional. Focused.

Jordan squinted. "Huh. No denial. Interesting."

"If you keep talking shit, I'm going to staple your tongue to the blotter."

He grinned. "Spicy. My favorite flavor."

"Delaney," Harper called, not looking up from his computer, "don't make her assault you before 9 a.m. I haven't had enough caffeine to lie to HR convincingly."

"HR doesn't care," Jordan said. "HR stopped caring three mayors ago. We could get married in here, and they'd send a fruit basket."

I set my bag down, dragged my chair out from under Jordan's dramatic little hip, and dropped into it. He rotated to the corner of my desk instead, like some nosy desk gargoyle.

He dropped his voice. "So... was it good?"

"Jordan."

"What?" he whispered. "I'm asking for scientific reasons."

"You're asking because you're nosy."

"Yes," he said proudly.

I rolled my eyes and opened the case folder sitting on my desk. "We're working, remember? Bunch of bodies, same tox profile, same showy dump sites? I don't have time to rate my sex life for you on a scale."

Jordan went still for half a beat. "Oh my God," he breathed. "It's *that* good."

I aimed my pen at his throat. "I will ruin you."

He closed his mouth, but not before giving me the kind of grin that said this conversation absolutely was not over, only postponed for dramatic value.

Across the bullpen, Thibodeaux stuck his head out of his office. "Briefing. Five minutes. Homicide and Vice. Let's go, let's go."

Harper pushed back from his desk with a groan. Ramos grabbed his notepad. Jordan slid off my desk and did a quiet little happy dance that I chose to ignore for the sake of my blood pressure. Sanders and Nguyen shared a look before they both glanced at the door like they were planning an escape. I leveled a look in their direction, and they both sighed before slinking off to the briefing room.

I stood, grabbed my folder, and finally—finally—looked at Owen. He was already watching me. Of course he was.

Sergeant Owen Bishop, Homicide. Late thirties. Built like he bench-pressed moral dilemmas for fun. Shirt sleeves rolled, a couple buttons undone—that very specific kind of "casual" that only men with control issues could pull off. He looked like he'd tried to go home, then remembered he *was* home in chaos. Calm. Contained. Responsible. The kind of control that made you want to see what happened when it snapped.

Last night, I had him saying my name like a prayer and a threat. I could still remember what his short blonde hair felt like when I ran my fingers through it. What those ocean eyes looked like when he was whispering sinful things in my ear.

Fuck. Get it together, Case.

But I couldn't stop myself from glancing back at him.

Right now, he looked like nothing had happened. Which would've been convincing if I didn't see the muscle in his jaw tic when our eyes met. If I hadn't watched his hand flex on the file he was holding, like he was thinking about my skin instead of his paperwork. My stomach did a stupid slow roll.

I hated that.

No, I didn't.

Whatever.

He broke eye contact first. Good. Because if he'd held it another second, I would've blushed like a rookie, and that was not happening in front of this audience. We filed into the briefing room and pretended to be adults. The board at the front of the room hadn't gotten prettier overnight. The girls' photos. Drop sites marked in red. A list of overlapping tox hits: fentanyl analog, benzos, xylazine. Not-so-cute little cocktail designed to knock you flat and keep you quiet.

Harper flopped into a chair and kicked his boots up on the one next to him. Jordan sat forward like it was movie night. Ramos leaned against the wall, arms folded, expression bland. I took my usual spot near the front. The rest of the team, including Sanders and Nguyen, filled in the empty seats.

Owen didn't look at me when he started. "All right. We've got three bodies, plus the one from last week. Same signature cut, same disposal pattern. We're assuming it's the same actor until proven otherwise."

"Same showmanship," Harper added. "Busy overpass, drug den, law firm private parking? Guy's begging for attention."

"He's not hiding them," I said. "He's staging them. He wants cameras."

"Or he wants us," Jordan said, tapping a pen against his knee.

Owen nodded once. "That's one read."

"It's the right one," I muttered.

His look cut over to me, sharp. "Vice is still digging into that Bay Street seizure from three months ago?"

I lifted my chin. "Working on it."

"I'd like that yesterday."

Um, excuse me? I blinked at him, but he looked away. Dismissing me.

The way he said it—like I was still a rookie he could order

around, like the whole room wasn't watching—hit something raw. I hated how hard the man was to read. Hated how good he was at acting like there was nothing between us. It made me doubt... everything. Was I being a fool? My whirling thoughts built into a hurricane inside my head. Before I could stop myself, I turned fully towards him. He looked down at me, like he wasn't the slightest bit impressed, let alone intimidated by the anger I knew was all over my face. I had always been shit at hiding emotions.

"Careful, Owen," I said, sweet as heatstroke. "You keep talking to me like that in front of my squad, and they're gonna start thinking you're flirting with me in the workplace, and then we're going to have to make a whole training video."

The room went electric.

Ramos's head jerked up. Harper made a strangled noise. Jordan clapped a hand over his own mouth and made an actual squeak.

Owen stared at me for a beat. To his credit, he didn't flinch. He stuck his tongue in his cheek and leveled me with a look that would've wilted a spring flower. "Chambers."

"Mhm?" I tilted my head.

"That's 'Sergeant Bishop' in the briefing room."

"And it's Sergeant Chambers to you."

The whole team was watching us now, the air still and tight as a dry rotted rubber band. I felt the heat crawl up my neck immediately. *Nice work, Chambers. Real professional.*

Owen's eyes were flat, unreadable. "Briefing's over," he said evenly. "Get to work."

And just like that, it was business again.

I spent the next half hour snapping at anything that moved. The copier. The phone. Poor Harper, who made the mistake of asking if I wanted lunch. Jordan finally cornered me by the coffee pot.

"Okay," he said, "either you're possessed or you're trying to murder the Keurig with vibes alone."

"Both," I muttered.

He waited. He always waited. Eventually, I sighed. "He acted like it didn't happen."

"Yeah. That's what guys like him do when they don't know how to feel things." Jordan took the ruined coffee cup from my hand and refilled it. "Doesn't mean you gotta burn down the precinct over it."

I stared into the mug. "I wasn't trying to—"

"I know." His grin softened. "Next time, maybe don't roast him alive in front of everyone. Save it for the hallway. Or, you know, your next illicit rendezvous. You're scary when you're wounded."

I exhaled through my teeth, half laughing. "He brings it out in me."

"Then congratulations," Jordan said, patting my shoulder. "You've joined the club. Bishop's been making people crazy since the academy. Or so I've heard."

He handed me a fresh cup of coffee, grin back in place. "Now drink that, apologize to Harper before he files for witness protection, and try not to stab anyone until after lunch. Then go save the world, or whatever it is you two do when you're not making me live in a soap opera."

I smiled despite myself. "Thanks, Jordan."

"Anytime, my gorgeous bestie."

I rolled my eyes but headed back to my desk, the heat in my chest cooling into something sharper. He could play the stoic sergeant all he wanted. He could keep pretending nothing had happened. But sooner or later, one of us was going to break that silence—and I was starting to hope it'd be him.

The bullpen cleared out fast after the briefing. Harper and Ramos took the canvass detail; Jordan grabbed witness follow-ups; Nguyen muttered something about pulling more tower pings, then he and Sanders headed back to Vice.

I should've been happy. Fewer people meant fewer eyes on me. Instead, I felt like I was going to crawl out of my own damn skin. From my desk, I could see the side of Owen's face, the lines cut into his cheek, the way he pinched the bridge of his nose when he was thinking too hard. Every time I looked up, there he was—infuriatingly calm. Typing. Reviewing files. Acting like he hadn't had my back against his kitchen counter twelve hours ago.

I wanted to stab him.

I wanted to kiss him.

I wanted him to stop pretending we hadn't set each other on fire.

I tried to work. Really, I did. My laptop stayed open for twenty minutes while I stared at the same paragraph. Finally, I snapped it shut, grabbed my folder, and muttered something about getting real work done where people actually respected me. I was halfway to the door when I heard his voice.

"Casey."

I stopped. Didn't turn. "Busy, Sergeant."

"You leaving mid-shift now?"

I turned, slow, pulse spiking. "You need something?"

He leaned against his doorframe, arms crossed, sleeves rolled. The picture of control. "What was that in the briefing?"

"What was *what?*"

"That little outburst. You trying to get yourself written up, or just testing how far you can push me?"

The laugh that came out of me sounded more like disbelief. "Push *you?* You stood there giving orders like I was one of your rookies."

"I was giving direction."

"Direction," I repeated, stepping closer, folder tight in my hand. "We're the same damn rank, Bishop. You don't get to 'direct' me."

"I was keeping the meeting on track."

"By steamrolling me? Yeah, that's one way to lead."

His jaw flexed. "You done?"

"No. Not even close."

For a second, neither of us said anything. My heart was pounding like I'd just run a mile. Finally, I said, "You are the smartest, *stupidest* man I've ever met, Owen Bishop. And no, I am not fucking leaving. I am going to do my damn job somewhere I can think."

And before he could reply, I walked away.

Vice felt smaller after that. Quieter. The kind of quiet that hums in your ears. Nguyen looked up from his monitors when I came in. "You good, Sarge?"

"Fine."

He didn't buy it, but he knew better than to argue.

Sanders was in the corner, muttering to herself over call logs.

Ramos sat on the edge of a desk, scrolling through his phone. "You look like you could use a drink," he said.

"I could use results," I shot back.

He chuckled. "Same thing in this line of work."

I gave him a look that shut him up, then dropped into my chair.

The tox reports were spread out in front of me, the same

names, the same cocktail of poisons, and absolutely no new leads. Hours passed. The room thinned as people clocked out, until it was just me and the soft buzz of Nguyen's monitors. My eyes burned from the screen glow. My coffee was cold. My thoughts kept circling the same black hole: *He's acting like nothing happened.* I could do that too.

Around seven, a soft knock hit my doorframe. I didn't look up. "If you're selling something, I already hate it."

"Good thing I'm not."

His voice.

I froze. Then forced myself to glance up.

Owen stood in the doorway, hands in his pockets. "You're still here."

"It's my office. What are you doing here?"

He stepped in, dropped a file on my desk. "Pulled the IA requisition logs myself. Found discrepancies in the Bay Street paperwork—same batch, same signatures. Might be our link."

I looked at him, then at the file. "You mean *my* link."

"Right. Your link," he said, tone dry. "You've got good instincts, Casey. Even when your mouth runs ahead of them."

"Don't start."

"I'm serious," he said. "You're onto something."

It was infuriating how calm he could sound, like we were colleagues in sync instead of whatever the hell we were.

"Thanks," I said finally. "I'll follow up tomorrow."

"Don't overwork your team. They're already stretched thin."

I tilted my head. "Since when do you care about Vice?"

"Since you started running yourself into the ground for it."

The look he gave me wasn't professional. It wasn't friendly, either. It was protective, infuriatingly gentle.

"You should eat something," he said, already turning to leave.

"You think better when you're not starving."

"I think fine."

"Casey."

I glared at him.

"Come eat something. Please."

Please? *Please?* I didn't think he knew the word. I caved.

We ended up in the evidence cage, pizza spread between us, surrounded by old case files and the smell of dust and cardboard.

"Your people love you," he said after a while, quiet.

I gave a short laugh. "They tolerate me because I remember birthdays and bribe them with beignets."

"That's not tolerance. That's loyalty."

"Same thing."

He looked at me in that steady way he did so well. "You ever think maybe you're not as easy to read as you think you are?"

"Meaning?"

"Meaning you act like a hurricane, but you run your team like a shield. They'd follow you into hell because they know you'd drag them back out."

The words hit a little too close. I shifted, set down my slice. "I grew up in the system, Owen."

That made him look up.

"And for some godforsaken reason, instead of letting it turn me cold like it did everyone else, I let it fuel me. I wanted to be light and warmth and safety—the kind of person I needed back then." He didn't say anything. Just listened. The silence stretched, heavy but not uncomfortable.

"I wear my heart on my sleeve," I said finally. "And I'm not ashamed of that. I can't just turn it off like you can." His jaw tightened. He didn't look away, but there was something in his

91

eyes—a flicker, a fracture.

"Maybe that's what I like about you," he said. Quiet. Unplanned.

That pulled the air right out of me. I blinked once, slow, trying not to let it show how hard that landed. Then, "Careful, Sergeant. Sounds dangerously close to a compliment."

He huffed out something that might've been a laugh. "Don't get used to it."

It was well past midnight when I packed up my bag. The building was mostly dark, my thoughts louder than they had any right to be. I nearly jumped when Jordan appeared out of the shadows.

"Boss! Perfect timing. You're coming with me."

"What—why?"

"My husband's making dinner again, and you look like you're one minor inconvenience from committing a felony."

"I already ate," I said automatically.

His eyes went wide before I could even stop the slip. I sighed. "Don't say it."

"Oh, I'm *absolutely* saying it," he whispered. "You had dinner with Bishop. At work. Alone. Do you realize what this means for me? I get to be insufferable for *weeks*."

"Jordan."

He was practically vibrating. "You are living my dream arc. Forbidden workplace romance, emotionally unavailable older man—this is my Super Bowl."

"Get in the car before I arrest you."

"Drive me home and tell me everything."

The city blurred by in sodium glow and rain-slick streets. In between sips of iced coffee, Jordan talked the whole time—half gossip, half actual case analysis.

"Feels like it," I admitted. "Pattern's too neat. Like he wants us to see him getting better."

He nodded, thoughtful now, the gossip giving way to detective mode. "Then we catch him before he graduates to something bigger."

"Working on it," I said.

We pulled up outside his apartment. He unbuckled, then looked at me. "You know I'm right about Bishop, though."

"I know you're annoying."

"Same thing."

I rolled my eyes, but I was smiling. "Tell Marco I said hi."

He grinned, already halfway out of the car. "Will do. Try not to make out with your Homicide counterpart before breakfast, okay?"

"No promises," I muttered. He laughed the whole way up the steps. I sat there a second longer, engine idling, trying not to think about the way Owen's voice had gone soft when he'd said, "That's what I like about you." Then I put the car in gear and drove home, the city lights breaking up the night.

The next day, the lead came through a voicemail from one of Jordan's CIs—a salvage yard off Highway 90, just past the levee, where a local gang was supposedly moving again. Possibly moving our stolen bricks. Thin intel, sketchy source. Still, it was all we had.

"Let's roll," I said, grabbing my keys.

Owen was already sliding into the passenger seat before I could argue. Jordan and Harper piled into the back like kids on a field trip.

"Seat belts," I said, starting the SUV.

"You could've at least taken a second to breathe before barging out of the briefing room."

93

I shot Owen a look as I pulled out of the lot. "I did breathe. I *am* breathing. I've got a plan."

"Define 'plan,'" Harper said, clicking his belt in.

"Quiet entry," I said. "Recon first."

Owen shook his head. "And backup?"

"We don't need it."

"Yes, we do."

"So, we wait for SWAT," I said, eyes on the road. "Meanwhile, our dealer's halfway to Baton Rouge."

"It's called protocol."

"It's called sitting on our thumbs, waiting for a green light while the bad guy runs the red."

He exhaled, the sound halfway between frustration and disbelief. "You ever stop to think maybe being first through the door isn't a survival strategy?"

"You ever stop to think maybe you're just scared to be wrong?"

The silence stretched—thick, simmering, familiar.

Then Jordan stage-whispered from the backseat, "So... are Mom and Dad fighting again?"

Harper groaned. "Don't start."

"I'm just saying," Jordan continued, "the sexual tension's killing morale."

"Jordan," I warned.

"Sorry, *Mom*."

Owen's jaw ticked. "You wanna walk?"

Jordan snorted. "See? Dad voice."

The salvage yard squatted behind a sagging chain-link fence, every inch of it rust, oil, and bad decisions. The gate was technically locked. Technically.

"Looks abandoned," Harper said.

I wasn't so sure.

We slipped through, guns up, breath shallow. Rows of gutted cars created narrow lanes of shadow. Wind howled through the stacked shipping containers, making the place hum like a throat clearing. Then—gunfire.

The first shot cracked past my head, slamming into a car door. I dove behind a rusted-out pickup, Harper and Jordan scattering.

"Contact north side!" Owen yelled.

"Yeah, no shit. I figured that one out." I stuck my head over the hood of the pickup before ducking back down. "I see them!" I shouted. Returned fire. Two pops, fast. One silhouette ducked.

Jordan's radio crackled. "Fuck!" Followed by a solid *thud.*

"Talk to me, Jordan!"

"Vest caught it!" he gasped. "Hurts like hell, though!"

"Stay down!" I barked.

"Gladly!"

Owen's voice came through comms, steady even under fire. "We're boxed in. East and west lanes are both hot."

I looked toward the fence—chain-link, half-collapsed, and my SUV gleaming just beyond it.

"Owen," I said, already moving.

He looked over at me. "Wait—"

"Cover me!"

"Casey—"

Too late. I sprinted across open ground, heart pounding in my throat, bullets pinging off metal. Ducking through a gap in the fence, I dove into the SUV, jammed the key in, and floored it. The engine roared awake like it had a death wish to match mine. "Everyone get ready to move!" I shouted into comms. "On my mark—three, two—"

The SUV hit the fence full-speed. The chain-link screamed,

sparks flying as the gate folded under the grill.

"Come on!"

Harper dragged Jordan up; Owen fired cover shots until the last second before diving into the passenger seat.

"Drive!" he yelled.

"I *am* driving!" We both ducked instinctively when someone shot out the back glass. "Would you *fucking* shoot someone?"

"For fuck's sake, woman…" Owen leaned over, firing a few shots through the shattered window. We fishtailed onto the road, tires screeching. The city swallowed the gunfire behind us.

Jordan wheezed a laugh. "You two flirting or fighting? Ow—my ribs."

"Both," Harper muttered.

Owen braced a hand on the dash, chest still heaving. "You call that quiet entry?"

"I call that effective exit."

His mouth twitched. "You're impossible."

"Yeah," I said, breathless. "But you like that about me."

Thibodeaux was waiting by the garage, arms crossed like a disappointed parent. He was wearing the expression of a man who'd seen every brand of stupidity the badge had to offer—and was somehow still being surprised.

He took one look at the SUV, now ventilated like Swiss cheese, and groaned. "I should've retired ten years ago."

Jordan was slouched against Harper, still milking his injury for sympathy. "Hey, boss, you got any ice packs for emotional trauma?"

"Not unless you count the cold shoulder I'm about to give all of you," Thibodeaux said flatly. "Debrief in thirty. And somebody call the city before WWL reports another 'rogue police chase.' I am too old to explain chain-link carnage to the mayor again."

"Yes, sir," I said, trying not to smile.

He squinted at me like he knew I was enjoying this. "And Chambers?"

"Yeah?"

"Next time you want to make an entrance, try the gate code first."

"Technically, it was an exit. And I didn't see a gate. So, I made one."

He walked off muttering something about early retirement and blood pressure medication.

Owen leaned against the SUV, smirking. "You could've waited for backup."

"And miss all that character building?"

He huffed. "You drive like a lunatic."

"You shoot like one."

A beat of silence. Then his mouth curved, just slightly. "Quiet entry."

"Effective exit," I said, grinning back.

A few hours later, Harper was nursing coffee that had the consistency of tar, Jordan was doing his best "wounded hero" act with an ice pack and a grin, and Owen was pacing like he could wear a trench in the tile. Thibodeaux had already fled the scene, probably halfway to his car before we could give him another reason to drink.

The report writing was mind-numbing. Gunfire. Pursuit. Vehicle damage. Property destruction. "Effective exit" didn't translate well into official language, so I stuck with "tactical withdrawal" and called it a day.

By the time I signed the last page, it was dark out. The squad had filtered out one by one, Jordan milking his near-death experience for rides and sympathy. He leaned on my desk on his way out. "Hey, boss, tell your boyfriend thanks for the adrenaline rush. My ribs are writing him a thank-you card."

"He's not my—"

"Sure he's not," Jordan said, smirking. "Text me if you two start arguing again. I'll bring popcorn."

He whistled his way out before I could throw my pen at him. The bullpen went quiet, the kind of quiet that makes your heartbeat feel too loud. I could see Owen in his office through the glass—tie loosened, sleeves rolled, staring at the case board like it might finally blink first.

I told myself to just go home. Eat. Sleep. Pretend to be normal. Instead, I found myself standing in his doorway.

He didn't look up. "You should be off the clock."

"So should you."

"Someone's got to file this mess."

"Already did," I said, setting the folder on his desk. "Twice, actually, since you're too old-school to trust the digital system."

That earned me a look—the kind that was half irritation, half something else. "You ever get tired of pushing buttons?"

"You ever get tired of acting like yours don't exist?"

He leaned back in his chair. I could see the tiny tremor at the corner of his mouth when he forced calm. It was a lie, and I wanted to tear it off him.

"You could've waited," he said. It wasn't an accusation. It was a fact he wanted me to swallow so he could be right about something.

"And miss the part where we get results?" I shot back. "You act like the world's got a manual for courage. It doesn't. It's messy and loud and… human."

He blinked, the motion slow enough to be deliberate. "You make this personal."

"Of course I do." I stepped in. "I'm tired of you acting like everything is a business transaction. I want the man, not the badge."

A muscle jumped in his jaw. He steadied himself against the desk like a man who hadn't admitted he could be unmoored. "I don't show... I don't do that."

"No," I said softly, "you don't. You plaster on that indifferent thing for work and people thank you for it. But I know it's paint. I want you to chip it off." My voice sharpened. "I want you to break for me—not as a weakness, but as proof you can be something messy and still be damn good at your job."

He inhaled. It sounded huge in the quiet office. "You're asking me to be less professional," he said, and there was something in the tilt of his head that looked dangerously like the start of an answer.

I laughed, low and not unkind. "I'm asking you to be honest. For once. Beg me to stay. Admit you don't like the idea of me getting shot for the thrill of it. Say my name and mean it. Tell me I scare you. Tell me you want me. Say the things your face won't."

For a second his face did something I'd waited what felt like forever to see—it softened, and it was terrifying and lovely and unbearably intimate. He opened his mouth, then shut it. He swallowed something that might have been pride.

"Casey," he said finally, standing. Not a plea. Not exactly what I asked for. But the sound of my name out of him was soft enough to make the world tilt.

I let the silence hang there, delicious and awful. I turned, walked to the door as if I was leaving the conversation and the next act both to him. My hand closed on the handle. I paused, just long enough to let him think the walk-away was surrender. Then I locked it. The *click* echoed in the room like a verdict. He watched me as I came around his desk and stood in front of him. I placed my hand on his chest and pushed him backwards. He sat back in his chair with a look like he was trying to figure me out, but didn't have all the pieces yet. When I knelt between his spread knees and started to undo his belt, he tried to stop me. Not with a word, just a hand on mine. But I shook him off and kept going. I was going to find that chink in his armor. He didn't have to become soft in this too-often-cruel world. But I couldn't love a man who wasn't soft for me. He lifted his hips just enough for me to slide his jeans down. He was already half hard. And fuck, the man was huge. And to be perfectly honest, I had been dying to taste him.

I looked up at him then. Those eyes watched me, analyzed me. I smiled at him, then bent my head so I could run my tongue over the tip of his cock. He grunted, his hand coming up to cup the back of my head. I licked him again and then took him in my mouth. Hollowing out my cheeks and breathing through my nose, I managed to swallow almost his entire length. When he swore vehemently, fisting my hair in those rough hands, I hummed my approval. Bobbing my head, I placed my hand on his thighs. I pulled my head back and ran my tongue along his tip again, this time tasting precum. Still he didn't say anything, except for the muttered curses.

But the hand in my hair told me everything I needed to know. I sucked him to the base again and again, moving my head until he was raising his hips to meet me. Then he started speaking the filthy words I had grown to like so much.

"That's it, Casey. Fuck. Just like that."

I hummed again, and he thrust into my mouth. Once. Twice. Then he was shooting cum down my throat, and I did my best to swallow every drop. Still, when I rocked back on my heels, I could feel the mixture of spit and his seed on my chin. He ran a thumb through it, cleaning me, and then pressed his finger between my lips. I smiled at him after I sucked it clean, and he gave me a rare smile back. When I stood, he stood with me, pulling his jeans back up. Leaning down, he kissed me, and I opened for him so he could taste what I had just done. Like he didn't already know. Then, I headed for the door and unlocked it. Before I left, I turned back to him.

"Owen?"

"Hmm?"

"What does *'ma louve'* mean?"

He watched me for a minute, tilting his head. Then, after a beat, "My she-wolf."

"And *'mon péché'*?"

The way he looked at me felt like a claim, and I fought the urge to shiver.

"My sin."

"Hmm. Night, Owen."

"Good night, Casey."

CHAPTER 7 ◉ OWEN

The next morning I made it as far as my office doorway before my brain betrayed me. One step inside and she was there again: knees on the floor, my hands wrapped in her hair, her breath hot against my skin. And that wicked tongue that was divinely soft, despite all the sharp words it threw. Damn, she had ruined me for anyone else. Nothing could top that.

I gripped the frame hard enough to creak and turned my back to the rest of the room for a minute, readjusting myself like a lovestruck teenage boy. *Christ. Get it together.*

Turning back, I looked over the room that was oblivious to what had happened last night and the way it still affected me. The bullpen was already humming. Same circus. Same clowns. Except now I was one of them.

Because there she was—Casey Chambers, storm in a black blazer—walking in like she owned the place. Coffee in hand. *My* coffee. Or, technically, *her* coffee, courtesy of me. She didn't know that, of course. She just knew that every morning, her favorite drink appeared on her desk, hot and perfectly made, like divine intervention. She'd asked around once, half joking. I'd shrugged and said, "Maybe the caffeine fairy's unionized."

She'd rolled her eyes at my shitty attempt at a joke, and that had been the end of it. Now she took a slow sip, closed her eyes for a second like she was tasting heaven, and I felt smug enough to be arrested for it. I hadn't done stuff like this for anyone since my marriage fell apart. Nor had I noticed the absence until she walked in and filled it without asking. I leaned against my doorframe, watching her give orders to her squad.

"Nguyen, tox comparison and access audit—Bay Street batch first. If the timestamps drift, I want to know before lunch. Sanders, double-check overtime logs. Ramos, grab the call logs from evidence control."

Commanding. Focused. Gorgeous. Clueless to the fact that her secret coffee supplier was standing ten feet away, looking like a man who'd just pulled off a heist. I must've been smiling, because Jordan sidled up next to me with that too-pleased grin that usually meant trouble. He followed my line of sight, then the coffee cup, then me.

"Oh, oh," he murmured, eyes lighting up. "You?"

"Me what?"

He smirked. "You're the caffeine fairy."

I didn't answer.

"Don't bother lying," he said. "You've got that smug post-delivery look. Word of advice—next time, grab one of those strawberry scones from the display case. She'll love you forever."

I kept my face blank. "Don't know what you're talking about."

Jordan snorted. "Sure you don't. You're just standing here, staring at her like she's the first sunrise you've ever seen. Totally normal coworker behavior."

I shot him a look that would've shut most people up.

He grinned wider. "Oh, this is *so* fun."

Before I could decide whether to throw him out a window,

Thibodeaux's voice cut across the bullpen. "Bishop! Chambers! Get your squads. We're up."

Normally, I ran the morning briefings. But five bodies changed the math. When a case turned serial, and the mayor started dialing at sunrise, the deputy chief planted himself at the front of the room.

Five photos on the board.

Five victims.

Five different corners of the same city, each one dumped somewhere you couldn't miss if you tried.

Thibodeaux's tie was crooked, and he had a look on his face like someone had kicked his dog. "We've got another one— female, late twenties, found under the Calliope overpass. Broad daylight, rush-hour traffic right above her. Same chemical blend, same staging. This son of a bitch wants a spotlight."

Casey's expression hardened. "Any identifiers?"

"Wallet's gone, prints came back clean. Dental's pending." Thibodeaux rubbed his eyes. "Mayor's office wants updates by 5 p.m. Press doesn't have wind of this yet—keep it that way."

Ramos raised a hand from the back row, grin lazy. "Already ahead of you, boss. I called the lab first thing, got the tox rushed."

Thibodeaux frowned. "You're not lab liaison."

Ramos shrugged. "Just trying to save Sergeant Chambers the hassle. Figured I'd earn brownie points."

The room chuckled. Casey gave him a brief nod of thanks. I didn't laugh. I exchanged a look with Casey and could tell she was thinking the same thing. Nobody volunteered for extra work in this department unless they were trying to impress someone—or hiding something.

Thibodeaux sighed. "Fine. Since you're feeling ambitious, you can help Bishop and Chambers run down supplier records.

We need to know how this compound keeps slipping through evidence control."

"On it," Nguyen said, already typing something into his phone. Ramos leaned over his shoulder and got swatted at.

Thibodeaux's gaze swept the room before settling on me. "This stays internal. No leaks, no whispers. Mayor wants results, not excuses."

"Understood," I said. The meeting broke like surf. Chairs scraped, paper rustled, caffeine-fueled motion.

Casey crossed the aisle toward me, file in hand. "One of my people found something interesting. Ride with me?"

"Yeah," I said.

Jordan murmured as we passed, "Don't forget the scone next time, Romeo."

I ignored him. Barely.

Ramos called out, "I'll pull the manifests and meet you there." Casey threw him a thumbs-up without looking back. I watched him for a beat too long, that easy grin sitting wrong in my gut.

Casey drove us to a warehouse at the edge of the industrial district—a gutted shell of sheet metal and broken glass, condemned since the last hurricane. Perfect place to plan something like this. Hidden enough to buy time, open enough to make a statement. The CSU lights strobed off puddles of oil and rainwater, painting the walls in sterile blue-white. They crawled over the place like ants, and a few of them nodded at us when we walked past.

Casey crouched by the pallet stack, gloved hands brushing dust from a crate. Faded letters bled through grime: **NOPD EVIDENCE**.

"Tell me that's not what I think it is," she muttered.

"Looks like one of ours," I said. "Drug evidence container.

105

You ever see one go missing from Vice inventory?"

She straightened, pulling her hair back into a rough knot. "Not unless someone signed it out, which would leave a trail."

"That's assuming they used their real name," I said.

Before she could answer, Ramos and Harper came through the side door, flashlights sweeping. Ramos walked up to her, handing her a folder that matched the one stamped on the side of the crate.

"That was fast."

He shrugged. "I got a buddy in CSU. He gave me the heads-up."

I frowned at him as she flipped through the report. "This lot number's from a seizure three months ago. Should've been destroyed."

"Clerical error," Ramos said easily. "You know how evidence control is." He chuckled and walked off toward the coroner's van, too casual for a man who'd just found contraband marked "property of NOPD." Harper followed, giving me a look that said he noticed the weirdness too.

I waited until Ramos was out of earshot. "You trust him?"

Casey's jaw flexed. "I trust my team."

She took one more look at the crate before heading toward the exit. "Let's get this processed before the media sniffs it out. The mayor's already breathing down Thibodeaux's neck."

The drive back was quiet—not the comfortable kind. The city lights smeared into streaks of gold and red. Casey sat angled toward the window, posture textbook straight, tablet open across her lap. We rode in silence another few blocks. The wipers clicked time. Then she sighed and said softly, "You ever get the feeling we're just mopping up someone else's mess? Like we're always a step behind because somebody's feeding him our moves?"

"Yeah," I said. "And that somebody's gonna hang."

The precinct buzzed louder than usual when we walked in. Reporters had been calling all morning, and half the bullpen was pretending not to check social media updates. From what I could tell, no one had leaked any details, but reporters were like hound dogs on the scent, and this whole damn thing stank.

Casey dropped the crime-scene file on Nguyen's desk. "Pull every evidence requisition for Bay Street over the last year. Check for duplicates, overrides, or sign-ins outside normal hours. You know what you're looking for."

Nguyen cracked his knuckles. "On it, boss."

Across the room, two beat cops leaned up against the reception desk, animated and grinning like they were at happy hour instead of standing in the middle of a precinct. Casey brushed past them on her way to the bullpen. The kid she passed—patrol blues, maybe twenty-two—gave her a bright smile. "Morning, Sergeant Chambers. Hell of a takedown. Heard that fence didn't stand a chance."

She smiled back, polite but distracted. "Thanks. Keep your head on a swivel out there."

He grinned as she walked away, leaned toward his buddy, and said, "With an ass like that, no wonder she made sergeant so fast."

She kept moving like she hadn't heard him. But I did.

He barely saw me coming. I stopped in front of him, calm, even voice. "You got something to say about Sergeant Chambers?"

He stammered, color draining from his face. "N-no, sir. Just—joking around."

"Funny," I said. "I didn't hear a joke."

107

His partner tried to step in. "It's nothing, Sarge. He didn't mean—"

"I don't really give a shit what he *meant*. That shit doesn't fly here," I said. "And if I ever hear that kind of talk again, I'll make sure your captain hears it first."

The kid nodded fast. "Yes, sir. Won't happen again."

"Good."

I turned, and caught Jordan leaning against a file cabinet, coffee in hand, smirking. "Careful, Bishop. People might start thinking you *like* her."

"Watch it," I muttered.

He grinned. "Oh, I am. Closely."

Casey came back a minute later, fresh cup of coffee in hand, completely unaware of the exchange. She passed me the file she'd been holding. "Nguyen's already pulling the timestamps. If we're lucky, we'll have something soon."

I grunted before settling behind my desk. She watched me, that little half smirk that made me want to push her up against the wall. I watched her walk away until she stopped by Crawford's desk and started talking to him about a lead, waving Sanders over to join in the conversation.

By dusk, the bullpen looked like triage. Empty beignet boxes, case files, and half-drunk cups littered every surface. It was just me, Casey, Jordan, Harper, and Nguyen at that point. Nguyen's monitors flickered blue light across his face as he squinted at the screen. "There's a data pull from the evidence archive around 0200 Saturday. Big one. Video files, case summaries, full metadata packets."

Casey frowned. "Who requested it?"

"That's the thing—nobody. No logged user, no requisition ticket. Just a ghost process labeled 'System Maintenance.'"

Jordan snorted. "Because our IT department totally does routine maintenance at two in the damn morning."

"Could be an automated backup," Harper offered.

"Could be," Nguyen said, "except it routed through an unlisted node. Inside our firewall."

The bullpen went still for a beat.

Casey looked to Nguyen. "Lock it down. No copies, no server sync. This stays between us."

Nguyen nodded. "Who's 'us'?"

"Me, Bishop, Harper, Jordan, and you," she said. "Thibodeaux's under the mayor's microscope—until we know what we're sitting on, it doesn't leave this room."

Harper gave a low whistle. "Tight circle."

"Welcome to Vice," she said. "We keep our drama in-house."

Jordan grinned. "Family values. I love it."

The banter cracked the tension just enough. Someone had ordered pizza; grease-stained boxes were stacked on the corner of my desk. Casey sat back at her desk, where I was leaning up against it and watching the exchange. She took a slice when I pushed one her way and actually ate it without protest, which I counted as progress. Nguyen turned back to his screens. "If the same IP hits again, I can bounce a trace through the gateway, but it'll take time."

"Do it," Casey said. "And lock your workstation when you leave."

He gave a mock salute. "Aye, boss."

She leaned back in her chair, exhaustion cutting through the bravado. An hour later, Thibodeaux appeared in the doorway, tie loosened, expression halfway between pride and exhaustion. "You're all still here."

Jordan saluted him with a breadstick. "Dedication."

"Go home," Thibodeaux said. "All of you. I want brains that work tomorrow."

No one moved.

He sighed. "Fine. Two more hours, then I'm cutting power to this floor." He looked at me. "You, Bishop—brief me in the morning. Chambers, same. And tell your people to get some damn sleep."

"Yes, sir," we said in unison.

When he left, Jordan snorted. "You two even talk in sync now. Adorable."

"You know what, I think Thibodeaux was right. Go home," Casey said, pointing toward the door.

He grinned, grabbed his jacket, and slung it over his shoulder. "Night, family."

Harper followed, muttering something about therapy

Nguyen was the last holdout. The kid typed like the keyboard owed him money, a steady clatter filling the bullpen. Casey sat sideways in her chair, files spread like a paper halo around her.

"Trace is running," Nguyen said. "Firewall's slow, but I'll get a read by morning."

"Go home," Casey told him. "You'll code better when you've slept."

He blinked at her, then at the clock. "It's past ten. Damn. Yeah—okay." He saved his work, powered down, and slung his backpack over one shoulder. "Try not to burn the place down before I get back."

"No promises," she said.

When the door shut behind him, the room went quiet—just the hum of monitors cooling down and the soft buzz of the exit sign. Casey rubbed the bridge of her nose, shoulders heavy. "If this trace comes up empty, I'll start pulling requisition logs by hand."

"Don't," I said. "You'll be here till sunrise."

"I've done worse."

"Yeah. I know."

That stopped her for a beat. She looked at me—really looked, like she was deciding whether to fight or finally breathe. Instead, she just sighed and gathered her files.

"Walk you out?" I asked.

She didn't answer, but she didn't say no either.

The parking lot was slick and empty, sodium lights turning puddles into sheets of gold. She paused by her car, one hand on the door handle.

"Get some sleep," I said.

She gave a tired half-smile. "You too, Bishop. Sweet dreams."

"Can't dream without you." It was corny, and I wanted to kick myself the second the words left my lips. But then she smiled and walked back to me. Leaning up on her tiptoes, she kissed me. Just a quick press of her lips on mine. Then she got in her car, started the engine, and drove off. I shook myself, then turned to go inside, not quite ready to leave.

Back upstairs, the bullpen felt colder. The evidence file on my desk was still open—Bay Street, lot number 0432-B, Ramos's signature dated two weeks after the destruction order.

I took a photo of the page, locked it in the drawer, and reached for my phone. A new message flashed on screen as I did.

STOP DIGGING.

It had been three days since the text. Three days of pretending I wasn't waiting for another one to land. Number was junk—burner or spoof, nothing traceable. Just a warning sharp enough to slice through the static. I'd run it through every system I could touch without raising flags, and come up empty. Whoever sent it knew what they were doing—and how far to reach. That was the part that stuck under my skin. I thought about showing Casey. More than once. But she'd charge into the fire first and ask questions second, and if somebody wanted her rattled, I wasn't handing them the satisfaction. So I kept my mouth shut, buried the anxiety under paperwork, and told myself it was nothing but noise.

I was signing off on evidence logs when the door flew open hard enough to rattle the blinds. Harper barreled in first, still catching his breath, and Jordan right behind him, both talking at once.

"Boss—we've got something—"

"Not something, *someone*," Jordan said, grinning like a man who'd just solved the riddle of life.

I set my pen down. "One at a time."

Harper dropped a folder onto my desk. "Bryce Keller. Former Army MP. Dishonorable discharge in '21 after a domestic battery charge. Sister OD'd last year—Bay Street product."

Jordan added, "Same batch marker that's been turning up in our victims."

I opened the folder. Keller's ID photo stared back—flat eyes, crew cut grown ragged, a face carved out of bitterness. Everything about it made a cruel kind of sense.

"Good work," I said finally. "But a theory and a conviction are two different things. I want proof—chain of custody, purchase records, something that bleeds on paper. The mayor's already circling this like a shark. If we screw the landing, Keller walks."

Jordan and Harper exchanged a look, then Harper nodded once. "We'll lock it down. Warrants, receipts, everything clean."

"Do it."

They left with the restless energy of cops who could already taste the press conference. The silence they left behind felt heavier than before. Keller was our guy—every instinct said so. But instincts don't survive cross-examination. I'd seen too many airtight cases come apart over one loose thread.

Casey appeared in my doorway like she'd been summoned by the thought. "You really think Keller's behind the bodies?" she asked. Jordan must have already filled her in. Guy was nothing if not loyal to his sergeant

"I think he's as close to a bull's-eye as we've had," I said. "But I'm not hanging this case on gut feelings."

She stepped inside, closing the door behind her. The motion carried quiet authority—command presence, they called it at the academy. She'd turned it into an art form.

"Jordan's running point with Harper," she said. "They'll get us the hard links. Credit cards, travel records, maybe a supply trail for that compound."

I nodded. "Make sure it's airtight. Keller's smart. He wants attention, not capture."

"Thanks for the tip. With it being my first day on the job and all." Her gaze met mine, steady and unreadable. For a second, the room felt smaller—just the two of us and the hum of the old fluorescent light overhead.

"I'm old, Casey. Habits die hard."

She sighed, the fight leaving her as she said, "You've been quiet lately."

"Paperwork," I lied.

"Sure," she said, mouth curving the faintest bit. "Well, if your paperwork starts killing people, call me."

She turned to go. I caught her reflection in the glass—dark blazer, hair pulled back, posture like armor—and wondered how long before the job started cracking that armor for good.

When the door shut, I stared at Keller's photo again. His sister's death, his crusade, our mess. Some men drown in grief. Others build monuments out of it. Keller was building his out of corpses. I frowned. *Not in my city.*

Back at home, the house was too quiet, the kind that pressed in on you. I dropped my jacket, opened the fridge, and grabbed the only thing that looked vaguely edible. I'd just sat down and glared at my phone when it lit up. But the name on the screen killed my irritation in an instant.

Chambers.

I answered before the second ring. "Talk to me."

Her voice was calm, but that clipped calm that only comes after a shot of adrenaline.

"I think someone's following me."

My pulse kicked, and I suddenly lost interest in my sandwich. "Where are you?"

"Coming off the expressway near the river. Two cars back, silver Charger. They've been on me since I left the precinct."

I was already on my feet, coat half-on. "Don't go home."

"I don't really have anywhere else to go. Except maybe Jordan's."

"No. Come here."

"Owen—"

"Casey. Come to me."

There was a short silence on the other end. Then, "On my way."

I stayed on the line, talking her through every turn, every mirror check. She kept her voice even, professional, but I could hear the tremor underneath. When she finally said, "Think I lost them," I didn't believe her, not really. But ten minutes later, headlights swept across my front window, and I stepped out onto the porch. The Charger was gone. Just her.

She pulled up too fast, tires spitting rain. I met her halfway down the drive, scanning the street before she even killed the engine. The second she opened the door, I was there.

"You all right?"

She nodded once, sharp. "Yeah. Just—guess this means we're getting close."

I used my bulk to try and shelter her smaller frame from the rain. "Come on, let's get inside where it's dry."

She'd been here before. That night she came over on business—case files, evidence chain, nothing personal. I remembered how she'd stood in the same doorway then, scanning the room like she was cataloguing it for court. We had both needed a distraction then. And had found one. Tonight, she didn't even look. Just dropped her coat over the arm of the couch and let out a slow breath.

"Still looks the same," she said.

"I don't redecorate much."

"Yeah, I can tell." She gave a half-smile. "You live like you're in witness protection."

"Less cleanup that way."

That got a real laugh. Small, tired, but real.

She curled up on the couch, knees tucked. Her hair was damp, curling at the edges. I felt a part of me settle. Knowing that she was safe. That she was *here*.

Her gaze drifted toward the mantel, to the framed photo of my father. "That your dad?"

"Yeah."

"He looks like you."

I huffed. "Poor bastard."

115

She gave me that look—half amusement, half curiosity. "He was a cop, right?"

"Lieutenant. Retired early. Liver didn't."

Her expression softened. "I'm sorry."

"Don't be. He made his choices. Good cop, though. Just couldn't turn it off when he came home."

She nodded, understanding immediately. "Yeah. They never can."

For a while, neither of us talked. The only sound was the rain against the windows and the slow tick of the kitchen clock.

Then she said, quiet, "Must've been hard—growing up like that."

"Worse for my mom," I said. "She tried to keep it together until one day she didn't. Being married to a cop isn't easy."

Her mouth quirked. "Guess being one's not easy either."

"No," I said. "But at least we understand the hours, the ghosts, the silence."

She watched me for a second and I would have given my last dollar to know what was going on behind those brown eyes. Finally, she murmured, "Thanks. For, you know... answering."

"Didn't sound optional," I said. "You call like that, I'm showing up whether you like it or not."

She offered me a small smile. "Just take the thanks, Owen."

I hesitated before making my way down the hall and grabbing one of my T-shirts. She was soaked from head to toe. I handed it to her before dropping into the corner of the couch beside her. Not close enough to crowd, but close enough that the warmth between us filled the space. I tried, and failed, not to stare when she pulled off her top right there in my living room and slipped into mine. The TV stayed dark. We didn't need the noise. The house hummed softly around us—the fridge, the clock, the kind of silence that felt alive. She stole my sandwich off the table, and I didn't complain.

At some point, her head found my shoulder. Then my arm settled around her, and it just felt so damn right. Before I knew it, I was asleep too.

The next morning, my first conscious thought was pain. Not the kind that made you reach for a gun—more the kind that made you question your life choices. Every vertebra was writing a complaint to HR. My neck felt like I'd lost a fight with a cinder block. Casey, of course, was perfectly fine. Still asleep. Still tucked against my shoulder like it was custom-built for her.

I glanced down at her, hair mussed, breathing soft. She looked peaceful, which was... new. She didn't get a lot of peace. Neither did I. That's probably why I didn't move, even though my spine was threatening mutiny.

Then my phone buzzed. Once. Twice. Persistent.

I reached for it carefully, trying not to wake her. No number. No text bubble, no name.

Just a photo. Casey's car, parked in my driveway. The caption underneath:

Nice night, Detective?

My stomach dropped.

Whoever had been following her hadn't stopped when she got here. They'd stayed close enough to take the picture, close enough to know exactly how to twist the knife.

I looked at her again—still asleep, blissfully unaware—and slid the phone face-down on the table. My pulse wouldn't slow. Every instinct screamed to lock down the house, check the windows, call Harper. But I didn't move.

For the first time in a long time, the danger wasn't out there. It was right on my doorstep. And worse—this time, it was

117

personal. I spent the next five minutes staring at my phone, willing it to vanish. It didn't. Casey stirred beside me and mumbled something unintelligible, shifting just enough to dig an elbow into my ribs. I grimaced. She sighed, turned her face against my shoulder, and promptly went back to sleep.

I sat there another minute before easing out from under her. My lower back protested like I'd aged a decade overnight. The couch creaked, my spine popped, and I muttered, "Jesus Christ, I need new furniture."

In the kitchen, I started the coffee maker. The smell filled the house. My phone sat face-down on the counter where I'd dropped it. I didn't flip it over. Not yet. Instead, I leaned on the counter, staring at the slow drip of coffee like it might explain what the hell I was supposed to do next.

Tell her about the photo? Maybe.

Tell her someone knew she was here? Definitely.

Tell her it made my blood run cold? Not a chance.

Around the time the coffee finished, Casey wandered in. Her hair was a mess, eyes puffy with sleep, but she still somehow managed to look like she could interrogate a room full of felons and win.

"Morning," she said, voice rough.

"Morning," I echoed. "You sleep okay?"

She eyed the couch behind me. "Shockingly, yeah. That couch is comfy."

"If you say so," I said. "My back is filing for worker's comp."

That got a soft laugh out of her—small, but worth it. She leaned on the doorway, arms folded. I watched her, cataloging every movement without meaning to. The way she pushed her hair back with her thumb, the way she rolled her shoulders like she was testing how much weight she could carry today. I slid her a cup of coffee; she moaned at the first sip, and my dick perked up like Pavlov's dog.

I should've told her. I knew it. But for five more minutes, I wanted normal. The knock at the door killed that. Three sharp raps—cop knock.

She glanced up. "Expecting someone?"

"No."

I didn't like surprises before caffeine. I liked them even less after last night.

She stepped toward the door before I could say anything. "I'll get it."

"Casey—"

Too late. She swung it open.

Harper stood on the porch, mid-sentence before his brain caught up. "Boss, we've got—uh…"

He froze. Blinked once. Twice.

"Sergeant Chambers," he said finally, voice pitching up half a note.

"Morning, Harper," she said, calm as could be, wearing one of my T-shirts and holding my favorite mug.

The man looked like someone had just short-circuited his frontal lobe.

His eyes darted from her to me, then back to her. "I, uh… didn't realize Vice was… conducting field work here."

Casey sipped her coffee. "Multi-jurisdictional cooperation. You know how it is."

I rubbed a hand down my face. "Come in before you combust."

Harper stepped inside, still blinking like he was trying to reboot. His voice dropped to me in a whisper that was about as subtle as a grenade: "Boss, do I… need to leave? Or call HR? Or both?"

"Just give me the damn file," I said.

He handed it over without taking his eyes off Casey. "Right, uh, Keller update. Surveillance caught him at the Elysian motel—three nights in a row. Driving a silver Charger with stolen plates."

"Alone?" Casey asked, setting her mug down and instantly back in work mode.

"No. Woman in her twenties. CSU found her this morning." Her mouth flattened. "Same pattern?"

Harper nodded. "Yeah. And worse."

The humor drained out of the room like someone cut the power. I flipped through the photos. Another life stolen, another message painted in cruelty. "Get Keller on every camera between here and Baton Rouge. And I want a BOLO on that silver Charger."

Harper nodded quickly and turned for the door, still looking a little dazed. "Copy that, boss. And, uh… nice to see you again, Sergeant Chambers."

"Likewise," she said, smirking just enough to twist the knife.

When the door shut, I looked at her. She raised an eyebrow. "You gonna tell him he can breathe again?"

"He'll figure it out eventually."

"You really should warn your people before they walk into awkward domestic scenes."

"Yeah," I said. "But then I'd miss moments like that."

Her smile faded a little. "The car. You think it's the same one from last night?"

I hesitated just long enough for her to notice.

"Owen," she said, voice low.

"Maybe," I admitted. "We'll run it down."

She stared me down, that sharp, unblinking cop look. "You're not telling me something."

I met her gaze evenly. "You're imagining things."

She laughed under her breath—not amused. "You're a terrible liar." She grabbed her now dry shirt, pulled it on, and headed for the door. "No more secrets. I mean it."

"I'll do my best."

"You always do."

And then she was gone. The silence that followed wasn't peaceful. It was heavy. I turned my phone over again. The photo stared back.

CHAPTER 8 ◆ CASEY

Now that we had a name, everything changed. It wasn't theory anymore; it was a manhunt. Every detective in two divisions had skin in it, and the air in the bullpen buzzed like static before a storm.

Nguyen and Crawford were buried in Keller's digital trail—burner phones, old army contacts, bank activity that smelled like cash laundering. Harper and Bishop hit his last known job site, a construction company that hadn't updated payroll since the year of the OD. Sanders and Ramos were shaking down the detectives who'd handled his sister's case, trying to pry loose details that never made it into the original report.

And Jordan and I? We pulled the short straw.

Family.

Which was how we ended up on the steps of a weather-worn brownstone off St. Charles Avenue. Wind blew sideways in thin sheets, plastering my blazer to my arms. The neighborhood had once been proud, the kind of place where porches stayed painted and folks waved at their mailman. Now it sagged under the weight of years—quiet, tired, watching us like it knew what we were bringing.

Jordan checked his notes while I rang the bell. Inside, a dog barked once and went silent. A minute later, the door cracked open, and Mrs. Keller looked out—older than her file photo, grief etched deep into the lines around her mouth.

"Mrs. Keller?" I asked softly, flashing my badge. "Sergeant Chambers, NOPD Vice. This is Detective Delaney, my partner."

Her eyes flicked from our shields to our faces, wary but polite. "What's this about?"

"I'm sorry to bother you, ma'am," I said. "We're following up on a series of overdose cases. Your son's name came up in connection with the product involved. It's not a formal accusation—we just need to clarify a few things."

She hesitated at *son*, shoulders tightening. "Bryce?"

"Yes, ma'am."

After a beat, she stepped aside. "Come in, then."

The house smelled like lavender polish and dust—the kind of clean that came from habit, not energy. Lace curtains let in tired slats of light.

Jordan moved quietly through the living room, eyes scanning the photos lining the mantel. He didn't touch anything, just looked—cop quiet, gathering details without needing to ask. Bryce in uniform, a young woman in graduation robes, a family picnic frozen in better times, a man who I assumed was her husband. Other than her wayward son, this woman had no one. My heart hurt for her.

Mrs. Keller lowered herself into a floral armchair, twisting a tissue between her fingers. I stayed standing; sitting felt wrong.

"When was the last time you saw your son?" I asked.

"Couple weeks ago," she said. "He came by late, said he was working on something big. Looked lighter, like he'd finally found a reason to get out of bed again."

"Did he say what that was?"

She shook her head. "After his sister died, we stopped talking

123

about... anything. Every word turned into a fight." Her gaze drifted to the mantel, where a smiling young woman knelt next to a blooming garden. "He changed after that. Said he wanted someone to pay for what happened. I thought he meant the dealer."

Jordan glanced up from the photos. "Anyone come by asking about Bryce lately? Anyone you didn't recognize?"

"No. Just you two." She swallowed hard. "You think he's in trouble again, don't you?"

I chose my words carefully. "We're not sure yet. What we do know is people are getting hurt, and your son's name keeps coming up around the edges. We need to find him before someone else does."

She nodded slowly, voice barely above a whisper. "Bryce was a good boy once. The army straightened him out—or I thought it did. After she died..." Her eyes filled, but she blinked the tears back. "He's always been a wildfire, miss. But now? He's out of control."

I nodded. "If he contacts you again, or if you remember anything—even a word that sounded off—call me directly." I slid her my card.

Outside, the wind picked up like it had a point to prove. Jordan blew out a slow breath. "That was rough."

"Yeah." I watched the door swing shut behind us. "He's not hiding out of guilt. He's hiding because he thinks he's the hero."

Jordan shoved his hands in his pockets, eyes scanning the street. "Then let's hope the hero doesn't decide to make his grand finale before we find him."

I didn't answer. Just started walking.

The wind was starting to die down by the time we got to the precinct, which made me feel like we were in the eye of a hurricane. Inside, the bullpen was its usual chaos—phones ringing, printers whining, coffee cups breeding on every flat surface. Nguyen and Crawford were huddled over their monitors like twin gargoyles, the glow from the screens turning their faces corpse-pale. Sanders and Ramos were mid-argument over jurisdiction, while a beat cop played referee with a donut in hand.

I dropped my blazer on the back of my chair and started the debrief. "All right, Keller's mother confirms he's been in the city within the last two weeks. No mention of where he's staying, but he's running solo. Ramos, did you get anything from the old OD case?"

"Couple of bad statements and a missing evidence tag," he said. "I'm betting Keller's sister's batch was part of that Bay Street seizure."

Sanders nodded. "Fits with the timestamps Nguyen pulled. Somebody moved that product after-hours."

"Then we keep digging," I said. "Nguyen, check storage access again—cross it against the weekend rosters. I want names, not ghosts."

Nguyen cracked his knuckles. "On it, boss."

The energy was good—focused, electric. We were getting somewhere. I was about to grab a fresh cup of coffee when the door swung open, and the mood shifted.

Owen and Harper walked in, looking like they'd just crawled out of a twelve-hour stakeout—rumpled, tired, carrying that Homicide air of devil may care.

"Vice party?" Harper quipped.

Jordan smirked. "We call it 'actually doing our jobs.'"

Before I could answer, Crawford piped up from behind his screen. "Got back some info on those texts you got!"

Confused, I looked over at him and found him holding out some papers to Owen. Who was glaring at Crawford like he had just revealed the secret to life.

"Texts?" I said, my tone knife-sharp.

Crawford practically shrank under the weight of Owen's gaze. Owen didn't even look at me. "Nothing," he said.

"Doesn't sound like nothing," I said, already moving.

"Chambers," he warned, low.

I snatched the printouts out of Crawford's hand before he could even blink. The top page was a system trace report—timestamped, encrypted, and clearly flagged under Bishop's name.

Two different traces, two different messages from unknown numbers.

My chest went tight. "How long have you been sitting on this?"

Owen's jaw flexed. "Casey—"

"How. Long?"

He didn't answer me, so I flipped through the pages until I could find the dates. Almost a week. Almost a *fucking* week. I could feel the heat rising in my face—that slow, volcanic kind that started in your gut and worked its way up your throat.

"A week, Owen? Tell me I'm reading this wrong."

His voice stayed calm, infuriatingly so. "It was sent to *me*, Casey."

"About *our* case, dumbass! That is *my* fucking car in your driveway!"

The bullpen had gone dead quiet except for the distant hum of the air vents. Harper pinched the bridge of his nose like a man watching a train derail in slow motion. Jordan, meanwhile, had already leaned toward Harper, and out of the corner of my eye I saw a twenty change hands.

Owen stepped forward, lowering his voice. "I was handling it. The message was clean, no trace, no metadata. I wasn't about to send the department into a panic over a glorified scare tactic."

"A glorified scare tactic?" I snapped. "Someone followed me, Owen! You think that's a coincidence?"

A murmur rolled through the room.

He froze, and for the first time, that calm cracked. "You weren't supposed to know about this."

"Oh, no shit." I threw the papers down on a desk. "You think keeping me in the dark makes me safer? You think I don't know how to handle myself?"

"This isn't about what you can handle—"

"The hell it's not!"

I was aware, distantly, that half the bullpen had stopped pretending to work. Sanders's coffee froze halfway to her mouth. Even Thibodeaux's door cracked open halfway before quietly shutting again. The man probably decided no paycheck was worth refereeing *this*.

Owen exhaled through his nose, low and controlled. "You're angry, fine. But this isn't about ego—"

"Don't you *dare* call it ego."

He stepped closer. "I'm trying to keep you alive."

I took another step in too, close enough to feel the heat off him, and practically snarled. "Then maybe try trusting me to do my job instead of making me the goddamn damsel in your story."

The tension snapped taut—electric, razor-thin.

Jordan cleared his throat from behind me. "All right, that's enough foreplay for one morning."

"Shut up, Jordan," we both said at the same time.

127

Crawford muttered, "I think I need to transfer."

I didn't even look at him. "You keep anything else from me, Bishop," I said, voice low, "and I swear to God—"

"You'll what?"

"Find out."

I turned to leave, but his hand shot out—big, calloused—closing around my wrist. Not rough, not yet, but firm enough to stop me. "Casey—"

I don't remember deciding to move—just the feel of his sleeve under my fingers as he reached for me. Training took over. I pivoted, caught his wrist, used his own weight. He hit the floor hard enough to rattle a chair. "Don't touch me," I warned.

But Owen Bishop never knew when to quit. He sprang to his feet, moving a lot faster than a man his size should be able to, one hand raised like he could talk me down. "Would you just listen—"

"I would've listened. The second you got that first message about *our* case. But you chose to keep that from me." I was waving my arms around for emphasis, and he caught my arm again, reflex more than intent. Wrong move. My knee came up, my free hand caught his wrist, and in one clean motion I had his arm twisted back, shoulder locked. He grunted, trying not to wince.

"Jesus, Casey—"

"Let. Go."

"Not until you calm the hell down—"

I tightened the hold. "You first."

It should've ended there. But his instincts kicked in—muscle memory, years of control tactics—and suddenly he reversed the grip, his size and strength winning out. My back hit the wall, hard enough to knock the air out of me, his forearm braced just enough to pin, but not hurt.

We were both breathing hard. The bullpen had gone dead quiet again—a silent, collective *holy shit*. Somewhere behind us, Jordan muttered, "Yep. Should've brought popcorn."

"Casey," Owen said, voice low, all that authority bleeding through it. "You done?"

I glared up at him, close enough to count the flecks of blue in his eyes. "Not even close."

For a second, neither of us moved. We just stood there—locked in that stupid, dangerous standoff where anger started to blur into something else.

Then I shoved off the wall, breaking his hold. He let me, but not easily. I straightened my shirt, jaw tight. "Next time you grab me like that, you better be ready to lose teeth."

He exhaled, running a hand down his face. "Next time you pull that stunt in the middle of my bullpen, you better be ready for paperwork."

"Your bullpen?" I snapped. "Newsflash, Bishop—this case doesn't belong to you. I get you're used to being a one-man wrecking crew, but this is my case as well. I've got stake in this *too*."

Owen and I stared at each other for a long beat. Jordan clapped his hands once. "All right, folks, show's over. Break it up before Thibodeaux walks out and decides to try his hand at retirement again." I grabbed my jacket and stormed out, pulse pounding, hand still tingling from where I'd grabbed him. Vice was dark when I got back. The bullpen looked like a ghost town—half-drained coffee cups, cold monitors, and that faint hum of fluorescent lights that never really turned off. It smelled like burnt espresso and old stress. My team was still at Homicide's office, finishing what I'd walked out on.

129

Good. I could use the peace and quiet. I tossed my keys onto my desk and sank into the chair, the leather sighing under me. My hands still trembled—part rage, part leftover adrenaline. My pulse hadn't slowed since Owen had grabbed my wrist. Since I'd twisted out of it. Since I'd *let* him get under my skin again. The silence pressed in. I stared at the wall of case photos—girls who'd never make it home—and tried to remind myself what the hell all this anger was actually for.

A knock came at the door.

"Come in," I said without looking up. The door creaked open, and Captain Morales stepped inside, crisp uniform somehow immune to the city's humidity. She shut the door quietly, took one look at me, and sighed like a woman who already knew the story.

"I heard what happened."

Of course she had. Rumors in this department moved faster than fiber optics.

"News travels," I said.

"In this place? It teleports." She crossed her arms. "You want to tell me why Homicide's senior sergeant nearly ended up flat on his ass courtesy of *my* sergeant?"

I exhaled through my nose. "Disagreement about jurisdiction."

Morales arched an eyebrow. "Is that the new euphemism for trying to murder a coworker?"

I looked up finally. "If I'd wanted to murder him, he'd still be on the floor."

That earned the ghost of a smile, but it didn't last. "You're lucky I like you, Chambers."

I leaned back in my chair. The captain and I had bonded over being the only females with rank in the boys club that was

Vice. A lot of people called it favoritism when she promoted me. Others were less nice about it. As if she were reading my mind, Morales stepped closer, resting a hand on the edge of my desk. Her voice softened just enough to slip past my defenses. "When I promoted you, everyone said I was insane. Too young, too female, too loud. They said Vice needed a politician, not a fighter."

"I didn't ask for the job because I wanted to play politics."

"I know," she said. "That's why you got it. But every time you walk into a room, half the people there are waiting for you to prove them right. Don't give them the satisfaction."

I stared down at my hands. "You think I embarrassed you."

"I think you had a bad day. Don't make it worse by pretending it didn't happen."

I nodded once. "Understood."

She straightened, heading for the door. "Go home, Sergeant. Sleep. Think. And when you come back tomorrow, I want the version of you that terrifies the criminals, not the one who wrestles her allies."

"Yes, ma'am."

She hesitated in the doorway. "Casey?"

"Yeah?"

"You're one of the best. Don't let that temper be what people remember about you."

When she left, the office felt bigger than it had any right to. The lights buzzed. Somewhere outside, sirens echoed—faint, distant, constant. I rubbed a hand over my face and laughed once, sharp and humorless. Go home, she'd said. Sure. But the only place my mind kept circling back to wasn't *home*. It was Owen Bishop's front porch. I sat in that office for the longest time, even after the lights shut off. At some point, I found myself

131

moving before my brain had even caught up to what my feet were doing. And when I got in my car, instead of turning left for home… I turned right.

Towards him.

I had a feeling he would still be awake. I hadn't expected to find him on the front porch. He sat on the steps, elbows on his knees and tongue in his cheek. His eyes narrowed on my car when I pulled in, but he didn't move. I got out slowly, never taking my eyes from him. The sun had long since set, but the streetlights cast a glow over him. He was all hard edges, a sort of menacing confidence that came with age and experience. I stopped right in front of him and for a second, neither of us spoke.

"What are you doing here, Casey?"

"That's a damn good question." I folded my arms. "I'll let you know when I figure it out."

He tilted his head, those cool eyes assessing me the way he did suspects—measured, patient, looking for the crack. I forced myself to stand still.

"Don't ever pull that shit again," I said.

"I was—"

"Trying to protect me. Yeah, I know." My voice came out sharper than I meant it to. "Some misguided, knight-in-shining-armor crap. I don't need a babysitter, Owen. I need a partner. And I really, *really* hate liars."

"I wasn't lying," he said, too calmly. "I just left out a few details."

I frowned. "And how many times has a perp fed you that same line?"

He exhaled, looking skyward. "More times than I can count."

"But you let it slide, right? Because technically, they weren't lying."

His gaze dropped back to me. "Usually, I introduce their face to the wall."

I tried not to laugh, but my lips twitched anyway. His eyes caught the movement, lingered a second too long.

"I don't like being mad at you," I said quietly. Then, because I couldn't help it: "But you gotta admit—it isn't all bad."

That earned the faintest lift of an eyebrow.

I let the grin slip this time, slow and deliberate, before stepping closer. "I kinda liked the part where you had me up against the wall."

He stood slowly, before stepping forward until we were chest to chest. I had to tilt my head back to look at him. He tucked an errant strand of hair behind my ear. "Get in the house, Casey."

"What if I don't wanna?" I quipped.

He made a sound deep in his throat—half warning, half something else—and before I could blink, he scooped me off my feet.

"Owen!" I yelped, the word muffled against his back as he tossed me over his shoulder like I weighed nothing.

"Keep mouthing off," he muttered, heading for the door.

I started to kick, mostly out of pride. "Put me down, you overgrown—"

The sharp crack of his palm against my ass stole the rest of my words from me. I went still, shocked, pulse hammering. His chuckle rumbled through me a second later. So, I bit him—just a nip, just enough to make him swear—and he smacked me again, harder this time, muttering something about stubborn women and early graves as he carried me up the steps. I stopped struggling when he started rubbing the spot he had hit before trailing his hand until it rested at the top of my inner thigh.

Down the hall, past the wallpaper that still had the marks left by pictures that used to hang. When he tossed me on the bed, I bounced on the mattress before lying there and looking up at him. I raised an eyebrow when he removed his belt.

"What am I going to do with you, Casey?"

"I'm more interested in what you plan on doing with that belt at the moment."

He chuckled, and I was willing to guess the number of people who had heard this man laugh could fit on one hand. I was thrilled to count myself among them. "What do you want me to do with it, *ma louve?*" He held the belt in one hand, kneeling over me. Using the buckle as a sort of pointer, he traced the edges of my body with it. I couldn't help but shiver.

"Do you want me to put it around your wrists? Keeping you from touching me while I use you?"

His other hand started undoing the buttons of my shirt, as the belt made its way up and down my side, from my shoulder to my upper thigh, and back again.

"Do you want me to flip you over? And spank you for misbehaving?"

He had half my shirt unbuttoned and one of his hands cupped my breast, my nipple erect and trying desperately to make contact with his rough palm. He flicked it through the fabric, and I groaned.

"What if I made you kneel for me? And fucked your pretty little mouth while I used the belt around your throat for leverage."

Laying the belt across my hips, he leaned down and kissed my neck. He got to the edge of my tattoo, right above my collarbone, and bit me. Hard. I yelped then moaned when he licked the spot, soothing the sting. His hands unbuttoned my jeans while his lips worked my skin, covering me in love bites as he nipped and sucked every inch of me. I was melting in his hands, I was sure, my body putty under his experienced touch.

"Owen, please."

He slid my jeans down, tossing them to the side, and cupped my pussy, pushing the heel of his palm into me. The pressure on my clit had me whimpering and grinding against him, but he pulled away. I swore, watching through heavy eyes as he picked up the belt again. "I want an answer, Casey."

Shit, an answer? I could barely even remember my fucking options. I hadn't realized this was a damn pop quiz; my body had devoted every inch of power to the fire building in my core, leaving my memory in the dust. The last one? Maybe? I groaned, trying desperately to remember what he had said. Something about fucking me? Yeah, I was good with that.

Owen's hand came down on my pussy, hard. The slap made me levitate, and my curse was half whimper, half moan. "An answer, *mon péché*. Use your words. Tell me what you want."

This motherfucker. "The last one."

A devilish light filled his eyes, and I wondered what I had just agreed to. He pulled me to my feet, and I swayed under the sudden movement. He gripped my hips, steadying me. "You sure?"

I bit my lip. Whatever it was, I trusted him. "Yes."

He kissed me, his tongue clashing with mine for a minute before he pulled away. "Good girl."

I blinked. Good girl? Did I like that? Shit. Yeah. I liked that. I *really* liked that.

Owen apparently took advantage of my momentary distraction. Suddenly, the belt was around my neck, and I was on my knees before him. The belt tightened until I was forced to look up at him. His erection tented his pants and was right in my face. I realized what I had just agreed to. I licked my lips and reached for his waistband. He eased the pressure on my throat until the belt was almost slack against my skin. When his jeans dropped to the floor, followed shortly by his boxers, his cock sprang out. He was hard. So hard, I was sure it had to hurt.

The last time I had been on my knees for him, the light was dim, and I was more concerned about getting a reaction out of him than anything. Now, I took a moment to appreciate the sheer size of the man. And to marvel how the fuck that had ever fit inside me. I leaned forward, licking away the bead of precum at his tip. The belt tightened on my throat again, and I looked up at him.

"Open your mouth, Casey."

Feeling feisty, I pressed my lips firmly together and leaned back on my heels, a challenge in my eyes. The belt got tighter. And I got wetter.

The hand that was holding the belt gave a little yank, forcing me forward, and I nearly fell on him. I had to grab at his thighs to brace myself. His thick, ridiculously well-muscled thighs. The man was almost forty. And yet I knew guys my age who couldn't hold a candle to his physique. I squeezed him, digging my nails in just enough to make him grunt. His other hand fell to the back of my head, twisting itself into my hair. Then he yanked my head back, pulling on the belt at the same time, and with watery eyes, I looked up at him.

"Such a brat. You want to breathe, you'll open that mouth."

I swear I tried to hold out, but to be perfectly honest... I didn't want to. When I finally sucked in a lungful of air, he shoved his cock past my lips until he hit the back of my throat. I gagged at the intrusion, and he loosened his hold on the belt and allowed me oxygen. The grip on my hair remained firm, and after a few seconds, he began to move.

"Fuck, that's my girl," he groaned, and I grinned around his shaft. The belt tightened again, but didn't fully restrict my air flow, just forced me to tilt my head back so he could go even deeper. "Relax your jaw, *mon péché*. I know you can take me. Show me what you've got."

I licked him from base to tip, like I had that one night, and he jerked. Hollowing out my cheeks, I forced myself to breathe through my nose. Looking up at him, I watched as he closed his eyes and rocked in and out of my mouth. Fuck, the man was so damn fine I was sure there was going to be a wet spot on the carpet from where I was kneeling. I wanted him to use me. Grazing my teeth along the top of his cock, I moaned to get his attention. His eyes flew open, and he looked down at me. He smoothed my hair back from my face.

"I can't decide what's more beautiful. You in tact gear, kicking someone's ass. Or you on your knees for me, begging me to fuck you senseless with that look in your eyes."

I moaned in response, dropping a hand to the ever-building pressure between my legs. When I pressed a finger against my clit, I moaned again, and my eyes shuttered closed. "Are you wet for me, Casey?"

I opened my eyes, nodding. His cock was still in my mouth, and his movements got faster. "Show me."

I ran a finger through my slit, coating myself in my arousal before holding it up for him.

He groaned. "Such a good girl." He fisted the belt in one hand and used the other to hold the back of my head. Bracing me, keeping me from moving. "I'm going to fuck your mouth now, *mon péché*. And while I do, I want you to make yourself come.

Do you understand me? Three taps on my thigh, I'll stop. But otherwise..."

I shuddered at the dark promise before nodding. Then the belt got even tighter, the hand on the back of my head firmer. He began to thrust in and out of my mouth until I couldn't stop the drool from slipping past my lips. He was hitting the back of my throat, again and again. I could barely breathe, but moved my hand back down to my pussy, and began to thrust a finger in and out of myself to the same rhythm he fucked my mouth with.

For a minute or so, neither one of us said anything. I closed my eyes, focusing on his primal grunts and the sound of my fingers sliding in and out of my cunt. My eyes shot open when he hit the back of my throat, and I choked. As I forced myself to breathe through my nose, he didn't let up the pace, and I continued to gag on his cock. But I never even considered tapping out.

I would've probably fallen over backwards when I came, but the belt and his hand kept me in place. My chin was coated in drool by then, my eyes watering from the force he was using. He came soon after I did, shooting his seed down my throat in hot, salty spurts. I did my best to swallow every drop, and when he pulled out of my mouth with a pop, he dropped the belt.

For a minute, I didn't move, then he pulled me to my feet. "On the bed, love. I'm not done with you yet."

Gently, he guided me until my knees hit the edge of the mattress and I sat down dutifully. He spread my legs then knelt between my knees, pulling me down for a kiss. He made a sound deep in the back of his throat when he tasted himself on my tongue. Pulling away, he ran his thumb across my chin, cleaning up the mess of spit and cum I hadn't been able to swallow. Then he kissed me again before dropping a hand between my legs and shoving two fingers inside me. I jolted in surprise, my body hypersensitive to touch, but he began to push his fingers in and out in a slow and steady pace. Eventually, I started rocking my hips against him, throwing my head back on a moan.

"Owen. Baby. Yes." The last word came out on a hiss as he replaced his hand with his mouth and sucked my clit between his teeth. I fell backwards onto the bed, fisting the sheets and cursing when he bit the tender flesh. He braced one arm across my thighs and began to eat me out in earnest, thrusting his tongue in and out of me at the same rate at which he had thrust his cock in and out of my mouth. I rubbed my pussy shamelessly against his face, chasing the high his wicked tongue promised me. When I found it, I felt ethereal, as though my very being seemed to levitate above the bed. He licked my slit from top to bottom, lapping at the juice that was the result of his attentions.

He pulled away, blowing a breath of cold air over my pussy, and I shivered in response. I closed my eyes and lay there, my legs dangling off the edge of the bed. When he grabbed my ankles, I grudgingly opened them to see what he was doing.

"I'm going to make you come again, Casey. And when I do, when I fill you with my seed, and you scream my name, I want you to remember something. Everything I do, I do for you. I want to protect you. And if that makes me a bad man, if that makes you angry... well, frankly, I don't give a damn. You can toss my ass to the floor anytime you want, *ma louve*. But you'll remember who you belong to. Won't you?"

As he talked, he placed my ankles on his shoulder. My thigh muscles protested the strain, but I was too busy watching him line his cock up to my entrance to complain. I marveled at how

139

he was hard again, while I also marveled at his words. I had never considered myself to be the girl who belonged to anyone. I was fiercely independent, always had been. But something about this man made me want to be soft. To let someone else take the lead for once.

It was at that moment that I realized I wanted to be his. That I might just be falling in love with this bullheaded man.

He pulled me from my thoughts as he rubbed his cock across my clit and pussy. I was so damn wet, he nearly slid into me several times. I knew what he wanted to hear, but I was determined to play it coy. Even as my hips rose to meet his touch. I bit my lip but refused to say a word.

He slapped my breast then, and I almost came off the bed. "Fuck... Owen." He slapped the other one, and I writhed. "Owen motherfucking Bishop," I gasped.

"Yes, baby?"

He began to rub my breast then. One rough palm cupping me, before sliding over my nipple, soothing the hurt, and moving to the other. *Fuck.* I could feel my resolve breaking, and I knew he heard it in my voice.

"I want—"

"What, love? What do you want?"

Fine, you win.

"Asshole," I gasped, and he smirked at me. "I want you. Inside me. Now. Please, Owen, please."

"That's my girl." He slid into me in one thrust, his lip curling in a way that was almost feral as he settled his cock deep inside my cunt. "Fuck, you take me so well."

My body was fire and ice, every touch heaven and hell. He pushed even further inside me, using the position my legs were in to his advantage. My eyes rolled to the back of my head, and he flicked my clit as he began to move. "You were mine the second you ground your ass against me in that damn bar, baby. Mine the second we saw each other in Chief's office. Mine the second you drove your SUV through that fence."

"Mine."

Thrust.

"You."

Thrust.

"Are."

His hand came up to my throat, rubbing at the slight red mark the belt had left.

"Mine."

He squeezed and I fractured, screaming his name and cursing him in the same breath. With a snarl, he came inside me and fucked me through yet another orgasm. When he collapsed back onto the bed beside me, he pulled me with him until I was on top of his chest. We were both coated in a fine sheen of sweat, and I couldn't help but shiver. I was sore. So deliciously sore. And I couldn't even think about walking. Tomorrow was going to be interesting. But for now, I just wanted to sleep. He traced the edges of my tattoo, and I shivered again, so he lifted us both just enough to pull a blanket out from underneath. When we were wrapped in it, I curled my head under his chin and tangled my legs between his.

Right before I fell asleep, I said, "Owen?"

"Yeah, love?"

"I will still put you on the floor when you piss me off."

His chuckle vibrated through us both. "I know, *ma louve*. I wouldn't want it any other way. Now, be a good girl and listen for once. Get some sleep."

My eyelids grew impossibly heavy, but I muttered, "I *am* a

141

good girl."

He chuckled again, and the movement lulled me off to sleep.

CHAPTER 9 ◆ CASEY

Owen and I drove separately to the precinct, but I managed to steal a kiss before we made our way inside. I was surprised when he returned the gesture, and we lost ourselves in the familiar taste of each other until someone cleared their throat. Blushing like a schoolgirl, I darted inside. He held the door to the bullpen open for me and Jordan smiled at me over his mug.

"Somebody tell Facilities the electricity in here's messing with my hair."

Harper didn't even look up. "You don't have hair, Jordan."

Laughter rippled through the room, but it was the kind that made you feel warm. Somehow, Homicide and Vice had learned to not only coexist but to get along. Someone get me a lottery ticket, stat. I shook my head, grinning. Nguyen's monitor light painted his face ghost-pale as he pretended not to eavesdrop. Crawford kept typing, slower than usual, clearly hoping not to be collateral damage. Again. Poor guy.

Owen made his way to his office, the picture of composure. Rumpled shirt, coffee in hand. I hadn't noticed the coffee until he set it on my desk in a way that told me he had done it before, and it dawned on me who my "caffeine fairy" was. I glanced at Jordan, who waggled his eyebrows at me.

Dropping my bag beside my desk, I sat on the edge and turned to face the room. "All right, children. Who's actually doing their job?"

"Time to impress Mom!" Jordan spun in his chair until he was also facing the room, and Sanders shot him a look before Harper said, "What if we want to impress dad?"

"I think you're a bit late on that, my friend. I do believe someone else has dibs on the whole 'dad' thing."

I frowned at him. Please tell me he wasn't going where I thought he was. Sanders looked scandalized, but Harper scratched his neck.

"I don't get it."

Jordan snorted. "Think about it."

Crawford buried his face in his hands. "Please don't."

I was dimly aware of Owen stopping beside my desk, but I couldn't tear my eyes away from the conversation.

A light bulb apparently went off over Harper's head, and he straightened like he was the winner on *Wheel of Fortune*. "Oh, you mean someone calling him *Daddy*!"

The room promptly imploded. Owen choked on his coffee. Sanders turned the color of a radish. Jordan blinked and then started howling. Harper looked like he wished the floor would swallow him. I couldn't move. I didn't dare glance at Owen. Crawford made a sound like a dying man, his head still buried in his hands.

Nguyen spun around and cleared his throat loudly, always the first to defuse tension with data. "Anyways." He waited for the room to settle and frowned when it didn't. "Anyways! Jordan, shut up. Guys, listen. I got something. Keller's bank pulls put him in the same ZIP as the Canal Street Kings three days before his sister's anniversary."

I cleared my throat and made a show of straightening the files on my desk. I could feel Owen looking at me. I refused to meet his eyes.

"Street crew?" I asked.

He nodded. "Mid-level gang. Mostly run counterfeit IDs and move dope out of laundromats. But get this—our boy didn't just score a gram or two. He bought them out. Cash."

Jordan whistled low. "So, he cleaned out a street crew. That's... ambitious."

Harper raised his cup in salute. "Let's pay the Kings a royal visit."

Owen put his cup down on my desk then headed for the door. "Let's go."

No hesitation. No look in my direction. Still, every step he took made the air buzz hotter.

The Canal Street Kings staked claim to a crumbling row of shotgun houses and an old gas station that smelled like diesel and burnt grease. A couple of guys leaned against a wall, a rust-red Camaro in front of them. They were passing a blunt and pretending they weren't watching us cross the street.

Jordan and Harper peeled off toward the next block. That left Owen and me. He had divided us before we left, and Jordan waggled his eyebrows at me before climbing in the SUV with Harper.

The closest dealer eyed my badge, then my hips. "You lost, sweetheart? Vice don't usually come sightseeing down here."

"Not sightseeing," I said. "Looking for information. You remember a guy named Keller—white, mid-thirties, military cut, cash in hand?"

He grinned. "White boy? Yeah, he came by. Wanted it all, paid up front. What the fuck else did we care? We weren't about to ask for his social card, little mama. What you want—a background check? I got something you can check."

Before I could blink, Owen had him by the jacket and slammed him into the brick wall hard enough to pop a few old posters loose. The guy's head smacked the mortar with a hollow *thunk*. Owen's voice was a low growl. "You open that mouth again, and you're done talking for the week."

Blood streamed down the dealer's face, glistening on the collar of Owen's shirt. The other Kings took a step back.

"Bishop!" I snapped.

He released the guy, not gently. "Next time, think before you talk."

The dealer held a hand to his nose, glaring through watery eyes. When he spoke next, it was garbled by the apparent broken nose. "He said he wanted everything left from that Bay Street haul. That's all I got."

That one line was enough to set the hook. "Bay Street haul?" I repeated.

"Yeah," the man muttered. "Big stash got lifted. Didn't stick around long enough to ask where he planned to take it."

I looked at Owen. "We're done here."

He gave a curt nod, eyes still sharp, but otherwise the picture of calm. We turned and walked back toward the cars.

Two blocks over, Harper and Jordan were finishing their own canvass, leaning on the hood of Harper's SUV when we pulled up. Our vehicles idled nose to nose, flashers off but ready. Jordan eyed the smear of red drying across Owen's shirt. "Do I even want to know whose blood that is?"

Owen glanced down at his chest like he'd just noticed it and shrugged. "Not mine."

Jordan shook his head. "Right, yes. 'Cause that's what I was worried about. When Thibodeaux notices, that's exactly what I'll tell him."

"Good luck with that," I said, climbing into the driver's seat.

The sarcasm covered the tension, but just barely. We'd gotten our lead. We'd also just reminded half the squad that there was a reason Vice and Homicide kept separate coffee pots.

When night rolled around, the squad group chat had reached consensus: the only thing more dangerous than the Keller case was another night sober. The 10/7 was a cop institution—dim, loud, and forgiving of bloodstained shirts. Harper claimed a high-top near the back. Nguyen and Sanders were already nursing beers, arguing about whether *Die Hard* qualified as a Christmas movie. Jordan was at the jukebox, threatening the room with early-2000s rap.

I headed for the bar to grab the next round. The bartender, a woman who'd seen more bad nights than most of us combined, smiled knowingly. "Long day?"

"Long week," I said, sliding bills across the counter. "Make it six beers, six shots of something strong, and something with an umbrella, please."

While she filled glasses, a stranger slid onto the stool beside me. Civilian. Clean hands, nice watch, no badge bulge under his jacket. He smiled, and I felt a bit bad for him cause he might have had a chance a few months ago. He wasn't unattractive, but he just wasn't doing it for me.

"You look like you could use company," he said.

"Do I?" I kept my tone neutral.

He leaned closer, breath warm with whiskey. "I'm just saying, someone that pretty shouldn't drink alone."

"Someone who thinks they're that smooth should find a new line."

147

He chuckled, undeterred. "Maybe you and I—"

A hand settled at my waist, firm and unmistakable. The voice behind me was calm, quiet, and absolute. "She's taken."

The man froze. I didn't have to turn to know who it was. Owen's heat pressed against my back, his body angled just enough to box the guy out. Possessive. Territorial. And God help me, effective. My would-be suitor muttered something under his breath and disappeared toward the pool tables. Owen didn't move his hand.

"You planning to let go anytime soon?" I asked.

"Eventually."

I turned to face him, ready to lecture him on boundaries and professionalism, but the words stalled when I caught sight of Jordan across the room. He was holding up his phone. The screen read a bright, bold *10*.

Next to him, Harper flashed a *7* on a napkin.

Sanders, ever the overachiever, held a *3*.

Nguyen stared at the ceiling like a man praying for a lightning strike to end his suffering, an *8* scrawled on his palm.

A laugh burst out of me before I could stop it—loud, genuine, breaking the tension like glass.

"What are they rating?"

"Us, dumb ass. They are rating us."

Owen glanced toward them, then back at me, a reluctant smile tugging his mouth. "Us." He said the word like it was foreign, but savored it like it was sweet. "Nosy sons of bitches," he said.

I swatted his chest. "Be nice."

"I'm not paid enough to be nice."

"Don't I know it."

He leaned in, close enough that his breath brushed my ear.

"And yet you keep showing up."

The bartender slid me a tray of drinks and I busied myself with grabbing them so I didn't have to reply. He relieved me of two and followed me to the table.

The rest of the night unspooled in laughter and low music, stories that got louder with every round. For the first time in days, the case faded into the background. The static between Owen and me didn't. It hummed quietly under every word. At some point, liquid courage buzzing in my veins, I pulled Owen towards the dance floor, and our entire table went quiet when he actually followed. He spun me around a few times, the noise of the bar fading until it was just the beat of the music and us. The way he pulled me to him was definitely not work-friendly, but for once, neither of us cared. Back at the table, Jordan gave me a thumbs up, and Owen did his best to silence the teasing with one of his signature looks.

When they called last call, half the squad had left. The neon sign outside flickered like a dying heartbeat. I stepped into the cool night air, phone in one hand, keys in the other. Owen was leaning against my car, sleeves rolled to his elbows, eyes soft for once.

"Following me now?" I asked.

"Making sure you don't start any more fights with people twice your size," he said.

I tilted my head. "Big talk for someone who nearly redecorated a brick wall with a suspect."

He gave a one-shouldered shrug. "He earned it."

I snorted. "You're going to have to start a punch card—nine assaults gets you a free therapy session."

"Tried therapy," he said. "Made the shrink cry."

I snorted, his rare humor surprising me and I leaned next to

149

him. "I can't believe you got jealous."

He eyed me. "I don't do jealous."

I rolled my eyes. "I think that guy in there would disagree."

Owen raised an eyebrow as I dropped my voice lower, mocking him. "She's taken."

"You are."

There it was again—that low, dangerous tenderness. I opened my mouth to argue and never got the chance. He turned towards me, brushed a loose strand of hair from my face, and kissed me. Slow, steady, deliberate—nothing like the chaos that usually defined us. Just heat, restraint, and a promise neither of us had any business making.

When he pulled back, he rested his forehead against mine. "Go home, Chambers."

"Bossy."

"Always."

I huffed a quiet laugh, slid into the driver's seat, and shut the door. He stayed there, hands in his pockets, watching until I turned out of the lot. The streets were empty, washed clean by a late drizzle. I kept one hand on the wheel, the other absently tracing the ghost of where his fingers had been on my waist. The night was thick with humidity and something else—guilt, maybe, or craving.

I told myself I didn't like it when he pulled that possessive crap. I'd worked too hard to be taken seriously to let a man—any man—stake a claim. But the pulse in my throat said otherwise. I hit the interstate, grinning like an idiot. Not because of the drinks. Because of him. Because of us. Because the smartest thing I could do was run the other way, and every instinct I had was already turning back.

Sleep came in fits, shallow and unsatisfying. When my alarm

finally went off, I was already awake, staring at the ceiling and wondering when coffee had stopped working as a cure-all. The city outside my window was still half-asleep—a gray haze of humidity and headlights.

I gave up pretending I'd rest and shuffled into the kitchen. Coffee first. Always coffee.

The first sip burned just enough to feel alive again. I sat cross-legged on the couch, body cam footage playing on my laptop. The Canal Street Kings, Keller's name scrawled across every page of my notes, and Owen's voice drifting through the speakers—calm, clipped, efficient. Then the part where he slammed that dealer into a wall.

I paused, staring at the frozen frame of his jaw set hard, blood across his collar. I told myself I was annoyed. My pulse disagreed.

"Professional," I muttered. "You're a damn professional."

I added another note to the margin of my file: *Keller – Canal St. – all cash. Military past. Find connection.*

By six-thirty, I'd traded pajamas for pressed slacks and mascara. The drive to the precinct was quiet. The bullpen wasn't.

Harper was halfway through a rant about football stats. Nguyen had three screens open and the kind of focus only caffeine and mild panic could produce. Sanders—balancing a coffee in one hand and a pen in the other—was the first to spot me.

"Morning, boss. Hope you're caffeinated—we got something."

I dropped my bag by my desk. "If it's breakfast tacos, I'll marry whoever brought them."

"Better. But I do not accept the marriage proposal. Bit soon for that." Nguyen spun one monitor toward me. "NCIC

151

hit overnight. Keller popped for assault and battery out of Charleston, South Carolina."

That made me pause. "How far back?"

"2015," Sanders said. "Bar fight near Fort Jackson. Charges dropped after restitution. No follow-up."

"Who handled it?"

Nguyen scrolled. "Contact of record—Lieutenant Jason Hartwell, Charleston PD. Still active. I sent him a message, and he replied this morning. Said he's free for a quick video call."

"Good work." I glanced toward the door. "Bishop in yet?"

"Just walked in," Sanders said, smirking as Owen appeared with two coffees like he'd read her mind.

He handed me one and leaned against my desk, expression unreadable as usual. "What'd I miss?"

"Old case," I said, gesturing to the screen with my coffee. "Keller's got history in Charleston. Bar fight, clean getaway."

"Guy's got a type," Owen muttered.

Nguyen started the call. The Charleston PD logo blinked onto the monitor, followed by a tired-looking man with graying hair and a loosened tie. He was in the middle of hitting the screen when the camera focused.

"There. Ya damn thing. Learn to fucking cooperate." He turned his attention from berating the computer to us. "Lieutenant Hartwell," he greeted. "Morning. Who am I talking to?"

"Sergeant Chambers, Vice Division, New Orleans PD. This is Sergeant Bishop, Homicide."

He nodded once, glancing between us. "Appreciate you reaching out. You're chasing Keller, huh?"

"Yes, sir. We've got him linked to a counterfeit operation down here. We're trying to fill in some blanks from his military years."

Hartwell scratched his jaw. "Yeah, I remember that one. Keller got drunk, picked a fight with the wrong guy at a bar outside the base. Broke a jaw. Case disappeared when the victim wouldn't press. I figured he'd fallen off the grid after that."

"Any chance you remember who took the initial report?" I asked.

He frowned and looked off-screen. "Hell, that was a decade ago." He looked up and appeared to be scanning the room. He did a double-take and then frowned. We were forgotten for a moment.

"McGrady," Hartwell said sharply, "didn't the doctor tell you to take it easy?"

The answer was instant. "He *suggested* I take it easy."

Another woman snorted. "Want me to shoot her in the other leg? Even her out? Hey, who you talking to this early?"

Hartwell frowned at them, "None of your business." But two women leaned into his screen. One was a lithe redhead, the other a woman with long black hair done in cornrows.

Hartwell shooed them off camera but then stopped. "Vaughn, you worked that area off base, right? Back when you were a beat cop?"

The woman with black hair turned back to him. "Yes sir, what about it?"

"You remember a soldier named Keller? Bar fight?"

"Sir, if I remembered every bar fight involving a soldier, I would petition the mayor for a medal." The two women vanished out of screen, arguing loudly.

Hartwell turned his attention back to us, "Apologies. My detectives haven't mastered the concept of an indoor voice. Or minding their own damn business."

Owen's mouth twitched. "Can't say we don't understand."

Hartwell flipped open a file on his desk. "Anyway, I'll dig up the report and send it over. Looks like Keller settled his restitution fast—no follow-ups after that. We didn't hear from him again."

"Appreciate your time, Lieutenant," I said.

"Anytime. And if you figure out why this guy's name keeps crawling back out of the woodwork, let me know. The bastard owes me a bottle of scotch."

The call ended.

Nguyen grinned. "That sounded fun."

Jordan, having made his appearance later than usual, nodded sagely. "Yeah, that one girl reminded me of a certain cop I know. Can't imagine who."

I stared at the blank screen a second longer, half a smile tugging at my mouth. Whoever those two were—McGrady and Vaughn—they had that same bite we did. Probably gave their lieutenant heartburn daily. Jordan was right, the environment was familiar. Guess departments had their similarities, no matter the state.

"All right," I said, pushing up from my chair. "Nguyen, pull Keller's financials again. Sanders, recheck the body cam timestamps from last night. If Keller's running with out-of-state money, I want a trail before noon."

Owen gave me a sidelong look. "Sleep much?"

"Barely."

"Coffee'll only get you so far."

"Then it's a good thing I've got a whole pot."

He smirked, just barely. "You're impossible."

"Efficient," I corrected, already turning toward my desk, but I offered him a small smile that I hoped was at least somewhat reassuring.

CHAPTER 10 ◆ CASEY

By 10 a.m., the precinct was one cigarette and a bad headline away from a riot. Thibodeaux was already screaming at somebody important on the phone, pacing like a man on a countdown.

"No, I'm not *ignoring* the goddamn mayor— I'm *telling* him!— If he wants miracles, he can buy a rosary!" He slammed the receiver down so hard the front desk sergeant flinched.

Every TV in the bullpen blared the same story on loop: *Another Keller Victim Found.* Reporters were stacked outside the glass doors like seagulls around a landfill, cameras flashing every time one of us moved. I shoved through them earlier just to get inside—nearly brained one with my coffee cup in the process—and I was already five seconds from snapping a neck if one more mic came within biting distance.

Jordan came storming in from the hallway, dragging a twitchy guy in cuffs by the collar. "Guess who decided to brag about knowing Keller's supplier?" He shoved the man into the nearest chair. "Smile for the cameras, jackass."

The perp spat onto the floor. "I want a lawyer."

"Yeah, and I want eight hours of sleep and a winning *Powerball* ticket," Jordan said, shoving him again. "We all suffer."

Owen appeared from somewhere behind me, cool as ever

despite the chaos. He didn't even raise his voice—just snapped his fingers toward Harper and Sanders. "Interview room two. Now."

Harper grumbled something about "not my circus," but went anyway, dragging Jordan's perp along while Sanders followed with her clipboard already out. At the far end of the room, Nguyen and Crawford looked like they'd merged with their monitors. Lines of CCTV feeds flickered across the screens—street cams, ATM footage, even grainy traffic light captures.

Nguyen's fingers flew over the keyboard. "We're patching into every camera south of Canal. He's gotta show up somewhere."

Crawford didn't even blink. "He's changing cars every forty-eight hours. That plate's useless now."

"Then find out where he's getting the cars."

"Right. Why didn't I think of that?" Crawford jabbed angrily at his keyboard, "Oh, wait. Cause I already did!"

He and Nguyen started arguing vehemently. I chose to ignore them, pinching the bridge of my nose.

Across the room, Harper and Sanders were also arguing. Something about procedure. Or maybe sports. With those two, it was a coin flip.

"I'm telling you," Harper said, waving a folder, "we hit the warehouses first. Keller's using them to funnel cash—"

Sanders cut him off. "And I'm telling you if we keep chasing his ghost network instead of the man, we'll be knee-deep in paperwork while he skips the state!"

Harper's eyes narrowed. "You got a better plan?"

"Yeah. One that doesn't involve you playing hero in front of a news camera." The two squared off. Sanders's pixie cut was growing long, and I swear she looked puffy. Like a Halloween cat.

"Kids," I called over. "Play nice or I'll separate you."

Harper snorted. "She started it."

Sanders flipped him off as she walked away. "And I'll finish it."

"Nguyen, tell me you've got something before I strangle both of them."

He tapped a few keys, squinting at the feed. "Wait—pause that."

Crawford shot him an irritated glance but did so. Nguyen enhanced the image until it finally sharpened—two faces, both familiar from the evidence board. Street-level runners we'd been trying to track for a week, stepping into a black pickup near the docks. Not Keller. But close enough to shake loose answers.

My pulse kicked. "Freeze it. Send it to Patrol. Get units rolling."

Owen was suddenly beside me, already pulling on his jacket. "We're going out?"

"Damn right we are."

Thibodeaux chose that exact moment to re-emerge from his office, tie crooked, eyes bloodshot. "Nobody's going anywhere until I get an update."

"You just got one," I said. "Two associates tied to our missing stash, spotted near the docks. We're checking it out."

He pointed at me with the kind of rage only caffeine and ulcers could create. "If this turns out to be another homeless guy with a beard, I'm turning your badge into a coaster."

"Understood, sir," I said sweetly, already heading for the door.

"Don't 'sir' me, Chambers! And tell Bishop to keep his goddamn temper in check— last thing I need is another use-of-force complaint!"

Thibodeaux's bellow followed us down the hall: "Get me Keller before I retire or die, whichever comes first!"

The parking lot was swarming with reporters. They pressed against the barricades, shouting questions:

"Is Keller targeting cops now?"

"Has Vice lost control of the case?"

"Sergeant Chambers! Is it true—"

Owen opened my car door for me before I could commit assault by microphone. "Ignore them."

"I was gonna," I said, climbing in. "It's you I am worried about. Didn't I hear you threatening to rip their vocal cords out earlier?"

He smirked. "You spying on me?"

"Bite me."

"Tempting."

I slammed the door just to stop smiling.

Inside, the tension followed us like a shadow. Every radio channel was alive with chatter— patrols fanning out, SWAT on standby, uniforms pulling overtime. By the time we reached the staging area, the sun was a white knife in the sky. The heat made the asphalt shimmer, and my patience had officially evaporated.

Harper met us at the curb, wiping sweat off his brow. "We splitting warrants between teams?"

I nodded. "Yeah, so let's not waste daylight."

Owen's jaw flexed. "We hit hard, we hit fast. No warning this time."

Sanders arched an eyebrow. "You mean *less* warning than last time? Because we practically showed up in a marching band."

Owen's glare shut her up.

Jordan jogged over, vest half-fastened. "You two gonna brief us, or are we winging it again?"

I slid my sunglasses on. "Winging it's faster."

Owen gave me a look that could have peeled paint. "This isn't your first rodeo, Chambers. Keep your head."

"Don't tell me what to do," I said, climbing into the driver's seat.

He didn't respond. Just shook his head and muttered under his breath as he got in the other SUV. Nguyen forwarded them to my tablet with a soft ding. "Merry Christmas," he said. "Two stash spots tied to Keller's runners. Utilities, burner numbers, and a whole lotta shady Venmo history. Sending info to your phones now."

Owen scanned the addresses over my shoulder. "I'll take Claiborne. You take the one off Alvar."

"Why do you get Claiborne?" I asked.

"Because Claiborne backs up to an alley and yours opens onto a courtyard." He gave me a look. "You like having neighbors with line of sight, remember?"

"Yes, I know. Why do you know?"

He winked, and I think my brain malfunctioned. "I know a lot about you, Casey."

I sputtered before saying, "Try to not get shot."

"You too."

We split at the cars. Harper and Jordan fell in with me; Sanders grabbed her vest and jogged after us. Owen took the other SUV with two uniforms and a SWAT liaison who already looked like he regretted his career choices.

Both SUVs peeled out of the lot. The storm was coming. I could feel it in my bones. And for the first time in days, I was ready to hit back. My knee bounced the whole way. I told myself it was just adrenaline. It wasn't only that.

We parked a block from the Alvar address, a two-story brick

building that had seen better centuries. Laundry hung from rusted balconies. Someone's music thumped through too-thin walls. Sanders checked her phone. "Warrant's clean. Utilities in a fake name that's been used on two other Keller-related addresses."

"Good," I said. "Harper, you're with me on the door. Sanders, you take Jordan. Cover the stairwell, and the back. I don't want anyone slipping out a window while we're making introductions."

Jordan nodded, already pulling his vest tighter. "Yes ma'am."

We stacked on the door, guns out. I took a breath, felt the familiar coil of focus settle in. My world narrowed to the crack under the door and the muffled voices inside.

I hesitated, taking a second to steel myself.

Harper raised his brows. "Nice weather we're having."

"Knock it down," I said.

He kicked. The door exploded inward, slamming into the wall with a satisfying crunch. We poured in, shouting, "Police! Search warrant!"

Two men in the living room jerked upright—one on a stained couch, the other halfway through a line of something off the coffee table. A third tried to bolt for the kitchen.

Bad choice.

I went after the runner. He grabbed for the counter, knocked over a stack of dishes, then turned and swung wild. I ducked under his fist, drove my shoulder into his ribs, and heard the air leave him in a shocked grunt. He tried to grab my arm. I twisted, planted my foot, and kicked sideways—hard. The ball of my foot connected with his knee and he howled, stumbling back against the fridge as his leg gave out. "Stay down."

He spat at me. Literally. The glob hit my vest.

I grabbed the front of his shirt, yanked him forward, and introduced his face to the cabinet door. Not enough to break anything vital—hopefully—but enough to make him rethink his life choices. Blood smeared the peeling paint. The perp sagged, groaning. I spun him, slammed him chest-first against the fridge, and cuffed him while he wheezed.

"You're under arrest," I said. "You have the right to shut the hell up. I strongly suggest you use it."

"I want a lawyer," he mumbled through blood.

"That's nice."

In the living room, Harper and Jordan had the other two face-down on the floor, wrists zip-tied, assorted baggies and cash scattered like confetti. I heard what I assumed was Sanders rummaging around on the upper floor.

"Nothing big," Jordan said, breathless. "But it's Keller-adjacent. Burner tied to one of his shell numbers."

"Good enough. Let's take them back."

Outside, a couple of neighbors watched from their doors, eyes wide. One woman folded her arms, shook her head, and muttered, "'Bout damn time," as we hustled the three men down the stairs. I shoved my guy into the back of the car, slammed the door, and leaned on the frame for half a second, catching my breath.

Nguyen's voice crackled through the radio. "Bishop's team hit paydirt. Confiscated cash, some uncut dope, and a ledger with Keller's initials all over it. They're headed back in."

"Copy," I said. "We're en route with three."

Booking was a zoo when we got back. Front desk swamped, holding full, the stale smell of sweat and disinfectant clinging to everything.

I yanked my guy out of the backseat. He tried to plant his

feet; I jerked him forward anyway. "Move it," I said.

Owen's voice cut through the din behind me. "Chambers."

I looked back. He stood there, another suspect in cuffs at his side—taller, thick neck, sleeves rolled to show off bad tattoos and worse judgment. The guy was grinning like he thought this was a party. Owen glanced at the guy I was holding, taking in the dried blood and glancing back at me. He raised an eyebrow, then gestured for me to go in front of him.

The desk sergeant buzzed the gate open. I marched my perp down the row, ignoring his commentary about my mother, my badge, and what he'd like to do to both. I shoved him into an empty cell. He stumbled, caught himself on the bench, then turned back to the bars, chin lifted. "This ain't gonna stick."

I smiled without warmth. "We'll see."

I stepped back as the door clanged shut and locked. For a second, the noise of the bullpen fell away. It was just me, the pulse in my ears, and the weight of every bad decision in this building. Footsteps approached. Owen, escorting his own prize down the hallway. I leaned against the opposite wall, arms crossed, watching. Our eyes met for a heartbeat—his dark, steady, something hot flickering just under the surface.

My perp saw the look, saw the connection, and laughed. "Oh, I get it now. Little miss cop likes it rough, huh?"

He slapped his hand on his bars, rattling them. "Hey, big man, you hittin' that? That why she's all wound up?"

The entire corridor tightened. Even the air seemed to go still.

I moved toward the cell, ready to shut him up the old-fashioned way, but Owen stepped in front of me, blocking my path.

"Don't," he said quietly.

I bristled. "Don't tell me—"

"—what to do, yeah," he murmured. "I know. Just trust me for five seconds."

I swallowed whatever I was about to say and forced myself back a step. My fingers curled into fists at my sides.

His perp chose that moment to lean into Owen's space, chest puffed. "You gonna stop me, Sergeant? You don't scare me. Bet without that badge, you're nothing."

Owen's face didn't change. His eyes did. They went flat, dangerous.

"You sure you want to test that theory?" he asked.

The guy laughed and shoved him, cuffed hands not stopping him from making dumbass decisions. Full-on palm to the chest, a hard, deliberate challenge.

Two uniforms down the hall swore and started forward. I didn't move. Neither did Owen.

For half a heartbeat, I thought he was going to let it go. Take the high road. Be the professional one for once.

Then he stepped in, fast and controlled. He caught the guy's wrist, twisted it down against the bar in a joint lock that made the perp grunt and drop to one knee. With his other hand, Owen grabbed the back of his neck and leaned over him.

"Don't touch me," he said, voice low enough to make the hairs on my arms stand up. "Ever."

The guy struggled. Owen shifted just enough to tighten the hold, and the fight leaked out of him in a hiss. "You done?" Owen asked.

The perp muttered something unintelligible that sounded a lot like *yeah.*

"Good." Owen released him, took a step back. The man struggled to his feet, panting, holding his wrist.

One of the uniforms cleared his throat. "We're gonna, uh, log that as resisting."

"Write whatever you want," Owen said. "He's not going to file a complaint."

I believed him. So did the perp, judging by how quiet he'd gone.

Owen turned back to me. For a second, we just looked at each other. The corridor hummed with fluorescent lights and restraint.

"You all right?" he asked.

"I was fine," I said. "You're the one making new enemies."

He huffed something close to a laugh. "Guy was already an enemy."

We started back toward the bullpen. Halfway there, he dipped his head, speaking low enough that only I could hear.

"And thank you," he added.

"For what?" I asked.

"For listening for once. For not jumping in when I told you not to."

"I didn't do it for you. I did it because Internal Affairs gives me hives."

"Whatever gets you there." He leaned closer, just enough that his breath grazed my ear. "Still listened, though."

My skin prickled. "Barely."

His mouth brushed my temple—almost nothing, almost an accident. "Good girl," he murmured.

The words shot straight through me. My feet kept moving, but my brain shorted out for a full three seconds. Heat flooded my face, my chest, lower.

I hated how much I liked it. Hated that my body lit up like he'd flipped a switch he had no business touching.

I managed to find my voice. "Don't—"

165

"Relax," he said, stepping away, his expression already back to neutral as we hit the bullpen. "No one heard."

I wasn't entirely sure I had, either. It felt half hallucinated. Owen freaking Bishop breaking his macho cop persona? At the precinct? Definitely a hallucination.

I watched him towards the bullpen like nothing had happened. Son of a... Oh, I was getting him back for that. Somehow. I hurried after him.

The second I stepped inside, eyeing the coffee pot in the corner, Nguyen called out to us both.

"Chambers! Bishop! Hope you're ready to go right back out. We've got something. Possible Keller sighting on the riverfront."

Just like that, the temperature in the room shifted.

The game was back on.

The lead hit like a jolt of caffeine straight to the veins. Screw the coffeepot. This was better.

"Shit, we just got back," I grumbled, but my pulse was racing. This was what I lived for. "What do you have?"

"Riverfront camera picked him up ten minutes ago," Nguyen said, already pulling footage onto the main screen. "Dock 17, by the old grain warehouse."

Keller. Real, breathing, moving Keller.

The bullpen went silent for half a second, the collective inhale before the chaos. Then everyone moved at once.

Thibodeaux burst out of his office, red-faced and already sweating. "I want him alive, and I want him now! No more near-misses, no more screwups. If somebody lets this son of a bitch walk again, I'll personally staple their resignation to their forehead!"

"Yes, sir," I said, already halfway to the door.

The drive downriver felt like one long drumroll. The closer

we got to the docks, the heavier the air felt—like even the humidity knew something was about to explode.

Nguyen's voice came in over comms: "Thermal shows at least four heat signatures inside. Keller's one of them."

"Copy that," Owen said. His tone was the kind that made people obey without thinking.

We killed the lights two blocks out and rolled the last few yards in silence. The warehouse loomed ahead—corrugated metal and broken windows, graffiti bleeding down its sides. Somewhere inside, Keller was either panicking or setting another trap. Seeing as how we just took down a few of his buddies, my money was on the latter.

I chambered a round. "What's the plan?"

"Same as always," Owen said. "I go high, you go low."

We split at the entrance. Harper, Jordan, and Sanders fanned wide, flanking the loading dock. Owen and I took the front.

The first thing that hit me when we stepped inside was the smell—oil, rust, and something metallic that had nothing to do with machinery.

Voices echoed ahead.

"…told you they'd come," a man said.

Keller.

I crept forward, gun up, heart slamming. He was maybe thirty yards away, arguing with two men armed with SMGs. Guns for hire. Great.

I motioned for Harper's team to circle right. Owen moved left, silent and deliberate, his steps barely scuffing the concrete.

"Police!" I shouted. "Hands where I can see them!" I would like to say that they immediately dropped their guns and complied. Tragically, that would be a lie. Bullets tore through the air before the echo of my voice even faded. Sparks showered

167

off the metal crates. I dove behind a forklift, the impact ringing in my ribs.

"Chambers, right flank!" Owen barked through comms.

"On it!"

I rolled out, fired twice. One gunman dropped; the other ducked behind a pillar. Keller bolted for the side exit.

"Movement!" Sanders shouted.

Owen was already moving, sprinting through the gunfire like it was rain. He caught the second shooter in a shoulder tackle that sent them both crashing into a stack of pallets. I took the opening, sprinting after Keller.

He hit the door, shoved it open, and vanished into the alley beyond. I chased him through the storm-wet dark, boots hammering against slick pavement. He was fast—desperate fast—but I was faster.

"Stop!" I yelled.

He didn't.

We barreled through puddles and trash piles until he hit a chain-link fence and turned to face me, breath coming in sharp bursts.

"Don't do it," I said. "You're done, Keller. It's over."

He smiled—a thin, feral twist of a mouth. "You don't even know what you're part of, Detective."

"Sergeant," I corrected.

He raised the gun.

I fired first.

His weapon spun from his hand with a metallic clang, skittering into the shadows. He staggered, clutching his arm, blood seeping between his fingers. Behind me, I heard the pounding of boots—Owen, Jordan, Harper closing in.

Then the truck came out of nowhere.

A black pickup screamed around the corner, fishtailing through water, engine roaring. Keller dove sideways, rolled, and hauled himself into the passenger seat before any of us could close the gap. What the fuck? He had been *right* there!

"Shit!" I sprinted for the alley mouth. "He's getting away!"

Owen fired three shots at the tires. One hit, but not enough—the truck fishtailed again, sparks flying, and vanished downriver. I tried to hit another, but the rain made it hard to see. Silence crashed down, broken only by the sound of rain and our ragged breathing.

Harper slammed his gun down onto a crate. "We had him! We *had* him!"

"License plate?" Nguyen's voice demanded over the radio.

"Didn't have one," Owen practically snarled.

"He's gone!" Sanders shouted. "No plate, no tag, no goddamn anything!"

I just stood there, water dripping from my hair, shoulders tight. Breathing hard and staring into the dark like it had personally offended me. Which, frankly, it had. I kicked the fence hard enough to make it rattle. "He had backup. Professional backup."

Jordan swore. "How the hell does a dishonorably discharged grunt afford mercenaries?"

"Same way he bought the Kings," I said. "Someone's funding him."

Owen shook his head, water droplets flying. "And now they'll know we're closing in."

He looked at me then—really looked at me—and there was murder and guilt and exhaustion in his eyes. His voice was low, meant only for my ears. "Not your fault, Case."

Anger flared red hot. "I know that." The man knew me well

169

enough to know I was blaming myself, but it didn't stop me from snapping at him.

He watched me a second longer, then turned and headed for where we had parked our SUVs. Jordan was already calling for CSU. Maybe Keller had left something behind.

Back at the precinct, the victory buzz that usually followed a raid was gone. Everyone looked wrung out, tempers fraying. Thibodeaux was pacing in front of the murder board like he had to bone to pick. With it, or with us? Probably both. He turned to face us as we walked in. "Three warrants, two gunfights, one blown lead, and a fugitive who's now *press fodder*. Do you have *any idea* how bad this looks?"

"Only every time the TV plays it," Harper muttered.

Thibodeaux ignored him. "The mayor's ready to crucify someone. He wants Keller by tomorrow morning. Alive. No excuses."

Owen's voice was quiet, which was always worse than loud. "We'll find him."

"See that you do," Thibodeaux said. He stalked off, barking at the front desk about statements.

The room stayed heavy even after he left. Sanders kicked a chair that spun and slammed into a desk. Jordan threw his empty coffee cup against the trash can and missed. I walked over to my desk, pulling off my wet vest and top until I was just in the thin tank underneath. I shivered before grabbing the jacket I had hanging off the back of my chair.

Owen came over, leaned his hip against the edge of my desk. "You good?"

I laughed once, sharp and humorless. "Define good."

"You didn't freeze. You didn't miss. You chased him down alone."

"Yeah, and he still got away."

He studied me. "You'll get another shot."

I wanted to believe that. I wanted to believe a lot of things.

But right then, all I could feel was the ache in my chest and the echo of Keller's words—*You don't even know what you're part of.*

I turned away from him before the exhaustion cracked through the rest of my composure. "I need a shower and a drink. Preferably in that order."

Owen leaned down around me, hands on my desk on either side of my chair. Boxing me. Forcing me to look at him.

"Casey," he said quietly, "stop beating yourself up."

I met his eyes. "And where would the fun be in that?"

Something flickered in his expression. Pride. Frustration. Maybe something darker. "You're impossible."

He backed away, heading towards his office. I watched him go.

The bullpen hummed back to life around us—radios, typing, the dull roar of a department refusing to sleep. But under all of it, the failure hung heavy.

We'd had Keller in our sights. And now the whole damn city would know we'd lost him.

CHAPTER 11 ⊙ OWEN

The microphones were multiplying.

That was my first thought as I stood off to the side of the press room and watched some reporter in a wrinkled dress shirt shoulder his way to the podium and clip on yet another black foam-tipped mic. The stand already looked like a metal porcupine—cords, logos, blinking red lights—all of it feeding on the city seal like a parasite.

The mayor stepped up and the room went fake-quiet. Not respect, not grief—just the hush that falls when a hundred people decide the sound bite is about to start. Hot lights. Too many bodies. The smell of coffee and stress trapped under a ceiling that hadn't seen fresh paint since Katrina.

"Good morning," he said, hitting that practiced baritone like he'd been rehearsing in front of his bathroom mirror. "Thank you all for coming on such short notice."

I'd already heard this speech. Thibodeaux had muttered the bullet points at me over the phone sometime after midnight. Optics. Narrative. Progress. All PR-speak for: We nearly had the bastard and still let him get away, so now we need to lie to the city until we catch him. I didn't bother listening to the opening fluff. My eyes were on the riser, but not on the mayor.

I watched Casey.

She stood to his right, half a step behind—prime camera framing. NOPD blazer, white shirt, hair pulled back. Somebody in makeup had done what they could with the bruise at her temple, but I still saw the edge of it under the concealer. Her posture was regulation neutral. Hands clasped in front of her. Chin level. To anyone who didn't know better, she looked steady.

I knew better.

Her fingers were laced together too tight, knuckles just a shade too white. Her shoulders sat a little higher than usual, locked instead of loose. When the mayor said "near apprehension," a muscle in her jaw jumped once and vanished.

It hit me, in that moment, that at some point I'd started cataloguing her tells. Watching close enough to know the difference between baseline tension and the particular kind of guilt that dug its claws in and didn't let go. She was dragging the latter around like it was chained to her ankles.

"Last night," the mayor was saying, "thanks to the tireless efforts of our Homicide and Vice divisions, NOPD disrupted an attempted abduction outside a warehouse in the Industrial Canal and came within a breath of apprehending the suspect believed responsible for these brutal homicides."

My molars ground together. "Within a breath" was one way to describe it. I had my own version playing on repeat. Dark loading dock. Rain coming down in sheets. Keller running full-tilt, cutting between pallets and rusted containers like he'd rehearsed the route a hundred times. Casey on his heels, breath harsh in my ear over the radio, voice edged with adrenaline.

He'd hit the chain-link fence at the perimeter, turned, and realized he was boxed in—nothing but steel and her gun between him and handcuffs.

173

For one second, I'd believed that was it.

"...and I want to assure the people of New Orleans," the mayor went on, "we will not rest until this predator is brought to justice and our streets are safe again."

Beside him, Thibodeaux looked like a stroke waiting to happen. His suit was rumpled, his tie was crooked, and the bruised circles under his eyes made his whole face look carved out of granite. His hands were clasped behind his back in that classic command pose, but on him it read more like self-restraint than discipline. Hands in pockets, he'd beat someone to death with a microphone.

A hand shot up in the front row. "Mayor Dupree," a reporter called, "is it true that NOPD had this suspect cornered against a fence and still allowed him to escape in a vehicle? Can you explain what went wrong?"

There it was. Not even a pretense of subtlety. Who the *fuck* had told the press that?

The mayor's smile went tight around the edges. He angled slightly toward Thibodeaux, ceding the floor. Thibodeaux glared at the reporter. "Our officers prevented an abduction and brought back evidence that significantly advances this investigation," he said. His voice was rougher than usual—too much coffee, not enough sleep. "We are not going to break down tactical decisions from an active scene—"

"But Sergeant Chambers had the suspect at gunpoint, correct?" The reporter cut in. "Was there an error in judgment when she chose to fire at the suspect instead of disabling the vehicle or the driver?"

Casey didn't move. Her hands got a shade whiter. She clenched her jaw so hard I was sure it hurt.

I stepped forward before Thibodeaux went nuclear on live

174

TV. I didn't take the podium. I wasn't in the mood to be anyone's official mouthpiece. I just shifted enough that the front row had to tilt a little to see me, cameras reframing to drag me into the shot.

"You don't get to Monday-morning quarterback a split-second decision from the safety of a chair," I said. My voice came out low, flat, the way it always did when I'd decided I wasn't going to bend. "Last night, Keller had a getaway truck we didn't know existed. Sergeant Chambers fired center mass on the man who's been hunting women in this city. That was the right call."

"Sergeant Bishop," another reporter jumped in, "are you confirming she hit him?"

"I'm confirming we have every reason to believe he's injured and running," I said. "He's bleeding, he's desperate, and his options just got a lot smaller. That's what you should be printing."

"Is it true there have been multiple near apprehensions since this investigation began?" someone else asked. "At what point do those 'near' arrests become failures?"

"Near arrests kept people from dying," I said. "They disrupted his pattern. They forced him to change his routine. You want a list of everything that went wrong from a tactical standpoint, wait for the official report. You want the truth? We disrupted God knows what in that damn warehouse last night. That's what matters."

Phones lifted higher. A low murmur rolled through the room. Thibodeaux shot me a look that said, *We're going to have a long conversation about this later, but I'm not mad at you right this second.*

"The focus today," the mayor said, grabbing the reins back with both hands, "is on the progress our officers have made.

175

We are narrowing this suspect's movements and we are committed—"

I tuned him out again. My gaze slid back to Casey. She stared straight ahead, still in formation, but the death grip had eased off her hands. Her shoulders dropped a fraction. The iron band of guilt hadn't disappeared; I doubted anything short of an arrest would crack that. But it wasn't strangling her quite as hard. I shouldn't have been able to read that much from tiny shifts in muscle and posture.

I did anyway.

The conference dragged another twenty minutes. Questions about curfews, patrol numbers, overtime budgets. The usual crap from people who'd never had to stand over a body and call the family. When it finally ended, the mayor did his slow walk off the stage, still shaking hands, still smiling. Cameras chased him, then pivoted toward the exit doors, already thinking about the next fire to aim a lens at.

Thibodeaux stalked down from the riser like a storm cloud slid into a suit. "Bishop. Chambers." He didn't slow; he just shot the words at us on his way past. "My office. Ten minutes. If I don't see both of you, I'm canceling every day off on your calendar from now to Mardi Gras."

"Looking forward to it," I muttered.

"I heard that," he snapped, without turning.

Casey stepped down beside me, letting out a slow breath now that she wasn't under direct floodlight. Up close, the bruise at her temple was darker than I'd thought. She had that hollow look around her eyes—sleepless, wired on adrenaline and shame. "You didn't have to do that," she said quietly.

"Do what?"

"Step in," she said. "They asked me the question. I'm a big girl.

I could've handled it."

"I know you could've," I said. "Doesn't mean I'm gonna let them hang this around your neck because they like the story better that way."

Her mouth twitched. "Pretty sure that's not how media relations works."

"Pretty sure I don't care."

We were almost to the side door when Thibodeaux's assistant appeared, weaving through the last of the camera crews. Tablet under one arm, headset crooked around his neck, hair doing its best impression of a bird's nest. "There you are," he said. "Chief's office. Five minutes ago. His words, not mine. He's chewing drywall."

"Told us ten," I said.

"Yeah, he lied," the guy replied. "Something about you hijacking his presser."

"Sounds like him," I started to answer, but radio chatter interrupted us.

"Dispatch to any available Homicide or Vice unit," the dispatcher said, tone brisk. "Caller at Magnolia Arms Motel on St. Charles reports long-term guest paid cash under a name matching a known alias in the serial investigation. Neighbor reports crying and banging from the adjacent room overnight. Units, please advise."

The three of us went still. Magnolia Arms. Cash. Alias. Crying. Casey was already thumbing her mic. "Dispatch, 9-Victor-12 and 5-David-21 responding. ETA ten minutes."

"Copy, 9-Victor-12 and 5-David-21," dispatch replied. "Caller reports room two-twelve. Manager will meet you with a master key."

The assistant blew out a breath. "You do realize Thibodeaux

is going to skin us," he said. "Slowly. While filing paperwork."

"He can get in line," I said. "If this is Keller's spot or one of his dump sites, we're not handing it off to whoever's closest in the area."

I looked at Casey. Some of the self-hatred had receded behind her eyes. Something sharper had slid into place over it—purpose. "We need the win," she said.

"Yeah," I said. "We do."

We pulled up to Magnolia Arms, which looked like a place hope went to die. Three stories of tired stucco, the color of old nicotine stains. Balconies with rusted rails. A flickering VACANCY sign over the office that couldn't quite make up its mind. The kind of half-motel, half-extended-stay place where people paid by the week and nobody asked for last names.

A patrol car idled out front, red-blue lights turning lazily, bleeding over the wet asphalt. A uniform stood under the office awning, cap low against a half-hearted drizzle.

He straightened when we pulled in. "Sergeants," he said, nodding to both of us. "Manager's inside. Neighbor's back in his room like we told him. Says your suspect's been here about two weeks."

"Name?" Casey asked.

"Registered under 'K. Lawrence,'" the cop said. "Manager didn't think anything of it until his wife connected it to the news. Long-term guest, paid cash, doesn't want housekeeping. You know the type."

Yeah. I did. "What about the noise?" I asked.

"Unit in two-ten," he said. "Guy says he heard crying and thuds through the wall late last night. Thought it was a fight, then realized it sounded wrong. Went over, knocked on the door. Man in two-twelve cracked it, told him to mind his business. Manager went this morning to ask about the complaint, got the same treatment. Waited until the guy left for a smoke break out back and called it in."

"Description?" Casey asked.

"Male, white, late thirties maybe, ballcap, hoodie up. Not much to go on," the cop said.

"Manager says he went down the back stairs toward the alley. Doesn't know if he came back."

So: we had an alias Keller had used before, a long-term room, no plates, and now a possible holding spot. No confirmation it was him. Plenty of reasons to assume it could be.

Harper's unmarked car slid into the lot while we got the quick download. He climbed out, big frame moving with that deceptive calm of his, eyes already running the building like a schematic.

"Sorry I'm late. Stuck behind a damn trolley car of all things. What've we got?" he asked.

"Alias on the register and a neighbor hearing crying," I said. "Manager saw the guy in the room, got a bad feeling, called it in after he left. Two-twelve."

Harper's mouth hardened. "You thinking Keller?"

"I'm thinking I'm done underestimating coincidence," I said. "Let's move."

Inside, the manager was waiting behind a cloudy plexiglass barrier, a ring of keys jingling in his shaking hand. Jordan talked him through the basics, showed him Keller's composite. The guy went pale and nodded too fast.

"Second floor, back corner," he said. "Two-twelve. There's a connecting door to the next unit, but it should be locked. I never rent adjoining rooms together."

"Today you might've made an exception without knowing

it," I said. "Stay downstairs with the patrol officer. No one up unless they've got a badge." He nodded like his life depended on obeying and backed away. We hit the stairs in a stack: me and Harper up front, Casey just behind, Jordan bringing up the rear with the key, radio clipped hot to his shoulder. The second-floor walkway smelled like bleach, fried food, and stale cigarettes. Somewhere down the row, a TV blared an infomercial about miracle cookware.

"Two-twelve," Jordan whispered, stopping next to a door with flaking numbers screwed on crooked. He held the master key up. I took my spot to the left of the door, back to the wall, gun low and ready. Harper mirrored me on the right. Casey set up a half step behind him, angled for cover and crossfire. Jordan stayed farther back, out of the hallway's fatal funnel, ready to move or talk or both. I listened.

No TV hum. No male voice. Just a faint, ragged hitch in the air—like someone trying very hard not to cry and failing. My jaw tightened. I knocked, hard enough to rattle the frame. "NOPD," I called. "Sergeants Bishop and Chambers. Open the door."

Silence. Three seconds.

"Last chance," I said. "Open it, or we do."

Nothing.

I met Harper's eyes and gave a short nod. He slid the key in, turned, and felt the bolt thunk. He left the key there, hand on the knob, waiting. "On me," I said quietly. "We cross. Harper, take the bathroom. Casey, you've got my right. Jordan, you stay in the hall unless we call you in."

No one argued. We'd done this dance too many times at this point to quibble about who called the steps at the door. "Now," I said. Harper shoved the door, and we flowed in.

180

The smell hit me first. Bleach, sharp enough to sting my nose. Underneath, the metallic tang of old blood, sweat, and the sour edge of fear. The curtains were mostly closed, the room lit by a single lamp listing on the nightstand. A chair lay on its side on the carpet, one of the legs splintered clean through. Duct tape clung to the seat and armrests. On the bed, tied spread-eagle to the headboard, was a woman. She was young. Twenties, maybe. Dark hair stuck to her cheeks. Duct tape chewed angry marks into her wrists and ankles. Bruises everywhere the sheet didn't cover. A line of dried blood from the corner of her mouth down to her collarbone. Her chest hitched in shallow, panicked breaths.

Alive.

"Police!" Harper shouted. "Don't move!"

"Clear left," Casey called, sweeping her side with her Glock.

"Bathroom's clear," Harper said a beat later, standing in the open doorway, gun up. "No one else in here."

Of course Keller wasn't. He never stayed for the aftermath. He just left bodies and ghosts. I holstered and moved to the bed, careful of where I stepped. "Hey," I said, dropping my voice. "Hey. Can you hear me?"

Her eyelids fluttered. A hoarse sound scraped up her throat, not quite a word.

"You're safe now," I said. "We're cops. We've got you."

"Jordan, EMS," Casey said without looking back. She stepped closer to the headboard, keeping her body between the girl and the door. "Priority."

"Already requested." Jordan's voice came from the hall. "Three to five minutes."

Casey holstered her gun to pull a folding knife from the back of her belt. She slid the blade under the tape at the girl's wrist, angling it so the sharp edge faced the rope of adhesive and not the skin. "You're gonna feel a pull," she murmured. "Don't fight me. We're getting you out."

The girl made a broken sound, tears leaking sideways into her hair.

I wanted to reach out, to steady her, but stopped myself. A strange man's hand was the last thing she needed. So, I crouched low instead, keeping my voice even, soft but clear. "You're safe now," I said. "We're the police. No one's going to touch you until the medics get here, all right?"

My eyes kept sweeping the room out of habit—duffel bag half packed by the dresser, bathroom light still on, empty takeout containers on the floor, a narrow door on the far wall with a cheap brass knob and a tired-looking deadbolt. I clocked it, filed it away. Separate room, technically. Separate warrant. Something we'd deal with after we got the victim out. I was just telling myself we'd have patrol knock on the neighbor when the lock on that door rattled. Metal clicked. The deadbolt turned from the other side. Everything in me went cold and hot at the same time.

"Hold—" I started.

The adjoining door blew inward and hit the stopper hard enough to bounce.

A man came through that gap like he'd been launched. Not Keller—this one was shorter, thicker through the middle, messy hair, scruff—but the eyes were the same kind of empty I'd seen in too many men who'd convinced themselves they were just "helping the boss." Knife in his right hand. Momentum behind him. He saw Casey cutting tape and went straight for her. She pivoted on instinct, bringing her own knife up. Steel met steel with a sharp, ugly scrape. For a heartbeat, the blade in his hand

182

arced toward her throat.

I didn't think. My body moved.

I hit him from the side, shoulder slamming into his ribs. The impact drove him into the wall next to the connecting door. The door itself bounced and slammed shut again, rattling in its frame. He grunted, knife arm flailing. The blade snapped sideways and kissed along Casey's forearm instead of opening her neck. She swore, short and vicious.

My jaw caught a wild elbow. Pain flared bright. I shoved it aside, drove my knee into the guy's thigh hard enough to feel something give. His knife hand went loose. The blade clattered to the carpet. Harper was there a half-second later, hauling the guy's arms back and slamming him face-first onto the ugly motel carpet.

"Don't move," Harper growled in his ear, cuffing him with the kind of efficiency that came from a career of not having patience for idiots.

I turned back to Casey. Blood ran in a thin line down her forearm, already starting to drip off her fingers onto the carpet. Not spurting, thank God, but enough to make my stomach twist.

"You good?" I asked, already knowing she was going to lie.

"It's fine," she said automatically, looking down. "Barely—"

"That is not 'barely,'" I interrupted.

Jordan looked over at us, eyed the blood, and winced. "I'll call for a second ambo."

Casey glared at him. "Don't you dare."

The cut ran along the outside of her forearm, just below the elbow. Long. Shallow. Ugly. It would scar, but it hadn't hit anything vital. Relief made my knees feel hollow. I grabbed the nearest clean-ish towel I could find—a folded one sitting on the little sink counter by the door—and pressed it over the wound, wrapping my hand around her arm to hold pressure.

She flinched once, then steadied. "You know, I gotta say... If blood loss equals weight loss," she muttered, deadpan, "I am killing this diet."

It punched a laugh out of me I hadn't expected, half hysterical and half genuine. Jordan cocked a smile before shaking his head, like the gallows humor was something he had come to expect from his sergeant.

"Yeah, well, you're not dropping a size on my crime scene," I said. "Hold that."

She took over the pressure with her good hand, fingers firm. I kicked an empty Styrofoam box out of the way and dragged a straight-backed chair away from the wall with my boot. "Chair," I said. "Sit. You face-plant.'"

"Equal rank, remember?" she said, but she did. Her skin was a shade paler than ten minutes ago, but her eyes were sharp. "Keep bossing me around, I'll file a grievance with HR."

On the bed, the girl whimpered again, and Jordan finished cutting her free. Casey leaned forward, careful not to smear blood or touch anything she shouldn't, and brushed hair from the girl's face with the back of her knuckles.

"Hey," she said softly, voice doing that thing where it turned from razor to velvet. "You're okay. EMS is almost here. You're getting out of this room today, you hear me?"

The girl's eyes cracked open, pupils huge. "He said I wasn't... leaving," she rasped. "Said...no one cared..."

"He's a liar," Casey said, and there was more steel in her voice than there'd been when she'd answered the reporters. "We're here. We care. He doesn't get the last word."

Harper walked the cuffed idiot out past us a minute later,

handing him off to the patrol unit in the hall with a terse list of charges that was going to take up half a page. Jordan stood just outside the doorway, face a little too pale, fingers flying over his tablet as he logged times, locations, everything CSU would need. The medics arrived, bringing a wave of organized chaos with them. Oxygen mask, vitals, tape cut, IV started. They transferred the girl to a backboard and then a gurney, rolling her out past the broken chair and the dirty carpet toward something that didn't smell like bleach and fear.

Jordan rode with her in the ambulance. It felt right. He was steady like that.

Casey and I watched the ambo leave, after she had practically threatened the medics to leave her be.

"I'm taking you to the ER," I told her.

"You ordering me, Sergeant?" she asked, arching an eyebrow.

"Strongly suggesting it," I said. "You bleed on my car, I'm making you detail it."

"That's extortion."

"Yep."

She shook her head, glancing at the temporary bandage the EMTs had put on her arm before climbing in the SUV.

At the hospital, the ER waiting room was the same as every other ER waiting room in every city I'd ever worked in—bad chairs, worse coffee, and a TV tuned to a daytime show where strangers screamed about paternity tests while the world fell apart outside. Jordan paced for the first ten minutes, then gave it up as a bad job and dropped into the plastic seat beside me. Harper texted updates from upstairs between dealing with CSU and the patrol units. Ramos showed up at some point, flirted with a nurse, and kept glancing at the door before sitting next to Harper with a sharp sigh.

185

"You know Thibodeaux is going to absolutely lose his shit," Jordan said finally, rubbing a hand over his face. "You blew up his press conference and then skipped his lecture to go hero-mode at Magnolia Arms."

"I responded to a tip that might be Keller," I said. "He can yell at me all he wants. He wasn't the one listening to a girl cry through the wall."

Jordan's mouth tugged sideways. "No argument here," he said. "I'm just saying, if he strokes out mid-rant, I'm not doing CPR. That's above my pay grade."

Harper glanced up at him. "You're a terrible human being."

"I am hurt," Jordan said, clutching his chest. "Words hurt, you know."

Harper rolled his eyes before returning to his phone. The double doors squeaked open. Casey walked out, blazer draped over one arm, sleeve on the injured side cut up to mid-bicep to make room for white wrap and butterfly bandages. The bruise at her temple looked worse under the hospital lights, but the line of her mouth was less brittle.

"How many?" Jordan asked, nodding at her arm.

"Seven stitches," she said. "New personal record. I do believe I am owed seven gifts now."

"Funny," I said dryly. "What did the doctor say?"

"No heavy lifting for a few days. Otherwise I'm fine."

Jordan squinted at her. "Define 'fine.'"

She ignored that, looking past us at the doors that led to the upper floors. "The girl?" she asked.

"Stable," I said, standing and stretching. "They've got her on a floor upstairs. She's eating, took a shower. That's usually a good sign."

Relief washed over Casey's face so openly it hurt to look at.

"Good," she said quietly. "That's...good."

"All right," I said. "Harper and Jordan, back to the precinct. Start the reports, get CSU synced, hand the chief the headlines he's gonna pretend were his idea. I'll take Chambers home and then let him scream at me until he feels better."

"I can go to the station," she said.

"You're going home."

"I'm not on painkillers," she argued. "They gave me a tetanus shot and some gauze. I'm fine."

"For now," I said. "Give it a couple hours; that thing's gonna throb like hell. You're not white-knuckling a steering wheel like that. I don't feel like scraping my sergeant off a guardrail tonight."

She made a face. "You know equal rank means you don't get to order me around, right?"

"Good thing I'm not ordering," I said. "I'm just refusing to take you anywhere but home. You didn't drive here, remember?"

Jordan snorted. "He's got you there."

She sighed. "Fine," she said. "But if Thibodeaux throws anything during your little chat, I want a live replay."

Harper snorted, and Jordan gave me a thumbs-up as they headed out the door. The fog had gotten even thicker by the time we pulled out of the lot. It came down like a thin blanket, turning the world into a smear of streetlight glare and brake lights.

Casey cradled a flimsy hospital coffee cup in her good hand, the bandaged arm resting carefully in her lap. I drove, watching the road and the mirrors, part of my brain still back at the motel, still at the fence, still in every place Keller had been and slipped away.

"You're quiet," she said after a few blocks.

187

"You're the one with a fresh hole in her arm," I said. "I could say the same."

She huffed something that might've been a laugh. "I'm thinking," she admitted.

"Dangerous habit."

"About last night," she said, ignoring that. "And today. The fence. The truck. That girl. Just keeps looping."

"Yeah," I said. "Same channel over here."

She turned her head, watching the city streak past her window. "Every time I close my eyes, I see him turning," she said. "Back against the chain-link, rain in his face, smiling like he'd already won. I had him. And then that truck shows up, and I hesitate for half a second—am I gonna hit the driver, is it clean—and he's gone. And now there's a girl upstairs who almost died because he was still breathing this morning."

There it was. The whole weight of it, dragged into the open.

"You didn't let him go," I said. "He had a backup plan. We didn't know about the truck. You took the shot you had and you tagged him. He's bleeding. That matters."

"Doesn't feel like it," she said, voice low. "Feels like I failed and someone else paid the bill."

"There's a girl upstairs who's not in the morgue because you took that shot," I said. "Because you chased the lead from the warehouse to Magnolia Arms. Because you walked into that room and cut her loose even when your brain was screaming Keller's name in the back of your head."

She didn't say anything for a full block. "You really believe that?" she asked eventually.

"I don't say things I don't believe," I replied. "Ask IA. Or my ex-wife."

A corner of her mouth lifted despite herself. "You know that's the second time you've used IA as your character witness today," she said.

"They're very familiar with my inability to shut up," I said.

"Do you keep a list?" she asked.

"Of my ex-wives?"

"No, smart-ass. People you save. People you don't."

I exhaled through my nose. "I used to," I said. "Early days. Tried to balance the numbers. Thought if I closed enough cases, put enough bad guys in boxes, I'd sleep better."

"And now?"

"Now I know the math never adds up," I said. "No matter how many you save, there are still names on the wall. So I take what I can get. Today? Keller lost a victim. He didn't get to finish what he started. That's a win."

"Small victory," she murmured.

"Sometimes it's the only kind we get."

The light ahead turned red. I eased us to a stop.

"You always do that," she said after a second.

"Do what?"

"Show up," she said. "When it's bad. When it's sideways. When I'm standing in front of a fence or a room or a press conference trying not to fall apart. You step in front of the cameras. You tackle the moron with the knife. You drive me home even when we both know I could Uber and you could go let the chief tear chunks out of you."

"That's my job," I said.

"No," she said quietly. "Your job is solving murders. You don't have to carry everybody while you do it."

I didn't know what the hell to do with that. Compliments sat about as comfortably on my skin as handcuffs.

"You're not exactly dead weight," I said finally. "Contrary to popular belief."

"Oh my God," she said, mock scandalized. "Was that—was that you admitting I'm good at my job? Do I need to record this?"

"Don't push it," I said. The light turned green. I rolled us through the intersection.

She smiled into her coffee, but the smile didn't reach her eyes all the way. Not yet.

"You still think about the ones you lose?" she asked.

"Every day," I said. "Difference is, I've stopped pretending I could've saved all of them if I'd just done one thing differently. That way lies madness."

"Feels like I'm halfway there already," she muttered.

"Then don't give Keller the satisfaction of finishing the job," I said. "He wants you in your own head, second-guessing, pulling your punches. Don't let him live rent-free in there."

She snorted. "In this economy? Hardly."

"Good. Extend the same policy to serial killers."

We turned onto her street. Small houses, tiny yards, too much history crammed into too little space. Her place sat in the middle of the block—faded siding, a railing that had seen better days, porch light off. I pulled to the curb and put the car in park.

"You need help getting inside?" I asked.

She shot me a look. "I got stabbed in the arm, not the leg, Owen."

"Humor me."

She rolled her eyes but didn't argue when I got out and walked with her up the path. She fumbled her keys with the bandaged hand; I caught them before they hit the porch, dropped the ring into her good hand without comment.

"Thanks," she said. She was close enough now that I could see the flecks of green in her hazel eyes, the fatigue tucked into the corners.

"You're not fine," I said. "But you're breathing. That's enough for today."

She huffed a breath that wasn't quite a laugh. "We did good," she said, more to the door than to me. "Didn't catch the monster, but we stole one back from him."

"Yeah," I said. "We did."

Before I could think better of it, I leaned down and cupped the back of her head. I used my other hand on her chin to tilt her head back and kiss her. I fucking loved the taste of her. Coffee and cinnamon, and something fruity. She groaned, parting her lips for me like I knew she would. I wanted to take it further. Damn me but I did. However, I hadn't been lying when I said she would be feeling that wound once the adrenaline wore off. So, I stepped back, and she tracked my movement with hooded eyes.

"Come inside?"

I shook my head, "Tempting, *ma louve*. But you need to rest. We've got a killer to catch. Get some sleep, beautiful."

"Bossy, bossy." But she pressed another kiss to my jaw, standing on her tippy toes to do so, before winking at me. She put her key in the lock, then paused and glanced back at me. "Try not to get yourself suspended before I'm back on duty," she said. "I'm not training a new Homicide sergeant."

We were close enough now that every step forward felt like walking into a tighter circle. Keller would strike again—I didn't doubt that. But for tonight, there was one woman in a hospital bed instead of on a slab because we'd shown up at that motel. And another who had gotten under my skin, who would fight

191

for them with a dogged determination that put most people I knew to shame.

Sometimes that had to be enough to get you to the next shift.

"I'll pencil 'don't get fired' into my day planner," I said.

She gave me one last tired, real smile, then opened the door and slipped inside. It clicked shut behind her. I stood on the porch for a second, listening to the sound of her movements inside, the city humming in the distance. Then I turned, walked back to the car, and slid behind the wheel.

The engine rumbled to life as I headed back to the precinct. Small victories. I'd take them. And when I found Keller, I'd make damn sure he didn't get any more.

CHAPTER 12 ◆ CASEY

The stitches pulled every time I straightened my arm, a neat little reminder that Keller had teeth even when he wasn't in the room. The slash ran from elbow to wrist—seven stitches, ugly but shallow. Functional. Amy from Medical had told me to take it easy, which I translated as *don't bleed on the paperwork.*

After the press circus, I decided morale had gone to hell. People were snapping at each other in the halls, coffee consumption had tripled, and the homicide bullpen smelled like exhaustion and printer toner. So, naturally, I declared war on morale the only way I knew how: food. The text went out before sunrise.

Potluck tomorrow. Attendance mandatory. Bring something edible or I assign you to paperwork until you cry.

Jordan answered with a skull emoji. Harper sent, "define edible." Owen, of course, just sent a thumbs-up.

By the next afternoon, the homicide floor looked like somebody's half-remembered family reunion—tables dragged together, crockpots lined up like soldiers, paper plates stacked in uneven towers. I'd expected pushback. Instead, there was actual laughter, the kind that sounded like people remembering how to breathe.

Vice and Homicide had been stuck together for almost two

months now. At first, it was like trying to make cats and dogs share a bed. Harper and Crawford hated sharing cases with "the narcs," my squad griped that Homicide acted like they'd invented the concept of evidence. The first week we'd run two separate coffee pots out of spite. Now they were arguing over hot sauce.

I leaned against the corner of the breakroom doorway, nursing a Styrofoam cup of something that had started its life as coffee and evolved into tar.

Jordan was terrorizing Harper with his "secret recipe" brownies, Sanders had somehow coaxed Smythe from the evidence locker into a debate about the Saints' defense, and Nguyen was half working on his laptop between bites. And then Owen walked in, carrying a pot the size of a toddler. The smell hit first—dark roux, shrimp, smoked sausage, the kind of spice that crept under your skin and reminded you why people still called this city home. Conversations stopped.

Harper's eyes went wide. "You can cook?"

Owen set the pot down on the counter like it was no big deal. "It's my grandmother's recipe," he said. "She was a Dupuis."

Of course she was. I grabbed a paper bowl and spoon, already heading for the pot. Owen took my bowl from me, filled it to the brim, and handed it back.

"Is your grandmother the one who taught you French?" I asked around a mouthful of food.

He froze for half a second. Just long enough.

Harper's eyebrows tried to escape his forehead. "You speak French?"

Owen shot me a look over the rim of the gumbo pot. Slow. Heavy. Full of heat and warning and a very specific memory of him murmuring things against my throat that were absolutely not fit for the breakroom.

Jordan caught the look and nearly choked on his brownie. "Oh, he knows French, all right!" he said loudly.

Owen's voice dropped an octave. "Jordan."

"Just saying," Jordan muttered, grinning.

Everyone laughed, except Owen, whose mouth curved in that almost-smile that meant *we'll talk later*. Ramos and Sanders fought over the last chocolate chip cookie. Harper ate so fast, he was going to be complaining of heart burn later. I focused on ladling more gumbo into a bowl so I didn't have to meet his eyes.

Thibodeaux appeared in the doorway like some sort of stressed-out cryptid, eyes scanning the food with laser focus. While everyone was still snickering about the French thing, he made a beeline straight for Jordan's deviled eggs, lifted the entire tray, and walked off with it without breaking stride.

"Did he just—" Jordan started.

"Yes," Harper said. "Yes, he did."

Nguyen was at one of the tables, a plate balanced next to his laptop. He was smacking the side of it with the flat of his hand, muttering under his breath.

"Stop beating up the tech," Crawford said, annoyed. "Those things cost more than your car."

"It's glitching," Nguyen said. "I run the Keller cross-check, it shows one thing. I run it again, it shows another. The system logs are—" He smacked it again. "Broken."

"Or you put too much hot sauce on your fingers and gummed up the keys," Crawford said.

I watched them argue, spoon halfway to my mouth. The gumbo was stupidly good—deep, layered heat, just enough kick. Of course, Owen could cook. Of course, he'd show up with something that made the rest of us look like amateurs.

He caught my eye from across the room. There was still that flicker there from earlier, that warning: we don't talk about the French.

I shouldn't have started it. I did it anyway.

'Cause damn I loved when he spoke French.

The room blurred into noise and heat—people laughing, swapping stories, griping about the mayor. For the first time in weeks, nobody mentioned Keller, or the girl in the hospital, or how close we'd come to losing everything.

I ducked into the evidence closet an hour later because we were out of tamper bags and because I needed ten seconds without everyone watching my face every time someone mentioned the word "warehouse." The closet was more of a narrow hallway with a door, lined with shelves— boxes of forms, boxes of seals, spare printer cartridges, things we pretended were organized. The air smelled like paper and dust and something stale.

I found the box I needed on the top shelf and immediately regretted not bullying someone taller into coming with me. My arm protested when I tried to reach. "Dammit," I muttered, stretching anyway. A hand appeared over my head and slid the box forward.

I didn't have to turn around to know who it was. No one else moved that quietly and still somehow managed to make the air feel heavier when they walked into a room.

"You know," Owen said behind me, "normal people ask for help."

I turned, hugging the box against my chest. "I'm not normal people," I said. "And I had it."

He glanced pointedly at the bandage peeking out from under my sleeve. "Sure you did."

196

The closet felt smaller all of a sudden. The hum of the fluorescents overhead sounded louder. He was close enough that I could smell the spice of the gumbo still clinging to his shirt, undercut by soap and sweat and the things I tried really hard not to catalog anymore.

I cleared my throat. "You cook, you speak French," I said. "Anything else you want to reveal to the class? Secret opera career? Knitting circle?"

His mouth curved, but his eyes didn't soften. "You really had to bring up the French?" he asked.

I shrugged, trying for breezy and landing somewhere around awkward. "What, I'm not allowed to be impressed by your... multilingual skill set?"

"The only times I've ever spoken French to you," he said quietly, "did not involve other people in the room."

Heat crawled up my neck. "Well, they don't know that. I was just putting together clues like any good cop. Gumbo. Dupuis grandma. French."

He stepped closer. The box of tamper bags dug into my ribs. "Casey." His voice was a low rumble that immediately had my mouth dry and other parts of me decidedly *not* dry. "Sounds to me like you've been missing me."

"Owen..."

"What? Just putting clues together. Like a good cop. Not my fault you're thinking of that. But you are, aren't you?"

That.

He didn't specify what "that" was—those nights, that argument, the way we'd burned up and then slammed the brakes hard enough to give ourselves whiplash—but we both knew.

"No," I lied.

He called me on it without saying a word. Just raised an

eyebrow at me, using his height to lean over me.

We'd been dancing around this for days. The near-misses in hallways. The too-long looks over case files. The way my stomach dipped every time he said my name in that low, aggravatingly calm voice. We stared at each other in the narrow strip of space between shelves. My heart was beating too fast, which was stupid, because I'd faced down a serial killer at gunpoint and not felt this rattled.

"This is a bad idea," I said.

"Probably," he agreed.

Then he kissed me anyway.

It wasn't gentle, like last night. It was like he'd been biting back the impulse for weeks and finally run out of leash—one hand braced on the shelf next to my head, the other hovering like he wanted to touch my face and couldn't quite let himself. His mouth was hot, demanding, every line of his body saying, "I'm still here, you're still here, we're still alive."

The box slid out of my grip, wedged against the shelf by his hip. I curled my good hand in his shirt, heat spiking low and steady. I moaned into his mouth, which shattered what little restraint he had left. He picked me up, setting me on the shelf behind us, and I wrapped my legs around him. Untucking his shirt, I ran my hands along his defined abdomen as his fingers dug into my hip. The stupid little closet, the fluorescent hum, all of it dropped away. It was just him and me and the taste of gumbo and coffee and something that felt a lot like reckless relief.

My stitches tugged when I shifted, and I hissed against his mouth. He pulled back a fraction, eyes dropping to my arm. "Careful," he murmured.

"You started it," I said, breathing hard.

"Yeah," he said. "I did."

Down the hall, Nguyen yelled for me. We both ignored it. Every rational part of my brain was screaming about workplace boundaries and timing and Keller and all the reasons this was a terrible decision, and none of them were winning. Then he was kissing me again, pressing himself up to the sweet spot between my thighs. His belt buckle dug deliciously into me, and I whimpered.

"Owen..."

He trailed kisses along my jaw, then nipped my ear. His breath was hot on my skin as he whispered, "Can you be quiet for me, *mon péché*? You want release, baby, I will give it to you. But you've gotta be a good girl, and stay quiet."

Oh, yeah. This was a horrible idea. But not one I was going to regret anytime soon. I nodded, and he kissed that sweet spot where my neck met my shoulder. Then his hands traveled to my belt which he undid. After my pants were undone, he slid a hand down the front of my jeans. Cupping my pussy, he kissed me again, and I shuddered in anticipation. The reckless thrill. Addicting. Wrong. But so right. "I can stop, Casey."

I threaded my fingers through his hair, "Don't you dare."

His answering chuckle was all sin and promise. One capable finger traced me from clit to bottom, and he swore. "So wet for me, baby. Remember what I said... quiet." Then he flicked my clit, and I bucked, biting my lip to hold back a moan. "Good girl."

He pushed a finger inside me, then another. Slowly, he pumped his fingers in and out of me. Stretching me, playing me. I began to rock my hips, throwing my head back as the desire to moan warred with the need to not be caught. He slid another finger into me and I whimpered. "Shhhh, *mon péché*."

199

His other hand slid to my throat and he squeezed, the lack of oxygen ensuring my inability to speak and spreading a fire through my belly. I looked at him through lowered lashes and on the fourth finger, my body spasmed. He almost had his whole damn hand inside me and still it wasn't enough. But then he began to pump his fingers in and out of me, faster and faster. He scissored his hands, twisting and thrusting, never stopping. On and on he went. The pleasure built in my body like a wave.

My eyes shuttered closed but he gave a firm squeeze on my neck and murmured, "I don't get to hear those little sounds you make when you shatter around me. But I do get to see the way those pretty eyes turn molten. Come for me, baby."

His thumb pressed against my clit as he thrust his other four fingers deep in my pussy, and I bucked so hard, the shelf trembled. He watched me as I coated his fingers in my arousal, dimly worried that I was going to have a wet spot on my jeans. He kept pumping his fingers, riding me through my orgasm, and kissing me when I couldn't fight back my moan. He swallowed the sound with a searing kiss, and my whole body turned to putty under his touch. Letting go of my throat, he pulled his hand from my pants and licked each finger clean.

After helping me down from the shelf, he spanked me on the ass, and I jumped before smacking him on the shoulder. Nguyen yelled again, and we both smirked at each other. On my tiptoes, I pressed a kiss to his jaw, then to his lips. Then pressed myself against his very hard cock that was tenting his jeans.

"You might want to fix that."

"Oh, I plan to. Later."

"Is that so?" I tilted my head at him, a smile playing on my lips.

Before he could say a word, Nguyen's voice carried down the hallway outside again. "Chambers! You still on this floor? I need you to look at something before I throw my laptop out the window!"

I closed my eyes. "You have got to be kidding me."

Bishop stepped back, just enough that the air could move between us again. His jaw flexed. He looked like he wanted to punch the wall and knew better. I headed for the door as he adjusted himself. I wanted to say something clever. I wanted to not be shaking. I settled for, "We can't do this again. Not here. Not like this."

"I know," he said.

"But," I added, because apparently I hated myself and enjoyed ruining my career, "I'm not saying I didn't...want to."

His eyes caught mine, dark and unreadable and way too aware. "Go see what Nguyen wants," he said. "Before he commits a felony against government property."

I grabbed the box from the shelf, straightened my shirt, and tried to pretend my mouth didn't feel swollen. Or that there wasn't a damp spot on my panties. Then I stepped out into the hallway and left the closet behind me. For now. I passed the box to Ramos, who passed it to Sanders, who looked scandalized by it and watched as she dropped it on some rookie's desk. Then I headed over to Nguyen.

Nguyen's "office" was really just a corner of the evidence tech room with three monitors and a collection of stress toys that had all seen better days. I found him hunched over his laptop, glasses slid down his nose, Crawford standing behind him with his arms folded.

"If you smack that thing one more time, I'm calling IT and asking them to install a shock collar," Crawford was saying when I walked in.

"It's glitching," Nguyen insisted. "Tell him it's glitching, Sarge."

"Depends," I said. "Is this about your fantasy football league or my serial killer?"

He pushed his glasses up. "Keller. And I swear I wasn't snooping. I was just trying to solve your favorite little mystery about why his supply chain looks like Swiss cheese."

That got my full attention. "Show me."

He spun the laptop toward me. On the screen was the evidence management system, a digital labyrinth I'd spent way too many nights lost in. "These are all the Keller-adjacent exhibits," Nguyen said, tapping one column. "Overdose kits, lab samples, seized product, the whole buffet. I'm cross-checking them against who logged them in, who checked them out, who signed them for court, the usual. Clean so far—until this."

He clicked a filter. Half the list disappeared.

"What am I looking at?" I asked.

"Everything tagged as destroyed in the last ninety days," he said.

Destroyed. My stomach tightened. "On an active serial case."

"Yeah," he said. "That's red flag number one. Red flag number two is this." He pointed at a name in the "Officer ID" column.

Ramos, D.

My thoughts stuttered. "That's...that can't be right." I looked up, but Ramos had disappeared from his usual spot. Glancing around the room, I found him over by the vending machine. He kicked it, and I returned my attention to the screen in front of me. No way.

"Believe me, I wanted it to be a typo," Nguyen said. "So I checked the raw access logs. These items were marked for destruction from an internal terminal, using Ramos's credentials. The system logged his ID and his password hash."

Crawford nodded grimly. "We did a physical check," he said. "Those exhibits are gone. Not in the cage. Not in off-site storage. Not mis-shelved. Gone."

The room tilted for a second. Item numbers and dates swam.

"That bust is what put us onto Keller's supply in the first place," I said. "We've been chasing that connection for weeks."

"Yeah," Nguyen said. "And now most of the physical evidence tying Keller's favorite cocktail back to that seizure has been 'lawfully destroyed' by a guy who, last I checked, still works under you."

"He does still work under me," I snapped. "And Ramos wouldn't do this."

Nguyen held his hands up in surrender. "I'm not saying he did," he said. "I'm saying the system thinks he did. Either he's dirty, or someone's riding his login like a stolen car. Both options suck."

"He's not dirty," I said automatically.

The words came too fast. Too easy. Crawford watched me with that calm, cop's gaze that always felt like an X-ray. "You sure?" he asked.

Ramos was cocky and a pain in my ass on a good day. He popped his gum too loud and flirted with anything that made eye contact. He cut corners on paperwork and called it efficiency.

But he'd also pulled me out of a bar bathroom when an undercover meet went sideways. He'd sat with victims for hours while they shook and wept and tried to remember faces. He'd taken the worst shifts without complaining—much.

"I know my team," I said. "He wouldn't destroy Keller evidence. Not after what we've seen."

Nguyen's shoulders slumped a little. "Then your system's haunted," he said. "Because as far as the logs are concerned, your boy's been busy."

I leaned closer, forcing my brain to focus. "Timestamps."

He enlarged the column. The dates jumped out—two weeks ago. Six days ago. Last night, while we'd been hip-deep in press conferences and Magnolia Arms.

"He was out on surveillance those nights," I said slowly. "At least, that's what the duty roster says."

"Surveillance on what?" Crawford asked.

I opened my mouth, then shut it. I couldn't remember. A nuisance Vice case? A follow-up on one of Keller's associates? It was all a blur of long nights and bad coffee.

Nguyen cleared his throat. "Just so we're clear," he said, "this isn't me calling him dirty. It's me saying something's wrong, and if we don't figure out what, Keller stays three steps ahead."

"Okay," I said. The word tasted like grit. "You did good flagging this. Don't talk to anyone else about it yet. Not even Ramos. I'll take it from here."

He nodded, relief and worry wrestling behind his eyes. "You want me to pull more logs?" he asked. "See what else his ID's touched in the last quarter?"

I thought of Keller's smug smile at the fence. The empty truck bay. The girl on the bed at Magnolia Arms, tape burns on her wrists.

"Yeah," I said. "Every log, every access, every time he sneezed near a keyboard."

Nguyen saluted with his pen. Crawford gave me a look that said he would pretend he hadn't heard anything and still somehow know all of it anyway. As I left the tech room, the food smells from the potluck had faded, replaced by the usual station stink. My gumbo was a heavy weight in my stomach. My moment in the closet with Owen, as earth shattering as it was, a distant memory.

Ramos wouldn't do this, I told myself.

Would he?

The bullpen had emptied out by the time I sat down at my desk with my own terminal. Most of Vice was in the field; most of Homicide was pretending not to be hiding from report writing. The overhead lights were on the dimmer setting we all pretended didn't exist, casting everything in a tired yellow. I logged in and pulled up the same evidence management screen Nguyen had shown me. The timestamps stared back, accusing. I cross-referenced them with duty rosters, radio logs, patrol allocations.

Ramos signed out a pool car thirty minutes before the first destruction entry. No GPS, of course—the unit was one of the older ones. He'd listed "surveillance" as his reason. He'd been logged into the evidence system from an internal terminal five minutes after that.

You can be in two places at once, sure. If you lie about one of them.

"Tell me you're seeing something other than the worst-case scenario."

I looked up.

Owen stood on the other side of my desk, the faint remnants of the day's headache pulling at the corners of his eyes. He had just come from Thibodeaux's office and was doing a damn good job acting like the closet hadn't happened, but then his eyes dropped to my mouth. He leaned up against my desk, his knee brushing mine. Neither of us moved away. He had that look I'd learned meant Thibodeaux had screamed himself hoarse and everyone was still somehow alive.

"How bad?" I asked.

"He wanted to fire me, then remembered he can't replace me mid-homicide spree," Owen said. "You know. The usual."

"He steal any more eggs?"

"He stole the last brownie," Owen said darkly. "Jordan may never recover."

I huffed out a breath that wasn't quite a laugh. "Nguyen found something," I said. "Sit."

He did, lowering himself into the chair beside my desk with a faint wince I pretended not to see. The warehouse, the motel—none of us were at a hundred percent. He pulled the chair closer, until our knees were brushing again.

I swung the monitor slightly so he could see and walked him through it: the destroyed evidence, the timestamps, the Ramos ID.

He listened without interrupting, eyes narrowing, jaw tightening a fraction with each new piece.

When I finished, he sat back. "You're sure these are Keller-adjacent," he said.

"One hundred percent. The pills from that club bust are the same formulation as what his victims have in their system. We lose that chain, we lose a direct route from him to the street-level supply."

"And Ramos is the one who logged them for destruction," Owen said.

"The system says he is," I said. "I'm saying that doesn't make sense."

"Walk me through why."

"Because he's not an idiot," I snapped. "Because he's been busting his ass on this case. Because he was there the night we pulled that girl out of the motel and he looked like he wanted to rip Keller's throat out with his bare hands." Because no way could I have a dirty cop in *my* unit and not notice.

"People are complicated," Owen said. "You know that better than most."

"He's not Keller's guy," I insisted.

Owen watched me for a long beat. "You mentored him," he said. It wasn't a question.

I looked away. "He came over from Patrol two years ago," I said. "Didn't know the difference between an informant and a stool pigeon. I taught him how to write a warrant that wouldn't get laughed out of court. I taught him how to talk to girls who thought cops were just another kind of threat."

And I didn't want to believe I'd misjudged him this badly.

"Could somebody else be using his login?" Owen asked.

"Sure," I said. "If they knew his password, had access to an internal terminal, and decided to impersonate a specific detective instead of grabbing a generic admin ID. That'd be a lot of work when most people just write 'clerical error' and hope no one checks."

"Could Ramos be working angles you don't know about?" he countered. "Side deals. Skimming. Feeding Keller intel for cash or favors."

My stomach twisted. "No," I said. "I mean—I don't want to believe that."

"That's not the question," he said. "The question is whether you're willing to consider it."

I dug my fingers into the edge of the desk. The stitches in my arm burned. "I know my squad," I said. It came out softer than I meant it to. "They're not perfect, but they're mine. If there's rot, I need it to be outside my house."

"Wants and needs aren't the same thing," he said.

"Thanks for the fortune cookie."

He let that roll off. "Look," he said. "Best case, someone is using Ramos as cover. Worst case, Ramos is in bed with Keller or someone close to him. Either way, we've got a leak that explains why this son of a bitch keeps slipping us. That's progress, ugly as it is."

"And if it is him?" I asked. "If he sold Keller the first batch, if he's been wiping evidence, if he's the reason half our trail is missing—"

"Then we deal with it," Owen said. "We shut it down. We close the holes and put Keller in a box anyway."

"You say that like it's easy."

"Nothing about this is easy," he said. "But pretending it's not happening doesn't make it go away."

I stared at the screen. Ramos's name looked wrong in that column. Like someone had taken a piece from a different puzzle and forced it into the gap.

"He wouldn't do this," I said. "He wouldn't risk his badge on a scumbag like Keller. He—"

Images flashed—Ramos laughing too loudly at some dumb joke, bragging about his latest undercover score, rolling his eyes at my lectures on procedure. Ramos coming in with a nice new watch he couldn't quite explain. Ramos disappearing on "surveillance" that never produced usable intel.

I'd written half of it off as ego. I didn't love what the other half looked like under this light. I blew out a breath that shook more than I wanted it to. "Okay," I said. "Here's what we're doing."

Owen nodded once, the way he did when he'd decided to back my play on principle and argue about it later if necessary.

"Nguyen's already pulling more logs," I said. "I want every access record tied to Ramos's ID for the last six months. Evidence, cameras, door swipes, the works. If he's moved a paperclip, I want a timestamp."

"Internal Affairs?" Owen asked.

"Not yet," I said. "Nguyen flagged this because he's good at his job, not because he wants to be thrown into a meat grinder. We drag IA in without more than a handful of suspicious entries, they'll blow the doors off this place and Keller will hear about it before we have a chance to figure out what he's done."

"You're playing close to the chest."

"I'm playing the only way that makes sense," I said. "We have a leak tied to the one detective I cannot afford to be dirty. I am not handing that to a bunch of suits who think statistics are an investigative tool."

He studied me for a moment. "When this goes bad," he said, "it's going to go very bad, Chambers."

"You and I realized weeks ago we had a leak, remember? We knew we had one. We got distracted. Focused on Keller. You backing out now?" I asked.

"Hell no," he said. "I just like to know how deep the water is before I jump."

"Deep," I said. "With sharks."

He almost smiled. "My favorite."

I turned back to the monitor, fingers hovering over the keyboard. The cursor blinked in the search bar, patient and merciless. "Pull every log he's touched," I said. "Every case, every exhibit, every shift. If Ramos is clean, I'm going to prove it. And if he's not…"

I swallowed the rest. *If he's not, I'm the one who missed it. I'm the one who brought him into my house and didn't see the rot.*

Owen didn't say anything. He didn't have to. The hum of the computers filled the silence. Somewhere down the hall, Jordan yelled about his stolen brownie. The normal noise of the squadroom rolled on, oblivious.

I hit enter. If the system was going to tell me one of my own had betrayed us, I was damn well going to make it say it to my face.

CHAPTER 13 ◆ CASEY

The beginning of the end came suddenly. Part of me had hoped Keller would go quiet, which was stupid. Nothing about this case had been easy. Why start now? We boxed him in behind a shuttered strip mall that smelled like old grease and bad decisions. The front had a faded mural of bent-backed dancers and stacked yoga mats. The back lot was all cracked asphalt and weeds. A perfect place to reinvent yourself as a murderer.

I sat in the passenger seat of the unmarked, eyes on the rear door. My stitches tugged every time I shifted in the seat. I cursed the pain, but welcomed the reminder.

"Bravo team in position." Jordan's voice crackled over the radio. "Side door's ours. Harper's trying not to cry about the smell."

"It's like a gym and a fryer had a demon baby," Harper replied.

"Focus," I said into my mic.

Beside me, Owen watched the same door, forearms braced on the steering wheel, jaw set hard enough to crack a tooth. The streetlight carved shadows under his eyes. We'd both been living on coffee and adrenaline for too long.

We hadn't talked about the closet.

We hadn't had time.

I was still hyper-aware of him, though. The way his knee brushed mine when he shifted. The faint spice of his aftershave on his shirt, the calluses on his palms that were evident when I was standing right next to him in a briefing, and definitely not staring at them. The memory of one of those hands around my throat, his other hand—

No. Not now. Dammit. I squirmed in my seat; Owen glanced at me. I gave him a tight smile.

"Crawford's in the alley," Nguyen reported. "Fire escape's clear. No other exits."

"Okay," I said. "This is it." I glanced at Owen, "Owen and I are taking the front. Jordan, you and Harper on the side. Sanford, you plug the rabbit hole. We want Keller breathing and walking."

"Preferably not armed," Harper added.

"Preferably," I agreed. "But unlikely. On my go. Three... two...one."

We moved.

The cold hit as soon as we stepped out of the car—sharp, damp, cutting through my thin station sweater. My boots scraped gravel as Owen and I crossed to the front door, guns out and low. Old flyers peeled off the bricks, fluttering like ghost-skin in the breeze. Owen took the hinge side; I took the handle. We exchanged a quick look. His was all professionalism. Mine probably had too much fury in it. What can I say? I've got just a smidge of anger issues. Bless the department therapist for trying to work it out of me. But hey, rage worked sometimes. Like now. When I used that rage to kick in the fucking door.

It didn't fly open clean. The cheap frame bounced, then gave, slamming back into the wall. A hallway stretched ahead— cinderblock, old paint, a dim light flickering at the far end.

Voices carried down it. One low, one wheedling, both male.

"Police!" I shouted, already moving. "Hands where I can see them!"

Jordan and Harper burst in through the side door at the same time, our timing finally working for once. Sanders's silhouette appeared at the far end, blocking the back exit like a pissed-off linebacker.

The studio space had been stripped down to bare bones. Mirrors still lined one wall, smeared and streaked. The outlines of yoga poses were ghosted on the far side, half-covered by cheap shelving. A folding table in the middle held pill presses, plastic tubs, baggies. Keller's signature scattered in neat, lethal rows. He stood behind the table, halfway into a duffel bag, box cutter in one hand, spine stiffening when he saw us. The other guy—a twitchy runner type—froze, eyes wide.

For half a beat, everything paused.

Then Keller bolted. Again.

I swore.

He didn't sprint for the closest exit. That would've put him into Crawford's arms. He went sideways instead, cutting between the table and the wall, boots skidding on scattered powder.

"Don't!" I snapped, training my sights on his center mass. Last time I'd said that, he'd run, and I'd put a bullet in his shoulder. He'd lived, learned nothing, and graduated to overdosing girls in motel rooms. This time, he glanced at me, saw the gun, and changed tactics.

He came *toward* me.

He moved fast for someone with a bullet hole in his recent history. He kicked the table hard as he went, sending tubs and baggies skittering across the floor, a cloud of powder puffing into the air. The box cutter flashed in his hand as he angled in.

"Casey!" Owen barked.

I shifted my aim, trying to track center mass without putting one through a tub of God-knew-what and contaminating the whole scene. Keller came at me, arm swinging. Box cutter gripped in his hand. I was *not* about to get cut twice in one week.

The blade caught my sleeve as I jerked backwards, and my stitches screeched in protest. If I broke them, Thibodeaux was going to have my ass for not listening when the doctor told me to take it easy. But that was a later problem. Right now, I focused on Keller as he went to make another swing at me.

Then Owen hit him. He didn't go for some gentle, textbook tackle. He slammed into Keller from the side like a truck, driving him into the mirrored wall. Glass shuddered, then cracked. Keller's head bounced off it with a dull smack. Keller went down hard. Owen went with him, riding him to the floor, knee in his back, forearm across his neck. The box cutter skittered away.

"Stop resisting," Owen barked.

"I'm not—I'm not—" Keller wheezed, already twisting.

Owen yanked his arm up between his shoulder blades, with enough force that I might have winced. Keller yelped.

"Bishop," I snapped, moving in, gun still out, adrenaline burning. "He's done."

"He came at you with a knife," Owen snarled.

"Yes, I noticed that. Jordan—cuffs."

Jordan was already there, dropping to a knee, snapping metal around Keller's wrists. "You are under arrest," he panted, breath fogging in the cold air. "For the murders of Ashley Price, Kelsey Harris, Gracelyn—"

214

Keller laughed, breathless and ugly. "You had to bring the hero squad," he rasped. "Gotta say, Sarge, I'm hurt. I thought we had something special. Just you and me."

I flipped him off. He laughed again as Jordan tried to drag him to his feet, but was hampered by Owen's weight still on Keller's back.

I saw Jordan's eyes flick up, over to me, a quick check-in.

"Sergeant," I said.

Nothing. Deaf, stubborn old bastard.

"Dammit, Owen. Get off him."

Owen's gaze cut to mine. I held it. Slowly, like it physically hurt him, he eased off, letting Jordan haul Keller to his knees.

Keller grinned up at me through blood and smeared powder. His lip had split again. "That one's got a temper," he said, jerking his head at Owen. "You should put a leash on your pet."

"Shut up." But I took a small step towards the three men, angling myself just so between Owen and Keller. Tragically, he ignored me and kept talking.

"You finally decided to clean up your mess," he said. "Bit late for that, don't you think?"

"Walk," Harper ordered, taking one arm while Jordan took the other.

Keller dragged his heels just enough to make it annoying. "You really don't get it," he said, loud enough for all of us to hear. "You think this ends because you put cuffs on me? I'm a symptom, Sergeants. You haven't even found the disease yet."

"Shut up," I said.

He laughed. "You don't even know who paid for the show," he said. "You're not in the right decade yet. The lady with pearls? She writes bigger checks than you've ever seen."

The phrase hit like ice water poured down my spine. Lady

with pearls? What did that mean? Ramos. Keller. And now someone else? Fucking hell.

"Keep moving," Owen growled.

Keller went, still chuckling under his breath. We had him. Finally. It didn't feel like a win. It felt like the opening act.

By the time we got Keller processed, booked, and sitting in Interview Two, my arm ached, my head hurt, and the coffee in my stomach had turned to something acidic and mean.

Homicide's interview rooms were exactly as cheerful as you'd expect: gray walls, bolted table, two chairs, mirrored glass. The air always smelled faintly of institutional cleaner and bad decisions.

Keller sat cuffed to the table, wrists chained to the ring. He'd cleaned up a little—someone had wiped the worst of the powder off his face—but his lip was still split. The bruising around his old shoulder wound peeked above his collar. He had a butterfly Band-Aid over a deep scratch on his forehead, which I assumed came from the glass. He looked...settled. Like a guy about to give a speech.

"You sure you want to do this yourself?" Owen asked quietly outside the door.

"I'm not giving him to anyone else," I said. "He wants an audience. Fine. He gets us."

We went in together.

Keller's eyes lit up when he saw us. "Look at that," he said. "My favorite double act."

"State your name for the record," I said, dropping a folder onto the table and sitting opposite him.

"Fuck you."

"I genuinely doubt your mother named you Fuck You Keller. I met her, by the way. Nice lady."

He chuckled. "Still got jokes. That's good. You're going to need them."

Owen stayed standing, back to the wall, arms folded. To anyone else, he looked calm. I could see the tension in his shoulders, the way his jaw ticked when Keller's gaze slid over me.

I flipped the folder open. Autopsy photos. Tox reports. Scene shots. A greatest hits album of Keller's work.

"You know the drill," I said. "You've been Mirandized. You asked for a lawyer, then un-asked. You talk, that's on you. You shut up, that's on you too."

"I said I'd talk," Keller said. "You cops never listen."

"Then say something worth listening to," I said.

He leaned back, as far as the chain would let him, and studied me. "You ever watch a building come down, Sergeant?" he asked. "Real demolition, charges placed just so. Not the shit on TV."

"Answer the damn question," Owen said.

"That *is* the answer," Keller said, glaring at Owen. "You don't start with the roof. You start with the beams. The supports. The things nobody ever looks at until they're gone. Then one day, boom. Whole structure folds in on itself like it's tired."

"You calling those girls beams?" I asked. My voice came out flatter than I felt.

"They were symptoms," he said. "Like me."

"Her name was Lily," I said. I didn't look at the file. I'd seen it enough. "Your sister. We've had her in this case folder from day one."

Something flickered behind his eyes. "You remember her?"

"She overdosed two years ago," I said. "Wrong cut, hot batch. You want to tell me what that has to do with the girls you've been killing?"

"She was sixteen when she got hooked," he said quietly. "Seventeen when she died. You know how we found out it wasn't just 'wrong place, wrong time, wrong dealer'?"

I didn't answer. Sometimes you got more when they filled their own silence.

"She OD'd in our bathroom," he said. "Tile Mom couldn't scrub clean. At the hospital, they said bad batch, super potent, not her usual. They said it like it made it better somehow, like it meant she hadn't *meant* to die. Like that helped."

His tone didn't crack. That made it worse.

"Couple months later," he went on, "there's a little write-up in the paper. Big Vice raid. Photos of a table full of product. Some detective smiling for the cameras. The numbers in the article? Purity, composition? They sounded real familiar." He tapped his temple with a cuffed knuckle. "So I asked around."

"Around where?" I asked.

"Corners. Clubs. People who actually know where the dope comes from," he said. "You know what they told me? That some of the hot new shit out there was straight from a cop seizure. 'Back from the dead,' they called it. Funny, right?"

"People talk shit," I said. "Half of what you hear on the street is bravado."

"Yeah," he said. "And half of it's snitches trying to stay alive. Thing is, I didn't need them to be right about everything. Just the one thing: that there was a batch taken by cops, waved around for the press, that somehow made its way back onto the street."

"We already know that batch exists," I said. "We found an old crate in a warehouse. Same formulation as the stuff in your victims. The part we're missing is how *you* got your hands on it."

"You're missing a lot more than that," he said. "But sure, we'll pretend supply chain is the issue."

"Who sold it to you?" Owen asked. "Name."

Keller smiled slowly. "You think I'm just going to sit here and give you all the answers?" he said. "Come on, Sergeant. You're smarter than that. But, I'll throw you a bone. This batch was cop retirement fund shit. It was people with badges deciding dope looks better as cash."

"It's convenient for you," I said, "blaming your hobby on some hypothetical dirty cop."

"It's not hypothetical," he snapped. "I watched my mother sign paperwork for the coroner's office that said 'accidental overdose.' Then I watched a dealer three blocks from my house brag about 'cop-cut' product that'd put three people in the ICU. When my sister's old crew started dropping from the same shit, you know what I realized?"

"That you needed therapy," I snarked.

"That you people don't feel anything until it lands on your doorstep," he said. "So I took it there." I let that sit for a moment. The hum of the fluorescent fixture filled the space between us.

"We already knew you were using that old batch," I said. "We've got tox reports. We've got the crate. You're not giving us anything new there."

"Yeah?" he asked, tilting his head. "Did you know why I picked the girls I did?"

"Because they were easy targets," I said. "Girls nobody would notice until long after they were dead."

"Exactly," he said. "You know how many times my sister tried to get into rehab and got told there were 'no beds, no funding'?" He did air quotes with his cuffed hands. "But you always have beds for the good ones. The right ones. Your sorority overdose? You know she got a news story and a GoFundMe. My sister got a toe tag and a backlog on some detective's desk."

"So you enjoyed making us look at them," I said.

"I enjoyed making you admit they existed," he said. His lip curled. "You built this machine that chews people up and then you act shocked when somebody points out what's in the gears."

"Spare me the martyr complex," Owen said, voice low. "You didn't expose a problem. You slaughtered victims."

"Victims of victims," Keller said. "That's the whole point. You lose some batch off a truck because some bastard in your nice little world decides to turn it into cash? That's one sin. Every corpse it makes after that? That's interest."

"Then why use the same batch?" I asked. "Why not something new? Why not disappear into the sea of fentanyl and heroin like every other asshole who's ever decided God made a mistake?"

He smiled again, small and mean. "Because it's poetic, Casey," he said. "Because every time you pull tox, you see that number and you *know*. You did this."

Owen pushed off the wall when Keller used my first name. He didn't say anything. Just flattened his palms on the table and leveled Keller with a look that would've sent lesser men screaming.

"You're not God," I said.

"Neither are you," he shot back. "You just play him on TV."

I swallowed down bile. "Let's get to the part where you stop preaching and start answering questions. We have you on scene. We have your victims. We have your weapon of choice. What we don't have is who gave you access to that particular poison and who bankrolled your little crusade."

"You think a guy like me rents yoga studios with his own

credit?" he asked lightly.

"Yes," I said. "Because you're arrogant."

He laughed softly. "God, I like you," he said. "You keep pretending this is about ego."

"Isn't it?" Owen asked. "You monologue like it is."

He shrugged. "Maybe a bit," he said. "Mostly it's about balance. You took something from me. I took something from you."

"We didn't sell that batch," I said. "We weren't even on that raid."

He looked at me like I'd missed the point. "Uniforms change," he said. "Badges turn over. The machine stays the same."

"The machine didn't fund warehouses and hired muscle," I said. "Someone did. Someone with money. Who?"

He smiled, slow and secretive. "You heard me in the parking lot," he said. "You're not deaf."

"The lady with pearls," I said.

His eyes lit with that same fever-bright amusement I'd seen at the fence. "See?" he said. "You do listen."

"Who is she?" I pressed.

He shook his head. "Casey, Casey," he said. "You got to figure some things out for yourself."

"You haven't told us anything we didn't already know," Owen snapped.

"The right question," Keller said, like Owen hadn't even spoken, "is why she gave a damn in the first place. Most people look at someone like my sister and think, 'one less problem.' She didn't. She understood what you people did. What you *didn't* do. That's why she paid attention when I told her about the batch."

"So she just...what?" I asked. "Showed up out of nowhere with a checkbook and a hit list?"

"You ever been to a funeral where nobody important shows up?" he asked instead. "No politicians, no cameras, no reporters? Just a few sad folding chairs and a priest who forgets the dead girl's name halfway through the homily?"

I thought of too many nameless services. Too many mothers with hollow eyes.

"Sometimes," he went on, "one person actually looks at the body and realizes the whole thing's rotten. Sometimes she wears pearls."

"You met her at a funeral," I said.

He smiled, the corners of his mouth ticking up in a way that wasn't quite yes and definitely wasn't no. "She knew it was your business that killed Lily," he said. "She knew your people took that batch and turned it back into poison on the street. She decided that if the city bought itself a future with my sister's life, it could damn well pay interest."

"That still doesn't tell me who she is," I said. "Or how to find her."

"Then maybe you should look in your own files. You've been sitting on the answer since the day Lily died. You just didn't care enough to read the fine print."

"We're going in circles," Owen snarled.

Keller's gaze flicked to him. "You know what you are, Sergeant?" he asked. "You're the good dog. They kick you, they starve you, they send you after people like me, and you still think you're on the right side. Meanwhile, they're selling the bullets."

"You don't know a damn thing about me," Owen said.

"I know you've got a temper," Keller said, glancing at the mirrored wall where the ghost of his impact still smudged the glass. "I know you'd feel better if you could put me through that a few more times. And I know if you push much harder in here, the suits are going to have a field day with your disciplinary file."

Owen's shoulders tightened almost imperceptibly.

"Enough," I said. "You wanted to talk, you talked. You gave us motive. Congratulations, you're very tragic. But right now, all you've done is confirm what we already suspected—that you're using a batch that should've been buried in an incinerator, and you did it to make a point. That doesn't keep you out of prison."

He smiled faintly. "You think I care?" he asked. "I've already done what I set out to do."

"You haven't," I said. "Because whoever helped you? Whoever sold that batch back to the street, whoever picked out the wrecks you turned into messages—they're still out there. You're going to rot while they keep cashing checks."

That lit something mean in his eyes. Good. I'd been fishing for it.

"They're not untouchable," I pressed. "Whoever took that evidence out of our chain of custody, whoever backed you, we *will* find them. With or without you. If you give us a name, you might get to watch."

He stared at me for a long beat. His jaw worked. "Lawyer," he said finally.

I sat back. "Sure," I said. "We're done."

We left him with his ghosts and the mirrored glass.

The rest of the day was spent tying up loose ends. But when Owen's captain lightly suggested we all call it an early night, no one took him up on that offer. We were all so damned tired, I was sure every report was filled with spelling and grammatical errors. But we were all ready for this to be over.

The next morning, the bull pen felt wrong. Too bright, for

one thing. A hard, clear light came through the grimy windows, exposing every stain, every scuff. The board with Keller's victims was still up, red string and photos and dates anchoring the horror in place. Someone had put a Post-it over his mugshot that said "ASSHOLE" in block letters. Jordan's handwriting.

My arm was stiff, my head was pounding, and I'd had three hours of sleep on my couch with my gun on the coffee table. Owen looked worse. He was already at his desk when I walked in, collar undone, staring at a report he clearly wasn't reading. I took a small second to appreciate just how incredibly handsome he looked. Even half dead with exhaustion like the rest of us.

"Morning, Sergeant," Jordan said as I dumped my bag on my chair. "How's our friendly neighborhood serial killer?"

"Waiting on a lawyer and practicing his martyr monologue," I said. "You need to work on your handwriting." I gestured at the board.

"Rude. I don't know what you're talking about," he said.

Nguyen rubbed at his eyes behind his glasses before waving me over. "I stayed late going through logs," he said. "I've got more on Ramos." Jordan, Nguyen, and I all took a second to ensure Ramos wasn't in earshot. Shockingly, he wasn't even in the room. A problem for later.

"Hit me," I said.

"His credentials have been used to log into the evidence system after hours eight times in the last six months," Nguyen said, already pulling up a window. "Each time, there's movement on seizures that are either Keller-adjacent or connected to his supply line. It's the same pattern as the batch we found in the warehouse."

"All from internal terminals?" I asked.

"Yeah," he said. "No remote access. No VPN. You have to be

in the building. Half those timestamps don't line up with his duty roster. He's listed as on surveillance or off shift."

"So either he's lying about where he is at night," Jordan said, "or someone's playing dress-up with his login."

"Either way, it's bad," Nguyen said.

"Keep digging," I said to Nguyen. "Ramos's logins, last year. Every access, physical or digital. Cross it with duty rosters and video. If someone's riding his ID, I want to see where they're standing when they do it."

Nguyen nodded, hair sticking up at weird angles. "On it," he said.

I was about to sit down when the mood in the bullpen shifted.

It's a real thing—cop radar. Noise drops just enough, air pressure changes, and everyone looks up at once. Like some internal alarm goes off. The reason hit a second later: two men in suits stepping out of the elevator. Not detectives. Not ADA. Different kind of predator. Neat ties, bland expressions, eyes that scanned like emotionless tools. Internal Affairs.

"Fuck," Jordan muttered under his breath. "It's too early for this."

"Language," Harper said automatically, then saw the suits and muttered something worse.

Thibodeaux emerged from his office like he'd scented blood. He'd changed shirts from his earlier coffee-stained one, but his tie was still crooked. The lines around his eyes looked deeper. "Gentlemen," he said, striding toward them. "Not to be rude, but I really try not to deal with paperwork and shit storms before ten."

"Captain Thibodeaux," the taller suit said. "We're here regarding an anonymous complaint filed last night."

"Of course you are," Thibodeaux said. "Because God forbid

225

anyone in this building ever be *happy* for five minutes. You couldn't call?"

"This needed an in-person response," the man said. His gaze skimmed the room and locked onto Owen. "Sergeant Bishop."

Ice water slid down my spine.

Owen stood slowly, made his way from his office. "That's me," he said.

"We're placing you on administrative leave pending investigation," the suit said. "We'll need your badge and firearm."

"On what grounds?" Owen asked. His voice was calm. Too calm.

"Allegations of excessive force during the apprehension of a suspect last night," the shorter suit said, flipping open a folder. "As well as an inappropriate personal relationship with another cop assigned to the Keller task force."

Every muscle in my body tried to seize at once. The bullpen went so quiet I could hear the vending machine humming.

"Anonymous complaint?" Jordan said tightly. "That's cute."

The taller suit didn't look at him. "This is an administrative action, not a criminal one," he said to Owen. "You'll be on full pay while we review."

"Generous," Owen said dryly. His eyes flicked to me for half a second. Enough for me to read things I didn't want to see: apology, anger, something that felt dangerously like guilt. He unhooked his badge from his belt and set it gently on his desk. The little clink when it hit the wood made my throat hurt. His gun came next. He cleared it out of habit, ejected the magazine, racked the slide, then handed it over grip-first.

"This is bullshit," Jordan said under his breath.

"Detective Delaney," the short suit said without looking up, "if you'd like to be part of this investigation, keep talking."

Jordan all but snarled at him, muttering a few choice things under his breath.

Thibodeaux was still trying. "We are in the middle of an active serial case," he said. "We finally have the bastard in custody. Can you maybe wait until we get through arraignment before you start cutting my legs out from under me?"

The taller suit's expression didn't change. "We're following protocol, Captain," he said. "You can direct any concerns to our office."

"That's great," Thibodeaux snapped. "Y'all just have the best fucking time. So glad you are on the case. Real fucking threat you've got there."

Owen straightened. Without the badge on his belt and the gun at his hip, he looked wrong. Not smaller. Just...unarmed in a way I wasn't used to seeing. "It's fine," he said, and he was talking to me more than to them. "You keep working the case, Sergeant. You don't need me to catch this son of a bitch."

"That's not the point," I said. It came out sharper than I meant.

The IA suits flanked Owen like they were escorting a suspect. They led him toward the elevator in a little procession of quiet authority and institutional arrogance. He had given more blood and sweat and energy to the entirety of the NOPD than half the damn cops in the city. This was *wrong*.

The doors slid shut on him with a soft, final thunk. The bullpen stayed frozen for a beat.

Then Thibodeaux muttered a string of curses that probably would've gotten him suspended too if anyone from IA heard it. He turned to me, his face a mix of fury and exhaustion. "Sergeant Chambers," he said. "Can you run this op without Bishop?"

Did I have a choice? No.

227

Did I like it? Also no.

"Yes, sir," I said. My voice didn't shake. I was stupidly proud of that.

"Good," he said. "Because unless I can convince those clowns upstairs to pull their heads out of their collective ass, you are officially running this solo. Bishop's team now answers to you. Finish this." He jabbed a finger toward Keller's mugshot on the board. "That bastard does not walk because the department decided to eat its own."

He stalked back to his office, slamming the door. The low murmur of the bullpen slowly resumed, thinner and more brittle than before.

Nguyen looked like he was about to puke. "This is bad," he said quietly.

"Understatement," Harper said.

Jordan's gaze flicked to me. "You know that complaint didn't come out of nowhere," he said. "Someone had details. Someone who knew about last night and the warehouse."

"Yeah," I said. "No shit."

Ramos's name pulsed in my skull like a headache. Anonymous complaint. Destroyed evidence. Borrowed login.

I took a breath that tasted like burnt coffee. "We keep going," I said. "We've got Keller. We've got questions about old evidence. We've got a potential leak tied to Ramos's credentials. IA can do whatever the hell they want with Owen's file; they don't get this case."

"If they pull you next," Jordan said, "we're screwed."

"Then let's not give them a reason."

The rest of the day blurred into motion—reports, calls, lawyers, Keller being his usual delightful self off-camera. I did what I always did: kept moving so I didn't have to think too hard about the hole where Owen should've been. It wasn't until late afternoon, when the bullpen had thinned out and the overhead lights had taken on that tired, yellow tinge, that Jordan found me alone. I was at my desk, staring at the evidence system login screen without really seeing it. The little cursor blinked in the password box, patient and unforgiving. Jordan dropped a coffee on my desk. It smelled like it had come from the machine down the hall, which meant it was terrible. I took it anyway.

"For you," he said. "Liquid sadness."

"Thoughtful."

He sat on the corner of my desk, legs dangling, looking more serious than he usually allowed himself to in public. "You know IA only said Bishop's name," he said. "They didn't suspend you. They didn't even say your rank out loud."

"That's not remotely comforting."

"I'm just saying," he went on, "the way they worded it? 'Inappropriate relationship with another cop.' That's vague as hell. Could be anybody. Could be half of Patrol. You're not on paper. Yet."

"Jordan," I said, "if the rumor mill gets even half of that complaint, 'vague' is not going to be the word anyone uses."

He grimaced. "Fair. But still. If they were gunning for you specifically, they'd have name-dropped you. Someone panicked and tried to cut Bishop out of the picture because he's the one most likely to figure out who's pissing in our water supply."

"Ramos," I said.

He didn't flinch. "Maybe. Maybe somebody else. Point is, this smells like strategy, not morality."

"That's supposed to make me feel better?" I asked.

"No. That's supposed to make you mad in the right direction."

229

I stared at the screen a second longer, then nodded once. "Nguyen's still pulling logs?" I asked.

"Yeah," Jordan said. "Crawford's shadowing Ramos without making it obvious. Harper's pretending not to notice any of this so he doesn't punch someone in a meeting."

"And you?"

He shrugged. "I'm here to tell you that if IA tries to spin this like you seduced poor, innocent Sergeant Bishop into misconduct, I will personally staple their complaint forms to the inside of their skulls."

A laugh cracked out of me before I could stop it. "Graphic."

"I'm adapting to my environment," he said. "Also, for the record? If they suspend you, I'm walking."

"No, you're not," I said automatically.

"Try me. I'll go sell insurance. Or open a taco truck. Something with less paperwork and fewer psychopaths."

"Insurance has plenty of psychopaths," I said. "And you'd eat your profits."

He grinned. "You know me so well."

I shook my head, but some of the weight in my chest shifted.

"Look," he said, sliding off the desk. "We can't fix IA. We can't fix whoever's playing games with Bishop's badge. What we *can* do is what we always do: find the goddamn leak, plug it, and build a case so strong they can't knock it down without everyone seeing the rot."

"Optimistic," I said.

"Realistic," he countered. "We're good at our jobs, Casey. That hasn't changed just because some asshole wrote 'anonymous' on a complaint form."

He walked away before I could say anything else.

I turned back to my terminal. My fingers hovered over the

keyboard. Keller's words echoed in my head. *Dirty cops. Dirty city. You built this machine.*

I wasn't going to let him be right. Not without a fight. If the system was going to tell me one of my own had helped arm the monster we'd just caged—and maybe tried to take Owen out of play to protect themselves—I was damn well going to make them say it to my face.

I logged in and started to dig.

CHAPTER 14 ◆ CASEY

The morning after Owen's suspension, the whole precinct felt like it was holding its breath and pretending it wasn't. The coffee tasted worse. The lights seemed harsher. Every conversation stopped a half-second too fast when I walked by.

IA had come in like a firing squad the day before—walked straight to his desk, asked for his badge and gun in front of everyone. People pretended to work while they watched him walk out with that detached, controlled look on his face, like he'd decided not to give them the satisfaction of seeing him bleed.

I'd spent the night replaying it in my head on a loop. His jaw set. The IA investigator's monotone voice. Thibodeaux swearing under his breath.

Anonymous tip: inappropriate relationship with a coworker.

Anonymous tip: excessive use of force.

I knew damn well who the coworker was. And I was pretty sure I knew who the anonymous tip was. The rat was in my house.

Now I was sitting at my desk with Keller's trial file spread across it like a paper explosion. Photos, transcripts, witness lists. All of it important. None of it sticking.

Thibodeaux's voice rumbled through the thin office walls, half muffled, half not.

"—you don't waltz into my house, suspend my best detective on hearsay, and expect me to kiss your ass for it—" Some IA suit said something I couldn't make out. Thibodeaux's tone sharpened. "Then charge him or get the hell out of my bullpen. But you're not using him as a scapegoat because your PR's in the toilet."

I flipped a page I hadn't read. Owen's empty desk sat in my peripheral vision like a missing tooth. The chair was pushed in. His coffee mug was still there, chipped at the handle. Someone had put his little desk plant on the floor so IA could go through his drawers and never put it back. It sat there, leaves drooping, like even the damn plant missed him.

"Hey, boss lady." Jordan's voice cut through the static in my head. He slid onto the corner of my desk like he lived there, nursing a cardboard coffee cup. "You good? You've been glaring at that file like it kicked your dog."

"I'm fine," I said, too fast.

He sipped, eyes flicking up to the glass of Thibodeaux's office, where his shadow paced. "Uh-huh. And I'm a ballerina."

I made a half-hearted swipe for his cup. "Give me that."

He jerked it out of reach. "Get your own. This is the last of the halfway decent pot."

"Then I outrank you."

"That line only works on people who haven't been drunk at 3 a.m. with you."

Normally, I'd volley back, enjoy the snark. Today, it just grated. I gathered a stack of photos and forced myself to look at Keller's smug face instead of the absence across the aisle.

I could still hear the whispers from yesterday.

"Did you hear?"

"IA walked Bishop."

"I told you something was off with them."

I'd wanted to tear every gossiping tongue out with my bare hands.

"Sergeant?"

I looked up. Nguyen stood at the edge of the bullpen, tablet in one hand, the other doing that anxious flex thing he did when he was about to say something he thought I wouldn't like.

"What?"

"Lab just confirmed the last set of samples in the Keller case. I emailed you the report."

"Good. Thanks."

He lingered. "You, uh... need anything else?"

"No."

A lie. I needed about a week of sleep, a bottle of whiskey, and for time to rewind twenty-four hours.

Nguyen nodded anyway and retreated.

Movement at the far end of the room snagged my attention. Ramos, jacket slung over his shoulder, sauntering toward the exit like it was any other Thursday.

"Where are you going?" I called.

He pivoted with that easy, practiced smile. "Gonna run a quick errand, Sarge."

"Define quick," I said.

"Fifteen, twenty tops. Chief of detectives wants a file pulled from records. I can swing it."

The words were innocuous. The way he said them wasn't. Too casual. Too smooth. A little too ready.

The anonymous tip had been detailed. Somebody knew about the night I spent at Owen's place. Knew about the suspect he'd taken down a little too hard after the guy came at me. Knew enough to wrap it all in just enough righteous concern to make IA listen. Someone on my team had sold him out.

"Jordan," I said, not taking my eyes off the elevator as it closed behind Ramos. "Harper."

Harper looked up from his computer, already half sighing. "What did I do?"

"Follow him," I said. "Eyes only. No contact. I want to know where 'records' is today."

Harper groaned theatrically. "You realize I just sat down, right?"

"You can sit in the car," I said. "Luxury accommodations, right out front."

Jordan was already grabbing his jacket. "You want this on comms or off the books?"

"Off," I said. IA had bugs in half the building lately. "Text me if you find something. Don't get burned."

Harper thumped his cup down on my desk with a put-upon sigh. "If I get shot for this, I'm haunting you."

"Join the line," I muttered.

They headed out after Ramos. I watched them until they disappeared from my line of sight, that oily unease in my gut spreading. I went back to Keller's trial file, but the words wouldn't land. Every time I tried to focus, my mind slid back to yesterday—Owen's hands steady as he put his badge on the desk, the way he'd caught my eye and given the slightest shake of his head. *Don't.*

Like I could've stayed silent if I wanted to.

The thing about guilt is it doesn't care that you're busy. It just sits in your chest, heavy and patient, and waits for you to slow down.

By the time my phone buzzed, my left eye was starting to twitch.

I grabbed for it automatically, expecting some meaningless email, another lab update, anything I could pretend to prioritize over the noise in my head.

Jordan's name glared up at me.

Jordan: Get ahold of your man before I do.

My stomach dropped hard enough I actually heard myself exhale. I typed back with stiff fingers.

Me: What does that mean?

The reply came fast.

Jordan: Means your sergeant's out here playing Batman with Ramos.

For a second, the bullpen dimmed at the edges. I had to blink to clear it. Owen. Suspended Owen. Out in the field. With Ramos. Of course he was. The man didn't know how to sit still if you nailed him to a chair. I could feel eyes on me, some instinctive ripple of attention anytime a captain looks like she's about to murder her phone. I turned my back, hunching over the screen.

Me: Are they together?

Jordan: No. Separate cars. Separate shadows. Pretty sure Bishop thinks he's being subtle.

A bitter laugh got stuck somewhere behind my teeth. Subtle was not one of Owen Bishop's spiritual gifts.

Me: Stay on Ramos. Do NOT engage. Bring Harper back to the precinct when you can break off without spooking anybody.

A pause.

Jordan: Copy. Might be a while. You sure you don't want us to grab Bishop by the ear and drag him home?

I pictured it—Jordan and Harper frog-marching Owen into

his house while he swore at them. The image might've been funny if my skin didn't feel two sizes too small.

Me: No. I'll handle Bishop. Just keep this off comms unless someone starts shooting.

I fired off a quick text to Owen, asking him what the hell he was doing and if he had left his senses at home. I glared at my phone when I didn't immediately get a reply.

"Casey?" Nguyen again, hovering in my doorway with his tablet clutched to his chest like a shield.

"What?" I snapped.

He flinched. "Sorry. Thought you'd want to know the DA called. They want you prepped to testify as lead in Keller by Monday."

"Yeah." My voice sounded far away. "Right. Email me the witness list again."

"You already—"

"Email it again."

He nodded and vanished.

I set the phone down carefully, like it might explode. My brain felt like static. Owen was out there working a shadow case he wasn't allowed to touch. Ramos—who'd sat in that IA interview room yesterday and looked shocked, shocked that someone would accuse a fellow officer of misconduct—was now the one being tailed like a suspect. And I was stuck in the middle, with Keller's smirking mug shot staring up at me like he knew the whole circus was my problem. I picked up one of the trial photos and stared at it until my vision blurred.

Guilt sat heavy in my ribcage.

I was the captain. This was my unit. My responsibility. My mess. And the rat was in my house.

The day dragged like it had weights on its ankles. Jordan and

Harper checked back in once, quick, just enough to say they'd done their job and hadn't been seen. Ramos had gone home. Owen had peeled off somewhere else. Hopefully home.

"Did he see you?" I'd asked.

"Nope," Jordan replied. "We're ghosts."

"That'd be a first," I muttered to myself.

The rest of the shift was a blur of motions I'd done a thousand times: sign forms, skim reports, answer calls, pretend everything was fine while the ground tilted under my feet. Every noise felt too loud. Every glance felt loaded.

Twice I caught people looking away from me mid-whisper. Once I heard my own name and Owen's in the same sentence and didn't trust myself to ask what the hell they thought they knew. By the time the bullpen started thinning out, the sound of Thibodeaux's voice had faded. His office light was still on, but the door was closed. No more shouting. Just the low murmur of a man fighting a losing battle with bureaucracy. My phone stayed stubbornly silent.

No message from Owen.

No: I'm ok.

No: I'm working an angle, trust me.

He'd gone radio silent on me. And I couldn't even call him into my office and tear him a new one because IA had put a nice, neat wall between us and called it "procedure." I stayed later than I had to, because the alternative was going home and sitting in my apartment with nothing but my thoughts for company. Eventually, even busywork ran out. At some point, Nguyen and Sanders wandered back by my desk. They looked tired in a way that had nothing to do with lack of sleep.

"You need anything, boss?" Sanders asked.

"Confession and a time machine," I said.

She huffed a humorless laugh. "That all?"

I glanced at her. "Jordan debrief you?"

"Yeah. Bishop was playing follow-the-leader. Looked like he was trying real hard not to get caught doing it." Sanders studied me for a beat. "You know it's not on you he got benched, right? IA was already gunning for him. Tip gave them an excuse, that's all."

"My detective made that call," I said. "From this unit. My unit. That's on me."

She didn't argue, which almost pissed me off more.

"Go home, Sanders," I said. "That's an order."

She saluted with two fingers, mock lazy. "Yes, ma'am. Try not to explode."

No promises.

Nguyen showed up in my doorway again just as I was contemplating whether falling asleep on my desk was an option. His eyes were too wide, pupils blown in that way that usually meant bad news or something very illegal.

"Boss. You got a minute?"

I wanted to say no on principle. "What is it? I thought I told you and Sanders to go home."

He came in and shut the door behind him. That got my attention. Nguyen hated closed doors. He set a folder down, open, pages already clipped to specific spots with neon sticky flags. "So, I was doing the Keller prep you asked, going back over any side seizures we logged during the original investigation."

"Uh-huh."

"And I got to Ramos's reports from last week. He logged a half kilo pick-up on a car stop. Same cut, same packaging as Keller's distribution chain. But..." He tapped the page. "It never hit evidence."

I straightened. "You're sure?"

"I cross-checked intake logs, chain of custody, lab submissions. There's nothing. It's like the drugs never existed once they left his report."

My skin went cold. "Maybe he mislabeled it."

Nguyen shook his head. "I checked for that too. That weight never shows up anywhere."

I stared at the page until the numbers blurred. Half a kilo wasn't nothing. And Ramos knew the Keller case inside and out. He knew exactly how much heat was on any dope tied to it.

"We'll ask him," I said, though the words felt brittle. "See if there's an innocent explanation."

"Yeah, about that..." Nguyen swallowed. "I might have looked at his phone."

I dropped my pen. "You what?"

"I mean, not look-looked. I didn't go scrolling through his Tinder. I cloned some metadata off the last backup. It's... fine," he said weakly.

"Nguyen."

He winced. "Technically, if we're being super strict about it, it might be considered a minor violation of like... a few federal laws."

I rubbed my temples. "So yes, you committed a crime."

"On your behalf," he said quickly. "And for the greater good."

"Those words don't go in the same sentence as 'felony,'" I said. But there was no real heat in it. I was too tired to pretend I had the moral high ground anymore. "What did you find?"

He brightened, relieved to be on the part where he was useful. "Texts from an unknown number. Talking about 'moving the rest' and 'last batch tonight.' Attached pinned location for a warehouse near the docks. Time stamp about an hour ago. Meet's set for 9 p.m."

I checked the clock. 7:45.

The guilt shifted, made room for something sharper. Anger.

Ramos had turned Owen in for doing his job too hard and loving too loud, then walked back into my unit and used that chaos as cover to run his own side hustle.

"Print everything," I said. "Screenshots. Logs. His report. I want a packet that would make a DA salivate."

Nguyen nodded fast. "On it."

"And Nguyen?"

He paused in the doorway.

"If anyone asks," I said, "you didn't touch his phone."

He exhaled like I'd just thrown him a life raft. "Yes, ma'am."

The door clicked shut behind him. I stared at the wall for a long beat, jaw clenched, heart beating too hard. Anonymous tip, my ass. Ramos wanted Owen gone. Why? Less oversight? Personal grudge? Fear he'd stumble too close to whatever this was? Didn't matter. He'd made his move. I was going to make mine.

The briefing room felt wrong the next morning—too cold, too bright, too damn quiet. Harper stood near the whiteboard with his arms crossed, staring at the printed photos like they'd personally offended him. Sanders sat stiff in one of the metal chairs, knuckles white around her pen. Nguyen hovered near the doorway, shifting his weight like he wanted to walk out of his own skin. Jordan and Crawford waited by the far wall, unreadable in that way only seasoned detectives could manage, but even they weren't hiding it well.

We'd all worked with Ramos. And now we were about to raid one of his secret little hideaways.

I set the warrant folder down on the table, the slap of paper sounding way too loud. "We're hitting the warehouse off Dauphine," I said. "We've got probable cause, and we have a narrow window before whoever Ramos was working with realizes he's missing."

Nguyen let out a shaky breath. "Can't believe he did this, Sarge."

"Yeah," Harper muttered. "Feels like shit."

I didn't argue. "Look, none of us wanted this. But wanting doesn't matter right now. We follow the evidence. We do this clean." My voice was steady, even though my stomach hadn't unclenched since last night. "We're not going after Ramos. We're going after whoever he was protecting."

Sanders finally looked up, eyes raw. "It still feels like we're kicking down the door of our own house."

"I know," I said, and I meant it. "But this is where he left us."

Jordan shifted, pushing off the wall. "Just tell us how you want to run it."

That got all their eyes on me. My team, and Owen's—hurting, betrayed, still solid under the grief. I picked up the warrant again, not because I needed to, but because it grounded me. The words were clear. The job was clear. My heartbeat... not so much.

"Crawford takes entry with Harper," I said. "Sanders, you and Nguyen run secondary. Jordan's with me. We'll sweep the east side. No one breaks formation, no one goes cowboy. We're doing this by the book."

A beat passed—not quite agreement, not quite acceptance. Something in the middle. Something heavy. Then Harper nodded. Sanders straightened. Nguyen swallowed and gave a tight, miserable "Yes, ma'am." Jordan met my eyes and gave the smallest nod, the kind that said he'd follow me even if the world was on fire.

"Gear up," I said, pulling the warrant back into my vest. "We roll out in five." And as we filed out of that room, the weight of Ramos's betrayal walked with us. But we walked anyway.

The warehouse down by the docks was the sort of place horror movies used for establishing shots. Long, low, and ugly. Humid air coming off the river. Smell of oil and old fish.

We rolled dark, no sirens. I put Nguyen on comms from the car with a laptop and a headset, Harper at my shoulder. A couple of uniforms we trusted took positions watching the side exits. Thibodeaux knew where we were in vague terms— "following up on a lead"—but I hadn't exactly mentioned the hacked phone or the missing kilo.

One crime at a time.

"We're early," Harper murmured as we hugged the shadow of a cargo container.

"Good," I said. "I want eyes before he even thinks about pulling up."

He peered around the corner. "The hell do you think he's doing, anyway?"

"Best case? Skimming," I said. "Worst case? He's every druggie's new best friend."

Harper grimaced.

Nguyen's voice crackled quietly in my ear. "We've got a ping. Ramos's phone just hit the tower nearest your location. ETA about three minutes if he's coming in straight."

"Copy," I whispered.

Three minutes stretched. Every drip of water, every distant engine, every click of metal as the building settled sounded like a gunshot. My hands felt steady. My heart didn't. Headlights finally swept across the cracked pavement, blinding for a second as a dark sedan turned into the lot. It rolled slow, like it knew it was somewhere it shouldn't be.

"Showtime," Harper muttered.

Another car followed—a black SUV, windows tinted too dark. That one parked closer to the docking bay.

Ramos climbed out of the sedan, silhouetted in the harsh glow of a single security light. No jacket this time. Just a hoodie and jeans. Off-duty clothes for off-book business.

The buyer stepped out of the SUV. Too far for me to see his face clearly, but the body language read confident. Like he'd done this dance before.

They met halfway, near a stack of pallets. The buyer said something, gesturing with one hand. Ramos handed over a duffel bag. The buyer unzipped it, checked the contents with a practiced glance.

Nguyen's voice was barely more than a breath. "I've got him on the camera feed I hacked into. That's definitely our boy. Looks like bricks in the bag, consistent size with half-kilo seizures."

I drew in a slow breath. "On my signal," I murmured into my shoulder mic. "We go loud. Ramos first, then buyer. I want them both breathing."

Harper nodded. "Breathing, resisted arrest. Got it."

I waited for the moment, watching their hands, their faces, the distance between them and their vehicles. When the buyer zipped the bag closed and reached for his waistband—whether for money or something less friendly—I moved.

"Police!" I shouted, gun trained center mass. "Drop it and show me your hands!"

Everything exploded at once.

The buyer jerked, hand flashing out with a gun. The night lit up with muzzle flashes. Bullets sang past, sparking off metal. Someone cursed. I dove behind a concrete pillar, shoulder slamming into it hard enough to send pain down my arm. I returned fire, controlled bursts, aiming for center, not head. Through the chaos, I caught a flash of Ramos. He'd dropped to one knee behind a stack of crates, gun out, eyes wide. For half a second, our gazes locked.

He looked terrified. And guilty. And pissed. A cocktail I knew too well.

"Ramos!" I yelled. "Drop it! It's over!"

He hesitated, gun wobbling just enough to tell me he was thinking about it.

Then the buyer shouted something I couldn't catch over the gunfire. The SUV's engine revved. Doors slammed. Someone laid down suppressing fire from the passenger side window.

Harper swore. "They're peeling off!"

"Take the tires if you can!" I snapped.

I had a clear line on the SUV's rear wheel, brought my sights up—and Ramos darted between us, sprinting for his own car.

"Ramos!"

He looked back at me over his shoulder. For a heartbeat, everything narrowed to that one flicker of eye contact.

Five years working shoulder to shoulder.

Five years of paperwork, coffee, bullshit, good arrests and bad days.

He was my friend. But he was choosing to run.

I could've taken the shot. I knew my aim. I trusted my hands. Center mass, he'd go down, probably live if EMS got there in time.

My finger tightened.

And stalled.

I pictured IA again. Owen standing there while they recited the allegations. The anonymous tip. Ramos sitting in that same room later, all offended concern. *Of course we have to hold ourselves accountable, Captain. We can't afford bad optics.*

My gut clenched.

I didn't pull the trigger.

Ramos hit his car, dove in, and the sedan screeched backwards, fishtailed, then shot out of the lot, following the SUV's taillights into the dark. Gunfire died away by degrees, leaving the ringing in my ears and the taste of copper in my mouth.

"You okay?" Jordan called, breathing hard and running over to me.

"I'm good," I lied.

We secured the scene—what there was of it. A few shell casings. Tire skids. The faint chemical smell of cut product that had been there and now wasn't. No bodies. No bricks. No Ramos.

No clean endings.

Nguyen's voice crackled, thin. "His phone just went dead. Either he tossed it or smashed it."

"Of course he did," I muttered.

I stood in the middle of the warehouse, gun heavy in my hand, and wanted to scream. I'd had him. I'd had the shot. I hadn't taken it. Guilt burned hot in my chest. Not the neat, moral kind. The ugly, selfish kind.

Because for all the anger and suspicion, a part of me still recognized the man who'd shared my desk cluster for years. Who'd eaten my cookies at holiday potlucks and bitched about overtime and written condolences letters when we buried victims. I lowered my gun and holstered it with hands that didn't feel completely steady.

"Let's pack it up," I said. "We'll log what we can. And then we're going back to write a nice, clean report that makes this clusterfuck look like we did everything by the book."

Back at the precinct, the silence was worse.

We came in through the side entrance, trailing damp warehouse smell and frustration. The bullpen felt oddly hollow. The usual late-night diehards had thinned out, leaving pockets of empty desks. The ones that remained looked up as we walked through, curiosity sharp, then quickly pretended not to stare. Thibodeaux's door flew open before I even reached my desk. He'd taken off his tie and rolled his sleeves up, which meant he was at "about to commit homicide" levels of pissed.

"You want to tell me why I'm getting a call from dispatch about shots fired at the warehouse docks before I get one from my own unit?" he demanded.

I didn't bother sugarcoating it. I stepped into his office and shut the door behind us.

"We followed a lead on Ramos," I said. "Missing seizure. His report doesn't match the evidence log. Nguyen found texts arranging a sale tonight. We set up an ambush."

Thibodeaux's jaw worked. "And?"

"And we confirmed he's dirty," I said. The words tasted like ash. "He got away."

Thibodeaux swore, low and vicious. "You sure?"

"Yes."

"How sure?"

"IA-sure," I said. "If they'd done their damn jobs and looked at him half as hard as they looked at Owen, they'd have caught a kilo-sized red flag."

Thibodeaux dropped his hand and looked at me. Really

looked. Behind the fury and exhaustion, there was something like sympathy. I hated it. "This unit is leaking," he said quietly. "And it's not Bishop."

"No," I said. My voice was steady now. Anger had cooled into something harder. "It's not."

He nodded once. "Write it up. Clean as you can without lying. You know how this game works."

"Yes, sir."

"And Casey?"

"Yeah?"

"Don't you dare shoulder all of this," he said. "Ramos made his choices. IA made theirs. You're doing your job."

I held his gaze. "My detective turned right under my nose. That's on my leadership."

"That's on his conscience," Thibodeaux said. "Assuming he's still got one."

I didn't answer. There was nothing left to say.

Jordan met me at my desk. I tried really, really hard to not look at Owen's empty office and failed miserably.

"Well," Jordan said. "Ten out of ten do not recommend that field trip."

"You okay?" I asked, purely out of habit.

He shrugged. "Got shot at, didn't get hit. That's a win in my book."

"You clipped anyone?"

"Nicked the SUV, maybe. Not sure." He hesitated. "I, uh, saw you had the shot on Ramos."

"Yeah," I said.

"And you didn't take it."

"Thanks for the play-by-play, Jordan."

He held up his hands. "Not judging. Just... asking if you're good with that."

No.

Yes.

I don't know.

"I'm good with the fact that he's not dead on a slab downstairs," I said finally. "I'm less good with the fact that he's out there, running scared and dangerous."

Jordan nodded slowly. "Fair enough."

He pushed himself up. "I'm gonna go start my report before my memory turns this into a John Wick movie. You need anything else?"

I stared at the blank report form glowing on my screen. "Confession. Names. A reason this doesn't feel like my failure."

"This isn't on you, Case."

Everyone kept saying that. I wish they wouldn't. When I didn't respond, Jordan sighed and left me to my thoughts.

The bullpen emptied out by ones and twos until it was just me and the night shift dispatcher in the corner, humming under her breath with one earbud in. The hum of the fluorescent lights pressed at my temples.

I finished my report, scrubbed it twice for anything that might give IA a reason to drag me into an interview room and pick at the corners. By the time I hit send, I felt hollow. I shut down my computer and sat there for a moment, staring at the dark screen, listening to the rain start outside. My phone buzzed once. My heart jolted—hopeful. Stupid. Spam email.

Not Owen.

Of course not.

I thumbed over to our message thread anyway, like maybe if I stared at it long enough a new text would magically appear.

The last one was from me, sent yesterday: *Call me when you*

can. We need to talk about IA before they decide your fate for you.
Read, no reply.

I could hear IA's dry little summary in my head: Detective Bishop has displayed a pattern of disregarding protocol, both in the field and in his personal relationships.

Never mind that the use-of-force complaint came from Owen defending me from a suspect who'd tried to make this case my last.

Never mind that the "inappropriate relationship" was two consenting adults who happened to carry badges and work the same floor.

The anonymous tip hadn't been about ethics. It had been about leverage.

I grabbed my jacket and headed for the stairs. The air outside hit me like a damp slap—cool, misting rain, the kind that soaked you slowly without you noticing until it was too late. Streetlights smeared in the wet. I stood there on the sidewalk for a second, not moving, keys in my hand, the weight of the day pressing down.

Ramos was gone.

Keller's trial was hanging over us.

Owen was on the sidelines because someone in my house had decided to use him as a shield. When he wasn't sitting compliant and was instead risking his entire career to follow a rat on *my* team. I wasn't sure which was worse.

And I'd just let him run because I couldn't quite bring myself to shoot a man I used to trust. The guilt twisted with anger until I couldn't tell where one ended and the other began.

IA had walked Owen out like a perp. My team had watched. No one had said a word. Including me. I'd told myself I was playing it smart, waiting to see the full picture before I made any moves. Screw that.

I slid into the driver's seat and shut the door. The car felt too small, too quiet. Jordan's earlier text still sat at the top of my notifications. *Get ahold of your man before I do.*

My jaw clenched. "Fine," I muttered. He could ignore my texts. He could shut off his phone. He could pretend he was protecting me by keeping his distance while IA tore his reputation apart.

But he was not getting rid of me that easily. I turned the key. The engine rumbled to life. Wipers squeaked, then swept the rain aside.

"Fine," I said again, louder this time, to the empty car and the wet street. "He won't answer my texts, but I am making that son of a bitch talk to me." I put the car in drive and pulled away from the curb, heading straight for Owen Bishop's house.

CHAPTER 15 ◉ OWEN

Suspension my ass. They could take my badge, my gun, and my parking spot, but they weren't taking my brain. I'd spent the better part of two days surrounded by files I wasn't supposed to have, a half-empty pot of coffee, and a wall of notes that would make any defense attorney salivate. Ramos was dirty—hell, the whole precinct stank—and if IA thought benching me would stop me from proving it, they'd clearly never met me. I'd gone through the motions of "resting." Shaved. Did some laundry. Even pretended to watch TV. But every time I tried to disconnect, my mind went right back to the case—to her.

The sound of tires crunching over gravel snapped me out of my head. My stomach dropped, instinct taking over. I swept the open files into a pile, flipped a folder closed with my elbow, and covered the rest with yesterday's newspaper just as a car door slammed.

Then came the footsteps. Fast. Determined. When I peeked through the curtain, a familiar flash of black hair hit me square in the chest. Casey. I exhaled, relief and dread tangling somewhere behind my ribs. Of course it was her. Nobody else barged into a suspended cop's driveway like they were delivering divine judgment.

The pounding on the door started before I even reached it. I opened it mid-knock, and she all but stormed inside, a force of nature in jeans and righteous fury. Her words hit me in rapid fire—no preamble, no breath between shots. "You don't get to ignore me, Owen! I am so sorry, I never meant for any of this to happen, but you can't just disappear on me like that! I know you're pissed, and you have every right to be, but that doesn't mean you shut me out! Or that you go off half fucking cocked following a dangerous idiot who, unlike you, still has a badge! We are partners—on paper, off paper, whatever this is—but you don't get to ghost me when it's our case on the line—"

She stopped only long enough to inhale before launching right back in. Hands flying, eyes bright with exhaustion and guilt, she was unraveling faster than she realized. I let her go. Let her vent. I'd seen suspects crack slower under interrogation lights. But underneath all that fire was guilt—raw, frantic guilt—and it gutted me.

"Casey."

Nothing. No reaction.

"Casey."

She froze mid-sentence, eyes snapping up to mine.

I took a slow step closer. "Breathe."

Her shoulders rose, fell. Barely.

"You done?"

She made a strangled sound—half laugh, half sob. "No, I'm not done! You got suspended because of me!"

I shook my head. "IA made that call, not you."

"You think they don't know it was me?" she shot back. "They didn't have to say my name. Everyone knows."

"Then everyone knows we're two consenting adults," I said, my voice dropping low enough to still the air between us. "And

253

that's not on you. It's on both of us. And fuck IA. No one, and I mean no one, is making me choose between the job I love and the woman I love."

I saw my words, words I hadn't even meant to say yet, hit her like a freight train. She almost staggered back a step but caught herself. She looked up at me, those bright, intelligent eyes softening in the dim light of my living room. "Love?"

It was one word. One simple word. But we both knew it changed everything.

"Yeah. Love." I said it like a challenge. Like a man who'd been holding his breath for too damn long. "You think I don't know what that means? Casey, I spent years convincing myself I was fine. That this"—I gestured around the empty house at the stack of case files and the cold coffee on the counter—"was enough. That love was something for younger men with fewer scars and fewer regrets. I had my shot. It ended in court papers and a silence I got too used to."

I took a step closer to her, eyes locked on hers.

"Then you came in—loud, reckless, smarter than you have any right to be—and you woke me the hell up. You reminded me what it feels like to *want* again. To fight for something that isn't written in a report. So no, I'm not gonna sit here and let some pencil-pusher tell me I have to pick. Because I'm not choosing."

She still didn't say a word, just watched as I ran my hands through my hair. "I love my job. It's who I am. But I love you. And the two aren't mutually exclusive, no matter what they say. I can chase down killers by day and come home to you at night. I can carry the badge and still hold you. They don't get to decide that for me. They don't get to tell me I can't have both."

Casey made a small sound, and I stepped even closer to her.

I took her face in my hands, forcing her to look up at me. "So yeah—let them talk. Let them file their complaints and whisper in hallways. They can kiss my ass, because I've already made my choice. I'm keeping my badge. I'm keeping my woman. And anyone who's got a problem with that can take a number."

Her pretty pink lips parted, and I was sure I was the first person ever to put Casey Chambers at a loss for words. Then she smirked, that familiar half-grin that lit a fire in my gut every time. "Is that so?"

"Damn right."

She stepped back, and for a second, my heart stuttered. Then she turned towards the hall. Her back to the dark, she took a step backwards. Never taking her eyes off me. Then another. I just watched her. Watched as she took her shirt off and let it fall to the floor. Her boots were kicked off. Her jeans fell around her ankles, and as she stepped out of them, another step backwards. Towards my room. "Prove it."

Say. *Fucking*. Less.

I closed the distance between us in a few strides, but right as I reached her, she gave a completely uncharacteristic and adorable squeal as she darted just out of reach. She bolted to my room, and for a brief second, I almost felt bad for the guys she chased on duty. Woman was fast. I frowned when I heard the door click as it locked.

I tried the handle, which didn't budge. Did she just lock me out of my own room?

"Casey."

"Yes?"

"Open this door."

"No."

Excuse the fuck out of me? "Casey, you've got two seconds

255

to open this damn door."

"Or what? You're going to kick your own door down? What a mess that would make."

"Don't test me."

"You know, since you're on one side and I'm on the other... I gotta tell you, it's kind of cold in here."

I waited to see where she was going with this.

"I think I may need to warm up. And I know just the way. All the tension this past week. Really has a way of working a girl over."

I frowned. Yanked on the handle again. I heard her giggle.

"Better hurry, Owen. I might just make myself come before you even get in here."

She was right—kicking the door down would be a mess. I pressed my shoulder against the frame, testing how much it gave under my weight. Then froze when a familiar sound reached my ears. She moaned. Then again.

I swore, then turned and headed towards my kitchen. I kept a drill under the sink. And she had severely underestimated me. I grabbed it and returned to my door just in time to hear her groan and curse. I was going to make her pay for that.

The sounds coming from the room came to a sudden halt when the drill started whirring. One hinge fell to the floor. Then the second. The last hinge let go with a squeal. The door sagged, caught by the bolt for half a second before the jamb cracked and the whole thing crashed forward in a shower of splinters.

I put the drill down, then stepped through the gaping hole. She lay there, in my bed, legs spread and pussy wet. Her hand was still resting on her thigh, her arousal on her fingers. I looked deliberately from it to her. Raised an eyebrow. Pointed at her.

"Baby girl, you just fucked up."

She stuck her tongue out at me. I chuckled darkly, turning from where she lay on the bed and heading for my closet. The sheets rustled as she sat up, probably trying to figure out what I was doing. A smile made its way across my face as I grabbed a couple of the ties I had hung from the back of the closet door. I never wore them, didn't have much use for them. Until now.

Turning back to her, I ran the smooth fabric through my hands. She tracked the movement, pupils dilating as she quickly realized my intent. She didn't move from the bed as I made my way to her. For a second, I just stood there and stared at her. Taking in every inch of every delicious curve. Fuck, she was beautiful. And she was mine.

Quick as lightning, I grabbed her ankles. She yelped, eyes widening as I pulled her legs out from under her. She kicked at me, but I could tell it was half-hearted. She had put me on the floor before, and I had seen her take down guys twice her size. If she wanted to stop me, she would've. Her foot made contact with my shoulder as I wrapped the tie around her ankle. I grunted and flipped her over onto her belly.

"Keep fighting, *ma louve*. I love it when you fight. You really thought you were going to lock me out of my own bedroom?"

I tsked, then spanked her. Her yelp dissolved into a moan as I rubbed the red mark on her ass. I leaned over her, pressing kisses along her spine and tracing her tattoo. Her ankles were firmly tied together, and I leaned back to watch her test the strength of the tie. The muscles in her legs bunched as she tried pulling her legs apart. When she realized she wasn't getting out of it, she twisted her head until she was looking at me.

"To be honest, I hadn't expected you to take the thing off the hinges." She eyed the doorway, and I glanced over, too. Yeah,

257

that would need replacing. But I didn't regret it.

"I just think it's adorable that you thought you could play with yourself, in my bed, and I would just, what? Standby and listen? Baby, when you come, it's only going to be on one of three places. My fingers. My tongue. Or my cock."

"Is that so?"

I shook my head at her, "Who knew you would be such a brat?"

She laughed, using her free hands to roll herself over onto her back. "Think you can keep up, old man?"

I raised an eyebrow at her, "What did you just call me?"

She didn't answer, just grinned at me. I grabbed her bound ankles and yanked her closer to the edge of the bed before grabbing her wrists. Taking the other tie, I wrapped it around her wrists as she watched me.

"Here's what's going to happen, baby. I am going to play with you. I'm a fast learner, and I know all the little things you like. I'm going to take you to the edge, and drag you back. Again and again and again. And when you are begging, pleading for release... I'll consider giving it to you. But not until I have reminded you just who you belong to. Try and keep up, *mon péché.*"

She raised her eyebrows at the challenge, her eyes growing impossibly dark with lust and desire at my words. Her wrists were bound, legs too. She was mine to play with, to use. I pulled her by the ankles until the lower half of her body dangled off the mattress. I leaned over, kissing her breasts before sucking one of the stiff, pink peaks into my mouth. She groaned, and I grinned when I felt her try and free her hands.

I licked her nipple, dragging my teeth across it. I trailed kisses up her neck, capturing her lips with my own. She opened for me, and I practically drank in the taste of her. Grabbing her bound wrists, I raised her hands above her head. I had to be mindful of her damn stitches, which was part of the reason I had bound her in the first place.

"These stay here. Understand?"

"Owen...."

I slapped her breast, and she bucked. "Understand?"

She licked her lips, "Yes... sir."

Fuck. I liked the sound of that.

"Good girl."

She threw her head back on the bed, closing her eyes. I grabbed her hips, which still dangled off the bed. I bit the dimple in her hip, then the scar above her thigh that I knew was sensitive. She shuddered. Then I bit the top of her bare pussy. With her legs bound, I had just enough room to slide a finger over her clit. I flicked it, and she cursed. I braced myself next to her head, using the other hand to play with her clit. She moaned and tried rocking her hips.

When she went to move her hands, I pinched her. Hard. She shouted a curse, eyes flying open to glare at me. I kissed her.

"I told you those stay up there. Eyes on me, love."

Casey's eyes were nothing if not expressive. And while I played with her clit, until it was so tender she jerked at the slightest touch, I watched as they grew brighter. The brown was practically a warm amber now, lit from the fire I had stoked in her. So I stopped, and she swore.

"Fuck. No, Owen. I am so close."

I chuckled. "I know."

She thrashed, trying to rub her legs together for a bit of friction, but I slapped her tit again. She stilled, and I grabbed her hips before pushing her further back on the bed. I loosened the tie at her ankle just enough that I could part her thighs. She was soaked. I knelt, blowing cold air across the warmth of her wet cunt.

"Owen... fucking... Bishop."

I looked up at her. "Regret being a brat yet?"

"No."

Fine, then. Stubborn-ass woman. I pressed my nose to her slit, inhaling her scent before taking my tongue through the addictive cream that coated her lips. *Yes.* All week. That damn IA suspension. That son of a bitch Keller. That worthless rat Ramos. All the tension and the stress. It had been building inside us both, begging for a release. Before her, my release had been late nights and bourbon. Barely enough to take the edge off. But now?

The nights were filled with the taste of her. The sounds she made. The way her body responded to me. She was more than enough. I could do this forever. I dug my fingers into her hips, holding her in place as I pressed my tongue inside her. I glanced up at her, ensuring her hands were where they were supposed to be. She began to moan, then to shake, and then to rock her hips against my mouth. She soaked my chin as she whimpered my name. Then, just when she tensed, I stopped. She tried locking her legs around my head, but I stepped back before she could maneuver the tie on her ankles.

"Owen. You son of a bitch." She was covered in a sheen of sweat, little pieces of her hair clinging to her forehead. I had never seen anything so beautiful. She began to lift her hands towards me, but I raised an eyebrow at her, and she froze. Then she glared at me.

"You regret it yet?"

She raised her chin. "You like it."

I flipped her over again, until she was fully on the bed and on her belly once more. "That's not what I asked, love. Are you ready to be a good girl?"

Her pupils dilated again, and she squirmed. The movement made her ass jiggle and I spanked it, just because I could. She cried out and then finally, "Yes."

"Yes, what?" I wanted her to say it again.

"Yes, sir."

"You wanna come for me now, *mon péché*?"

"Yes, sir."

I leaned over her, moving her hair to the side and kissing her neck. Untying her ankles, I raised her ass into the air until she was on her knees with her tits pressed against the pillows. "How's your arm?"

"I—What?"

"Your arm, Casey. Does it hurt?"

She squirmed again. "Dammit Owen, I'm not really thinking about my arm right now."

I grinned. "Good." Then I took off my jeans, tossing them and my shirt to the floor.

She looked over her shoulder at me, and a smile played on her lips. "Fucking finally."

I spanked her again and she buried her face in a pillow as she groaned. I loved how she liked it rough, how she let me take control. Even if she did mouth back ten ways to Sunday. I wrapped my hand around my painfully hard cock before lining myself with her entrance. "Let's see how quickly you come."

When I thrust into her, I wasn't gentle. I braced one hand on her hip, and grabbed the back of her neck with the other. As I slammed home inside her, her entire body bowed as her pussy clenched around me. I muttered a curse as her tight cunt strangled my dick, then pulled back out and slammed into her again. The third time, she rocked backwards, rolling her hips into my waist.

I cursed again, "That's it, *mon péché*. Such a good girl for me. You take me so well. Come for me, baby."

"Owen! Oh fu-uu-uck!"

She came so hard, her pussy gripped my cock like a damn vise. So tight it almost hurt. I wrapped my hand in her hair before settling deep inside her and groaning as I filled her cunt. My cock twitched, and I rolled my neck as she finally relaxed under me. I reached for the ties on her wrists, undoing them before rolling us both until I was under her. She was fluid, her body completely spent, and she sprawled out over me before tucking her head under my chin. She sighed, scratching absentmindedly at her stitches. I smacked her hand, and she chuckled before nestling into me until we might as well have been one.

"Casey?"

"Mhm?"

"You'll catch Ramos."

"I know."

"And I'll come back."

She yawned, "I know that too."

"Good."

"Owen?"

"Yes, *ma louve*?"

"I think I love you too."

CHAPTER 16 ◆ CASEY

The sun broke through the blinds with a vengeance. I groaned, rolling over with a yawn. And found myself face to chest with a very, very naked Owen Bishop. Yum.

Stretching, I ran my hand over the rigid lines of his stomach and chest, and watched him breathe deeply, still sound asleep. He grumbled, and I smiled before dragging myself as quietly as I could from under the sheets. I looked around for my shirt, remembered it was in the hallway, and grabbed Owen's before making my way to the kitchen.

I hated his coffee pot, and I was pretty sure the damn thing hated me too after it spewed on me last time. Maybe that was what I would get him for Christmas. A nice, simple Keurig. I managed to wrangle the machine into submission and grinned triumphantly when the smell of fresh-brewed Folgers filled the house. I turned at the sound of footsteps behind me.

Owen had put on a pair of gray sweats which hung low across his hips and was leaning against the doorway, watching me. "I see you figured out the coffee pot."

"I'm feeling pretty proud of myself, not gonna lie."

I went over to the cabinet where he kept his coffee cups and was struck by the realization that Owen's house was as familiar to me as my own. I glanced at him over my shoulder, and found him still looking at me. "What?"

"Nothing. Just like watching you in my kitchen. You hungry? I can make some eggs before you have to go."

Go. I didn't want to go. It felt wrong wearing a badge when he didn't. But there was still so much to do. I sipped my coffee and tracked his every move as he started making some scrambled eggs.

He glanced over his shoulder, mouth curved in that slow, dangerous way that had ruined my self-control twelve hours ago. I wrapped his flannel tighter around me. The shirt smelled like smoke and cedar and the ghost of whatever cologne had survived the night. What was it about men's clothes that were just so much better than our own? I would happily torch my entire closet if it meant getting a closet full of clothes that smelled like him.

Well, except that cute green turtleneck Jordan got me for Christmas last year. Oh, and my boots. And my jeans that were worn to that perfect level of softness. Ok, so maybe not my whole closet. But still.

I sat at the table, crossing my legs and watching Owen at the stove. I should've felt shame. We were supposed to be partners. Nothing more. We were breaking approximately a hundred department rules. Hell, he had gotten suspended over it. Instead, I felt alive—raw, wired, stupidly at peace. The guilt that hovered wasn't about what we'd done; it was about the fact that I wanted to do it again. What had started as a one-night stand had turned into nights where I couldn't stand being alone. Without him. And, somehow, this grumpy, broody, stubborn man... felt the same way?

I'd fought for everything. Nothing in my life had ever come

easy—not safety, not trust, not a home. I was a foster kid with more placement numbers than birthday candles, the kind people wrote off before they bothered to learn my name. I learned early how to blend in, how to survive, how to smile just enough to keep people from asking questions. Every door I ever walked through, I had to kick open myself. No one was going to hand me anything, so I stopped waiting.

College before twenty, academy right after. While everyone else my age was out getting drunk or figuring out who they were, I was memorizing criminal codes and running on caffeine, sheer will, and spite. I worked every shift they'd give me, took every class they'd let me in, pushed until people twice my age couldn't ignore me anymore. I earned every damn inch I climbed. And maybe that was why I never made time for relationships— because when you built a life from nothing, you didn't risk it for something that might burn down everything you fought for. Jordan was the exception. He bulldozed his way into my life, loud and loyal and too stubborn to scare off. He became the brother I never had, the one person who kept me standing when the job or the ghosts tried to knock me flat.

Outside of that? It was easier to keep my distance. A few hookups, nothing personal, never another cop. I'd worked too hard to let whispers undo it. "She slept her way up." I'd heard that line too many times, whispered behind clipped smiles and coffee cups. I made sure nobody ever had reason to believe it. But then came Owen—older, steady, carrying his own scars. And for the first time, I wanted to stop fighting long enough to just *feel*. To be human. Lying there in his shirt, in his house, I realized I wasn't chasing survival anymore. I was chasing something I'd never let myself want: peace. And maybe that was the most dangerous thing of all.

He plated the eggs, set them between us, and gave me a knowing look. Like he could see the stampede of thoughts racing through my mind. "Eat before you go full existential crisis."

"Bossy," I muttered, stabbing a forkful. I groaned around the creaminess of the eggs. Owen fucking Bishop. Cop. Sex god. Gourmet chef. How the fuck was I supposed to resist?

For a few minutes, we just ate. The silence wasn't awkward—it was full, stretched thin by everything we weren't saying. The precinct, IA, Ramos, the whole mess we'd built around us like crime-scene tape.

He finally broke it. "What's on your mind, love?"

"I'm thinking I really screwed this up."

"You didn't screw it up. You made a choice."

I met his eyes. "You lost your badge for me, Owen."

He shook his head. "No. I lost my badge because the system's rigged and Ramos knew exactly which thread to pull. Don't give him that power by blaming yourself."

I swallowed the lump in my throat. "You love me."

He said it without hesitation. "Yeah."

"Say it again."

"I love you, Casey."

It should've terrified me. Instead, it steadied something inside I hadn't realized was shaking. "Then I guess we're both idiots, because I love you too."

The words came out small, but they landed like a confession. His eyes softened, and for a heartbeat, the world shrank to just us—the smell of coffee, the busted door that still lay on the floor, the promise we hadn't meant to make.

He reached across the table, rough fingers catching mine. "You focus on Ramos," he said quietly. "I'll handle clearing my name. We both fight the battles we can win."

I nodded because arguing with him was pointless, and because I needed distance before I forgot every rule I'd ever sworn to follow.

The shower at home scalded. I stood under it until my skin flushed pink and the mirror fogged over. The water beat against my shoulders, washing away sweat, smoke, regret.

Not regret.

Never that.

I braced my hands on the tile and closed my eyes. Last night hadn't been weakness—it had been release. Months of pressure, fear, pretending I didn't need anyone. I'd cracked, and he'd caught me. Simple as that. Like he always did.

But wanting him and *keeping* him were two different wars. IA was circling. Keller's trial was days away, rushed into the courtroom by the mayor. And Ramos... Ramos was the splinter under every fingernail.

I shut off the water and stared at my reflection. My hair clung to my cheeks; bruises bloomed along my collarbone like dark fingerprints. My damn stitches itched like something that crawled under my skin. I ran a finger gently along the seam of my skin, and whispered, "Time to end this."

The precinct was louder than usual, the kind of chaos that meant everyone was pretending not to notice how close to collapse we were. The Keller files had exploded across every surface—warrants, statements, maps marked in red.

Jordan looked up when I walked in. "You're supposed to be taking a personal day."

"I'm bad at instructions."

He smirked. "No kidding."

Nguyen sat at the far desk surrounded by empty Red Bull

cans and the glow of three monitors. His eyes were glassy but sharp. "Sergeant," he said, pushing his glasses up. "You got a minute?"

I glanced at Jordan. He shrugged. "Go easy on him; he's been digging through Ramos's trash for two days."

Nguyen looked like he'd seen a ghost. "It's not trash. It's... something."

We followed him down to Evidence B. The air down there always smelled like dust and old coffee grounds. He shut the door, drew the blinds, and stuck a thumb drive into the computer.

Static. Then the faint whir of a camera booting up.

A holding cell appeared on screen—gray cinderblock walls, flickering fluorescent light. My stomach tightened.

Nguyen said, "Pulled this from a corrupted file. Ten months old. Booking number #45317. Recognize the name?"

"Miguel Tovar." My mouth was dry. "Petty dealer, caught up in a sting. Ramos brought him in."

"Yeah. And the next morning, Tovar was found hanged with his shirt. Suicide, supposedly."

Jordan crossed his arms. "Supposedly?"

Nguyen clicked play.

The door opened. Ramos stepped in—same casual swagger, badge flashing. The audio hissed, then steadied.

TOVAR: "I didn't say nothing, man. I swear."

RAMOS: "Then why'd my name come up?"

TOVAR: "They asked who's taking the cash. I told 'em—"

RAMOS: "You didn't see a damn thing."

Ramos moved closer, half off-camera now. His voice dropped, a low growl you could feel more than hear. The picture jittered. A brief struggle. A sharp metallic clang. Ramos glanced up at the camera. Then nothing. Jordan swore vehemently, probably making his grandmother roll over in her grave. I just stared at the screen. What the fuck had I just witnessed?

Nguyen paused the footage. "That's where the file ends. Timestamp 23:46. The system shows it was deleted at 00:01 from Ramos's login."

I stared at the frozen frame. The shadow of Ramos's hand was still on Tovar's shoulder.

Jordan whispered, "Son of a bitch."

Nguyen swallowed. "What do we do with it?"

My throat burned. "He murdered him. In our own damn cellblock."

Jordan rubbed a hand over his face. "We take it to IA."

I laughed—short, bitter. "IA? They're the ones who cleared him. They benched Owen because of his lies. You think they care?"

Nguyen took a step back. Jordan didn't. He moved closer. "Case, listen to yourself."

"I *am* listening. He killed a man and got away with it because everyone looked the other way. Not this time."

"I see what you are thinking. I know you. And you can't go after him alone. You know that."

"I don't care."

"Yes, you do." His voice cracked on it, raw. "You care, because you're the best damn cop I've ever met, and this isn't you. This is not your fault."

I met his eyes, saw the fear under the anger. "How? How is it not my fault?"

"Casey—"

"Jordan, move."

He didn't. For a second, we just stood there—partners,

269

friends, staring across a line neither of us wanted to draw.

Finally, he stepped aside. "You walk out that door, you're not coming back the same."

"Maybe I'm ok with that."

I left without another word, passing the case board on my way out. Keller's face stared back at me from half a dozen printouts, smug as ever. Beside it, the mug shot of Ramos—smirk crooked, eyes daring the camera to accuse him. I had never viewed that familiar half-grin as anything other than friendly. Just something that made Ramos *Ramos*. But now? Now, someone had hung that picture up next to Keller's because... because Ramos was dirty. Guilty. Just as much a criminal as Keller. And that stung more than the damn stitches.

I yanked my badge from my belt and stared at the metal catching the light. It had weight, history, everything I'd bled for. My hands shook once before they went still. I wasn't angry—anger had burned out hours ago. What was left was heavier. A kind of hollow ache that settled in the bones. I'd trusted him. We had sworn the same oath, undergone the same training. But at some point, Ramos had stopped taking down the bad guys and become one. And I had missed every damn sign. I traced the letters on my badge. NOPD. If I'd paid attention—if I'd looked harder—maybe these girls wouldn't be dead. Maybe Owen wouldn't be suspended. Maybe none of this would've fallen apart.

The guilt came in waves, and I let it. Sometimes pain was the only proof you were still human. Then I clipped my badge back to my belt and headed to my car.

I drove without knowing where I was going. Ended up at the docks, like I always did when my brain needed quiet. I loved this city. Growing up, the vibrancy was the only thing that made me feel alive some days. One of the homes I had lived in was over on Camp St. Fifth grade. A woman named Mrs. Moreau would bring the group home fresh bread and sneak us chocolates. Tell us stories about princesses and dragons. Most of the girls wanted to be the princess, but I never wanted to be the girl who needed saving. I wanted to *do* the saving. What I would give for some of her wisdom now. The night was thick with the smell of salt and motor oil, the slap of water against pilings, the low hum of the city fading behind me. When the wind blew, I swore I could smell a hint of her lilac perfume.

I parked and walked until I reached the edge, where the boards creaked under my boots. The lake stretched black and endless. Somewhere out there, lightning flickered behind a curtain of clouds, silent and far away.

I sank onto an overturned crate and stared at the water. The reflection of the city lights rippled, distorted. It looked the way I felt—recognizable but broken.

For a long time, I didn't move. Didn't think. Just breathed. The wind picked up, carrying the smell of rain. I pulled my jacket tighter and tried to rewind it all in my head.

Where did it start?

What had I missed?

Images flickered—Ramos leaning against his desk, lazy grin, always one joke ahead of the tension. The way he brushed off paperwork, laughed too easily, the gut feeling I'd buried more than once because *he's just like that.*

God, I'd let it slide. I'd let *him* slide.

Now, innocents were dead. Owen was benched. Jordan was looking at me like he didn't know who I was.

I whispered to the dark, "What the hell am I supposed to do now?"

No answer came—just the gentle lapping of water against the dock.

I rubbed my hands together for warmth and tried to think like a cop again. If Ramos was running, he'd go somewhere familiar but forgotten. Not far—he wasn't built for disappearing. He'd want a buffer, not exile. Somewhere off the grid but still reachable. Somewhere no one would think to look.

And then, like a slow bleed of memory, it came back. Almost like the water had summoned it.

A barbecue. Summer heat. Ramos half-drunk and telling stories about his uncle's fishing cabin up on Pontchartrain. Said it was old, half rotted, a good place to "unplug." I remembered laughing, telling him the mosquitoes would eat him alive.

He'd grinned and said, *"If it ever all goes to hell, that's where I'm running. No one ever looks for trouble by the water."*

My breath caught. The words slid into place like a puzzle snapping shut.

Of course.

The cabin. The one just on the other side of this very same lake.

I stood, heart pounding—not from anger this time, but from certainty. Every instinct I had screamed that was where he'd gone.

I didn't know what I'd do when I found him. I wasn't sure I even wanted confrontation. Maybe I just wanted to see his face and ask *why*. Why the lies, the bodies, the betrayal. Why he'd traded everything sacred for a little power.

Lightning flashed again, closer now. Rain started in thin lines, cutting through the reflection of the skyline. I didn't move. The city behind me kept breathing, oblivious. The lake stretched out ahead, black and waiting.

And for the first time all day, I felt something like clarity—bitter, fragile, but real.I turned back toward my car, rain dripping off my hair, the echo of his voice still tangled in my head.

Pontchartrain.

If the world was going to give me answers, that's where they'd be.

CHAPTER 17 ◉ OWEN

C asey Chambers pulled out of my driveway at 7:14 a.m. I knew the exact time because I stood in the kitchen, watching her taillights disappear between the houses, one hand braced on the counter, the other wrapped around a mug I wasn't actually drinking from. She'd kissed me once at the door—quick, decisive, the kind of kiss that said *I care about you, but don't ask me to say it again right now,* and then she was gone.

The house went quiet in a way I didn't trust.

I wasn't used to quiet anymore. Not after having her inside these walls. She'd filled the place like oxygen—leaning against my counter in my shirt, cursing my coffee machine, rolling her eyes when I insisted on making her breakfast even though she was clearly three minutes from stealing my keys and driving herself to the precinct.

I looked at the barstool she'd been sitting on an hour earlier. The plate she'd used was rinsed and in the sink. Her smell was faint in the air—my shirt on her skin, the lingering trace of her shampoo.

It hit harder than it should have.

It was too damn early for that kind of nonsense, so I turned away from the kitchen and focused on something I could actually fix.

The bedroom door.

Or what was left of it.

The frame was a splintered crime scene—wood cracked around the bolt, hinge screws bent, the whole thing leaning against the wall like a drunk who'd lost a fight with gravity. I crouched beside the jamb and examined the break.

Yeah. Definitely splintered clean through.

I dragged a hand down my face and exhaled through my nose.

She'd locked herself inside last night. Not because she was pissed—Casey didn't get petty when she was mad. No, she had heard me tell her I loved her for the first damn time and short-circuited like the feral gremlin she was. Instead of saying it back, she made it a game. It was a dare. A "show me," or a "prove you mean it."

And I had.

With power tools.

I picked up the detached section of the frame and tested the break. It'd need wood glue, clamps, sanding, and maybe a prayer. I wasn't talking some hardware-store prayer either. I was talking Latin, candles, and a willing priest.

I stood and carried the broken piece into the living room. The whole time, the echo of last night played—her laugh, her hands in my hair, the way she'd let herself just... be with me. No armor. No badge. No bullshit.

That alone was enough to put a knot under my sternum.

I set the broken frame down on the coffee table, something my ex-wife would've killed me for, and grabbed my tool bag. The good one. The one I used when things actually mattered. I'd been a homicide sergeant for long enough to know how to reconstruct things—timelines, crime scenes, shattered truths.

Wood wasn't much different. You put the pieces back together and hoped the seams held.

I grabbed the wood glue, twisted the cap off, and started working it into the break. The smell hit immediately. Stingy chemical, familiar in a "spent half my twenties fixing rental apartment doors after fights" way.

The glue spread smooth, but as I pressed the pieces together, a hairline crack stayed visible. Not deep. But there.

Just like me.

I clamped the frame and leaned back on my heels.

The house was still too quiet.

I stood up, stretching the tension out of my shoulders. The IA meeting yesterday had left a sour taste in my mouth. The anonymous tip about "excessive force" and a "relationship with a coworker" had clearly landed. They weren't saying it, but they were circling.

And I knew exactly why.

Excessive force? I'd taken suspects down harder than regulation liked. He'd deserved worse.

Relationship with a coworker?

Yeah.

I'd earned that one.

IA knew who the coworker was, but everyone they talked to refused to crow. They had no way to prove it—and I was going to keep it that way until they pried it out of my cold, suspended hands.

I glanced toward the door she'd walked out of.

I'd told her I loved her last night.

Not planned. Not tactical.

It just came out—sharp, honest, raw—while we were standing in the dim light of my living room.

My badge. My woman. I'm keeping both. They don't get to make me choose. I love you.

It hadn't been romance.

It had been truth.

And she'd kissed me like it hadn't blindsided her at all.

That memory got shoved down deep before I could start thinking too hard about it. Thinking too hard about things was how a man got himself twisted up. I preferred action. Movement. Tasks. So I went back to the door. I lifted the actual slab off the hallway floor and inspected the hinge side. Not cracked. Just scuffed. It'd survive.

Which was more than I could say for my patience.

The door shifted in my hands, nearly slipping.

"Don't," I muttered at it. "Not today."

I propped it against the wall and pulled out the power sander. Two minutes of sanding later, the frame already looked better. A couple more passes and it'd look like the door had always been meant to come off the goddamn hinges.

My house was covered in dust.

Great, now I had to vacuum.

I set the sander down and picked up my coffee instead. I took one sip, grimaced, and dumped it in the sink. Casey was right. My machine was a relic from the 90s that sounded like it was brewing resentment instead of coffee.

She'd bullied it into cooperating this morning, which impressed me more than it should have. I poured myself a new cup from the French press sitting on the stove and leaned against the counter. My phone buzzed. IA. I didn't need to answer to know the tone. Tight. Clinical. Accusatory. I answered anyway.

"This is Bishop."

"Sergeant Bishop," the voice said. Detached. Clean. Probably wearing a tie too tight for oxygen flow. "Following up on yesterday's preliminary review."

I kept my voice flat. "Go ahead."

"Concerns remain regarding use of force and potential conduct violations unrelated to the Keller investigation."

Translation:

"We know you're screwing someone at work."

"And you've got a temper."

"What kind of conduct violations?" I asked, just to hear him dance.

"We received an anonymous report alleging a personal relationship with a coworker that may have influenced your actions."

I said nothing.

Silence was powerful. And dangerous. And in this case, necessary.

"You should know," the investigator continued, "that failure to disclose such a relationship is itself considered a breach of policy."

"There is no such relationship," I said.

Technically true. No *disclosed* relationship. And I wasn't about to tell IA anything that would bench Casey. Not when she was carrying half the Keller case alone.

"And the force complaint?" I asked.

"The allegation states you escalated a controlled takedown without supervisor approval."

"That's funny," I said. "Because last I checked, I am the supervisor."

"Sergeant—"

"You want my statement? It's the same one I gave yesterday. Suspect resisted. I responded. End of story."

"That's… insufficient."

"That's all you're getting," I said, and hung up.

I tossed my phone on the counter harder than necessary.

IA didn't bother me. I'd been in this game long enough to know when a review was real and when it was just politics in a cheap suit. This was the second kind. Somebody had filed that tip to throw a wrench into the Keller case. Maybe Keller himself. Maybe someone higher up. Maybe Ramos. That man had his fingers in too many pies and dirt under every fingernail.

But for the life of me, I didn't want Casey anywhere near IA until this was over.

She'd already given more blood to this case than anyone else.

I finished my coffee and went back to the bedroom. The frame still looked stable. The glue had begun to set. I pressed a fingertip to the seam—not perfect, but solid.

Just like her.

The thought made my stomach pull tight.

I didn't like that realization. I wasn't built for big emotional epiphanies. I solved crimes. I fixed messes. I used my badge like a shield and my presence like a threat.

Feelings were messy.

And she'd made a mess of me.

My phone buzzed again. This time, the sound sliced clean through the house, too sharp, too sudden. I grabbed it off the table, expecting IA again. It wasn't.

It was Jordan.

A call, not a text. Something in my chest shifted. Jordan never called unless something was wrong. Very wrong.

"Bishop," I answered.

"Owen," he said. "We got a problem."

Jordan didn't sound like himself. He usually had this easy-going, sarcastic, half-awake tone that made you wonder if anything actually rattled him. But today? Tight. Controlled. Off. That set every alarm I had ringing.

"What happened?" I asked.

He drew in a breath so shaky I could *hear* him trying to hide it.

"It's… look, I'm gonna start with the simple part."

Simple. Right.

"Nguyen found something," Jordan said.

"Found what?"

"A video."

I straightened, tension sliding cold and sharp through my spine. "Details, Delaney. What kind of video?"

"A holding cell recording. Ten months old."

That made me frown. "Ten months? This case isn't that old."

"Exactly," he said. "This predates the Keller mess. Before the joint case. Before any of it."

"So what's on the footage?"

The silence that followed wasn't hesitation. It was dread.

"It's Miguel Tovar."

Name didn't ring a bell. "Who?"

"Small-time dealer. Used to run the edges of the Quarter. Got picked up on drug possession, resisting, some low-level shit. He died in holding. Suicide by shirt."

I didn't like the way Jordan said suicide. Like he already didn't buy it.

"And?" I prompted.

"And," he said carefully, "Ramos brought him in."

"Okay," I said. "Keep going."

"I am trying. Hush and listen."

I grunted but didn't say anything.

"Nguyen was deep in the archives, pulling Keller-adjacent timestamps. Stumbled on a corrupted file. Thought it was nothing. Patched it anyway." He blew out a breath. "It wasn't nothing."

"What did it show?"

"You don't see everything. There's static, glitches, the audio's shit. But you see enough." He paused. "Ramos went into the holding cell alone," he said. "Tovar panicked. Tried to talk. Said somebody in Vice was taking cash off the top. Said he tried to tell detectives last time he was brought in. He mentions our unit. Casey. Ramos. By name."

My jaw clenched because I could already connect the dots.

"Ramos killed him," I said.

"Not on camera," Jordan said slowly. "All we can see is Ramos shoving Tovar. Hard. He pushes him off camera. The camera jumps. There's a scuffle. Then Tovar stops making noise."

My grip tightened around the phone. "And Ramos?"

"Looks straight up," he said. "Right at the camera. Like he's making sure it's still rolling. Then he hits the button panel. Video corrupts. And twelve minutes later, the system logs the file as deleted from Ramos's credentials."

A low, quiet anger started boiling under my ribs.

"And Tovar is dead the next morning?" I asked.

"Yeah," he said. A murder hidden as a suicide. In our own precinct. Ten months before any of us even got close to Keller's operation. A dirty cop doesn't wake up dirty. That kind of rot takes time.

"She saw it, didn't she?"

Jordan took too long to answer. "Yeah," he said. "She saw it."

I pressed a hand against the kitchen counter to steady myself. "When?"

"Maybe two hours ago," he said. "She came in early—no surprise there. Nguyen flagged her when he realized what the hell he was looking at. I told him to wait. She told him to hit play."

Of course she did.

"What'd she do after?" I asked.

"She didn't yell," he said. "Didn't cry. Didn't throw anything. She just... changed."

"How?"

"She's not just my sergeant, she's my best friend," he whispered. "She's funny and smart, and she's got this huge damn heart, but this... this turned her cold. It was like watching gasoline being poured. Nguyen was looking for exits before the match fell."

"Then what?"

"She left. I tried to stop her."

The floor felt like it tilted under me.

"She blamed herself," I muttered.

"She blamed all of us," Jordan corrected. "But mostly herself. And you know how she gets when she thinks something's her fault."

Yeah. I knew exactly how she got. Self-destructive. Laser-focused. Reckless in a way that made survival look optional.

"Where did she say she was going?"

"She didn't. I told her she couldn't handle this alone."

"And?"

"She told me to move."

I shut my eyes for a second. Casey Chambers didn't just walk away when she was that angry. "Jordan," I said quietly, "she's going after him."

"I know," he said. "I tried to get our captain, but he's in with IA. Keller's trial prep is eating everyone alive. And Ramos—Owen, you know how deep he is. You know how many people he's got backing him."

"Not enough," I said.

"Owen—"

"She's going to confront him. And she thinks she has the moral high ground, but he has a ten-month head start and a hell of a lot less to lose."

"That's what I'm afraid of."

Silence stretched. Heavy. Suffocating.

"Where is she now?" I asked.

"We don't know. She shut her radio off."

Of course she did.

"Phone?" I asked.

"You know I can't—"

"Don't say it," I snapped. "Don't say you can't. I'm not asking for a warrant. I'm not asking for IA permission. I'm asking if Nguyen is in the room with you."

Jordan hesitated. A small, guilty inhale. "He is," he admitted. "He's staring at his shoes like he's about to commit a felony."

"Good," I said. "Put me on speaker."

"Owen—"

"Now."

A shuffle. A click. Then Nguyen's anxious voice. "Uh—hey, Sarge."

"Nguyen," I said. "Track her cell."

"Oh God," he groaned. "Okay, that is nowhere near legal."

"That's why I'm not telling you to do it," I said. "I'm telling you to think real hard about how much you care about her."

"I care a lot," he said immediately. "She's terrifying. And my boss."

My voice sharpened. "And she's walking into the lion's den. Find her."

Keys began clacking. "This is such a bad idea," Nguyen muttered. A few seconds later:

"All right, I've got something. Nothing live, but last ping logged at 10:42 a.m."

"Where?" I demanded.

"Uh… lake-facing tower," Nguyen said. "Which means she headed north out of the city. Toward Pontchartrain."

"Nguyen," I said carefully, "is there anything on her phone that suggests where she's headed next? Route? Speed? Anything?"

"No texts, no calls," he said. "But her phone connected to a tower near Old Ferry Road."

Old Ferry Road.

The rural side of the lake. Sparse traffic. Abandoned fishing cabins. Unincorporated land where jurisdiction went fuzzy. A perfect place to leave a body, or two. Jordan swore vehemently.

"Fuck. *Fuck.* I know where she is going. I know where Ramos is," Jordan said, voice low. "His uncle has a cabin on Pontchartrain."

And for the first time all morning, fear punched straight through me—fast, sharp, and cold. "I'm going after her," I said.

"Owen—"

"No," I snapped. "She stepped into this thinking she had justice on her side. Ramos has a head start, a familiar hideout, and a reason to kill her. She needs backup."

"You're suspended," Jordan said. "You can't touch this."

"You called me, remember?"

"I know. Regretting that now. You could lose your badge."

"I'd rather lose my badge than lose her."

It came out before I could stop it.

On the other end of the line, Jordan didn't speak for a moment.

"All right," he said finally, voice heavy. "Then go. And Owen?"

"Yeah?"

"Be fast. Be careful."

I hung up the phone. Didn't bother with goodbyes. He didn't expect one anyway. Shoving my phone into my back pocket, I grabbed my keys off the hook, and was out the front door in seconds. I jogged down the steps two at a time and slid into my truck. Engine roared to life. I tore out of the driveway so fast the back tires spat gravel before punching in the coordinates Nguyen had texted on my GPS.

Old Ferry Road.

The kind of place you chose if you wanted no witnesses.

The kind of place Ramos would go if he knew he was cornered.

Or worse—if he planned to make sure the corner never got closed.

I gripped the wheel, knuckles white. Casey didn't know that terrain like I did. She didn't know what kind of shit people buried out there. Didn't know how many times the lake swallowed evidence whole. She thought she was walking into a confrontation. But she had zero control over the situation which would've scared just about anyone into stopping before they went too far. That was what fear was for. It kept you alive. But Casey? *Ma louve?* She was fearless.

The city blurred behind me. Buildings thinned. The smell of the river gave way to clean, cold lake air. Storm clouds stacked heavy in the distance, the sky that off-gray shade that made the

285

water look darker. My phone buzzed. Jordan again. I hit speaker. "What?"

"Just checking you didn't crash your truck trying to get there."

"Not yet," I said. "That the only reason you called?"

"...Nguyen pulled one more thing," he said. "Wanted you to know."

"Talk."

"After the file corruption, the system logs show two attempts to access that feed. One last week."

"Who tried?"

"Someone using admin credentials," Jordan said. "But the routing makes it look like it was scrubbed. Someone smarter than they should be. You know what that means."

"Ramos knew his cover was slipping."

"Yeah."

"And now Casey knows he's a murderer."

"Yeah."

"And she's alone."

A beat. "...yeah."

"That's just fucking great," I growled. "I'm almost there."

Road narrowed. Trees thickened. Asphalt turned patchy, then rough, then cracked. I eased off the gas to keep from breaking an axle. I took the left fork at the faded sign that said "OLD FERRY—PRIVATE ACCESS." The road dipped, then wound along the water. The lake came into view between gaps in the trees—dark, flat, waiting.

A cluster of old fishing cabins emerged ahead, sagging wood and rusted tin roofs. Most hadn't seen life in years. One sat farther back, half-hidden by brush, dock slanting toward the water like it had given up. I spotted her car before anything else. Parked crooked. Driver's door shut. Lights off. I slammed the truck into park so hard the transmission protested and was out the door before the engine fully died.

"Casey!" I shouted, breath cutting white in the cold air.

No answer.

Nothing but the quiet lap of the lake and the distant rumble of thunder.

I hit the bottom step.

And then—

POP.

A gunshot cracked from inside the cabin, close and vicious, the sound punching through the trees hard enough to shake loose a string of birds.

I stopped breathing.

"Casey!"

Two more shots followed—**POP. POP.**

Shorter, sharper, too loud and too fast.

My body reacted before my brain did. Before caution. Before training. Before anything that resembled sense. I charged the stairs, boots hammering against the rotted wood, heart slamming into my ribs so hard it hurt. One board collapsed under me—I didn't slow. I vaulted the last two steps, grabbed the railing, and threw myself at the door just as—

The world tunneled. Sound thinned. Nothing existed but her name roaring in my skull.

"Casey!"

I hit the door with my shoulder—wood cracked under the impact.

I hit it again.

The lock groaned.

One more hit—

The door splintered.

287

I stumbled inside just as the echoes of those two shots faded into a ringing, suffocating silence. And for a split second, I didn't know if she was alive. Didn't know if I still had a reason for breathing. Didn't know anything past the all-consuming need to get to her.

CHAPTER 18 ♦ CASEY

I knew I was doing something stupid long before the cabin
came into view.

That was the thing about terrible decisions—they usually
didn't arrive like hurricanes or sirens. They arrived quiet. Slow.
They started as a thought you should've shut down quickly, but
didn't. Then a second one that made the first easier to justify.
Then a third. And suddenly you were alone on Old Ferry Road,
edging toward the kind of mistake cops whispered about in
locker rooms. But I wasn't turning around. Couldn't. The
moment Nguyen hit play on that corrupted footage, something
inside me broke open.

Not rage. Not shock. Not grief.

Something... older. Something bone-deep.

A man murdered in our own cellblock. Criminal or not. A
cover-up. A dirty cop smiling into a camera he thought he
controlled.

And I'd missed him. Missed it. For months. Years, maybe.
People had died because I hadn't connected the threads fast
enough. So yeah—I was crossing a line. I could feel it with
every mile the tires chewed through. The patrol radio was off.
My phone on silent. Badge resting heavy at my hip. I wasn't on
duty. This wasn't sanctioned. This wasn't smart.

But the guilt pressed down so hard I could barely breathe, and guilt was the one thing I couldn't outrun. It had teeth. Claws. A voice that didn't whisper so much as hiss: *If you'd been sharper, louder, braver... Keller wouldn't have gotten this far. Those girls wouldn't be buried. Owen wouldn't be suspended. Tovar wouldn't be dead.*

So I drove.

The trees thickened as the road narrowed, branches reaching overhead like fingers. A storm was stacking over the lake—dark clouds bruised purple, the kind that made the air heavy, electric. Lightning flickered somewhere beyond the water. I rolled down the window. Cold air knifed in. Didn't help. The closer I got, the more everything sharpened—my breathing, my pulse, the grip of my gun beside me.

"You're being reckless," I muttered to myself.

Reckless wasn't new to me. But this? No backup. No plan. Just me and the man who'd dragged half my department into hell. When the cabin appeared through the trees, I killed the engine and sat for a moment, gripping the wheel, staring at the sagging porch and the half-rusted tin roof.

I got out, circled around the back, gun drawn. The hinges on the back door were rusted through; one quiet push and they gave, the frame groaning like it resented being disturbed.

The smell hit me first: old coffee, mildew, lake rot. A duffel on the table overflowed with cash, clothes, burner phones. He was running. I slipped inside, silent. Ramos was near the counter, back turned, phone in hand. "Don't move."

He froze. Slowly—so slowly I felt my finger tighten on the trigger—he turned. And his face said everything. He knew why I was here.

"Chambers," he breathed. "I hoped it wouldn't be you."

"Hands up," I said.

He raised them. Not enough.

"All the way."

Jaw clenched, he lifted them higher.

For a heartbeat, we just stared at each other—two cops trained under the same oath, standing in the ruins of everything we'd sworn to protect.

"You saw the video," he said.

I didn't ask how he knew. What difference it made. "Explain it," I demanded.

He laughed—a bitter, empty sound. "Explain it? Casey, I've been trying to explain it to myself for almost a year."

"You murdered a man."

"He was a liability."

"He was scared. He was trying to talk to us—"

"Exactly," he snapped. "He knew things. About Vice. About me. He was going to sell me out."

"And you silenced him."

"I protected the department," he shot back. "Protected you. My job."

"You don't get to say that," I hissed. "You don't get to hide behind our badge after everything you've done."

He dragged a hand down his face, laugh breaking like glass. "You think I wanted this? You think this was the plan? It started as nothing. A little extra cash. Turning a blind eye here. Passing intel there. I told myself it wasn't hurting anyone."

"It did."

"I know," he whispered. "I know."

He lowered his hands a fraction—not enough to grab a gun, but enough to tell me he wasn't fully surrendering.

"You could've come to me," I said. "I would've helped you."

291

"Helped me?" He barked a humorless laugh. "Casey, you have the tightest moral compass in the damn building. You would've dragged me by the ear into our captain's office."

"Because you needed help."

"I didn't need help!" he snapped. "I needed a chance. We sell our souls to this city and for what? Nothing. Nothing but pain and regret and loneliness."

That made something sting deep in my chest.

"You still had a choice."

"No," he said quietly, defeat settling on him like dust. "I stopped having choices the moment Keller realized I could be useful."

Silence.

Thick. Heavy.

We were so locked on each other—the gun, the truth, the betrayal—that the shift in the air didn't register. Not the faint crunch outside. Not the shadow crossing the doorway. Not the presence slinking through the frame like a ghost. Not until Ramos's eyes moved. Not toward me.

Past me.

I turned instinctively—

POP.

The gunshot slammed into the cabin like a grenade.

Ramos dropped before I even understood what happened—head snapping sideways, blood painting the wall behind him in a wide, terrible spray.

I barely had time to inhale. Time froze. My heart lurched.

I started to turn—

POP. POP.

Two more shots tore through the air.

Pain exploded through my side and back so violently the

world blinked white. I stumbled, breath ripped from my lungs, knees buckling as fire bloomed under my ribs. My gun slipped from my grip, fingers suddenly numb.

The second bullet hit lower—a white-hot punch that stole all the air I had left. My vision stuttered, my body refusing to stay upright. Every nerve screamed. My legs gave.

I hit the floor hard—hip, shoulder, cheek—a wet warmth spreading fast beneath me.

I gasped, but the air wouldn't come. My lungs spasmed uselessly. The pain was *everywhere*—sharp, crushing, radiating down my spine and into my ribs like someone had set me on fire from the inside out. The metallic taste of blood climbed up the back of my throat. My fingers twitched, reaching for my gun on instinct.

Footsteps crossed the cabin. Measured. Calm. Almost… elegant.

Mrs. Keller stepped fully into the doorway like she was arriving for brunch—tan coat, neat bun, gun still raised with a surgeon's precision. Pearls around her throat. Not a single tremor in her hands.

My stomach dropped through the floor.

"Pretty good shot, aren't I?" she said lightly, as if commenting on the weather. "Who do you think taught my son how to shoot?"

A cold shock tore through me, stronger than the pain.

Mrs. Keller?

No.

No, that wasn't right. She was grieving. She was a victim. She'd wept in my arms.

My lips parted. "You…"

"Tsk." She stepped over the blood delicately, like she didn't want to scuff her shoes. "Please don't look so shocked. I was just coming to tie up loose ends. I told myself I'd only deal with that one today—but imagine my good fortune… two pests in one nest."

My body curled involuntarily as the pain sharpened, tearing through my abdomen in waves. A strangled groan slipped out before I could stop it. She smiled. Like she enjoyed it.

"I would've gotten you cleanly," she mused, "but you turned at the wrong second. Such a shame your reflexes are good. A little twist of your spine, and those bullets dipped lower than I intended. You'll bleed out slower."

I tried to lift my head, but the room swayed so violently I had to slam my palm against the bloody floorboards to keep myself from blacking out right then. My breath hitched. My chest seized. Every heartbeat was a knife. I could feel warmth soaking my shirt, sliding down my waist, pooling beneath my hip. My sight tunneled—edges going dark, narrowing to the shape of her boots, her gun, her smile.

"You're…" My voice cracked. "You're behind all this."

"Oh, sweetheart." She crouched beside Ramos's body, brushing a strand of hair off his bloody forehead as if comforting a child. "All this? I've been behind this for *years*. My daughter, a victim of a city that never cared. My son, a soldier who tried to do everything right and was still shunned. When he came to me with the idea, well… he got that intelligence from me, if I do say so myself."

My pulse hammered wildly—from pain, from fear, from the horrifying puzzle pieces snapping together. Mrs. Keller. The sweet mother. The grieving widow. The quiet woman in pearls and soft cardigans.

The puppeteer.

The room tilted again. A ringing settled in my ears, drowning out her footsteps as she moved toward me.

I couldn't breathe.

Couldn't think.

Could barely keep my eyes open.

"I should thank you, really," she said. "I didn't expect you to come out here. Saves me a drive."

I forced my hand toward my holster, even though I knew my gun was out of reach. Muscle memory, desperation—didn't matter. She saw it and laughed.

"Oh, darling," she said. "That's adorable."

Pain ripped through me again—a sharp, squeezing agony under my ribs that made my whole torso jerk. A choked cry tore from my throat, unbidden. I was going to die here. Alone. Unarmed. On a rotten floor. With a bullet in my lung and another in my side. Killed by a woman who had fed me lies in a darkened living room.

I blinked hard, fighting the black creeping into my vision.

And then—

CRASH.

The front door exploded inward. Boots hammered the wood. A shadow filled the doorway. "Owen?" I whispered, disbelief cutting through the pain. He was suspended. He wasn't supposed to be here. He couldn't have known where I'd gone. How the hell—

"CASEY!"

His voice cracked on the second syllable—fear tearing through it. Real, gut-deep, raw fear. Through the blur, I saw him—wide-eyed, jaw clenched, gun raised, shoulders coiled like a man bracing for hell. Mrs. Keller's head snapped toward him. My hair stuck to my cheek.

Blood trickled into my mouth. I tried to lift my hand toward him—just a little—just enough.

He shouldn't be here. He shouldn't see this. I had to warn him, she was armed. My vision buckled. The cabin tilted sideways. My body folded, collapsing into the spreading warmth beneath me. Owen shouted my name again—louder this time, desperate—but the darkness swallowed the rest.

And I let go.

CHAPTER 19 ◆ CASEY

The world came back in pieces.

First was sound. A slow, steady beep. Then another. Then the faint hiss of air somewhere above me.

Next was weight. My body felt like it'd been poured full of cement. Heavy, wrong, like I'd been sleeping under a collapsed building instead of some blankets.

Pain drifted in last. At first it was just a pressure at my side and along my back, dull and distant. Then it sharpened as I tried to breathe deeper—a hot, stabbing slice under my ribs that shivered through my whole chest. I groaned before I could stop myself. That was when I realized my throat felt raw. Dry. Like someone had scraped it with sandpaper and then dared me to swallow.

"Hey." The voice was low, gentle, a little frayed around the edges.

"Casey. You with me?"

I tried to pry my eyelids open. They felt glued down. A couple of blinks later, the room slowly swam into focus—white ceiling, dim light, a curtain half-drawn. A monitor glowed to my right, lines dancing in time with the beeping. Hospital. I was in a hospital.

Great.

I turned my head, just enough to find the source of the voice, and nearly swallowed my tongue. "Marco?"

Jordan's husband was sitting in the chair by the window, big frame slouched forward, hands clasped loosely between his knees. His dark hair was pulled back in a ponytail, scruff heavier than usual. He looked tired as hell, but when I focused on him, his whole expression eased. "Hey, there," he said, standing up. "Welcome back."

It took effort to get my tongue to cooperate. "What... the... fuck?"

The words came out rough, half-whispered. Even that tiny movement made my chest twinge.

He huffed a quiet laugh. "I'd say 'watch your language,' but after the last forty-eight hours, you've earned it."

"Forty-eight...?" My brows tried to knit together. That hurt too.

He moved closer to the bed. Not crowding, just... there. Calm. Solid. The kind of presence you could lean on without feeling weak for it. "You've been out a couple days," he said softly. "On and off. Mostly off."

A couple days. My brain felt sluggish, like it was trying to run through molasses. I chased the last clear memory I had—the cabin, the lake, Ramos, the gun— Mrs. Keller. The shots. My heart spiked hard enough that the monitor tattled on me with a shrill jump in tempo.

Marco immediately lifted his hands in a slow-down gesture, eyes on mine. "Hey. Hey. Breathe. It's all right."

"Ramos," I rasped. "Mrs. Keller—"

"Not yet," he said firmly. "You try to sit up or solve a case right now, and Jordan is going to kick my ass for not stopping you."

298

I swallowed. It felt like trying to drag gravel down a straw. "Water?"

He grabbed a plastic cup from the bedside tray, slipped a straw toward my mouth. "Tiny sips, Casey. Not a chugging contest."

I took a small drink. Cold water hit the back of my throat like heaven and razor blades. I let my head sink back against the pillow. Everything hurt. Not in one place. Everywhere. My side burned, my back throbbed, there was an ache in my shoulder like I'd fallen wrong. My left hand had an IV taped in place, a pulse ox clipped to my finger. There was tape on my chest I didn't want to think about. "Did I... lose?" I managed.

He raised a brow. "Lose what?"

"Felt like... someone dropped a truck... on me."

"That would be the gunshot wounds," he said dryly.

Right. Those. Memory flickered again. Ramos's eyes when he realized I'd seen the video. His hands half-raised. His voice saying *I never meant for it to go this far.* Then the sound—that first gunshot, too close, too loud. The way his head snapped sideways. The blood. The spray. Then the second and third shots. The fire ripping through my side and back. The way the floor had rushed up to meet me. Mrs. Keller's face, calm and cold as she stepped over a body. Her smile. My stomach lurched. The heart monitor beeped an alarm.

"Casey." Marco's voice sharpened. "Stay with me."

I realized I'd shut my eyes. Forced them open again. "Sorry," I muttered.

"Don't be sorry," he said. "Just don't code on me again, yeah?"

"Again?" I croaked.

Something flickered across his face. "Yeah. You, uh... gave everybody a bit of a show on the way into surgery."

I tried to shift, and white-hot pain tore through my ribs so viciously I sucked in a breath and immediately regretted it. A broken sound escaped—more animal than human.

Marco's hand hovered over the rail, like he wanted to grab me but knew he shouldn't. "Okay, that's your body reminding you it's full of holes. Do not move like that again unless you want to meet Jesus."

"Jesus... is gonna... have to wait," I wheezed.

"Good," he said. "Jordan would fight him for you, and that would be awkward."

"Where is he?"

"Jordan? He's fine." A quick, reassuring smile. "Pretty sure he wore a trail in the linoleum outside in the hallway."

I let my eyes fall shut for a second. Everything inside me throbbed. "And Owen?" The words slipped out before I could block them.

Marco's smile softened in a way that made something in my chest twist. "He's... around."

"Around?" I pushed. If he had been shot too, I would never forgive myself.

"Yeah. As in—I have personally witnessed that man sit in that same damn chair for so many hours my lower back started hurting out of sympathy." He pointed at the window seat. "It took both me and a nurse threatening to sedate him to make him go get coffee."

I swallowed. Hard. Pain shot down my throat. Owen was ok. Physically, at least. "He shouldn't be here," I murmured. "He's suspended..."

Marco tilted his head. "Yeah, well, he's also stubborn as hell, in case you haven't noticed. And Jordan wasn't much better, so I sent both of them to get food so someone sane could sit with you until you woke up."

"You?" I whispered.

He shrugged. "Jordan wouldn't calm down until I promised to stay. And Owen... well, I don't think he trusted himself not to break a chair if he stayed any longer."

I almost smiled. It hurt too much. "Ramos?" I asked before I could stop myself.

Marco's brows pulled together. "I don't know everything. Just what Jordan mumbled between pacing fits." A pause. "He said one suspect didn't make it. The other did."

Mrs. Keller. A chill skated down my spine. My breathing hitched. The monitor blipped loudly.

"Casey," Marco warned, "you do not get to have a panic attack while attached to that many wires."

I forced myself to breathe—slow, shallow, even though it felt like something sharp had lodged under my ribs. A nurse walked by the door, did a double-take through the window, then vanished down the hall—probably to grab vitals equipment.

Marco sighed. "Great. Jordan's gonna sense movement like a damn velociraptor."

I blinked at him, confused.

He nodded toward the door with a grimace. "He's been waiting for you to wake up so he can yell at you for scaring the shit out of him. It's his love language."

I opened my mouth to respond—the door swung inward. The nurse stepped in with her tablet.

And from the hallway came Jordan's voice. Already talking at top speed, "—I swear to God, if she's awake and you didn't tell me, Marco, I'm going to end this marriage either with divorce or murder."

Marco gave me a look of apology that said *brace yourself.* I didn't have time to. Because Jordan Delaney slammed into the

301

doorway like a Category 5 hurricane with emotional issues.

He hit the doorway like the hospital had called a code blue on *his* self-control.

"Casey Chambers, I swear to all things good and holy—"

The nurse barely got out, "Sir, you need to—" before Jordan barreled straight past her like she was a light breeze instead of a trained professional with needles.

He skidded to my bedside, hands hovering, eyes wild. "You brave, dumb, beautiful woman who I love more than is reasonable, what the *hell* were you thinking? I swear to God, I will chain you to a desk, I will handcuff you to your bedframe—wait, no, Owen would kill me—Casey, why would you—"

"Jordan," I rasped.

"And don't 'Jordan' me! Two days! Two days I've been in this building thinking you died! I have gray hairs now! I counted them! Marco counted them too! I—Casey, Jesus, you look like you got hit by a truck—"

The nurse cleared her throat sharply. "Sir, I *need* you to move so I can check her vitals."

Jordan swung around with the offense of a man personally attacked. "Ma'am, with all due respect, I have earned this moment—"

"Jordan," Marco warned from the corner, voice low.

Jordan huffed, hands flailing. "Fine. But I am staying in the room. You cannot stop me. Casey, blink twice if you want me to stay—"

The nurse gave him a single look over the rim of her glasses. A look that said she had ended bigger men than him with her clipboard alone. Jordan sat in the chair. Immediately. Like someone had shoved his strings down. "Sorry," he muttered.

She began checking the wires, IVs, monitors, the whole

routine. "How's your pain?" she asked me.

"Bad," I admitted.

Jordan's head snapped toward me, outraged at the idea that I might be in pain and he couldn't physically fistfight it. "She needs more meds," he declared to the nurse. "The good stuff. The stuff that makes you taste colors and ask strangers philosophical questions."

The nurse ignored him. "Any dizziness?"

"Some," I said.

"How's your breathing?"

"Terrible."

"Well, you were shot in the lung," she said calmly. "So that makes sense."

Jordan made a noise like someone was wringing his neck. Marco gave him a look like it was tempting. The nurse checked the dressing on my side, then the one on my back, then the drainage tube.

Marco stepped closer, leaning down to murmur in his husband's ear. "Babe, breathe."

"Don't tell me to breathe, she's the one who—"

The door creaked again. Jordan froze mid-rant. Even the nurse paused. Because there he was. Owen. Standing just inside the doorway, tall and broad and frighteningly still. His clothes were rumpled, eyes shadowed, jaw dark with a couple days' worth of scruff. He looked like a man who hadn't slept, eaten, or taken a full breath since the moment he found me bleeding out.

For a second, he didn't move. Didn't blink. Didn't speak. He just stared at me. And something in his face—something raw and wrecked—punched the air right out of my tattered lungs.

"Owen," I whispered. He finally stepped into the room, slow

and quiet, as if afraid I'd disappear if he moved wrong. He didn't go straight to me. He didn't shove Jordan aside. He didn't say a word. He stood at the foot of the bed like a man bracing against an earthquake.

The nurse finished up her checks, completely oblivious to the emotional pile-up unfolding around her. "I'm going to page the doctor," she said. "She'll want to know you're awake."

Jordan immediately stood. "Perfect, I'll go get her—"

"No, you won't," Marco snapped, grabbing the collar of his jacket before he could sprint into the hallway like a bat out of hell.

"Marco," Jordan protested, "my best friend almost died, I am allowed—"

"And now she's awake," Marco said patiently, "and she needs space to breathe without you reenacting a telenovela in her face."

Jordan's jaw dropped. "A telenovela?! I'll have you know this is—"

"Ok. Outside," Marco ordered, already nudging him toward the door.

Jordan turned back to me with wide, frantic eyes. "Casey, I swear I love you, but I am going to murder you when you can walk again—"

"Jordan," I breathed, exhausted but amused. "I'm okay."

"You are very much not okay!" He pointed at the machines. "You are plugged into more electronics than a RadioShack!"

Marco dragged him out by the elbow, still protesting, still talking, still dramatically offended. The door clicked shut behind them. And the room went quiet. Except for the silence stretching between me and the man who almost lost me. Owen still didn't speak. He simply stood there, breathing shallowly, like if he let himself fully exhale, he'd fall apart.

His eyes were locked on me—haunted, furious, relieved, all tangled up in ways that made my heart stumble. He looked... wrecked. Not physically. Physically, he looked like Owen Bishop: tall, broad, solid, carved out of concrete and bad decisions. But emotionally?

He looked like a man who'd been walking around with a bullet lodged in his chest for two days.

"Owen," I whispered again, softer this time.

Something in him cracked. Not audibly. Not visibly. But I felt it. He moved—slowly, like approaching a wounded animal. He walked up the side of the bed and stopped within arm's reach but didn't touch me. His hands hovered, hesitant, as if he wasn't sure he'd be allowed.

"You're awake," he said finally, voice low and rough.

"Apparently," I rasped.

A huff of breath left him. Not quite a laugh. Not quite a sob.

He dragged a chair so close to my bed, I was worried he would end up in it. Up close, he looked even worse. His eyes were bloodshot and his jaw was clenched tight enough to crack molars. There were faint scratches along his wrist, like he'd shoved through brush or broken wood. Probably from the cabin. I swallowed. It burned. He noticed and immediately grabbed the water, holding it to my lips without a word. His hand shook just slightly.

When I'd taken a sip, he set it down and rested his elbows on his knees, leaning in until his face was level with mine. "Casey," he said quietly, "you scared the hell out of me."

Guilt punched me in the ribs harder than the bullets had. "I'm sorry," I whispered.

The look he gave me could've stopped a charging bull. "Don't.

Don't you dare apologize."

"I shouldn't have gone alone—"

"No." The word came out sharp, almost snapped. "You shouldn't have. But you did. And I'm not mad at you. I'm—" He broke off, jaw flexing. "Jesus, I don't even know what I am."

I blinked at him. "You're... tired?"

That earned the tiniest, pained smile. "Understatement of the year."

He reached up like he wanted to touch my face. His fingers stopped an inch from my cheek. Trembled. Lowered.

"Owen," I murmured, "you can... it's okay."

His breath hitched. Just once. Then he touched me. His fingers brushed the side of my jaw, and the contact was so tender it hurt worse than the bruises. "You almost died," he whispered.

My throat tightened. "So did you. Running in like that."

His eyes flickered. "I didn't care. I didn't think. I just— I saw you on the ground and everything went silent. Except your breathing. Or what was left of it."

I closed my eyes, fighting back a wave of emotion I wasn't ready for. He wasn't done.

"They had to pull me off the EMTs twice," he said. "Jordan threatened to tase me. A nurse threatened to sedate me. I—" His voice wavered and he stopped, jaw tightening to restrain something raw. "I've never felt anything like that in my life."

I forced myself to meet his eyes. "I'm here. I came back to you."

"I know." He exhaled shakily. "But for two days, I wasn't sure you would." He leaned back only enough to look me over—my bandages, the machines, the bruising he could see above the neckline of the gown. "You were shot twice," he said quietly, as if I'd missed that part. "One near your kidney. One that collapsed your lung. You coded once in the ambulance and again in surgery. They weren't sure if—"

His voice broke. Actually broke. Hearing him choke on the words did something violent to my heart.

"I'm sorry," I whispered again. "I didn't want—"

"Stop." He shook his head, pain etched into every movement. "You don't get to be sorry for almost dying. You don't get to carry this one. Stop apologizing."

I swallowed hard. "Then what do I get to do?"

"Recover," he said immediately. "Stay alive. Let us handle the rest."

"Us?"

His jaw set. "Me. Jordan. Harper. Half the damn department. Even Thibodeaux."

That pulled a faint, baffled sound from me. "Thibodeaux?"

Owen scrubbed a hand down his face. "Yeah. He barged into IA like a bull in a china shop and ripped them a new one. Called them—" He cleared his throat. "A bunch of panty-twisting morons who wouldn't know real police work if it pissed on their shoes."

I let out a breathy laugh. "Sounds like him."

"Yeah, well. He also threatened to bury their careers if they didn't reinstate me."

My eyes widened. "You—you got your badge back?"

He nodded once. "As of this morning."

The relief hit so hard my eyes stung. We sat there for a moment, the quiet settling again. Not the panicked kind from before. Something softer. Heavier. Real. Then his expression shifted.

"What happened out there?" he asked, voice low.

307

I swallowed. "Ramos was there. He was running. He said he never meant for it to go this far. I think he was going to turn himself in or disappear—I don't know. But he wasn't the one who shot me."

Owen's hand fisted on his knee. "I know."

"Mrs. Keller," I whispered.

His jaw flexed. "Yeah. She's in custody."

I closed my eyes. "She killed him. Shot him before I could even—"

"Casey." His voice softened immediately. "You are not responsible for his death. Or for hers. Or for any of this."

"I should've seen it."

"No," he said firmly. "You should've been able to trust the people you worked with. That's it. That's the beginning and end of the whole damn story."

Silence. His hand reached for mine again. This time, he didn't hesitate. He took it gently, warm and steady against my cold fingers.

"Casey," he murmured, "I thought I lost you."

"You didn't," I whispered back.

"I almost did."

"But you didn't."

He bowed his head for a moment, shoulders shaking once— barely, but enough that I felt it through the mattress. When he looked up again, something had settled behind his eyes. Something fierce and unyielding. "I'm not going anywhere," he said. "Not now. Not ever. You don't get to leave me like that." It wasn't a plea or a demand. It was a vow.

"Hey," I whispered, "come here. Please."

He stood, leaned over the rails, and pressed his forehead gently to mine. Careful. Controlled. But trembling. I squeezed his hand weakly. He squeezed back. I reached up for him, and brought his face to mine. When he kissed me, it felt like coming home.

CHAPTER 20 ◉ OWEN

They wheeled her out of the hospital like she was fragile. Anyone who'd ever met Casey Chambers knew she was anything but. Still, after watching her bleed out on a floorboard with a collapsed lung, I didn't trust the air around her not to be too sharp. The nurse handed her a stack of discharge papers. Casey didn't look at them—just adjusted the blanket over her lap with a frown that tried, and failed, to look tough.

Jordan and Marco were waiting at the curb. Jordan immediately launched into a speech.

"You're alive! Barely! But alive! And therefore, we're doing things my way now—"

"Jordan," Casey croaked, "shut up."

He shut up. For three seconds. Then he pointed at me. "You're taking her to your house."

Casey snorted. "No. He's not. I live five minutes away."

"Casey, *ma louve*," I said as gently as I could. "You need someone to take care of you."

She gave me an offended, incredulous look. "That's bullshit."

"No, it's not. Read the papers," I said. I grabbed the bars of the wheelchair, pushing her towards my truck and using the opportunity to lean down and whisper in her ear. "You're not staying alone. Be a good girl and listen for once."

Silence. Not angry silence. More like: Goddammit, he's right and I hate it. But she wouldn't be Casey if she didn't argue. She lifted her chin. "Owen, I can take care of myself."

"Yeah," I said quietly. "And two weeks ago, you did. But right now, you can barely sit upright without swaying. You're coming with me."

She opened her mouth. Closed it. She looked... tired. Not defeated—Casey never quit—but bone-deep exhausted in a way that made my chest tighten.

"Temporarily," she said.

"Fine." A small lie I didn't feel guilty about.

The ride to my place was quiet. The kind of quiet that settled into your bones. She stared out the window, one arm wrapped around her rib cage like she was holding herself together. I didn't miss the way she flinched every time the truck hit a bump. When we pulled into the driveway, I got out and reached her door.

"Don't hover," she muttered, even though she offered me her hand when she stepped down.

"Not hovering," I lied again. "Just... supervising."

"You're a terrible liar."

"Funny. I used to be good at it."

She didn't smile, but her eyes softened.

Inside, I'd already set up a spot on my bed— pillows, blankets, her meds lined up with military precision, water bottles, remote within reach, the works. I'd even cleared my side table, which hadn't been cleared since the Saints were in the playoffs. She paused in the doorway, eyeing the split in the wood and smiling before sitting very slowly on the mattress.

Then she looked at all the prep work and muttered, "You're

311

nesting."

"You say it like it's an insult."

"It is."

"You being alive is worth nesting."

She rolled her eyes but didn't argue for once. She slept most of that first day. And most of the next.

I didn't.

I stayed close. Read over old case files just to keep my hands busy. Stared at the spot under her collarbone where the bruise from the bullet impact still bloomed purple and black. Listened to her breathing like a man who'd spent two days wondering if it would stop. She woke up twice gasping from nightmares. Once she pushed herself upright too fast and nearly passed out. I caught her before she hit the floor.

"I'm fine," she whispered.

"You're not," I said. "And that's okay."

She didn't answer, but she didn't pull away either.

They played Bryce Keller's arraignment on TV three days after she came home. The prosecutor laid everything out. How Keller's sister OD'd on a batch Ramos sold back onto the street, how Keller spiraled, how his mother bankrolled the entire operation out of revenge and resentment. When they showed Margaret Keller in cuffs, Casey's jaw tightened.

"I knew Ramos made mistakes," she murmured. "I knew he crossed lines. But this—"

She shook her head. "I don't know how to categorize this level of betrayal."

"You don't," I said. "You don't have to. He made his choices."

"And I was in charge of him."

"Casey—"

She held up a hand. Not telling me off—just stopping herself from spiraling. "It still feels like I missed something huge," she said.

"You didn't," I told her. "He hid this entire mess from all of us. And Keller? He didn't kill those girls because of Ramos. He killed them because he wanted someone to blame for the pain he couldn't understand." Her stare stayed locked on the muted screen—photos of Keller being led through the courthouse.

She whispered, "It still hurts."

"I know." There wasn't anything else to say.

Ramos's funeral was small. Quiet. Sparse. Wrong. No flag. No honors. No ceremony. Just a handful of people in dark coats standing around a coffin that looked heavier than the truth they were burying. A sister I didn't know he had, who refused to look anywhere but the hole in the ground, and a mother who couldn't stop crying.

Casey insisted on going. "He made terrible choices," she said. "But he was mine. He was my detective."

I stood beside her, close enough that she could lean if she needed to. She didn't. But she shook once when they lowered the casket. She whispered something. I didn't catch it. Didn't need to. I doubted the words were for me. When we got back to the truck, she sat there staring straight ahead. For a long time. Then: "I hate funerals."

"Yeah."

"And I hate what he did."

"Yeah."

"And I hate that part of me still feels responsible."

"You're responsible for your team," I said softly. "Not for their secrets."

Her eyes flicked toward me. "Feels the same."

"I know it feels the same," I said. "Doesn't make it true."

Her throat worked. "Thanks."

I nodded, and she curled her finger at me. A silent, "come here." I did so, helpless to do anything but obey. I kissed her gently, still mindful of her injuries, and she groaned then bit me when I refused to deepen the kiss. I chuckled and wrapped her hand in mine. We sat there listening to the rain on the roof until she finally leaned her head back and whispered, "Take me home."

I did. And that night, she didn't wake from a nightmare. The day after Ramos's funeral, Thibodeaux called me into his office. Normally, when he did that, I brace for one of three things: a lecture, a threat disguised as mentorship, paperwork he didn't want to do. This time? He was grinning. Which was alarming.

"Close the door, Bishop," he said. I did. He leaned back in his chair, hands folded over his stomach. "Head of Internal Affairs called me."

I blinked. "To fire me?"

"To praise you," he said. "Which was disgusting. I feel unclean."

I stared.

He smirked. "Called in that favor he owed me. Reminded him about San Antonio. And his wife. And the little secret we kept from her."

Great; now *I* felt unclean. "The fuck does that mean?"

"It means," he said, smug as hell, "Internal Affairs is officially choosing to be blind, deaf, and stupid about whatever is going on with you and Chambers."

I sat. Hard. He continued, tone even smugger now, "As long as you two keep solving cases at the rate you have been, IA doesn't care if you're braiding each other's hair at shift change."

"We don't—" I started.

He waved a hand. "Save it. I don't want details. I'm too old and too emotionally constipated for romance."

I rubbed my jaw. "They're just... giving up?"

He shrugged. "They don't want the PR nightmare. Keller's case blew up in their faces, Ramos made them look incompetent, and the mayor wants it over with. You two are the only part of this shitstorm that isn't an embarrassment."

I didn't know whether to laugh or curse.

He leaned forward. "Just don't be stupid. Don't give them a reason to change their minds. Don't start making out in the hallway."

My eye twitched. "We don't—"

"I said I don't want details."

I didn't dare mention the supply closet and left his office thoroughly confused and somehow more stressed. But IA stayed quiet. Real quiet. No more interviews. No follow-ups. No carefully-worded questions about "unprofessional relationships." They just... backed off.

Cowards. Any sign of a fight and they tucked tail. But I wasn't complaining.

Casey's recovery moved at two speeds. Glacial and wildfire. Some days she slept twelve hours straight and still couldn't keep her eyes open. Some days she sat at my kitchen table with her Vice laptop, glaring at her inbox like she could intimidate her lungs into working faster.

"Light duty only," the doctor warned her at every appointment.

Casey lied every time and said, "Of course."

The woman didn't know who she was dealing with. At home, she was still stubborn as hell. I'd walk into the living room and catch her trying to fold laundry.

315

"Casey."

"It's one towel."

"You got shot in the lung."

"It's a small towel."

"Sit your ass down."

She glared every time. Sat every time. If I wasn't careful, I was going to enjoy this power way too much.

Domesticity wasn't something I'd ever planned for. Not with anyone. Not after the marriage I'd tanked years ago. Not in this line of work. But with Casey? It just... happened. There was a second toothbrush in my bathroom. Her shampoo in my shower. Her books on my nightstand. Her boots by the door. She stole half my T-shirts. Slept on my side of the bed even when I was in it. Complained about my coffee maker until I bought a new one.

Every night after a shift, I'd walk in to find her asleep on the couch, blanket around her shoulders, chest rising and falling slow and steady. Sometimes she'd wake up and blink at me like she wasn't sure whether to kiss me or punch me. Other times, I would pick her up and carry her to bed. Both options worked for me. After a while, God apparently decided to test my patience in other ways, and I was soon having every ounce of willpower tested. I would remind her about the whole light duty bit, and she would get mad. Then sashay through the living room in nothing but her underwear. I couldn't decide if I was blessed or cursed.

A couple weeks into her recovery, Jordan insisted on a barbecue. "Everyone needs closure," he declared, hands on his hips like a suburban mom. "We're doing food. And feelings. And hamburgers."

"We are not doing feelings," I said.

"Oh, you aren't. You're hopeless," he said. "But Casey's getting emotional support therapy."

Casey flipped him off from the couch.

Jordan pointed at her. "That's a yes."

Casey looked at me. "If he tries to hug me, I'm leaving."

"He's definitely going to hug you. Besides, weren't you telling me you needed more physical contact to 'aid in your recovery' last night?"

She raised an eyebrow at my air quotes before glaring at me. "Not what I meant, smart-ass."

The barbecue was... weirdly nice. Jordan and Marco commandeered my grill. Harper brought potato salad. With eggshells still in it. Delightful. Crawford brought beer he insisted was "artisanal," which meant it tasted like someone had melted a pinecone. Nguyen brought a laminated three-page grilling safety checklist. Casey sat in a lawn chair wrapped in a blanket like an injured raccoon. Occasionally, she would try and get up to help with something she had no business helping with and we all took turns yelling at her. But still, she was smiling.

Jordan hovered. Harper teased her. Marco kept handing her water like she was an overheated toddler. Crawford made snide comments about my grilling technique. Casey attempted to throw a spoon at him, remembered her ribs, and settled for glaring. She laughed once. And it was like a dam that broke. Suddenly, her laugh was ringing throughout the still New Orleans air. My favorite sound on repeat.

Later, when the sun dipped and the mosquitoes came out, Nguyen stood up to leave and said, "Boss, don't come back to work until the doctor clears you. I don't want to train another new detective."

Casey blinked at him. "Nguyen... was that nice?"

"It was," Harper said. "He's deteriorating emotionally."

"I'm evolving," Nguyen corrected.

Casey smiled. My chest hurt more than hers did. Fuller than it had been in years. That night, when everyone had gone home and the dishes were stacked in the sink, Casey moved slow toward the bedroom.

"You good?" I asked.

She nodded, though the motion was small and tired. "Yeah. Just sore."

I stepped closer. "You overdid it."

"I always overdo it."

"I know."

She paused, fingers curling at the hem of one of my shirts she'd stolen. "I don't like being... useless."

"You're not useless."

"I feel like it."

I shook my head before going to her. Wrapping my arm around her waist, I used my free hand to tilt her chin up to me. I kissed her forehead, then her nose. Her jaw. Her lips. She grumbled, then groaned and sighed into me. "You got shot twice. And you're still bossing everyone around. I'd call that pretty damn impressive."

Her eyes lifted to mine. Something soft flickered there—something she didn't let anyone else see. "You're really not letting me go back to my house, huh?" she whispered.

"No," I said simply.

"Because you're worried I'll choke on my own spit?"

"Because I sleep better when I know you're in bed next to me."

Her breath hitched. Just barely. Then she whispered, "I sleep better here too."

I swallowed. "Come on," I murmured. "Let's get you lying down before your ribs decide to file a complaint."

She rolled her eyes. But she leaned into me when I helped her. And when we finally settled into bed—her on her side supported by pillows, me on my back, her fingers brushing my arm—I felt something I hadn't felt in years.

Home. Not the place. Her.

Three months later, New Orleans looked different. Not cleaner or softer. Not magically fixed. But *steadier*. Like the city finally let out a long-held breath.

Casey was the same way. Her scars had faded from angry red to quiet pink. Her strength had come back—not all at once, but in sharp, stubborn pieces. Her temper came back too, which Harper said was "the true sign Chambers is healing." She was cleared for full duty in mid-March. She tried to play it cool. Signed the paperwork, nodded along with the doctor, shoved the folder into her bag like it was no big thing.

But when she walked out of her captain's office later that day, badge clipped to her jeans, gun light as air on her hip... She stopped in the parking lot, closed her eyes, and just breathed. I had insisted on giving her a ride and, from my truck, could see the tension in her shoulders start to melt off. When she climbed in, I didn't say a word. Some moments weren't meant to be interrupted.

Her return to Vice shook the building a little, according to Jordan. Like when someone moved the furniture an inch to the left—noticeable, disorienting, and oddly satisfying once you adjusted to it.

That night she told me that the new detective was already waiting at his desk. Detective Mark Ruiz. Late twenties. Sharp jaw. Too pretty for his own good. Transferred from Baton Rouge. He stood when she walked in.

"Sergeant Chambers," he had said. "It's an honor. I've heard... a lot."

Casey gave him a flat look. "I'm not a celebrity. Sit down."

He sat so fast he nearly tipped the chair. The entire precinct still tiptoed around her for the first week. Not out of pity. Not out of fear she was fragile. More like... respect. A quiet, complicated kind. She took it in stride, ignored the whispers, ignored the hesitant glances. But the old wound—the one with Ramos' name carved into it—still throbbed in the background.

Every time she passed his empty desk. Every time she opened an old case file. Every time someone said "Detective," and her brain took a half-second to remember it wasn't him anymore.

She didn't cry. Didn't break. Didn't rage. But she mourned him. The man he had been. The friend she thought she knew. And the version of herself that thought she could save everyone.

Meanwhile, Homicide was thriving. My captain called me into his office twice a week to complain about how many cases my team was closing. "You're making the rest of us look lazy, Bishop."

"Then tell them to work harder."

He glared.

I smirked.

We had an understanding. Eventually, everyone relaxed. Vice did its job. Homicide did its job. And no one could blame a solved murder or drug bust on "unprofessional entanglements." People stopped whispering. Stopped side-eyeing. One morning, while I was in the break room pouring coffee, Thibodeaux walked in, slapped a hand on my shoulder, and muttered, "Bishop."

"Sir."

"Keep Chambers out of the hospital for at least six months. My blood pressure can't handle round two."

"No promises."

He sighed like a man twice his age.

Casey's first night back on full duty ended at my house. Her things had slowly but surely made their way over until there was no need to stop at her old apartment before coming here. She stumbled in after a fourteen-hour shift smelling like rain, gunpowder, and the kind of exhaustion you only earned doing real police work.

I took one look at her and said, "You look exhausted, *ma louve*."

She kicked off her boots and dropped her badge on the counter. "Just hungry as hell." She tugged her ponytail holder out. "You cooking or we ordering?"

I looked at her. Skinny jeans on long legs, her favorite boots giving her a couple inches. Hair black as night, brown eyes a man could get lost in. "I can make us dinner. Later."

Her eyes sharpened, that devilish grin of hers doing something to me. "Later?"

"You're not on light duty anymore." I took a step towards her. She took a step back. Then another. "No, I'm not."

My girl wanted to play. Had I mentioned that it had been *months*? She took off, bolting down the hallway. I gave her a couple of seconds before running after her. She tried shutting the door in my face, but I stopped it just in time. The wood groaned under my palm, and Casey squealed. I wrapped my arms around her from behind, lifting her off the ground.

She yelped, going nearly limp. "Ow! Owen, my side!"

I froze—shit—before depositing her gently on the ground.

321

"I'm sorry, love—"

I stopped when she took a couple of steps away before turning to face me. And winking triumphantly. "Gotcha."

Oh, really now.

This time, I bent low and grabbed her thighs, lifting her in the air. She laughed, and I adjusted my hold as she wrapped her legs around my hips. Lowering her face to mine, she kissed me with a fervor that told me it had been a long few months for her, too. I groaned, nipping her lips until she moaned, and I took the opportunity to sweep my tongue inside. She was the best thing I had ever tasted. I laid her down on the bed, her legs still wrapped around me, never breaking our kiss. I pushed my hand under her shirt, going gently over the fresh scars that those bullets left in her. A reminder of how close I had gotten to losing her. A reason to never take a second for granted.

She ground against me, and I unbuttoned her shirt before biting at the swell of her breast. Then kissed each scar before kissing the dip of her hip and sliding her jeans off. I kissed the wet spot on her panties, and she bucked.

"*Mon péché*. I know I should go slow—"

"Oh, God. Don't you dare."

She reached for my buckle and all but yanked my pants down. My cock sprang out, and she wrapped her hands around it before leaning forward to kiss the tip. I made a low sound in the back of my throat before pushing her back down into the blankets and grabbing her waist.

"Tell me if I hurt you."

"Owen?"

"Yeah?"

"Shut up and fuck me already."

I grinned, "Yes ma'am." I tore off the thin fabric still separating us before plunging inside her in one, smooth motion. She swore, hips rising to meet me, as her eyes fluttered shut.

"Eyes on me." Partly because I needed to know if it hurt. Mostly because I had missed the way her eyes shone when she came on my cock. I found a rhythm that satisfied us both without risking pain, and she trembled around me when I pressed my thumb on her clit. I flicked the bundle of nerves that set her on fire, swearing when her pussy gripped me like a vise. "That's it. *Mon péché. Ma louve. Mon tout. Laisse-moi te voir venir vers moi. Une si bonne fille.*"

"Owen, fuck. I don't even know what that means. But, *fuck.*"

I leaned down, kissing her throat. "It means be a good girl and come for me."

She did, screaming my name and shattering around me. I kept moving, before settling myself deep inside her and following her over the edge. She ran her hands up my back, fingers tracing the muscles in my neck before getting lost in my hair. I kissed her again and felt her smile.

Later, after the takeout I had ordered arrived, we lay in bed and talked. Of cases, old and new. Of what came next, of what could be, what might be. She stole my egg roll; I was more than happy to let her. Neither one of us was willing to get out of bed, so we stashed the trash on the nightstand for the time being. She picked some cheesy movie on the TV and eventually fell asleep on my chest, her bare legs tangled with mine.

I watched her breathe and kissed the top of her head before pulling her closer to me. She mumbled in her sleep, snuggling deeper into my side.

There were moments in your life you looked at a person and just… knew.

Knew you'd take a bullet for them.

Knew you'd burn down the world to keep them safe.

Knew that the universe had quietly rearranged itself when you weren't paying attention.

This was one of them.

Still breathing after Caught in the Crossfire?

Good. Because I'm not done with you yet.

If you liked the danger, the tension, the *"oh, this is going to ruin my life"* chemistry in **Caught in the Crossfire**, you might want to buckle up.

🏍️ *Riding the Line*

Steel Saints MC—Book One
An undercover detective. A motorcycle club with secrets. Two brothers who were never part of the plan—and became the biggest risk of all. Loyalty, found family, and choices that don't come with a clean exit.

🔥 *Hell of a Ride*

Steel Saints MC—Book Two
A woman who bites back. A Marine barely holding himself together. Addiction, recovery, and a love that refuses to be easy—but also refuses to die.

Same world. Same chaos. Same emotional damage.

Want bonus scenes, sneak peeks, and updates before everyone else? Or maybe even a signed copy to add to your collection...

You probably do.

☞ **Visit my website!** www.sarakmasonauthor.com

🐿 **Join the SKM Newsletter!** link on website

I write dangerous love stories about messy people who don't behave, don't heal neatly, and don't apologize for wanting more.

Thanks for reading. See you in the next bad decision.

— **Sarah K. Mason**